shopping
for a
billionaire

Collection the

JULIA
KENT

New York Times Bestselling Author

Interior Design & Formatting by:
Christine Borgford, Perfectly Publishable
www.perfectlypublishable.com

shopping
for a
billionaire

#1

chapter
one

I AM EATING MY ninth cinnamon raisin bagel with maple horseradish cream cheese and hazelnut chocolate spread.

Don't judge me.

It's my job to eat this.

It's a Monday morning, 9:13 a.m. on the dot, and the counter person, Mark J., takes exactly seventeen seconds to acknowledge my presence. He then offers to upsell my small mocha latte, which I decline nicely, and within seventy-three seconds my cinnamon raisin bagel with maple horseradish cream cheese and hazelnut chocolate spread is in my hands, toasted and warm.

I pay my $10.22 with a $20 bill and he counts back my change properly, hands me a receipt and points out the survey I can complete for a chance to win a $100 gift card to this chain restaurant.

Survey? Buddy, I'm surveying you *right now*.

No, I don't have obsessive-compulsive disorder, though it helps in my line of work. I am not a private detective, and I don't have an unhealthy stalker thing for Mark J., who loses points for ringing up a customer, touching cash, and not washing his hands before touching the next person's bagel.

I cringe at mine.

I'm a secret shopper. Mystery shopper. Or as the clerks and managers in the stores where I pretend to be a regular shopper call me: Evil Personified.

That's *Ms.* Evil Personified to you, buddy.

It really *is* my job to sit here on a sunny Monday morning, in my ninth chain store, buying the same exact meal over and over again, sipping each mocha latte and sliding a thermometer in the hot liquid to make certain the temperature is between 170 and 180 degrees Fahrenheit.

You try doing that without making people think you are that one weird customer, the one who talks to aliens through the metal shake cans, or who brings her teacup Chihuahua in to share a grilled cheese and lets the dog lick the plate clean.

I'm just as weird, except I'm getting *paid* to do it.

My best friend and coworker, Amanda, created a little thermometer that looks just like a coffee stirrer. I slip it in through the lid and in sixty seconds—voila!

One hundred seventy-four degrees. I reach for my phone and pretend to send a text. I'm really opening my shopper's evaluation app, to type in all the answers to the 128 questions that must be properly answered.

I enter my name (Shannon Jacoby), today's date, the store location, whether the front trashcan was clean (it was), whether the front mats were clean (they were), the name of the clerk who waited on me (Mark J.), and pretty much every question you could imagine short of my favorite sexual position (none of your business) and the first date of my last period (who cares? It's not like I could possibly be pregnant. Maybe the cobwebs are in the way . . .).

Did I mention this is my ninth store of the day? I started at 5:30 a.m. I'm very, very questioned and cinnamoned *out*. One hundred twenty-eight questions times nine stores equals a big old identity crisis and a mouth that can't tell the difference between horseradish and mocha.

This is not my fault. I am in management for a secret shopper company. That means my job is to find people to do what *I'm* doing. A year ago, when I was a fresh-faced marketing major with my newly minted degree from UMass and $50,000 in student loans at the ripe old age of twenty-three, the job seemed like a dream.

You know those ads you see online to "Get Paid to Shop!"?

Yep. They're real. You really can sign on as a mystery shopper with various marketing companies, and once you pass some basic tests, you apply for jobs. What I'm doing right now pays your $10.22 expense, gives you the free breakfast sandwich and latte, and you earn a whopping $8 in payment about a month after submitting your mystery shopper report to our office.

And people are *lining up* to do this.

Except . . . sometimes, supervisors can't find anyone to fill a last-minute no-show. I'm a full-time, salaried employee (which means I get to keep the sandwich, but not the $8 for each of these nine shops this fine, beautiful, bloated morning).

One of our flakier shoppers, Meghan, texted me at 4:12 a.m. to tell me the purple and green unicorn in her flying sparkly Hummer told her not to eat bagels anymore, and she couldn't make her nine—NINE!—breakfast shops on religious grounds.

Okay, then. Someone was eating something other than cinnamon raisin bagels last night, and I suspect it involved mushrooms of some sort.

That gave me one hour and eighteen minutes to find a replacement, which meant—yep—here I was. In a rush, I'd jumped out of bed, printed out all of Meghan's shops, made a driving plan and a map, and steadied myself for the biggest mystery-shopping blitz I'd done since—

Since being dumped by my ex-boyfriend last year. Steven Michael Raleigh decided that finishing his MBA meant he needed a trophy wife who could schmooze with all the hoity-toities in the Back Bay in Boston.

Me? A Mendon girl with only a BA who works as a "glorified fast food snitch" just didn't cut it, so he cut me loose.

So here I sit in this little coffee shop in West Newton, counting down the minutes until I can break into the men's room. That's right—the *men's* room. Did I mention I'm a DD cup? *So* not a covert Men's Room Ninja.

My *ninth* men's room of the morning. Every part of the store has to be evaluated, including the toilets. You've seen one urinal, you've seen them all . . . except that's not how it works when you're evaluating a store for a mystery shop.

Nineteen questions about cleanliness and customer service

are waiting for my answers. Neatly waiting inside my smart-phone's app.

And if I don't break in to the men's room?

The eval will be a "failed job." I shudder. A failed job is worse than eating nine cinnamon raisin maple horseradish bagels, be-cause when you work in my field, a failed job is like a failed date with a billionaire.

Whatever went wrong, it's always, *always* your fault.

Speaking of billionaires, *helllllooo* Christian Grey. In walks a man wearing a suit that must cost more than my rickety old Saturn sedan. Fine grayish-blue with fibers that look like he snaps his fingers and they conform to his body because he's *that* dominant. Trim body with a flat, tapered torso, and *oh!* His jacket is unbuttoned. The bright white shirt underneath is so be-spoke that it fits like a glove.

If I had echolocation I could map out the terrain of ab mus-cles through sheer force of will. His cut body is meant to be re-lief mapped the way Braille is meant to be read.

With my fingertips.

Parts of my body that have been in suspended animation since I dated Steve spring to life. Some of these parts, as I watch him reach out and shake hands with Mark J. and see the taut lines of sinew at his wrist, the sprinkle of sandy hair around a gold watch, haven't risen from the dead since my party days at UMass.

And then he opens his mouth and asks Mark J., "How's your morning going?"

Liquid smoke, whiskey, sunshine and musk pour out of that jaunty, sultry mouth and all over my body like I am standing un-der a waterfall of *oh, yeahhhhh.* Everything goes into slow mo-tion around me. My world narrows to what I see, and I can't stop staring at Mr. Sex in a Suit.

Mark J. says something to the man in what sounds like Klingon, and they share a laugh. Beautiful, straight white teeth and cheeks that dimple—*dimple!*—make me fall even more in lust with Mr. I Will Make You Omelets in the Morning Wearing Your Suit Jacket and Nothing Else.

I look down and nearly vomit, because my torn t-shirt may actually have remnants of omelets on it. From yesterday. I sniff in that secret way people try to surreptitiously look like they are not *so* hygiene-deprived that they don't know whether they're offending half the Eastern Seaboard.

Damn. I am.

My phone rings. People around me look as I stare at it, slack-jawed. I can see my open mouth in the glass and realize my hair is still in a loose topknot on my head. Is that my nephew's My Little Pony scrunchie?

I really sprinted out the door this morning, didn't I? Being made an honorary Brony by a seven-year-old with two missing front teeth meant I'd been named "Thparkly Thunthine Auntie Thannon." I smile at the memory.

"Hello?" No one calls me. They always text. And the phone number is new. I don't know this person.

"Shannon, it's me." Amanda. My co-worker. My best friend. My thorn in my side. A ringing phone is an anomaly these days. Most people just zombie text. Me? I have a twenty-four-year-old friend who uses her phone like it's 2003.

"Why do you have a new number?"

"Greg made me get a cheaper plan." Greg is our boss. He makes those crazy coupon queens who buy $400 worth of groceries for $4.21 with 543 coupons look like people from *Lifestyles of the Rich and Famous.*

"Huh. Well, you could have answered the phone when I called this morning and taken some of these bagel hell assignments, you know," I whisper. "I am going to name my reflux Maple Horseradish Amanda after you."

"Oh, thank God! You picked up the jobs."

A very attractive college guy walks in, wearing a lacrosse team shirt and a pair of legs that make me wish I were wearing my good underwear instead of my safe underwear. You could go fly fishing in these granny pants.

My eyes can't stop flipping between college dude and Christian Grey. Eight bagel shops, and on the ninth, God gave Shannon a smorgasbord of hot men.

"You took them *all?*" Amanda's voice is somewhere between a dog whistle and a fire alarm. She shakes me out of my head just as Mr. Sex in a Suit walks by, making me sniff the air like an animal in heat. Which I kind of am, suddenly.

He smells like a weekend in Stowe at a private cabin with skis propped against the back wall, a roaring fire in a stone fireplace that crawls from floor to ceiling, and a bearskin rug that feels amazing against all your naked parts.

Even the dormant ones.

Especially the dormant ones.

"On the ninth one right now, but you're blowing my cover," I hiss. "And you *so* owe me. I'm making you pick up those podiatrist evals next month." Podiatrist shops don't exactly feed a sense of sexual desire, so my mind makes me go there. Feet. Hammer toes. *Eww.* Mr. Sex in a Suit leaves through the main doors, coffee in hand.

But wait, I want to cry out. *You forgot to let me lick your cuff links.*

"You can't make me do the bunion walk!" Amanda protests. Yes, mystery shoppers evaluate podiatrists. Doctors, dentists, banks, and even—

"Then you can do all the sex-toy shop surveys," I say, biting my lips after. I can feel the heat from her blush through the phone. Or maybe that's my own body as I lean to the left to search for a glimpse of Mr. Sophistication.

"Bunions it is," she replies curtly. "Come to the office after. We need to talk. Clinching this huge account hinges on how well these bagel shops go." She pauses. "And I am *so* not doing those marital aids shops!" *Click.*

chapter
two

NINETEEN QUESTIONS COMPEL ME to wrap up the rest of my sandwich, throw my half-full latte away, and walk with confidence toward the restrooms, hands shaking from too much caffeine. So what if, in my rush out of the house, I'd forgotten to change out of my yoga pants and torn t-shirt?

I look down. I'm wearing two different navy shoes. Which wouldn't be a problem, except one of them is open-toed.

Whatever. I am fine. This is my last shop of the day. So what if I look like something out of People of Walmart?

Thank goodness Mr. Omelet Cashmere Jacket is gone. He didn't even look at me, which is fine. (Not really, but . . .). Living in my own head has its privileges, like pretending I have a chance with someone like that. What would he see if he looked at me? Crazy hair, a full figure in an outfit so casual it classifies as pajamas, tired but observant brown eyes, and the blessings of good genes from my mother, with a pert nose and what Mom calls a "youthful appearance," but I call a curse of being carded forever.

And the whole two-different-shoes thing, which could be a fashion statement, you know? It could. Don't question it.

The coast is clear. *Tap tap tap.* I knock softly on the men's room door, assuming it's a one-seater like all the other stores I've been in this morning. No reply.

Sauntering in, I do a double take. Damn! Two urinals and two stalls instead of the big old square room. Someone could walk in on me. A guy could come in here and whip it out if I'm not careful.

Then again, it's been so long, I'm not sure I remember what they whip out.

Last year, one of my shops for a gas station chain made me count the number of hairs on the urinal cakes. That was, I contend, the low point in my secret shopping career. Fortunately, this particular chain does not have an obsession with hirsute urinators.

How progressive.

I tap on my phone and open the app, scanning the questions. Enough toilet paper? Check. Faucets in working order? Check. Paper-towel dispenser full? Check.

Toilets and urinals in operating order? Hoo boy.

If you've never been in a men's room, and have only set foot in the ladies' room at most fine (and not so fine) establishments, you need to know this: store owners hate men. No, really—this is the one area where women get treated better. We may earn seventy-seven cents on the dollar compared to men, but, by God, our public bathrooms don't look like something out of a Soviet-era prison.

Or worse—a Sochi hotel during the Olympics.

My mind wanders as I try not to touch anything I'm not required to touch in order to do my job and get out of here. I recall the scent of aftershave and man on Mr. Perfect Blue-Gray Suit from a few minutes ago, instead of the acrid odor of moldy cheese, urine, and chemical deodorizer that smells like poison-ivy pesticide. How would it feel not only to touch a man so put together, so confident, so in control—but to be *allowed* to?

The overwhelming pleasure of being in a relationship isn't the actual affection, sex, and companionship. It's the permission to be casual, to reach out and brush your hand against a pec, to thread your fingers in his hair, to hold hands and snuggle and have access to his abs, his calves, the fine, masculine curve of a forearm when you want.

On your terms.

By mutual agreement. The thought of running my palms from his wrists to his shoulders, then down that fine valley of sculpted marble chest to rest on his waist, to slide around and embrace him, makes my mouth curl up in a seductive smile.

That no one will ever see. So why bother?

Besides, I have toilets to flush.

I check the back of the bathroom door for the cleaning chart. You know those pieces of paper on the backs of the doors, with initials and times written on them to verify that the restroom has been cleaned? Someone verifies that verification.

Me. That's who. Of course, I have no way to verify that JS (the initials down the line for the past four hours) has actually cleaned the bathroom. Only a video camera would be able to tell for sure.

And while modern society loves to videotape everyone in public, mostly for the purpose of catching Lindsay Lohan in an uncompromising crotch shot, corporations haven't begun videotaping bathrooms.

Yet.

And thank goodness, not only for privacy reasons, but because cameras put people like me out of a job. As much as my job drives me nuts on days like this, it's a paycheck. I have health insurance. Paid time off. A retirement plan.

At twenty-four, that's like being a Nobel Prize winner in today's economy. Most of my friends from college are working part-time at retail stores in the mall, being evaluated by secret shoppers like . . . me.

Question number thirteen stops me cold. "Is the bathroom aesthetically pleasing?" Um, what? It still makes me cringe, even for the ninth time. The walls are a pale gray, with tile running halfway up. Chips and stains on the tile make me wonder what men have done in here. How does taking a pee translate into broken tiles? And those yellowed stains. I shudder. Is it really *that* hard to aim?

Whoosh! Whoosh! I flush both urinals, then rush over to toilet #1. *Whoosh!* I stand in front of the stall to #2 and get ready to flush that one.

I'm in my own little world and let my guard down to ponder the question. I am also exhausted and most definitely not in top form, because I let a few seconds go by before realizing that someone is coming in the bathroom. Out of the corner of my eye I see a business shoe, and that becomes a blur as I scurry into one of the stalls and shut the door.

Heart pounding, I stare at the dented back of the stall door. Then I look down. Chipped red nail polish peeks up at me from my open-toed navy shoe. Aside from being outed as a transgendered person in here, there's no plausible reason why any men's room stall occupant should have red toenails.

I quickly scramble to perch myself on the toilet, feet planted firmly on either side of the rim, squatting over the open bowl like I am giving birth. Because I am genetically incapable of balance—ever—and as my heart slams against my chest so hard it might as well be playing a djembe, I lean carefully forward with one arm against the back of the stall door, the other clutching my phone.

The unmistakable sound of a man taking a whizz echoes through the bathroom. I can't help myself and look through the tiny crack in the door.

It's Mr. Sex in a Suit, his back to me. Thank goodness, because if I got a full-frontal shot right now, then how would I answer the "aesthetically pleasing" question from a strictly professional standpoint?

The tiny bit of shifting I do to peer through the crack makes my right foot slip, and I make a squeaking sound, then lose my grip on my phone as my arm flails.

Ka-PLUNK!

You know that sound, right? I know, and you know, that I've just dropped my smartphone in the toilet, but he thinks the man—he assumes it's a man—in here just delivered something the size of a two-hundred-year-old turtle into the toilet.

I look down. My phone is still glowing, open to the question "Is the bathroom aesthetically pleasing?"

Staying silent, I struggle to remain perched on the toilet and in balance. One palm splays flat against the stall door, one hand curls into a fist as it poises over the toilet water.

Four-hundred-dollar phone

or

Arm in nasty men's room toilet water.

I have the distinct disadvantage of seeing every dried stain on the inside of the rim that my feet occupy, and I know that launching my hand into that porcelain prison means gangrenous death in three days after male pee germs invade my bloodstream and kill me.

But it's a $400 phone.

A *company* phone.

Closing my eyes, I lower my hand into the ice-cold water and pretend I'm Rose in the movie *Titanic*, bobbing on that miraculous door as my hand fishes blindly around the bottom of the toilet for my phone.

I get it not once, not twice, but three times as it slips and catches, slips and catches, and then—

The stall door opens toward me, sending me backwards with a scream, my arm stuck in the toilet as I fall down slightly, my back pushing against the toilet-flush knob.

Whoosh!

chapter
three

MR. BLUE-GRAY SUIT SPRINGS into action, jumping into the stall with me and planting nice, big, beautifully-manicured hands under my un-deodorized armpits and lifting me off the toilet. It's like we're in a toilet ballet, my body leaping up above his, suspended for a few seconds, and all I can think is *My arm is dripping toilet water all over a cashmere suit that cost more than my student loan balance.*

My second thought: *This will be one hell of a story to tell at our wedding reception.*

Our eyes lock as the toilet roars, and if we were anywhere else I could imagine this was a waterfall on a deserted island in the middle of the South Pacific, the two of us the only people inhabiting the island, forced by pure survival to have sex like monkeys and procreate to save the human race.

A sacrifice we both suffer through.

Except I'm not on an island with this man, whose arms don't even seem to strain under my size-sixteen weight. My breasts bob as he makes split-second calculations without looking away from me. Somehow, he moves my entire body, which is now on fire from his sure touch and primal, animal strength, and sets me down without either foot falling directly in the toilet.

The pain of the toilet handle digging into my shoulder blade when I fell back is making itself known, and my arm is dripping, but—but!—Mr. Death by Toilet Rescue is looking at me with concern, and almost as good:

I am clutching my phone.

This all took about five seconds, so I'm panting, and the top-knot of my already unruly hair has come undone, leaving a curtain of long waves framing my face. The ends of some of it are wet.

Oh, gross. Toilet arm, toilet phone—toilet *hair*?

The first words we share finally fill the air. He initiates with a grin.

"We have better seats out in the dining room, you know."

"My phone needed a bath," I reply, combing my hair with my dry hand, and now it's wet, too. I wonder what I look like right now, but I'm afraid if I look in a mirror I will crawl back into the toilet and try to flush myself out of this mess.

"What, exactly, have you been doing with your phone to make it so dirty?" he asks with a leer.

He steps back out of the stall with a gentlemanly sweep of his arm, green eyes filled with a mixture of mirth and guardedness. As he moves, he reveals a full-length wall mirror, giving me my own nightmare.

Oh. *That's* what I look like. Anyone have a spare coffee stirrer? Because I could stab myself in the eye and maybe bleed to death right here.

Or embarrassment will kill me. No such luck. If embarrassment could kill, I'd be dead nine times over by now.

I study myself in the mirror. Time seems measured by increments of incredulity, so why not make Mr. Toilet Rescuer think I'm even crazier by looking at my reflection like a puppy discovering "that other puppy" in the mirror?

Long brown hair, wet at the ends in the front. Split ends, no less. Who has the money for a decent cut after I needed new tires for my ancient Saturn? My torn pink t-shirt and gray yoga pants make me look like your average college student, except my shoes bring me to a screeching mental halt.

Yoga pants and one loafer, one open-toed shoe make me look like Mrs. McCullahay down the street, dragging her trash-cans out to the road at 5 a.m. with mismatched shoes, a muu-muu, and curlers in her hair while an inch-long ash hangs out of her mouth.

"At least I don't smoke," I mutter. Then I remember where I am, and look slowly to my left.

Mr. Smirky Suit leans casually against the scarred, dented stall wall, his face settled into a look of amusement now, but he's not going anywhere. Feet planted firmly in place, I realize he's giving me that look.

No, not *that* look. I'd take that look from him any time.

I mean the look of someone who will not let me out of here without an explanation.

An explanation I am contractually obligated *not* to give. Outing myself as a secret shopper is *verboten*. Unheard of.

Grounds for termination.

See, the first rule of mystery shopping is like the first rule of Fight Club: don't punch anyone. Oh. Wait. No . . . it's that you don't talk about it. Ever.

Though, sometimes, that not-punching rule comes in handy, because there are some really weird people in stores.

And Mr. Suit looks at me like I'm one of them.

"Let me introduce myself," he says, taking the lead. His body moves effortlessly from leaning to standing, then he takes two steps forward and I retreat until the backs of my calves hit the toilet rim again. I'm backing away from him and I don't know why.

"Declan McCormick. And you are?" Instinct makes me reach my hand out, and he's clasping mine before we both realize it's the toilet-contaminated hand.

He pretends it's perfectly normal, keeping strong eye contact and pumping my hand like it's the handle to a well. Except his fingers are warm, soft, and inviting, the touch lingering a little too long.

His eyes, too. They study me, and not like he's cataloging my features so he can file a police report or have me Section 35'd for being a danger to myself and others.

I am being *inventoried* in the most delicious of ways.

As a professional whose job it is to inventory customer service in business, I have acquired a set of unique skills—but more than that, I now have a sixth sense for when I'm being detailed.

And oh dear . . . there goes that flush.

And not the toilet kind.

I realize we're still shaking hands, and his eyes are taking me in. "Uh, Shannon. Shannon Jacoby. Nice to meet you." I find my voice.

He looks around the room and bursts out laughing, a flash of straight white teeth and a jaw I want to nuzzle making me inhale sharply. That laugh is the sound of extraordinary want entering my body, taking up residence low in my belly, and now waiting for a chance to pick china patterns and paint colors to really consider itself at home.

Go away, want. I've banished you.

Want ignores me and settles in, cleaning out the cobwebs that have taken up residence where I used to allow desire and hope and arousal to live.

Squatter.

"Shannon, this has to be the strangest way I've ever met a woman." One corner of his mouth curls up in a sexy little smile, like we're on a beach drinking alcohol out of coconuts carved by Cupid and not in a ratty old bathroom with a fluorescent tube light that starts buzzing like a nest of mosquitoes at an outdoor blood bank.

"You don't get around much, then," I say. My toes start to curl as my body fights to contain the wellspring of attraction that is unfurling inside me. No. Just . . . *no*. I can't let myself feel this. You spend enough time trying not to feel something and all that work gets thrown away with one single flush.

He does that polite laugh thing, eyes narrowing. I decide to just stare openly and catalog him right back. Brown hair, clipped close, in a style that can only come at the hands of the owner of a very expensive salon. The bluish-gray suit, textured and smooth at the same time, shimmering and flat as well under the twitchy light. Skin kissed by the sun but also a bit too light, as if he used to spend a lot of time outdoors but hasn't recently.

A body like a tall tennis player's, or a golfer's, and not my dad with his pot-bellied buddies getting in a round of nine holes at 4 p.m. just so they can have an excuse to drink their dinner. Declan is tall and sleek, confident and self-possessed. He moves like a lion, knowing the territory and owning it.

Always aware of any movement that interests him.

I'm 5' 9" and he's taller than me by at least half a foot. Tall girls always do a mental check: *could I wear high heels with him?* Steve hated when I wore high heels, because it put me eye-to-eye with him.

"What are you doing in the men's room?" he asks, smirking at me.

I tuck my phone into the back waistband of my pants. If there's a chance in hell it's still on, he might see the screen and figure out who I am. My wits begin to return to me. A zero-sum game forms in my body: wit vs. a body part that rhymes with *wit* that starts with C and that stands for trouble.

Wit is losing.

"I must have gotten confused." I fake-rub my eyes. "Forgot to grab my glasses on my way to class this morning."

His eyes narrow further, staring into mine. Am I imagining it, or did his face just fall a bit with disappointment? My heart shatters into a thousand tiny shards of glass that I feel like I just swallowed.

"Class? You're a student?" His eyes rake over me and there's a flicker of comprehension there, like some details that didn't gel are making sense to him.

When you trap yourself into a corner, always take someone else's out when you can. "Sure. Yes."

"What class?"

My heart is still jumping around in my chest like my little nephews at an indoor trampoline park after drinking a full-caf frozen mocha. Now he wants to chat while we stand in front of a toilet? And ask me questions about a class I don't really take?

"Excuse me," I say, gesturing with the grace of a three-legged moose on skis. "While I am certain that meeting over a toilet in the men's room right after my hand has been in places that brothel workers in Mumbai won't touch is scintillating, I would prefer to step out of here and escape *Eau de Urinal.*"

"You haven't answered my question." He is immutable. Heat

on legs. His pulse shows on his neck, right under the sharp curve of his tight jaw, and I want to kiss it. Press it. Feel it and let my own heartbeat join in.

"I didn't realize I was under your command, sir," I retort, saluting him with a rush of sarcasm bigger than my pent-up frustration.

His eyes deepen as he pivots just enough for me to get past him, our bodies brushing against each other with a heat that seems to treble with each nanosecond. I move into the area around the sinks and grab a paper towel, then turn the faucet on, careful to make sure my fingers don't touch the gleaming metal.

"What are you doing?" Declan asks. *Why won't he leave?* Surely someone dressed so nicely has stocks to broker, people to doctor, or laws to lawyer. Women to wetten. You know.

"Do you have any idea how germy bathroom sinks can be? I always do this," I explain, even as my head screams invective and tells me I don't have to explain anything.

"Nice of you to protect the other patrons."

"Huh?"

"If anything is germy . . ." His voice fades out into a low sound in the back of his throat. It sounds like something you'd hear in a locker room or at a hunting club. He gestures toward my arm.

Damn. He's got a point. I can't even argue, because he's right—but that never stopped me before.

"Toilet water—clean toilet water, and that one had been flushed before I reached in—is surprisingly sterile."

"Sterile?"

"Okay," I backpedal. "Reasonably clean."

"Are you from the health department?" His question sounds like a threat.

"No."

"You just troll men's rooms and spout microbiology statistics like a professor for . . . kicks." He says it in that maddening way men have of making everything seem like it's a fact, even when they're really asking a question.

Which was worse: having him think I was Amy from *Big Bang Theory* or just some crazy woman who crashes men's rooms and has a fetish for sticking her hand in the toilet?

(Not that there's anything wrong with Amy.)

I finish washing my hands and turn to grab a piece of paper towel, only to find Declan holding one out for me.

"Aha! So now I understand," I say, nodding slowly as I accept the paper towel and dry my hands. "You're the bathroom attendant. Where's your tip cup? You've definitely earned a little something."

The air tingles between us, and it's not the deodorizer machine spritzing the room. "I've earned a little something," he echoes in a voice loaded with suggestion. It's not a question.

Just then, the door bursts open and Mark J. rushes in, eyes wild and frantic.

He sees me and gasps, making a high-pitched noise that you would expect from a forty-something middle-aged pearl clutcher and not a guy who looks like he last starred on some cable reality television show called *Fast Food Wars*.

"You!" he screeches. "A customer said they saw a woman walk into the men's room. I didn't believe it!"

Declan reaches out for Mark J.'s arm. I lose track of time. How many seconds did it take for this to go from bad to worse? My cover cannot be blown.

"She just wandered in by accident," Declan explains. "Or she has a fetish. We're sorting it out right now." I glare so hard at him the hand dryer spontaneously starts.

"Why is she covered in water?" My sleeve is soaked and the ends of my hair are wet. Mark looks at Declan and sees water spots on his jacket. "Oh!" The sound is so soft I barely hear it, but from the look on Declan's face he hears it, too. His eyes close and jaw tenses. This is a man who is not accustomed to suffering fools gladly.

So why is he even talking to me?

"I see, now. Fetish. . . . I didn't mean . . ." Mark J.'s eyes plead with Declan to help explain what is going on, because it's clear from the worker's panic that he has about three different theories, two of which involve me and Declan breaking public decency laws and one of which involves questions about my biological gender.

None of his scenarios, though, involve my dropping a smartphone while completing a mystery shop, so I'm safe.

"I'll leave you two to whatever . . . it was . . . you were doing," Mark J. says as his fingers scramble to open the door and get out.

"What do you think," Declan says, eyes still on the pneumatically wheezing door, "he thinks we're doing in here?"

"Twerking?" My mind races a thousand miles a minute, covering territory from remembering how many toilet paper rolls were in each stall to imagining Declan naked with a can of whipped cream and a bowl of fresh cherries beside the bed to reminding myself I haven't shaved in days.

I am a modern-day Renaissance woman.

Maybe my eyes give me away during that nude vision of Declan, because the room rapidly becomes warmer and his eyes go dark and hooded as he takes another step toward me. Two more and we'll touch.

Three more and I could kiss him.

"I don't twerk," he whispers, one hand twitching as if it wants to touch me.

"I don't do any of the things Mark J. thinks I do," I whisper back. And then I cringe, because . . .

"Mark J.? You memorized his name tag?" One of Declan's eyebrows shoots up, and it's the sexiest look ever, like George Clooney and Channing Tatum and Sam Heughan rolled into one.

"He's . . . uh . . ."

"Oh," Declan says, his nostrils flaring a bit, lips tight to hold back a smile. "I see. He's your . . ." The words go low and Declan makes a few guttural noises and nose twitches that either mean he has a mild case of Tourette Syndrome or he's suggesting that I'm doing the nasty with Mark J.

This is where the path diverges in the woods, and I? I took the path most likely to humiliate me.

For the sake of being a professional.

"Yes!" I shout as the door opens and in walks a very confused kid who looks to be about ten years old. He double-checks the main door, then gawks at me, slack-jawed and wide-eyed. I like that. Kids are honest. Declan's all smoke and whiskey with me, teasing and playing with me, and I have been up since 4:12 a.m. being texted by secret shoppers who dropped acid and saw unicorns.

Don't play games with me.

"Yes, that's right! Mark J. and I are doing it," I whisper in Declan's ear as the kid runs back to his table and I work on my own escape. "We do it in the walk-in cooler, right by the salad bins. He lays me out over the break table outside and always throws the cigarette butts in the ashtray away. A true romantic. On uniform delivery day he's right there in the truck with me, careful to keep the apron clean while meeting my needs. Mark J. is the man."

I inch over to the door and sprint out to my car as Mark J., now safely behind the front counter, shouts, "Have a good day!"

chapter
four

M Y HANDS SHAKE AS I climb in my unlocked car
and rifle under the driver's seat in search of my keys.
I find the giant screwdriver. Yes, that is my "keys."
The original key broke off in the lock a few months ago and my
mechanic—AKA my dad—stripped out the lock and now I shove
a giant flathead screwdriver into the ignition and turn and pray.

That's the closest thing in my life to something being insert-
ed into a hole every day.

The car turns over and I gun the engine. After backing up
slowly, the car vibrates as I make a right turn onto the main road
and head to the office.

The vibrations aren't from the car, which runs smoothly
once you actually get it started. Those are my nerves jangling a
mile a minute, my body in some kind of post-urinal shock.

I examine my hand. The toilet hand. And then I lean back
and feel a bulge at the base of my back. And not the fun kind.

Dirty hand reaches back and finds my sweaty smartphone.
The screen is not glowing, and it seems to have developed a
sheen of sweat. Or maybe that's from me. Running from the
restaurant to my car was about the most exercise I've had in
months.

As the familiar roads come into view and I guide my car
on autopilot back to my apartment, I try to unwind the crazy,
jumbled mess of threaded thoughts that can't untangle just yet.
Hot guy. Hiding in the men's room. Dropping my phone in the
toilet. Being caught with my hand in there. Being rescued and

dripping toilet juice on Hot Guy.

And that was the good part of the morning.

My phone makes a creepy bleating sound, like baby seals dying at slaughter. The screen flickers like it's the last known electronic signal after nuclear war.

I try to shut it off but it just continues making an anemic whirring sound. This is what robots sound like when they die. The noise will invade my dreams for the next few weeks.

A deep breath will cleanse me. No dice. How about two? Nope. Nuthin'. Ten don't really help. By the time I've tried twenty-three deep breaths, I am home and feeling a little faint, with tingly lips.

Let's not add syncope to my growing list of Very Bad Things That Happen on a Mystery Shop.

I park in my assigned spot next to the trash cans, kill the engine, and slowly bang my forehead against the steering wheel. Twenty-three bangs actually calm me. Dented brow and all. By the time I stop, I feel like I can handle a basic shower.

That's more than I was capable of ten minutes ago. Other than a shower with Mr. Suit.

Who are you, a voice asks me, *and what have you done with asexual Shannon?*

Sitting out here with my dented head and confused heart won't get me anywhere. Amanda's probably frantically trying to find me, and a search party worthy of a missing Malaysian jet is about to be triggered if she calls my mom.

My mom can be a bit dramatic. A bit. The way Miley Cyrus can be a bit controversial.

I sprint into my house, holding the phone like it's a bomb. My apartment is a garage. Mostly. I live above a two-car garage in a neighborhood right behind a college, a one-bedroom place I share with my sister. It requires actual exertion on my part to enter and exit. Twenty-seven nearly vertical steps get me to my front door. An actual key (as opposed to a screwdriver) opens the front door, and then *bam!*

I'm assaulted by a glaring cat.

My cat makes Grumpy Cat look like Rainbow Brite. If glares

could peel paint, I could hire out Chuckles to a paint contractor and quit my job, living off my pet's singular skill.

People who think animals have expressionless faces are like people who can ignore an open package of Oreos.

Not quite human.

Chuckles—who probably started glaring after we named him as a puffball kitten ten years ago—sits primly in front of the door, a sentry serving as witness to some oversight of mine.

With a guilty look, I survey my kitchen, which is the first room you walk into in my apartment. Water dish full. Food dish half full.

Litter box—full.

Ah. "I'm sorry, Chuckles. I was too busy putting my hand down a human toilet today. I've had quite enough of excrement today. But I'll change it anyhow, because if you look at me like that much longer I'll burst into flame and they'll find us in a few weeks, you noshing on my crispy legs."

"You should think about the fact that you say more to your cat than you do to your own mother," Satan says from behind my ficus plant.

I scream. Chuckles screams. I pick up Chuckles and fling him at the plant, which serves exactly three purposes. First, it reveals my stupidity. Second, it makes Chuckles plot my death on a whole new level. And third, it makes my mother sidestep the whole fiasco with the fluid movement of a woman who teaches yoga, leaving her to glare at me with a look that makes me realize exactly where Chuckles learned it from.

"Nice guard cat," my mom says. She holds her purse over her shoulder and keys in her hand. "Before you ask," she adds as I press my palm over my heart, willing it to stay in place as Chuckles' death ray of magnetic harm tries to pry it out of me, "Amanda called and told me she couldn't reach you."

"I've been unavailable by phone for no more than thirty minutes. Thirty minutes! And she sends out the National Guard."

Mom looks triumphant. Marie Jacoby is what all my friends called a MILFF—Mother I'd Like to Flee From. A little too tan, a little too blond, a lot too judgmental. My mother doesn't greet you with "Hello."

"You should" is her salutation of choice.

"You should consider yourself fortunate. Some young girls would be falling all over themselves to have a mother who cares so much," she grouses.

"First off, I'm not a girl. And second, you're right. How about I sell you on eBay as mother of the year? You'd fetch a great price."

One eyebrow shoots up. One perfectly threaded eyebrow, that is. No stray hair can live on Mom's face. She visits the mall weekly and the women at the threading spa not only know her by name, they know her preferred coffee order from the little espresso place next to the escalator.

She peers intently at me, her eyes that luminous sapphire I still envy. I got dad's dirt-brown eyes. "You've met someone," she crows, plopping her oversized fake Prada bag on my scarred thrift shop table.

Which means she is here to talk.

"How do you do that?" I screech, channeling the same inner fifteen-year-old she can conjure at will with just two sentences and one knowing look.

Her eyebrow climbs higher. "So I'm right." She stands and gives my coffee machine an appraising look. It is an espresso machine I'd gotten on a mystery shop for a high-end cookware store. "Make me a coffee and I'll only ask the basics."

"Blackmailer," I mutter, but I know the score. Do this and she'll leave me alone. Argue and I am in for the full hover-mother treatment that makes the NSA look like *Spy Kids*.

I grab the can of ground espresso out of the cabinet above the sink and she makes a guttural sound of reproach. Ignoring her, I fill the machine and make sure there is enough water. Sometimes, pretending she didn't make a noise works.

But not this time.

"Look at the food in your cabinets! Coffee. Sugar and sweetener packets. Ketchup and soy sauce packets. Sample-size cookies. Teeny packages of microwave popcorn."

"I eat a perfectly fine diet, Mom," I mutter as the machine

begins to hiss. Or maybe that's me. It's hard to tell.

She waves a perfectly manicured hand dismissively. The nail polish matches a thin line of mauve that runs as a single stripe through her shirt.

"Not for you. For the man you'll entertain! He can't see that. That's not wife and mother material. No woman who makes a good wife keeps a pantry like that!"

"Last week you were Feminist Crusader Mom, telling me how proud you were that I finished my degree and support myself!" This is a well-worn argument. Since she turned fifty a little more than two years ago, and as her friends are all getting to Momzilla their way through their daughters' weddings, Mom has become zealously devoted to finding me A Man.

Not just any man, though.

A man worthy of a Farmington Country Club wedding.

Mom's phone rings. "You Sexy Thing" fills the room and Chuckles makes a disapproving sound eerily similar to my mother's. I seize my chance.

"Gotta wash the toilet water off my arm!" I call back as I pad to the bathroom and turn on the shower, drowning out whatever comments she peppers me with. Stripping out of the pajamas I've been wearing for far longer than their shelf life feels like shedding a skin.

The tiny, hot pinpricks of escapism give me ten minutes to cleanse myself and to think. Or not think. Mom chats on the other side of the bathroom door, blissfully unaware that I am not listening. Or commenting. Or responding in any way, shape, or form.

That doesn't stop her.

I turn off the shower spray and hear her shout, "And so that's how Janice's daughter found out her and her husband's toothbrushes had been shoved up the robbers' butts."

Whoa. As I towel off, my reflection opens its mouth and closes it a few times, wondering how I am expected to respond to *that.*

Some things are best left to the unknown.

As I open the door, a plume of steam hits Mom. "My hair!

My hair!" she shouts. I inherited her limp hair and Dad's eyes, which is so totally backwards. Dad has lush hair that my sister, Amy, got—perfect spiral curls that rest elegantly in auburn tendrils against her back. And Mom has those blue eyes.

I look in the mirror and Declan's name runs through my mind, planted there by my subconscious. If I say a word about him to Mom then she'll be planning the wedding and have him in a headlock, demanding a two-carat ring before he can say "Hello."

I walk into my bedroom wearing a towel, and stop short. Clothes are laid out on my bed for me.

"What am I? Four?" I mumble. Then I grudgingly put them on, because Mom does have good taste. The adobe shirt she pairs with navy pants and a scarf I never use looks more stylish than I want to admit.

"I can color code your wardrobe for you, Shannon," she shouts from the hallway as I dress.

"You should start a clothing line. Garanimals for Adults. It would be very popular!"

She takes my comment at face value. "What a great idea! I'll ask Amy what she thinks. Maybe we can do one of those crowd-funding things to raise money for it like Amy does."

Amy is an intern at a venture capital company. *So* not the same thing as Kickstarter or Indiegogo. I don't correct Mom, because it's about as useful as correcting Vladimir Putin about the Ukrainian / Russian border.

"Who was on the phone?" I ask.

"Amanda. She wants you to call her. What's wrong with your phone?"

"I dropped it in a toilet on a shop this morning."

Mom's face freezes in an outrageous O. "You didn't . . . *retrieve* it?" The only thing Mom fears more than never marrying off a kid at the Farmington Country Club is germs.

"I stuck my hand in the toilet in the men's room and saved it, even as I flushed!" I say with glee.

She glares at me. Chuckles leaves the room, clearly outclassed. "Men's room?"

I smile. "Where do you think I'm meeting men?"

"Oh, Shannon," she groans, reaching for the espresso I made for her before the shower. It's likely tepid by now, but that's how she likes it. "Have you become so desperate?"

"I know the men's room is a bit—"

"No—the men's room is ingenious, actually. No competition, except with the gay ones." She drinks the entire espresso in one gulp and slams the cup down like it's a shot competition during Spring Break in New Orleans. "I mean, really? On a *mystery shop*?" She says the last two words like Gwyneth Paltrow says the word *divorce*.

"So let me understand, Mom. Trolling the men's room is a clever way to meet a man, but doing so during a mystery shop is debasing?" She quickly pulls my unruly hair into an updo and bobby pins appear in her mouth like she had them shoved up her nose the entire time, waiting for the perfect moment to correct my hairstyle.

"It's just . . ." She sniffs. "What kind of man will you meet at a burger joint? Or a car wash? Getting your oil changed or buying a bagel sandwich?" Her face perks up. "Is there an elite level of mystery shopping? Who are the secret shoppers for Neiman Marcus, or the Omni Parker House? What about Tiffany's?" Her eyes glitter. "Now that would be one way to meet the right kind of man."

"The right kind of man." I can't keep the disdain out of my voice, but an image of Declan flashes through my mind. That smile.

"You won't meet him on your eighth bagel sandwich dressed like a college student on the fourth day of exams with a bad case of lice," she adds.

"I don't have lice!"

"Well, honey, you looked like it."

"Mom." I steel myself. "This has been great. Really. But I have to go." I grab my purse and throw a few cups of white rice in a baggie, then shove my phone in it. "But I need to get to work."

"We need to talk, Shannon—"

"Bye! And change Chuckles' litter box for me, would you? He looks like he's about to go in the zen rock garden."

And with that, I run down every one of those twenty-seven steps, grateful for my escape.

chapter
five

THE DRIVE TO THE office gives my body a chance to settle in to the day. Awake since four a.m., it is screaming for some kind of break.

Or maybe that is my inner thighs. They begin to spasm and ache, and not in that stretchy-groany kind of way after a long weekend of incredible sex.

Squatting on the toilet has, apparently, led to a fair amount of injury. Great. Add this to the growing list of occupational hazards.

If only Declan had been responsible for this burning ache in a decidedly more delicious way. Daydreaming never hurt anyone, right? I let my mind wander, wondering what he looks like out of that suit. In bed. Under bright white sheets on a crisp spring day, windows open and gauzy curtains billowing with the breeze, the air infused with the scent of sensual time.

Would he be a patient lover, taking every curve and valley of my body with a slow touch that built to a crescendo? Or an intense, no-holds-barred bedmate, with fevered kisses and unrestrained hands that need and knead, fusing us together in sweaty promises of nothing but oblivion?

A new kind of ache emerges between my thighs, and it's closer to the kind I wish I'd had with him.

For the first time since our meeting a few hours ago, I let myself laugh. Really giggle, with belly moving, abs engaged, and chest whooping with the craziness of it all. Was he laughing, too? I feel a blend of incredulity and shame inside me, too, but there's a lot more amusement. Never one to shy away from self-effacing humor, this event will be reshaped and I'll retell it to my friends, crafted in a way that makes everyone think, *That silly Shannon.*

Is Declan even thinking about me at all? The laughter dies inside fast. Maybe I'm just some whacko woman he humored as he now tells scathingly nasty stories to his work buddies about the chubby chick he found squatting on the men's room toilet, fishing her phone out.

Am I the butt of jokes? Does he describe me with vicious derision, using me as a quick one-off story, the office equivalent of a viral BuzzFeed link that makes people pause, point and laugh, and move on?

A lump in my throat tells me I care way too much about what he thinks. Why am I fantasizing about a guy who trapped me in a toilet stall while I was on a mystery shop?

Because you're that desperate, my mother's voice hisses in my head.

I throw an imaginary cat at her.

The company I work for, Consolidated Evalu-shop, Incorporated, is in a building as nondescript as the business's name. If boring had a name, it would be Consolidated Evalu-shop. The building is made of block concrete. The interior steps are concrete as well. No carpeting anywhere, leaving the hallways to echo. If Stalin's army had designed an office building, this is what it would look like.

Fortunately, our actual office has carpet. Cheap industrial carpet that is about as thick as a gambler's wallet the day after payday, but it's carpet. It pads our feet and keeps the floor warm.

I open the main door and walk into the office. There is a reception area the size of two or three graves shoved together without any chairs, and then to the right a long hallway, with three offices on either side. At the end of the hall is something the owner, Greg, calls a "kitchen" but I call it a supply closet with a sink in it.

Want coffee? Get it from the donut shop next door. Same if you need to respond to nature's call. Greg doesn't provide fancy fringe benefits like bathrooms, microwaves, coffee machines, or even pens. He uses the freebies he gets at the bazillion marketing conventions he attends (on the company dime, of course).

To be fair, we get plenty of freebies in this line of work, too. You go to enough mystery shops at banks and open a new account, you get to keep your free pens, notepads, water bottles, can cozies, toasters, smartphone cases, and other assorted swag that you receive.

Greg is super-cheap about outfitting the office, but he doesn't skimp on health insurance. I might make slightly more than a full-time assistant manager at the Gap, but I have one hundred percent employer-paid health insurance, so I'm not complaining.

Plus, he pays mileage for all our driving. Which adds up, fast. You drive a piece of junk like I do and you need the fifty-five cents for each mile to feed the hamsters that keep it going.

"Oooh, someone got lucky last night. You're walking like a woman who got what she needed and then some," Josh says, winking as I limp into the office. Josh is the company tech expert, which means we all think he's a little bit shaman, a little bit magician, and mostly a nerd.

My glare should make him spontaneously combust, or at least turn into a hedgehog with a profound case of psoriasis, but no such luck.

"Not even close. I hurt my inner thighs sitting on the toilet this morning."

His eyebrows shoot up and disappear into his disappearing hairline. "You need more fiber."

"I need a lot of things, Josh." Limp. Limp. I feel like I've been riding a Shetland pony for three days. At least I don't have saddle sores. But Josh's original idea, of having a man do this to me in bed . . . Mr. Sexy Suit comes to mind. Not the pompous ass who made me flush my own hand and cell phone, but the one I turned into Mr. Dreamy before The Great Toilet Fiasco of 2014.

I have the second door on the left, sandwiched between

Josh and Amanda. My office smells like pine and vinegar, which means it must be Thursday. The cleaning crew came through the night before. I hang up my purse, pull out the baggie with rice and my phone in it, put it in my windowsill to bake in the sun, and flip my computer on.

Amanda's left a note on my desk: *Leave it for two days in a baggie full of rice. If it doesn't work, we'll get you a new one. Greg won't be happy, but too bad. Hope your hand doesn't fall off from germs.*

It's so nice to have a friend who really gets your OCD phobias. Or who understands your mom. Or both.

"Shannon? I recovered your data," Josh says, scaring the hell out of me. He moves like a vampire, suddenly behind you in your office. I think he likes it. Office sadist.

But I forgive him, because *what*? "You recovered my shops?" Hope springs eternal.

"It's all in the cloud now, so thank me for setting that app up and forcing Greg to spend money on something worthwhile. Everything is in there but the last one, because *you* didn't hit save." I get a scowl that makes me think Chuckles is more evolved than most humans. Josh looks like a lamb pretending to be mad.

"I was perched over a men's toilet trying not to watch a man whip it out. Don't you dare shame me."

"The only shame is that you didn't try to look when he whipped it out," Josh says, eyes twinkling.

"You recovered *all* eight shops?" I'm incredulous. This is making my day already, and it's only 11:37 a.m.

He nods. I throw my arms around his neck and hug him. "I would French kiss you if you weren't gay," I murmur.

"You keep this dry spell up and you'll start French kissing me even though I *am* gay," he mutters, shaking his head. "If the only action your inner thighs are getting is while hiding from a hot guy in the men's room of a shop, it's time for a lifestyle evaluation."

"Let's mystery shop Shannon's life!" Amanda squeals, appearing at the perfect moment. The perfect moment to go through another episode of *Let's Dissect Poor Shannon's Failed*

Love Life, that is. My mother would emcee it.

We're on Season Three, Episode Five by my count. Netflix should pick this one up. People could binge watch and point to the TV as they laugh, feeling a sense of relief while thinking, *At least I'm not as bad as Shannon.*

I could provide an important public service.

"What about Hot Guy? Did he ask for your number?" Amanda and Mom had clearly connected.

"I'm sure he hits on all the women he meets who have their arm flushed down a toilet in the men's room." *Does he?* Because if he's met more than me that way, then it's really not me. It's him.

"Sample size of one!" she chirps. "You stand out from the crowd."

"I'm the only one who could give him E. coli by feeding him grapes!" I look nervously at my hand. It looks the same.

"You didn't catch his name?" Josh asks.

I freeze inside. *Declan McCormick* is on the tip of my tongue, but I keep it behind my teeth, like a candy you savor and suck on. Heat creeps up my chest and neck as I think about things on Declan I could suck.

I shake my head hard, like a dog after a swim. "Nope. Just really rich, really confident, and enough of an asshole to make me want him."

All three of us wistfully sigh in unison.

They believe the lie. They should. We're all really good liars. You kind of have to be in this business, because you spend so much time pretending to be something you're not, all while evaluating the surface level of people.

It's a cold job when you think about it that way. Now I frown and Amanda looks at me with concern. Then I realize she has black hair again. Fourth color change in four months.

"What did you do?" I ask as she follows me into my office. Yesterday she was a blonde, and the shift is jarring, like she's gone from looking like a beach bunny to a dominatrix.

"Carol flaked on the hair salon shop, so I had to go to yet another color, cut, and style," she says sadly. She touches the ends of her hair. "I look like Morticia Addams."

I snort. "You look like Katy Perry." Amanda is the cheerleader type. Was in high school, still is. And yes, I'm lying a little, because Amanda actually has near-zero similarity to Katy Perry other than black hair and red lips. In fact, right now, she's staring at me in a creepy way with that new hairdo, like that woman on the *Oddities San Francisco* show.

Like she either wants to tell me a secret or stick me in a jar with preserved three-headed piglets from 1883.

"You got all your shops in?"

"Eight out of nine."

She looks at the wall clock in the hallway. "Twenty-three minutes to get the last one in and we get credit for exceeding client expectations."

"But—um—hello? Toilet water? Dead phone? Hot guy?" I can't catch a break.

"Hot guy or no hot guy, we have that big meeting at four today with Anterdec, and if we get this all in on time it makes it much easier to land a client so big Greg will have to start turning the heat up over fifty-five in the winter."

"You know how to improve company morale. Don't tease me," I say, pretending to fan my face. "Next thing you know you'll tell me we're allowed to turn the overhead lights on after sundown."

"Don't push it," she says in a fake flat voice. But with the new hairstyle she makes my abs tighten with fear. I flinch. She sees it and frowns.

"You look like something out of a BDSM novel," I explain.

One corner of her mouth hitches up. It's half adorable and half chilling. "Really? Too bad I'm not dating anyone right now. This is just going to waste." Her hand sweeps over her face.

"Ha."

"Twenty-one minutes! Hurry! Once we have all the shops in the system we can do a quality-control check and go to this big meeting with an unblemished record. And then maybe they'll give us the Fokused Shoprite account." Amanda says this with a triumphant grin.

My jaw drops. "We have a shot at sniping one of their accounts?" Fokused, or Foked, as we call them, is our archenemy . . . er, competition. Consolidated and Fokused are the biggest consumer experience and marketing firms in the city, and the rivalry is strong.

If my little toilet-hand fiasco had cost us this account, I would have not only cried, Greg would have sold my office furniture out from under me and spent the $17 it was worth on coffee for the rest of the staff out of sheer anger.

My computer boots up and I log in to the website interface, a *zing* of thrill flooding my extremities as I see all complete shops from this morning, except that red ninth one.

Incomplete.

Incomplete this, sucker. Ten minutes later, I am stuck with one final question.

"Is the bathroom aesthetically pleasing?" I let my mind drift to Declan, remembering those smoldering eyes, the tightly muscled jaw, how his cheeks dimpled when he laughed. The snug cut of his tailored jacket across those broad shoulders and how strong and sure his hands had been on me, making certain I didn't fall.

Into the toilet, that is.

Can a relationship develop from two people who meet like this? Am I hopelessly dreaming? Or am I doomed to live the rest of my life surrounded by men at fast food restaurants on $5 sandwich day, or guys opening new accounts at banks to get a free pair of tickets to a big amusement park, or—

I take a slow, deep breath and remember the heat of his fingers on my arm. The warm questions in those eyes. The willingness to laugh with—okay, *at*—me.

I click *Yes* and then submit, ready to perform the killer client pitch of my entire career.

chapter
six

AMANDA AND GREG LIKE to pretend that they're the experts at client pitches, but while they're good openers, I've become the closer.

And in business, the closer is everything.

I have this innate sense that tells me how to fine-tune my words and convince a wavering vice president of marketing, or director of consumer relations, or vice president of *let's invent a title for the owner's son*, that Consolidated Evalu-shop, Inc. will help their company usher in a new wave of business that positions them at the vanguard of a paradigm shift in the industry.

See? I'm good.

Marketing really isn't anything more than word salad, and I don't mean the schizophrenic kind. Learning to speak business jargon fluently is definitely an acquired skill.

Growing a penis is another one. Haven't mastered that just yet, though if I could, I would.

You know how many female VPs I meet? Maybe one in fifty. Presidents? One. Ever. A smattering of directors, more assistant directors, and then the glut of "coordinators," which can mean anything from an underpaid, overworked equivalent of a vice president but without the paycheck to a glorified secretary.

And when you walk into a meeting, you have no idea what you're dealing with.

Guess what my title is?

Yep. Marketing coordinator.

"They emailed me this morning," Greg says. I take a good

look at him. One thing I have to give to Greg—he cleans up well. He's a little younger than my dad, which makes him mid-forties or so. You know—old, but not ancient. Brown hair, thinning out, and cut super short the way guys who won't quite admit they're balding cut their hair. His wife made him ditch the old 1980s frames he used to wear for a sleek updated look, and his suit is tailored, which it has to be. The beach ball masquerading as a stomach needs to fit.

"Portly" is the genteel term for what Greg looks like. He's a great Santa at Christmas over at the Community Center, and today he looks like a distinguished gentleman ready to play hardball at the boardroom table.

"What'd they say?" Amanda is wearing a long, gray pencil skirt with a slit up the back. Nothing too racy, but with her curvy hips it looks business sexy. Red silk shell and black blazer. With the black hair and red lips, she has the look down. I have to stop myself from calling her Mistress.

"They want to expand the account by sixty percent. Into their high-end properties."

Amanda and I suppress twin squeals of excitement. Anterdec owns an enormous chunk of real estate, hospitality companies, and restaurants in the area. If they have fewer than two hundred properties, I'd be surprised.

An account this big, including their luxury hotels, fine dining, and elite transportation services, could turn Consolidated into a major player in marketing services for enterprise companies.

(See how I did that? I should be a highly paid copywriter. Instead, I spent the ten minutes after we got here using a lint roller to peel cat hair off Greg's back.)

"You want first dibs on mystery shopping The Fort?" Greg's words make my heart soar. Amanda's eyes open so wide I think one will fall out. The Fort is *the* exclusive waterfront hotel in Boston. Rumor has it the mints on the pillows have mints on them. Sheiks and royalty from around the world stay there when they are in town.

A night in a standard suite costs what I make in a month.

"Dibs!" I hiss. Amanda snarls.

"Down, you two. If this goes through, there will be more than enough shops for both of you and Josh. The luxury shops will be handled in-house. I might need to add employees."

"You might need to add heat and a toilet," Amanda cracks just as the receptionist catches our eye and motions toward the board room.

We are in the financial district of Boston, where people like me notice the nearest Starbucks or Boloco, but folks like the vice president for marketing at Anterdec notice which building has a helipad for helicopter landings.

Three suited men are turned away from us as we enter, their heads huddled in discussion. One head is gray, two are brown.

No women. Of course.

"Advantage already. No women," Greg whispers in my ear. He is the opposite of sexist. He pays all of us, male or female, the same crappy salary.

The office is gorgeous. I'd expected a sleek, black and gray glassed room overlooking the building across the narrow road; the financial district isn't close enough to the water for everyone to get their sliver of a view of the ocean.

But *this*. We are on the twenty-second floor and the window looks out over a rooftop terrace next door, covered with topiary filled with . . . PacMan?

"Is that a PacMan maze on that rooftop, or am I nuts?" I whisper to Amanda, who stifles a giggle.

"Big video-game development company next door. Their IPO just happened. I hear one of the perks of working there is that they deworm your dog or cat on site while you work."

I open my mouth to say something back, when the three men turn and stand, facing us.

My mouth remains open.

One of the men is Declan McCormick.

His eyes meet mine and five different emotions roil through that chiseled jaw, those sharp eyes, that sun-kissed skin. Most of them are scandalous. All of them make my toes curl.

And then his face spreads with the hottest, warmest, most

mischievous smile I have ever seen on a man who has taken over my damn senses, and he says:

"Toilet Girl!"

chapter
seven

THERE ARE SO MANY ways the next few seconds can unfold. I can pretend I don't know what he is talking about and remain professional, giving him nonverbal cues and hoping he is decent enough to play along.

I can turn around and run screaming from the building.

I can laugh nonchalantly and step forward with grace, offering my hand and telling the story with self-deprecating sophistication and wit so overwhelming that I clinch the deal right here.

Instead, Amanda blurts out, "That's Hot Guy?"

Declan's face goes from joyfully amused to ridiculously gorgeous as he tucks his chin in one hand and tries not to laugh. The gray-haired man looks from Declan to me with an annoyed expression, the kind you only see on men who don't like to be left out of knowing the score, and who are accustomed to having everyone make them the center of attention.

The other brown-haired man takes a step forward and offers his hand to Amanda, who is standing a step closer to them than I am. "Hello. I'm Andrew McCormick, and you are . . . ?"

"Amanda Warrick," she says with a clipped, professional cadence. The lingering handshake is mutual, though.

He seems to drop her hand with great reluctance, then turns to me. "My brother calls you Toilet Girl, but I'm going to assume that's a stage name?"

Amanda snickers. Greg looks like I just drop-kicked his Christmas morning puppy out the twenty-second-story window. Declan watches me with deeply curious eyes and a flame of interest that makes the room feel like we've moved to the equator, and the gray-haired man clears his throat.

"You look a bit . . . flushed," he says to me with a confused smile, but impish eyes. I can see what Declan will look like in thirty years.

The room descends into chaotic laughter.

"Shannon Jacoby," I say, ignoring the howling monkeys and reaching out to shake what I assume is James McCormick's hand. The CEO of Anterdec, I've researched him thoroughly, but never in a million years put the McCormick name together with Declan. Amanda does the personal background research, and I mentally kick myself for not reading her brief. Then again, I didn't exactly plan to have Meghan drop nine shops on me in the wee hours of this morning.

"I take it you two have met?" Andrew says to me and Declan, his hard stare at his brother making it clear he expects the full story later.

"Careful, Dad—you don't want to know where that hand's been," Declan says dryly as the elder McCormick and I grasp hands for a quick shake.

"May I speak with you for a moment?" I ask Declan through a gritted-teeth smile. Anger blazes bright in me, turning a heat that had been uncomfortably sultry into a fiery mix of professional offense and uncontrollable lust.

Declan comes over next to me and places his hand on the small of my back as if to guide me to a quiet corner of the room so I can hiss at him while the others introduce themselves.

We both freeze. The touch of his palm, polite but firm, makes my entire body pulse with electricity and groundedness. His hand represents some core I didn't know I lack. Our breath becomes one, and I will myself not to look at him, because if I do, what will I see in his eyes?

Anything but the same feelings I have right now will destroy me. And the not knowing is easier to live with than certain rejection.

He leans down, hot breath tickling my ear, blowing lightly on the strands of hair that escape my up-do.

"I've been thinking about you all morning," he rasps. A million snappy comebacks flood my mind, but I hold them in check. Deflecting this—this supernova of attraction—can only happen for so long.

Declan and I are at the vanguard of a monumental paradigm shift, all right.

And all the business jargon in the world can't stop me from what fate has in store.

"Toilet water has that effect on men. They ought to bottle it and sell it at the perfume counter of Neiman Marcus."

He doesn't react. At all. No snort of laughter, no eye roll of derision. Just a heat that radiates off him and makes me simmer.

"What were you really doing in that bathroom?" he finally asks, the hand on my back moving in slow circles. It's the briefest hint of touch, but it makes me lean in to him, and I smell him, a mix of musk, cloves, and sophistication. "You clearly weren't a student on her way to class."

"PlentyofFish.com wasn't doing it for me, so . . ."

"You're on the market?" Declan asks. "No boyfriend? What about Mark J.? All that sex in the cooler, next to the salad bins."

I am going to scream. "You called me *Toilet Girl* at a business meeting," I say, remembering my anger. All I want to do is to become a puddle of Shannon at his feet and evaporate magically to reconstitute in his bed. Especially if the sheets smell like him. But I am standing here in professional dress, having added a blazer to the outfit my mom coordinated for me, and Greg is staring at us like two giant dollar signs are popping out of his eyes.

"And I'm *Hot Guy*?" His voice has a touch of steel behind the amusement.

He's got me there.

"How about Hot Guy and Toilet Girl get a cup of coffee after this meeting and see what happens?" he asks, pointedly ignoring everyone else in the room.

"You're asking me out at a client pitch meeting?" I ask, incredulous. My career rests on this account. If Greg doesn't get this deal, I'm stuck mystery shopping podiatrists and insurance agents forever.

"Would it help if I confess you're my first?"

"You're a virgin?" I sputter, just as the senior McCormick clears his throat and Declan and I look up, startled. From the Mr. Bill looks of shock on everyone's face, they've heard my last question.

"If we could get back to business," James says, motioning all of us to sit at the large oak table. It easily seats twenty and has carved legs thicker than my thigh. And let me tell you, that means it's nice and big, like something from the Teddy Roosevelt administration.

The entire office reeks of *man*. Thick, brown leather couches and pub chairs. Ornate Persian rugs bigger than the entire footprint of my parents' house. Heavy wood fixtures and Frank Lloyd Wright-inspired glass lamps.

Make that *original* Frank Lloyd Wright designs, most likely.

My face on fire, among other body parts, I sit at the table. Declan takes a seat across from me. My view faces the window, and it's amazing. And the sky is damn nice looking, too.

Greg rambles for five minutes about marketing crap that used to be important to me, but now all I can do is sneak looks at Declan and wonder how on earth I can put the genie back in the bottle. I don't want to be attracted to him. I don't want to be attracted to *anyone*.

My good nights involve cuddling with Chuckles on the couch while I binge watch seasons of television shows on Netflix with my favorite Crab Rangoon and hot 'n' sour soup takeout from the place down the street. The guy knows me so well he lets me tip him an extra three bucks to hop over to the convenience store and get my favorite pint of ice cream.

Now *that's* love. Even if you have to buy it.

This kind of interest in and from a man is deadly. It kills hope. Because here's how it works: I like him. He likes me. We bump uglies in bed. I want to talk about emotions. He wants to talk about anything but. I want a future.

He wants another girlfriend.

See? I can write the script and deliver it done. Lather, rinse, repeat.

Steve dumped me because I wanted a future and he wanted the female equivalent of a hood ornament. Which, as I smooth my shirt over my ample hips, I am not—in Steve's eyes. The woman he turned to after me is poised, well-coiffed, has a master's in public health from Harvard, and comes from a family that was descended from the original *Mayflower* passengers.

My Mendon roots can't compete.

Why am I thinking about Steve right now? I wonder, though as I take in the surroundings as Amanda steps up and recites statistics about new product testing and upselling by clerks in the Anterdec fast-food chains, I realize why.

Because Steve should be sitting at a table like this. Probably is, right now, in fact. Negotiating some business deal with a group of smirking suits who view every woman they work with as a coordinator.

I watch Declan watching Amanda, and really look at him. He's serious now, eyes tracking the PowerPoint slides as she clicks through, graphs and charts aligned beautifully to nail the entire point of this meeting:

We know our stuff.

You want to improve customer service, cut down on employee theft, help raise retention, and grow your customer base?

Let me lurk in your men's rooms and report back what I see.

What I saw this morning is suddenly staring back with a wolfish look so deep that I feel raw and vulnerable, like our suits, the rugs, the business paraphernalia is all just a prop to cover up the fact that we're primal beings who simply want each other.

This is new.

This is too much.

Someone says my name. They say it again. Then I feel a massive pain in my ankle.

"Ow!" I utter. Amanda's glare is even sharper than her ankle as it crashes into mine again. She's kicking me.

"It's your turn, Closer," she whispers. I look around the table. James, Andrew, and Greg look at me expectantly.

I stand, completely rattled. The deck I prepared is on the same laptop Amanda's been using, but it's like I've lost all organizational capacity in my mind. Declan won't stop looking at me like that.

Like *that*. Like he's watching me naked and he's nude and rising up to meet every square inch of my . . .

James starts to frown while Andrew gives Amanda a knowing look. I clear my throat, but before I can say anything, Declan interrupts.

"We have another meeting to get to," he says.

"We do?" Andrew exclaims, then, "Ow!" I get the impression Amanda's not the only one kicking ankles, because Declan gives his brother a fierce look.

"We do. And as the new vice president of marketing, I'm the decision maker here, right?" He looks at James with a hard stare.

All the friendliness drains out of the room. Greg looks like he's about to throw up, then pastes on a sad smile.

"Is there a reason why you won't have me finish the presentation?" I ask, my voice spiked with ice. If he's going to be an asshole and cut me short, and this has all been some kind of game, I'm not leaving without having my say. I've been through enough presentations like this to know that if you can get the senior executive on board, even if the other two don't like it, you have a fighting chance.

"Oh, you'll finish it." Declan's voice is dismissive. It makes my jaw ache, and I bite my tongue. "But I can't now." He becomes a smartphone zombie, avoiding eye contact. He's blowing hot and cold like the old heater in Greg's office.

James stays quiet. I get the sense it's not his normal state. His eyes flick over me, then back to Declan. "Of course, it's your call."

"But my presentation has some hard data that could really affect your decision," I say. I'm not going without a fighting chance.

"I'd like to reschedule your presentation," Declan says as he strides toward the door. Andrew follows him, slowly and with the stance of someone who is not accustomed to being the follower.

"When?" Greg asks.

"Tonight. Shannon and I will have a dinner meeting. Seven. Wear something nice," he says over his shoulder as he walks out.

Fury washes over me and I stand, crossing the big room in seconds. My hand reaches out for his shoulder and he turns around, eyes cold, looking down on me.

"You can't just order me to go on a date with you!" I cry out. The receptionist cocks her head, listening.

"Who said anything about a date?" His face is inscrutable. "It's a business meeting. Leave your address with Stacia and she'll have a driver sent to your home."

And with that, he stalks out. I start to follow him, but Amanda and Greg appear.

"He can't do that!" I sputter to Greg. *Back me up, dude,* I think.

James McCormick comes out, a bemused look on his face as he stares at me. "Ms. Jacoby, I assume you can give a good show for Declan tonight?"

Show? What am I now? Auditioning for *The Voice*? Who cares about this stupid account? I've been turned into a boy toy in seconds by Mr. Asshole in a Suit, and I'm about to give the McCormicks a piece of my mind.

Greg pipes up, finally. Good. *Here we go, boss. Defend me.*

"Shannon would be delighted. I'm sure Declan will love whatever she shows him tonight."

And with that, James McCormick leaves us, disappearing back into the football-field office.

I spin in outrage to Greg. "Thanks for pimping me!"

He shrugs. "The guy said *business* meeting. If that's what it takes to land this account, you can talk about process flow and customer satisfaction over candlelight, right?"

"You ever been told by a VP of marketing to 'wear something nice' and had a limo sent to your home for a *business* meeting?"

Silence.

"Look at it this way," Amanda says, slinging her laptop over her shoulder and shooting me a sympathetic look. "It has to be better than the way you met for the first time."

"And you!" I hiss. "'Hot Guy'? Seriously? You just . . . I don't even know you people. It's like you've become my mother!"

They both shudder. "That's kind of low, Shannon," Amanda mutters as we walk to the elevator. Greg scurries over to Stacia the receptionist and I hear him giving her my address. My God. It's like my mother has been tutoring him.

"And whoring me out to the VP of Anterdec Industries isn't?"

"I'm sure he won't do anything inappropriate," Greg says as he catches up to us.

"Bummer," Amanda says.

Greg's turn to look outraged. He's old enough—barely—to be our father, and while most of the time he acts like a peer, this isn't one of those moments. A paternalistic air fills the space between the three of us. It's more what I'd expected back in that meeting, and I would have appreciated it then, but I'll take what I can get.

"You absolutely do not need to go to this business dinner tonight," he says, resolute. Amanda's neck snaps back with surprise at the firmness of his words. "I'll go instead."

"Wear something nice," Amanda chirps.

He scowls. My stomach sinks. I want him to say that, but I don't want him to follow through. Being alone with Declan on a date—er, business dinner—sounds like heaven. This is my big chance to prove I am more than Toilet Girl. More pragmatically, if we can mix business and pleasure, why not snag a multimillion-dollar account, too, while I am at it?

The entire conversation taking place in my head makes me need a shower to wash off how dirty I feel and to need a shower with Declan. *Mmmm*, Declan in the shower, soaping me up, and—

"See how distraught she is!" Greg whispers to Amanda. "Look at that blank stare."

Amanda snorts. "I think she's drooling, Greg. That's the look of a woman dreaming about Hot Guy."

He looks offended. "Why would anyone be . . . you women are so . . . I don't understand . . ." We climb on the elevator and he pushes the *Close Doors* button. He's still sputtering when we hit the parking garage level where his car is parked. "And besides, what do you think your mother would say if she knew?"

"She'd offer me up just like you did, Greg. And go home and cut an extra foot up the slit of any dress I have. She's a better pimp than you when it comes to dating a billionaire."

"He's not a billionaire," is all Greg can come back with.

"He will be when he inherits his share of Anterdec." Amanda speaks with the authority of someone who has snooped through every nook and cranny of a man's Google results.

A dizzy wave of overwhelm makes me cling to the iron-pipe bannister of the concrete steps near Greg's car. "A billionaire?" Mom would get her Farmington Country Club wedding and more if I . . .

STOP!

"You feeling faint, Shannon?" Greg pauses, looking at me intently. "You seem fragile today." A look of sheer horror passes over him while I struggle to keep down my bites of all those early-morning bagel sandwiches. "You're not . . . you couldn't be . . . you know?" He mimes a basketball in front of his already-basketball-sized belly.

"What? A sumo wrestler?" Amanda mimics with startling brutality.

"Pregnant," he whispers. The two of them look at each other with twin expressions of shock and dissolve into hooting laughter, the kind where you wipe your eyes and hope you don't pee your pants.

"Not funny," I say.

"We know. You can't be pregnant. It would be the immaculate conception," Amanda squeaks.

My dizziness passes. "Done making fun of me? Let's get going."

They compose themselves and Greg beeps his car to unlock it. We climb in. I take the front seat and Amanda grumbles. I summon a Chuckles-worthy glare and she cowers, climbing in without another peep.

"What's your rush?" Greg balks as I tap my foot impatiently.

"I have to find something nice to wear tonight."

chapter
eight

"**Y**OU SNITCH!" IT'S 6:45P.M. and I am being held hostage by terrorist extremists with a list of demands that make al-Qaeda look like preschoolers playing pirate.

"I didn't mean to tell her," Amanda insists. "She asked me about Hot Guy and—"

"I can hear you. I'm two inches from your mouth," Mom says, waving an eyeshadow wand like she's conducting the Boston Pops. Occasionally it actually hits my eyelid. She won't admit she needs bifocals; her glasses are pushed so low on her nose they might as well be in Albany.

She can't see a thing, and I'm rapidly fearing I look more like Pennywise the Clown than Olivia Wilde. Mom promised me she could make me look like her, or Scarlett Johansson, or Jennifer Lawrence, with enough time and high-end makeup.

Right now I'd settle for retaining full vision in my left eye, which she has now poked twice with the eyeshadow wand.

"You have to look good to catch a billionaire's eye," Mom says. Then she frowns and, Lord have mercy, puts down the eyeshadow wand.

"I know," I simper.

"What about the rest of you?" Her eyes comb over her work so far. I think she'd like to produce the Mona Lisa, but is going to have to settle for Lisa Simpson.

"The rest of me? I shaved my legs and armpits. Plucked my eyebrows—"

"Is that what's different? What did you use, honey? A weed whacker?"

I look at her. She flinches. I swear the corners of Chuckles mouth turn up a tad.

"You can leave now," I say for the umpteenth time. "It's a business dinner."

"Did you shave . . . you know?" She points vaguely at my crotch area.

"My knees? Yes." I'm playing dumb on purpose.

"No! Your pink bits."

I choke and cough uncontrollably. I am not having this conversation, am I? Seriously? What did I do in a past life to deserve this? I was Eva Braun, wasn't I?

"All the girls your age do it. You'd think having a pubic hair or three was some kind of social crime." She's talking, and the words are coming out, but I can't hear her over the lambs screaming in my head. "Then again, men your age have come to expect a smooth Chuckles, so . . ."

Chuckles arches his back, the hairs rising on end, and he opens his mouth, hissing.

"A smooth what?"

"Chuckles," she whispers, enunciating the word. He hisses at her.

"Huh?"

"P-u-s-s-y," Mom spells out. "That's the word your father likes to use now that we need to spice things up in the—"

"Hara-kiri! Give me a kitchen knife!" I shout just as my sister, Amy, walks in the door.

"To kill Mom, or you?" She's carrying a bag of groceries and an extremely large foam hand.

"Either. Both. Mom was just telling me *allllll* about how Dad likes to talk dirty in bed."

Amy blanches. "Mom? Boundaries! Please!"

"What? It's not like that time I told you about needing a new diaphragm because it kept slipping during sex and making those strange sucking sounds."

I think even Chuckles turned pale at that one.

Mom keeps going. "Your father said the sounds reminded him of Darth Vader. So then we had this whole role-play thing going on with Princess Leia and Han Solo. . . ."

My cell phone buzzes with a text. Sweet Jesus, thank you. Saved by the limo driver. "Gotta go!" I say. "What's with the foam finger? You got a date with Robin Thicke?"

Amy gives me a look like a dog having its eyes poked out by a toddler. "Where are you off to?" She tosses the foam finger at Chuckles, who flees. She never answers my question, though, because Mom decides to be the town crier.

"Shannon has a date with a billionaire!" Mom exclaims.

"Oh? And I'm engaged to the leprechaun from the Lucky Charms cereal!" Amy replies, clapping her hands with fake glee.

I'm out the door before I can hear more.

Except the limo driver isn't who greets me when I get down my twenty-seven steps in high heels made of what feel like five-inch hatpins.

It's Declan.

Mom insisted I wear a little black dress, with an emphasis on "little." I'm a DD up top. Her spaghetti-strap ensemble left the equivalent of Girl Scout badges covering my boobs.

My tailored blazer with scalloped edges works well. Mom's borrowed diamond necklace and earrings make the picture. As long as I don't twist an ankle or take out a small pet with my high heels, I should be fine.

Declan is wearing what looks like a tuxedo, but without the tie. He approaches, and there's a moment where the setting sun is behind him and frames his body, the hues of rose and violet streaking the gray sky. He saunters toward me with a look of total absorption, eyes only on me, hungry and appreciative. My core tightens and fills with an unfamiliar feeling.

Desire.

He reaches for my hand and just holds it. He smells like soap and cloves and aftershave. I want to taste him. He looks like he wants to devour me.

"Hello!" says someone from behind me. I close my eyes and wince as my mother breaks her *You should* rule and calls down to us from the top of my stairs. "You kids have fun."

"It's not the prom, Mom," Amy shouts through my open apartment door.

"Of course it's not," Mom snaps. "Shannon had those really bad cramps that night and her date got lice, so it's not like she ever even went!"

Amy's face appears at the door for a fleeting second before she drags my protesting mother inside. *Slam!*

I blink three or four times, silent. Declan's thumb begins to move back and forth, slowly, maddeningly, like it's gentling a spooked horse.

His hand is shaking a bit. Not from nerves.

Because he is laughing.

I jerk my hand away, remembering myself. This is a business meeting. Business. Pure business.

"I promise I don't have lice," he says.

I almost snap back, *And I don't have my period right now*, but I already want to crawl into a hole and die. Why add to it?

"Not having lice is a great quality in a VP of marketing. Especially since so many of them are louses."

"Ouch."

"Hey, I aspire to be one someday."

"Shannon Jacoby, head louse." His face hardens as he realizes what he's said versus what he clearly meant.

"That just sounds all kinds of wrong, Declan."

"How about we both stop talking and just get in the limo." It's not a question. His hand lands on the base of my back and we both freeze again. Electricity travels in a full circuit between our two bodies. His pulse becomes mine. The tiny hairs on the wrist I can see stand up slowly, as if summoned, just like—

Well, just like something else on his body, I imagine.

The hand on my back slides up my spine, over the fine wool of my jacket, sinking into my loose hair, respectful but sending one hell of a signal. There is no pretense here. I don't have to guess whether he's interested. And my signals are so clear that the only way I could be more obvious would be to rent a billboard and hang a twenty-foot color photo of myself naked with the caption "I WILL SLEEP WITH YOU, DECLAN."

It can't be this easy, can it? My mind spins as his fingers move along the tender skin of my neck, making me gasp. I'm looking up at him and his lips look soft. Tender. Commanding and tasty.

A distant sound of ringing glass fills the air. It's distinct and cuts through the spell between us.

Declan looks back toward my front door. My mother is standing next to the open window with a wine glass and a spoon, gently chiming it like she's at a wedding reception and calling for the bride and groom to—

"Kiss! Kiss! Kiss!" she chants.

Declan looks at me, and with a deadpan expression says, "I think your mother wants us to take this nice and slow."

Amy yanks Mom out of the window and I hear muffled yelling. I grab Declan's hand and pull him to the limo door. The driver opens it and I climb in so fast and so inelegantly I hear my skirt split up the seam in the back.

Declan hears it, too, but sits back in the beige leather seat and ogles the vast expanse of creamy skin my mishap now exposes. A scene from a movie I saw recently, where a couple has sex in a limo, the woman in a ball gown, straddling the man, picks this exact moment to make a re-entrance into my psyche, plaguing me.

"Nice legs," Declan says.

"I'll bet you say that to all the marketing coordinators." He starts to say something, and I add, "And to none of the marketing vice presidents."

He thinks about that for a second and says, "You got me there."

chapter
nine

OUR EYES LOCK. "WHERE are we going?" It's a relief to make simple small talk.

He names a restaurant I've always wanted to try, but needed to date a billionaire to afford.

Oh.

"Sounds good," I say, nodding. Leaning back against the buttery leather, I try to take in my surroundings without looking like a major gawker. The leather seats hug my body better than any knockoff Tempur-Pedic memory foam like Mom and Dad have on their bed back home. A small fridge and a few decanters of what I assume are spirits dot the edges of the enclosed space. The limo looks like it could seat six comfortably, eight in a pinch.

With just two of us in here, there's plenty of room to stretch out.

Go horizontal.

Or straddle.

I close my eyes, willing the sensual images that flood my brain to stop. Declan's steady breath doesn't help, cutting through me like he's syncing it with the pictures in my mind. The scent of him fills the air between us and I feel charmed.

And doomed.

Declan chooses to say nothing, just watching me as if it's the most natural thing in the world. His eyes take me in and I wonder how I appear to him. Loose, long hair. Makeup mostly where it's supposed to go. A curvy body in a dress meant to ooze sophistication. A tailored, feminine blazer that says I might be sexy underneath, but I'm all business on the outside.

My inner world is crumbling, brick by brick, and Declan's holding the sledgehammer that demolishes me. Women like me don't ride in cars like this. We don't get invited out for a dinner—business or pleasure—by men like Declan. And we certainly don't entertain wild ideas about happily ever after with men who will go so high in the business world that women like me are just, well . . . coordinators.

Whatever delusions I hold inside about his attraction for me are there only because he's looking at me like he really means it. As if I am as beautiful and desirable as his look says.

He's very good at pretending that I'm worth the attention.

His phone rings, making me jump. His breathing stays the same, and his sleek, fluid movement impresses me. Nothing seems to rattle him. With dulcet tones, he talks to someone named Grace, the cadence of their conversation quickly familiar to me. Scheduling helicopters and private jets may be out of my realm, but I know a logistics talk when I hear one. Grace is probably his executive assistant. Something about New Zealand, a reception, and then a return flight to the West Coast pops up through their twenty-minute conversation.

I spend the time willing my heart to stay in my chest.

If I weren't such a cheap date I'd knock back a shot of whatever is in the crystal decanter at my elbow, an amber liquid that looks good. But two drinks and I'm quite tipsy. Three and I'm drunk.

Four and I'm singing "Bad Romance" at full blast in a really cheesy karaoke performance. Whether there's a karaoke machine or not.

Declan shoots me apologetic looks every so often, and I just smile without teeth. A shrug here and there helps communicate that it's okay. I get it. And I do.

In fact, the phone conversation helps me to bring my overwrought self back to center. Business. This is business. I'm not on a date with him. We're talking about a few million dollars a year that his company wants to spend for a specific value premise, and my company would love to receive that money to offer services.

That's it.

This is a transaction. Not a relationship. And certainly not an affair.

"It'll be at the restaurant?" Declan murmurs into the phone, then his face goes neutral but the skin around his eyes turns up a touch, like a smile without his lips moving.

Grace says something. Declan replies, "Good," and hangs up abruptly. It would be rude if it weren't shorthand. I'm sure Grace is doing a dance she and Declan know all too well, keeping the ship running smoothly through the careful discarding of unnecessary social expectations for the sake of ruthless efficiency.

He tucks the phone inside the breast pocket of his suit jacket just as the driver slows the limo, bringing it to a gentle halt. I look out the window. We're here.

Except the entrance we use is most definitely not one for the *hoi polloi*. Wouldn't want the unwashed masses rubbing elbows with the richie-riches, right? My own bitterness surprises me, and I have a hard time looking at Declan for a minute or two.

His eyes shift; he sees it, and wants to say something, but doesn't. Instead, the driver opens my door and Declan's hand comes out to take mine.

My heart seizes with the touch of bare skin on bare skin. Jesus. If the man can get me this close to an O holding my hands, I'll stroke out if we ever make it to a bed, naked.

And there I go again . . . what is wrong with me? I don't do this. I don't think like this. Not only do I not randomly strip strange men naked with my mind and have little porno movies in my head about them, I don't even think about one-night stands.

The only guys I've ever slept with were friends first. Good friends. The slow, leisurely meandering to physical affection and something more, carefully measured out and talked through is more my speed.

I like to take things slow. To reveal myself layer by layer to men. To dip a toe in the water and pull back. I'm the kind of person who gets into a pool one inch of flesh at a time, pausing to shiver and acclimate.

Declan is the sexual equivalent of doing a cannonball. At 4 a.m. In March in northern Vermont.

As I climb out, my torn skirt shows so much thigh I might as well have given birth.

Declan's eyebrow arches with appreciation. Controlling my breathing is becoming a second job. I stand and he reaches for me again, his hand on my back, and he smells like cloves, cinnamon, and tobacco. Not cigarettes, though.

"Do you smoke?" I ask as he leads me to an enormous oak door that opens suddenly, a concierge standing there in full tux.

"No. That's Dad's pipe you smell. We were working late at the office."

It's cardamom and Bengal tea spicy yumminess. I want to brew him in hot water and drink him.

We enter a room with an arched ceiling so high I expect to look up and see God with his finger outstretched. The dusky night shines through rounded windows at the peak. Dark mahogany covers the walls and muted lighting gives the restaurant a womblike feel. I can see past the front desk into the main dining room, where thick burgundy curtains frame each table.

This is a place designed for privacy.

"Ms. Jacoby." The maître d' appears, a man who looks to be about my father's age, with gray hair and a salt-and-pepper goatee. He's shorter than Declan, but lean, like a triathlete. Dressed in a tuxedo slightly different from the man at the door, he exudes luxury and service.

In his hand is a small white box with a bow and a gold paper medallion on it. He holds it out to me.

Puzzled, I look at Declan, who just smiles. I slide my fingernail along the gold seal and open the box.

It's a corsage.

"What?" A sentimental laugh fills me, and suddenly I'm at ease.

"You missed your prom, so I thought . . ." Declan has been calm, cool, and collected until this moment. Right now, he looks like a nervous seventeen year old, though he covers it quickly, eyes going back to a hooded, careless look quite fast.

I pull it out of the box and pin it to my blazer. It's a tasteful set of small red and white roses with a sprig of baby's breath around it. Simple. Elegant.

Special.

I stand on tiptoe and kiss his cheek. My lips graze his jaw as I step down. He's clean-shaven, but the rasp of my skin against his makes my entire body fill with instant lust.

"This is the nicest gesture anyone has ever made for me at a business meeting. Normally I'm lucky to have my own laptop outlet." I can't say what I really want to say, a mixture of gushing gratitude and joy that my babbling adolescent self is screeching inside. The words *Thank you* and *He likes me!* echo a thousand times a second through my mind and heart.

The box disappears as if the maître d' were Dumbledore with a wand, and he leads us back to a table for four, shrouded on three sides by thick velvet curtains, a dim chandelier above us.

Declan pulls my chair out and I sit, scooching in, the press of cool leather a surprise on my upper thighs. Damn. My skirt's split *that* high?

I'm unnerved again. A corsage? The heady scent of roses and caring fills the air around me. Declan's looking at me with eyes that say this is *not* a business meeting, and my body responds to him like it has to no other man. Ever. Not even Steve made me feel like this.

"I didn't go to my prom either," he says as we settle in. A waiter fills our water glasses and a bottle of wine appears. Before I'm asked, a glass of red is poured for me.

I hate red wine.

"I would have thought that you were prom king," I say.

He shakes his head, eyebrows furrowed. Then he waves a hand as if dispersing a bad memory.

"What?" I ask. I feel bolder now, as if I have the right to make him tell me whatever it is he was about to dismiss.

"I . . . I missed it because of my mother," he says, reluctant, as if the confession is against his nature.

"Your mother?"

"She was in the hospital."

My mind races to recall all the details Amanda and I learned when we researched Anterdec after our meeting. I know the name is the amalgam of the three sons' names: Andrew, Terrance, and Declan. An Ter Dec. But Mrs. McCormick . . . I don't remember anything about her.

"She died the day after my prom," Declan says softly. Our eyes meet, and mine must be horrified, because he reaches out for my hand to comfort *me*. He's the one whose mother died.

"You lost your mother that young?" I can't help it. My throat fills with sympathetic tears. My mom may be a pain in the ass, but I don't know what I'd do without her.

"It's been ten years," he says thickly. "But thank you."

"For what?"

"For reacting like that."

"Like what?"

"Like you care. Most people don't let themselves have genuine reactions to anything emotional."

"I'm not most people." The words come out wrong. What I want to say is *I wear my heart on my sleeve,* but that seems too vulnerable. This is just a business dinner, right?

Right.

"I'm sorry," I say, pulling my hand away with great reluctance. He squeezes it and begins to run his thumb along the soft skin of my wrist.

He's not going to let me retreat.

"So tell me why you need more convincing to give this account to Consolidated," I say, trying to change the tenor of this encounter.

I fail.

"Tell me why you're so afraid of me."

I reach for the red wine with my open hand and twirl the glass. The last time I drank red wine was with Steve, at our final work outing for him. He dragged me along to a big dinner with his firm and I choked down a glass and a half as he sent me a million nonverbal signals throughout the entire dinner.

Most of which involved scowls and eye rolls, because I did everything wrong.

Declan takes a sip of his wine and returns his attention to me.

"I'm not afraid of you." I really want white wine. A battle inside emerges. *Let it go*, one part says. *Speak up and assert yourself,* says another. *Billionaire grandchildren,* says my mother's voice.

I take a big sip of the red wine and choke it down.

"Maybe you're afraid of yourself," he says.

"Maybe I'm afraid you think I'm just being whored out by my boss so I'll land this account."

"Maybe I don't need sex so badly I trade accounts for it."

"Maybe that was never an option."

"Maybe I'm more interested in knowing why you were perched on that toilet. You still haven't answered my question from earlier."

That makes me laugh. "Why do you think? I was finishing the last mystery shop of the day. Who do you think reports on the cleanliness of the bathrooms?"

That makes him pause and take another sip of wine. "Never thought about it." He's still holding my hand, but his thumb stops moving.

"Of course not. That's *my* job. Not yours." I lean in, lowering my voice. "And thank you for not asking me to count the pubic hairs on the urinal cake."

"You're welcome, I guess." He does a double take. "Our competitors do that?"

"And worse. Don't ask what I have to do when I evaluate a manicure salon and detail their anti-fungal procedures."

He closed his eyes, but he's amused. "How romantic."

"I wouldn't talk like this if we were on a date. But this is all business."

We both look at our clasped hands. Then our eyes meet and he starts to say something, but the waiter appears and introduces himself. A flurry of recited specials and then we order. I get the filet and Declan orders some complicated pheasant dish.

"No salad and fish?" he asks when the waiter leaves. We've dropped hands. It feels weird to be disconnected. We're sitting next to each other, yet the table is large.

"Was I supposed to? Is this a mystery shop and that's the required meal?" I'm teasing, but it occurs to me that this is the first time I've dined out in a long time where I get to choose exactly what I want.

He cocks his head and studies me. In the low light of the restaurant, I can see auburn highlights in his hair. "Tell me about your life."

"Wow. You start small, don't you?"

He smiles wide, flashing those perfect teeth. "Tell me."

"I'll tell you about the account," I insist, trying hard to bring this back to business.

He sighs. "You *have* the account."

"I do?" I squeak.

"Of course. Now I want more."

chapter
ten

WAIT. WHY DID YOU ask about salad and fish?"
First things first.

"Because that's what every woman I date orders when we dine."

"Seriously? There's a meal code? I'm breaking some rule by getting *beef*?"

"You ordered what you like. I find that appealing. No pretense. No affect. You're just being Shannon."

Which wasn't enough for Steve. "I'm being the marketing coordinator for Consolidated Evalu-shop, Declan. You've just told me we have the account. Thank you."

Deflect deflect deflect.

"No—thank *you*. Once I realized what you were doing in that men's room, I knew we needed to give your company the account."

I almost drop the wine glass in shock. A tiny splash of red wine stains the white tablecloth. It looks like blood.

"You knew who I was?"

"Not quite. I figured you were with Consolidated, though. We knew your company would perform shops this week. It's one of the reasons I was there. Just spot-checking stores."

"And you didn't say anything?"

"I said a lot of things. You kept your cover as much as possible. Even to the point of hilarity."

"And embarrassment."

"That, too."

"Most people find me uncouth." Okay, *Steve* found me uncouth. Why am I thinking about Steve right now? I should be pretending to need to use the ladies' room and running in there to frantically text Amanda and Greg the good news.

"Anyone who thinks that is an ass who doesn't know an authentic human being from a blow-up doll girlfriend."

"I never said anything about a boyfriend," I protest.

"You didn't have to."

I am torn between being offended and being attracted to him, the professional in me screaming that this is inappropriate, but the woman inside wanting to press myself against him and explore.

All I can do is make a funny whimpering sound of defeat and confusion.

A flicker of movement in the corner of my eye catches my attention. A couple has come in to the restaurant, the woman with long, straight blond hair that reaches the cleft of her ass. She's willowy thin and wearing a tight white dress with a bright red silk sash as a belt. Her date is bent over, face out of sight, but I stiffen as I recognize the body, knowing those broad shoulders, that nipped waist, and the cut of the Armani suit with the fraternity pin at the lapel.

And then Steve stands up and looks into the dining room. Craning his neck, he's playing the room, searching for someone he can network with and impress. Building a client base is important, he always said. But who you run into a dinner or a bar or the gym is worth so much more. His eyes land—

Directly on me. His face turns to the right as if he can't believe he sees what he sees. His hand on his date's waist tightens, like he's saying *I'm taken*.

No shit, Sherlock.

Declan follows my stare and his eyes narrow. He reaches for my hand again. Predatory. Like he's claiming me. Staking out his territory.

Maybe I'm taken too, Steve.

"Who is that?" Declan asks.

I watch as Steve's eyes move over to Declan. Instant

recognition kicks in. Steve is an opportunist at heart. He appears to know exactly who Declan is, and this is a script I can write, too.

"That's my ex," I say without moving my lips.

"Good ex or bad ex?" he mutters. I break away and stare at Declan now, because what kind of man gets the landscape of dating *that* well?

"Social climber ex. Mendon girls aren't his thing. He traded up for a nicer model," I whisper, my insides going cold.

Declan shifts his chair a tiny bit closer to me and says through a serious expression, "Don't do that."

"Do what?" Steve and his date are still chatting with the maître d', though Steve points to us. Her eyes light up when she sees Declan, and she chats animatedly with Steve.

"Let him dictate how you view yourself."

I snort. "Like it's that easy."

"It can be."

"It can be," I mimic. I reach for the wine glass and chug it all down in a few gags.

"If you let it, Shannon." His eyes are serious.

"Why did you go all cold billionaire at the end of the meeting earlier today?" I ask. What do I have to lose? Might as well just give in and be me at this point. My day started in the crapper, and as Steve walks slowly across the enormous dining room toward us, it looks like it's ending with a piece of shit.

"Because I learned a long time ago that it's better to have people react to *you* than to react to *them*."

Stunned, I sit and ponder this, his words reverberating in my head as Steve appears, gushing and complimentary.

"Shannon! What a wonderful surprise!" Steve's doing his best Tim Gunn impression. "Don't you look fantastic!" Air kisses follow as he bends down and awkwardly embraces me. I get a mouthful of blue wool lapel.

His date looks like she just ate a lemon.

"Jessica Coffin, this is . . ." Steve pauses. Declan's hand clasps mine hard. " . . . an old friend, Shannon Jacoby."

Old friend? All righty, then. If you call the woman you went shopping for engagement rings with and slept with for the better part of two years an "old friend" . . .

I don't stand. She reaches out and shakes my hand with a cold salmon she pretends is a palm and fingers. Coffin is an old New England/*Mayflower* family name. It fits her.

Steve looks at me, then Declan, then me, then Declan, clearly expecting me to introduce them. His eyes land on our clasped hands.

I've never seen a coyote at the moment its ears pick up the sound of doomed prey, but as I watch Declan watching Steve, I feel like I'm pretty close right now. It's like *When Animals Attack: Boston Brahmin Brawl*—coming soon on The Learning Channel, right after *Honey Boo Boo*!

Steve clears his throat. Jessica looks like a Scandinavian Barbie, bored to tears. Finally, Declan stands and lets go of my hand, but plants a very territorial paw on my shoulder. He gestures with his other hand.

"Why don't you join us?" I swear he growls. Just a little.

Chuckles would be *so* cowed by the look I give Declan. In fact, I think I'm channeling my cat via astral projection, because I become pure evil via my eyes.

Declan just winks.

Winks! How can he wink when I am killing him with my laser death stare?

Steve rushes to sit down next to Declan, leaving Jessica to stand there, the right corner of her lip twitching. Or a bubble of Botox broke free. Hard to tell.

She clears her throat. Steve ignores her, about to open his mouth and say something to Declan. He looks like a golden retriever puppy who can barely control himself from pissing all over the foyer as he waits to be let out.

"Ahem," Jessica says again, looking at Steve with an icy glare that even he can't ignore.

Declan remains standing the entire time and gallantly walks over to her chair, pulls it out, and inclines his head. Her face cracks into chunks of ice the size of glaciers, and a smile that could act as a backup disco ball emerges from her head.

Steve is oblivious. It's his job to remain so. He's a player, a mover and shaker, a guy with one foot on the next rung of the ladder no matter where he's at—as he reminded me a million times while we were together—and he's got his eye on the prize, and the prize isn't Jessica any longer.

It's Declan.

Who looks at Steve like he wants to deworm him.

Meanwhile, my heart is dancing the cha-cha and my legs start to shake from nerves. Just then, the waiter comes to offer wine.

"We'd love to get another bottle of whatever Declan's ordered," Steve says in an arched tone, one he reserves for interacting with "the help" when we're in front of bigwigs. That makes Declan pause and look down at Steve, who is now sitting across from me with a look that says, *Don't blow this.*

Declan recites a few words of French to the waiter, who turns as if to go.

"One moment," I say. The waiter stops. "I would prefer a lighter white wine."

"You ordered the beef," Steve says, frowning. "Of course you drink red with beef." He knows I'm a steak girl, but the way he says it makes me bristle, a streak of self-loathing fury rising in a straight line up from belly to throat. The assumption that I'm a rube who can't possibly know what she's doing was part of the foundation of our entire relationship.

Worst of all? I reinforced it. Not the rube part, but the belief part.

Declan says something else in French to the waiter, who nods to me and walks away. Then he turns to Steve and says, "You know my name?"

Steve laughs in his fakey-sophisticated way. He doesn't seem to realize how obviously pretentious he is. I see it, Dad saw it from the first handshake he had with Steve, Amy sees it, but so many people Steve worked with never saw it.

It was my mom's job *not* to see it. All she saw when she looked at Steve was Harvard and Farmington and little MBA-fathered babies all lined up and cute in their matching Hanna

Andersson pajamas while sleeping in their PoshTots nurseries.

Declan's tight jaw and cold eyes tell me he sees it quite clearly.

"Everyone who's paying attention in this town knows who the McCormicks are," Steve says blithely.

Wrong answer.

Jessica is sitting across from Declan and I'm across from Steve. Declan's hand slips under the table and he leans toward me, hot palm landing on my thigh. Although everything below my waist is obscured by the table, it's damn obvious what he's doing to anyone observing.

Steve's face turns a pale pink I don't recall ever seeing, and Jessica's eyes roll so hard she burns twenty calories with the motion.

"Paying attention is a good quality," Declan says, turning his eyes to me. He gives my thigh a squeeze. I put my hand on his and try to move it.

It is granite.

Something in me snaps and floods at the same time, desperation and attempts at maintaining an illusion of control all melting away with a rush of pleasure. Maybe it's the wine I guzzled. Maybe it's the feel of Declan's hand on my leg, half on the cloth of my skirt and half on my stockings. Yes, the split was that bad.

Bad never felt so good.

Steve is cataloging me now, his eyes done with resting on Declan, instead looking at me as if he'd underestimated the value of a discarded possession.

The waiter picks this exact moment to return, carrying a bottle of white and four glasses. He pours a small amount in a glass. Declan does the necessaries, sipping and nodding with approval. I receive a nice, healthy glass of white wine and then the waiter pours a twin glass for Declan.

He offers some to Jessica, who nods.

Steve declines.

After replacing the chilled bottle in its ice container in a stand that now sits at my left elbow, the waiter asks Jessica for her dinner order.

"I'll have a small field greens salad with vinegar and oil and the tilapia."

Declan makes a noise of amusement and I try not to laugh. Salad and fish. Boy, did he call it. The only way not to start giggling is to drink my wine, which I do. All of it. Like it's Gatorade. I decide right then and there to order the biggest dessert they have on the menu and eat it with gusto.

Because I *can*. And it won't have maple in it.

Steve's eyes bug out of his head while Jessica keeps her bored expression, Maybe it's a new Xanax-Botox combo. Perhaps they inject the Xanax directly under the skin, because whatever it takes to achieve a flat affect that is so utterly devoid of emotion can't be organic. It must be manmade. Someone patented *that*.

Except it all morphs when she talks to Declan. The ice queen becomes a sweet, warm princess and she is hot to snag him. Not that I have a claim on him or anything, though the way his hand is learning the terrain of my inner thigh makes me think he was a geography major with a keen interest in cartography.

I don't stop him. I don't want to. And he's showing no signs of wanting to, either, as his fingertips graze my skin, moving in light circles, taking their time as they feel their way through questions I know the answers to now, but can't quite put into words.

Good luck, Jessica. You can't compete with Toilet Girl.

But you just keep on trying.

Steve alternates between looking like a ferocious business insider and a wounded intern. I can tell the landscape of his internal sense of the pecking order of the world has been deeply shaken. Accustomed to treating me like a social necessary at dinners like this, he used to think he had to carefully coach me. As if I were a walking liability ready to spring a *faux pas* at any minute and ruin his chances for success.

And yet I loved him. Still kind of do. Because even now, with Declan's hand practically typing out all the sexy scenes from *Fifty Shades of Grey* on my leg in Morse code, a part of me wants to help Steve. Whatever that means.

"I saw the exhibit your brother has over at the Bromfield,"

Jessica tells Declan, taking the opportunity to reach out and touch his forearm. My eyes lock on her perfect, slender hand, and suddenly the only meat I want between my teeth are those fingers.

The possessiveness makes my body go on high alert, and Declan's hand stops moving. Even he can feel it. He shifts his arm just so, enough to make her drop her hand as he reaches for his wine glass, giving me a sidelong glance that tells me the message was most certainly received.

"The Bromfield is a gallery for modern art," Jessica says pointedly to me, leaning around Declan. She says it like she's a children's television show host explaining a new concept to an imagined four-year-old audience.

"I'm more a Fountain Street Studios kind of gal," I say as I reach for the bottle of wine in the bucket next to me. Steve's eyes widen a touch, the signal obvious. I'm supposed to wait for someone else to pour it, or to ask Declan or Steve to, or I'm supposed to disappear into a giant sinkhole created by the gravity of my lack of manners.

Instead, I pour the rest of the wine into mine and Declan's glasses, and gently return the bottle.

"Fountain Street?" Jessica says, eyes as wide as saucers, a sarcastic curl to her lip as she looks with fake helplessness between Steve and Declan. "I don't believe I've heard of them."

"They're in Framingham," I say, pretending not to notice the condescension. She sniffs, expecting the men to join in her game. Framingham is a former working-class town with a city center that is not even the kind of place where Jessica could imagine her cleaning lady would live.

"The old warehouse?" Declan asks. "The one that the artists took over as a sort of co-op?" His eyes light up. "We've had commercial photographers from that operation come and do beautiful work for our promo materials in the real estate operation. High-end, quality work."

Jessica's eyes open wider, but this time driven by something other than coquettishness. A sharp look at Steve makes him literally sink a bit in his chair, as if his balls were deflating by the second.

"Have you been to one of their open houses?" I ask. The place advertises every few months, and I've always been curious.

"No, but I think we're about to. It's a date," he whispers, loud enough for Steve and Jessica to hear. She leans back with her lemon face again and Steve reaches for her hand with a loving look on his face. She tolerates his touch like she's getting a pap smear. Including the shudder, as if cold steel slides along her skin.

Declan and I reach for our glasses of wine at the exact same moment, and he holds his out to mine. "A toast!" He looks at Steve and Jessica, and they both pick up their wine glasses, Steve letting out a sigh, as if he'd been holding his breath for too long.

"What shall we toast to?" Steve asks.

Declan looks down in contemplation, and his hand opens on my leg, massaging up and down. I don't even try to pretend to ignore it now, loosened up by the wine and his attentions—both public and private. Doubts fade as the scenario sharpens. Crazy as it sounds, Declan's got his hot palm on my skin, his eyes on me, and his words, I suspect, are about to center around me, too.

"To . . . shopping for a billionaire!" Declan declares.

chapter
eleven

JESSICA INHALES SO SHARPLY she sounds like she's having an asthma attack as she exhales. Steve greedily takes a sip or ten of his wine without clinking glasses with anyone.

Declan gently nudges my wine with a punctuated connection of glass on glass, and eyes that blaze with so many unspoken words. His hand that moves from my thigh, up over my hip, and to the small of my back speaks a few thousand of them, though.

"I thought you were going to say, 'To Toilet Girl,'" I confess quietly, leaning toward him. My lips are so close to his ear I could lick it. Only his slight movement backwards stops me, as he's out of reach with a shift of air that makes me want to breathe him in forever. He could bottle that scent. Pure Declan.

He chuckles softly. "Too easy. Besides," he murmurs, "if you really are on the hunt for a billionaire, you're batting zero with me. I'm not even close. But you're technically shopping for my father's company, and *he's* one."

Before I can answer, Steve interrupts, and in a loud, commanding voice says, "I can't compete. I'm only a millionaire." Fake self-deprecating chuckle. Jessica gives him a honey-cheeked smile, one I thought she reserved only for men like Declan, who are an order of magnitude beyond Steve. I know—and Steve knows—he isn't really a millionaire. "On paper," he used to say. Um, okay. Even I, a mere marketing major, know that if you have $1.5 million in assets you're not a millionaire if you also have $1.2 million in debts.

But what does a silly Mendon girl with a bachelor's from UMass know? I'm guessing Jessica is a Wellesley girl. Too fragile for Smith, and too moneyed for Wheelock. Then again, she has a graduate degree from Harvard.

Steve's gaze penetrates me, the look cold and hungry at the same time. As much as I hate it, he rattles me. It's been nearly a year since he dumped me, so while I'm not a raw pile of goo living on ice cream and espresso between healthy doses of self-loathing and a nice injection of desolation, he's still the man I thought I would marry. The guy who helped me have my first orgasm. The man who cheered me on at graduation. The one who patiently explained pivot tables on spreadsheets.

And *hello?* How rare is that? Because you can find anyone to have sex with you, but a pivot table expert who can explain it all in plain English? That's some precious stuff.

Declan feels exotic. Extreme. Like a crazy risk you can only grab at a handful of times in your life but that you regret not grabbing for. Steve was the dependable, rusty old lawnmower in the garage. You weren't riding it anywhere special, but it would start up every spring just like you came to expect it to, and it would always be there.

Until it wasn't one day.

My analogies are getting really stupid as the wine makes me stretch with an unexpected yawn.

"Size doesn't matter, right, Shannon?" That's Jessica's voice, coming from left field. "Size of the bank account, I mean," she adds, winking at Declan.

Even Declan seems shocked. I think that comment would shut my mother up, and make Chuckles give her a high five. It's so . . . catty. That thump you just heard?

The sound of Steve being dumped.

I feel kind of bad for him, but it's hard to do that when Declan's thumb is stroking my soft skin with whisper-light brushes that make me move slightly, just enough to make a rush of molten lava pour through my veins, my body one big thrumming pulse of need for him.

Wait! This is a business meeting. I'm not supposed to be leaning against a wall of muscle in a bespoke suit, the scent of my own rose corsage from my prom date . . . er, *business associate* making me tingly and open. I'm supposed to feel bad for Steve as his entire conceptual framework for how the world works flushes away (see how I did that?) as the waiter delivers our food.

I see he ordered the filet, too. We used to find that endearing, and yes, I ordered white wine with my steak back then. Until he was in his final year of his MBA, he found that endearing, too.

Right now, Steve is so focused on Declan he doesn't seem to realize that Jessica just insulted his penis and bank account, and somehow managed to make me her girlfriend confidante. Impressive to do all that in one sentence. Perhaps I've misjudged her. If Chuckles were here, he'd defect to Jessicaland, happy to be united with his ancestral tribe.

Another glass of wine is needed to fully dissect the layers of Ms. Jessica. And a scalpel, too. Though she looks like she's been under more than enough scalpels, if you know what I mean.

We all—except for Jessica—pretend she didn't say what she said, instead *ooohing* and *aahhhing* over the food. I am feeling more and more like this is a date, and Declan confirms it by taking my hand and putting it on his thigh.

Oh, yes. I can *feel* how much this is a date, all right.

"How long have you two been dating?" Steve asks out of the blue. Holy *non sequitur*. The question is directed at Declan.

Only.

"We're not dating—"

"Since this morning." Our voices ring out in unison. You can guess who says what. Jessica gives her version of a snort, which sounds like a kitten sneezing.

I give Declan a distinct WTF? look and Steve glances down into Declan's lap, obviously spotting my hand doing its own version of Magellan's circumnavigation of big, round objects.

No, it isn't that bad, but in dim lighting with an overcharged tension between the four of us that could power a small town for a week, it doesn't look very businesslike.

Which means I just fulfilled Steve's prophecy about me.

I just don't know how to act properly in these sorts of settings.

Then again, he may be thinking that I'd never felt him up under the tablecloth of a fancy restaurant, surrounded by big-deal makers, but I have no idea whether that is true, because my phone starts to buzz.

My purse is right next to my thigh, so I leap into the air a bit, startled, my hand on Declan's lap whacking the underside of the table and ricocheting back into his lap so hard he makes a very uncomfortable *ooomph* sound that makes Jessica and Steve both arch their right eyebrows, like synchronized cynics. If they make that a sport, they'd win the gold.

"Sorry," I whisper as I simultaneously unzip my purse and stand. Bad move. Three (or is it four?) glasses of wine plus stiletto heels plus my ex-boyfriend and his date and an overly attentive business colleague so fine I could suck shots out of his belly button and have it called art by the Bromfield Gallery folks means the room spins and I crash back down into my seat.

Except it isn't my seat.

"Business meeting," Steve says as Declan snuggles with me in his lap, his nose nuzzling my neck, his arms wrapping around me less out of a lascivious nature and more to make sure I don't slide off and land on his feet.

"The best kind," Declan says, not looking at him. Jessica takes one bite of her fish and looks away.

Bzzzz. My phone won't stop buzzing. I stand again, more sure-footed, and excuse myself, walking away as fast as I can. Fortunately, the restaurant is fairly empty, and my lurching goes without notice.

The women's room is down a dark hallway with fake candles lighting the way. Monastery wine cellar look. It works. I get to the entrance in front of the ladies' room and look at my phone. Amanda, of course.

Did you get the account? she asks. *And bring condoms?*

Yes and yes, I text back.

What? Of course I brought condoms. Bought new ones, too, because it's been so long the ones I have might have reverted to their original element forms. I might not *plan* to have sex with Declan, but I'm damn sure going to plan just *in case* I have sex with Declan.

Kind of like buying a lottery ticket. You can't win if you don't play.

And . . . ? she writes.

Yes, I text back, cryptic on purpose.

Make her freak out. Chuckles would be pleased.

To which? she types.

We got the account, I explain. *The other one depends on Steve.*

STEVE? Are you still carrying a torch for that asshole? We need to get you exorcised, Amanda types back.

It's so hard to read her. She keeps her emotions hidden so well.

Steve is here. At dinner.

My phone rings suddenly. I answer it.

"Where are you and what the hell is Steve doing on your date with Declan?" she snaps.

"Business meeting," I insist.

"You bring condoms to every business meeting you have? When we get the dental association account, you seriously bring condoms for dinner meetings with Dr. Jorgensson?" Dr. Jorgensson is the current president of the association and is in his late eighties. He looks like a nicely dressed orc. He has a home health aide attend all our meetings.

"Yep," I say. "Even with him. Can never be too prepared."

"Why is Steve there? And speaking of people I would sleep with before I'd ever touch your ex, Dr. Jorgensson looks damn fine compared to him."

"Hey! I slept with Steve and that's really insulting."

Silence.

Then: "I'd still choose the colostomy bag over that piece of—"

My phone buzzes with a text. "Gotta go. But we got the account!" I say in an excited voice.

"That is awesome," she says, not ready to let me go. "But what is STEVE doing there?"

"He and his date"—*bzzzzz*—"appeared out of nowhere."

"Where are you?"

I tell her.

She emits a low whistle. "Your car's Blue Book isn't close to the bill Declan will have for dinner."

"I know."

"And Steve brought—who'd he bring?"

"Some chick named Jessica Coffin. Boston Barbie."

"Jessica Coffin?" Amanda says her name like I'm supposed to know who she is. "Oh my God. Steve is fishing in big waters."

"Well, she clearly thinks his fishie is little."

"What?"

"Never mind." *Bzzz.* "I really have to go."

"Call or text me later!" Amanda says.

"Tell Greg the good news!"

"And you have fun, too. Let loose. Be wild, Shannon. It's about time."

Click. I tap over to messages. It's Steve:

I think fate brought you here tonight.

Oh my God.

chapter
twelve

AND THEN HE WRITES:
I've never seen you so vibrant. In command. You're perfectly poised and professional. I just want you to know I'm proud of you.

Huh? This is the guy who spent two entire days of a conference berating me for using the wrong fork at dinner and now he's saying this?

Shannon? He texts immediately, as if the handful of seconds have been far too long for me to pause before replying like an eager dog catching a bone.

I type back:

Nice to see you, too, Steve. Jessica seems like a great woman.

Gag.

Another text, except this one is from an unknown number.

I have a cold spot on my thigh. It needs your hand to keep it warm.

I type back:

Sorry, honey! I'm at a business meeting. The kids need a bath and Johnny's homework needs to be signed. I'll be home late! <3

And then texter's remorse kicks in, because it seemed funny when I wrote it, but now, as entire nanoseconds stretch into cavernous eternity, I eye the exit and wonder if I can actually walk that far with four glasses of wine (it's definitely four) and a heart that is attached to bungee cords that stretch two hundred yards with each adrenaline surge.

That's fine, Declan texts back. *I like to role-play, too. How about you wrap yourself in Saran Wrap and I'll get a pound of choc-olate-covered strawberries and we'll see what we can do with that after the kids are in bed?*

Dark or milk chocolate? I text back, heart now attached to the back of Evel Knievel's motorcycle on a jump.

There's only one right answer.

Silence.

Silence.

Silence.

Both, he replies.

"Goal!" I hiss, like an Italian football announcer, only quiet.

"You okay, miss?" A waiter walks past me with a frown on his face, brow creased with concern.

I hold up my phone screen. "Just reacting to a business text. Clinched a deal I've been waiting to land for a long time."

He smiles and walks away.

I look down to find a new text from Steve:

Can we do dinner tomorrow night? I'd like to catch up.

I don't want to answer that, so I lean against the thick, oak-paneled wall and take a deep breath.

"How long?" says a warm baritone attached to a (near) bil-lionaire. Declan appears suddenly, heat in his eyes.

"How long what?" My frantic mind rushes off to erotic plac-es all too quickly. Bad girl. Good, bad girl . . .

"How long have you been waiting to clinch a deal . . ." Declan repeats, closing the space between us through sheer will. I swear his body doesn't even move, but then it's there, warm and pulsing against mine. " . . . like this?"

His lips taste like grapes and hope, full and respectful, press-ing against my own with a lush connection that makes me eager for more. Stepping in to the kiss, his body meets every inch of mine from thigh to shoulder, one hand sinking into my loose hair, capturing the back of my neck as if I am about to fall, his other hand around my waist, splayed against my hip.

Instinct makes my own arms wrap around his waist, slid-ing under the smooth wool of his jacket to find cotton as finely spun as silk, my fingers dancing on it as they ride up. His knee nudges my legs open as he pushes me into the wall, searching for every spot on our bodies that we could touch in public without being charged with a crime.

The feel of his cheek against mine, his hands everywhere, his groan mingling with my own gasps transports me. Nothing else matters. No one else exists. The insanity of the day, from how we met to our business meeting to this business dinner . . .

We are getting down to business, all right.

I break away and meet his eyes, wanting to see that this is real. *Real*. Not part of my imagination or something I read in a book and transposed onto my life. That Declan isn't kissing me out of pity, or a cheap booty call, or for any of the rare reasons men used on me as their own drive and baser natures made them view me as a tool.

No. What I see in his eyes reflects what I feel, and then I am the one kissing him, reveling in the starbursts of ignited recognition that something truly unique—life altering—thrives between us, nurtured only by this shared joining.

Our embrace is so strong, so tight, the slant of his mouth commanding and fiery, tongues communicating through touch in a way his fingers had earlier, but with more urgency and so much passion I think we might break the wall if we push any harder against it.

"Shannon," he murmurs, pulling away. The withdrawal of his mouth feels like a kind of mourning. He looks at my chest. "I crushed your corsage."

That's not the only reason he looks at my chest.

I laugh, a throaty sound of delight, so genuine that my mind feels blank with a kind of clarity that seems unreal, even as it grounds me. I open my mouth and pure joy comes forth:

"You are the best prom date ever."

He dips his head down and our foreheads touch. His eyes turn to green triangles with his own genuine smile. We must look like complete idiots, and the idea that this is a business meeting went out the window a long time ago. Actually, I think that idea was flushed from the start.

"What made you kiss me?" he asks in a low voice that

promises to make coffee and bring it to me in bed in the morning.

"You kissed me!" I answer, my hands on his shoulders now. I bat him lightly with one hand.

"Why?" he insists. I can tell he won't let me squirm out of this one. My phone is buzzing like mad and I imagine Steve is about to send a search party after us. Big deal. Who cares.

I look up, a few inches between us, and his eyes change. He's taller than me, arms protective, and he wants me. *Wants.* Not just *desires* me, not just *likes* me. Wants. Craves. I am irresistible, and the part of me that finds that laughable is sitting back in wonder, thinking she got it *all* wrong for many, many years.

I close my eyes and sigh. "You had me at 'both.'"

shopping
for a
billionaire

#2

chapter
one

I WAKE UP TO the sight of three pairs of nostrils bearing down on me.

How much did I drink last night? Am I in some kind of Shayla Black/Lexi Blake dream where it's three on one? *Mmmmmm.*

One set of nostrils is decidedly feline. The other two are human.

None is male.

Damn.

"How did it go?" Mom and Amanda ask in unison. Both are hovering over me like a traffic helicopter at rush hour after a chicken truck crash on the Mass Pike.

"You brought a condom last night, right?" Amy shouts from the kitchen. I look up and see that my bedroom door is open. My eyes travel to Chuckles, who somehow manages to leer at me. Then he licks his absent balls.

Okay, so I guess one of the pairs of nostrils is male after all.

Sort of.

"Or more than one condom," Mom adds with a giggle. She sits on the edge of my bed and tilts the entire world toward her.

"What are you people doing in here?" I mumble, pulling the down pillow over my head and molding it around me like a space helmet. How much wine did I drink? Mom and Amanda make themselves at home in my bedroom, and I hope Amy is making me a coffee right now. I need about twelve of them.

"Inquiring minds want to know. Did you kiss him?" Amanda

asks in a voice so brimming with cheer that I want to remove her vocal cords with a lobster pick. When did the garage door start banging into the concrete over and over like that?

Oh. That's my pulse.

"And why did Steve text me last night and tell me how much he misses you?" Mom asks in a staged voice designed to turn her into the Queen of All Juicy Gossip.

Amy races into the room so fast that the cup of coffee in her hand sloshes on her thumb and she yelps. Chuckles pauses his vaguely obscene self-hygiene routine and narrows his eyes as if she's offended him.

"Steve?" Amy says with incredulity. "The snake senses when someone else wants her."

"When Declan McCormick, mover and shaker, wants her," Amanda adds, that peppy note in her voice transmuted into something like the evil witch in *Snow White*. Steve better not eat any apples today. Maleficent is on the loose.

"I like Steve!" Mom declares.

"You like Harvard degrees," I mutter.

"You can fall in love with a successful man just as easily as you can fall in love with a narcissistic slacker who convinces you that three jobs is fine and zero for him is the natural order of business," Mom sniffs.

She's describing our older sister Carol's ex-husband, who seems to have singlehandedly proven that there is an inverse relationship between how good a father is and the quantity of publicly displayed tattoos he has of his children's names.

Though, to be fair, we only have a sample size of one.

"Did you kiss him?" Amanda asks.

"I am not speaking to any of you until I've had my first latte, three ibuprofen, and a hacksaw for my head." I press my palms against my temples to show them my pain. No one seems impressed.

"You drank red wine, didn't you?" Mom says, not even waiting for an answer because she knows me too well.

I grunt in the affirmative.

"You know you can't handle the sulfites or the sulfates or

whatever it is you can't handle. Why did you drink it?"

"Because it goes with beef, and because Declan didn't know about me and red wine. But I switched to white halfway though."

"Even worse!" Mom chides. "If you mix red and white it curdles everything in your stomach and you'll end up with diverticulitis."

Amanda gives her the crazy-lady look and says, "No, it doesn't. The two are completely unrelated, and curdling . . . what?" She gives Mom a look Amy and I patented.

"Mom's been reading health articles on websites with medical experts who moonlight on psychic hotlines," Amy explains.

"Don't even try, Amanda. It's like her myth that eating the crusts of your sandwiches will curl your hair," I say, pulling my hands away from my head and hoping the seams of my skull remain in place.

"Worked for Amy!" Mom insists.

"Or that chewing your fingernails constipates you," I add with bitterness. Where's my coffee? What good are these pity groupies if they don't deliver hot caffeine? I refuse to trade my pathetic life stories for anything less than three lattes this morning.

"Those fingernails absorb all the water in your body, and when they pass through, it's like Freddy Krueger's claw on your intestines." She shudders.

"Who?" Amanda, Amy and I ask simultaneously.

"Freddy Kru—oh, never mind." Mom rolls her eyes and walks into the kitchen, mumbling something about being old.

"So did you . . ." Amy waggles her auburn eyebrows. She looks like Rose from *Doctor Who*, but with curly hair and bright blue eyes. "You know?"

"We kissed. And I think my hand memorized which side he dresses on," I confess. "Not one more word until I have a latte in my hand!"

Amy scurries off to the kitchen, where I hear her and Mom giggling and talking about me. How do I know they're talking about *me*?

Because they're both alive.

"You didn't sleep with him, though, did you?" Amanda asks. She clearly is both horrified and titillated by the idea.

So am I.

"Are you kidding me? I'm the one who runs a CORI background check on people who take care of my cat. I Google search through fifty-six pages of results. I practically ask for a credit report and a physical exam before I'll go to second base." I laugh, amused at my own joke. It makes my head echo with the pulse of an elephant.

She doesn't laugh, but instead nods solemnly.

"That was a joke."

"No, it wasn't," she adds in a pitying voice, patting my hand like she's expressing sympathy.

A flash of last night bursts into my pain-filled head. Declan's arms around me, my back up against the heavy oak panels. The glow of a candle in a tiny Tiffany lamp attached to the wall, making shadows of our connection, projecting every move in temporary reflection. The sharp intake of Steve's shocked gasp as he discovered us, Declan's hand following the split seam of my skirt, my own hands buried in his thick hair, waves of heat pouring off us as we touched and tasted and took.

That thumping elephant in my head decides to do the Funky Chicken and the Hokey Pokey at the same time. Damn elephant wedding dances. Who replaced my blood with flammable molasses?

I force myself to remember last night. Steve's strangled groan of recognition. The smile I felt on Declan's lips as we both heard it. How I tried to pull away and Declan tightened his grip. The hiss of his whisper as he said, "He has no power over you. He discarded you. Don't give him that power back. You are worth so much more."

The hurt look in Steve's eyes, the first genuine emotion I'd seen in him in over a year.

My own heart tugging me toward Steve, in search of more of the real him. Being torn between the two men, and letting paralysis win, which made it seem like, by default, I'd chosen Declan.

But . . .

"Earth to Shannon!" Amy says, bringing me my beloved nectar o' java. I take two large, hot sips and sigh, grateful. Amanda becomes my beta in the best-friend hierarchy. Blood—and coffee—is thicker than best-friend water.

Mom re-enters my bedroom and I get a good look at her. Lilac yoga pants cut to fit curves. A V-neck cotton white shirt with some lycra to it. A sports bra underneath. White Crocs. She looks so fitness-perfect. Her hair hangs in light layers around her face, cut with a whisper touch by a new stylist she found in Wayland. I can see why she makes the drive—he's *that* good.

There's a glow in her face that makes me think life is going well for her. I don't often think of her as Marie Jacoby. She's Mom. Just . . . *Mom*. Not an actual human being with feelings and hopes and her own tangled inner and outer life. Always a parent, my bedrock Mommy who attended to skinned knees, made Elmo cupcakes for my birthday treat when I turned five, and who steadfastly combed through my lice-ridden hair after my failed prom date gave me an apologetic kiss on the cheek.

And a bad case of lice.

Lice. Bad jokes. Declan. Last night. His mom dying the day after his prom. Tears threaten the edges of my eyes and a wellspring of unbridled emotion hits me, hard. The blend of his touch, his restrained storytelling, but the look on his face that said he wanted to talk, to share, to connect. Losing your mom so young had to make you vulnerable. Losing her the day after your senior prom must have been a form of torture.

A blast of clarity cuts through my throbbing head and makes me see how beautiful Mom really is.

"You look like an AARP ad," I say, admiring her.

Mom takes one perfectly manicured hand and places it over her heart, her face a mask of horror, my words clearly having the opposite effect as I'd intended. She's wearing very little makeup right now, which means she's still wearing more than I wore last night on my big date. Er . . . business dinner.

"What a cruel thing to say, Shannon!" she cries out, tears in her eyes. Mortified, I sit up, a cold rolling pin running from the base of my neck to my ass. I didn't . . . I wasn't trying to . . . oh, hell. I can't get anything right this morning. The tears choke my throat, my brain and body sending mixed signals through synapses and nerves and veins, rendering me stupid with heart palpitations and a sudden sweat that makes my armpits feel like swamps.

I take more sips, needing reinforcement, willing my internal disappointment at myself away.

"What? That was a *compliment!*" My words are sharper than I want them to be. I have to snap, or the tears will take over.

"AARP is for people fifty and older, Mom," Amy says, trying to help. "You look great for fifty-two."

"That's like telling a chubby girl she has such a nice face," Mom says. She's clearly recovered from her offended state and the claws are coming out. Chuckles winks at her. My tears dry up.

"Hey!" me and Amy shout, both representing the "chubby girl" sector in modern American society.

"See?" Mom says, triumphant. She's a chubby girl, too. "That's what the AARP comment felt like. A reminder that society has oppressive expectations for gender and age norms." She crosses her arms over her ample lilac bosom and gives me and Amy looks of disdain. She's Gloria Steinem in yoga pants and 3-D mascara.

"Mom's been reading Jezebel again," Amy says.

"You don't *really* think I look old enough to be an AARP member, do you?" Mom asks me.

"You *are* old enough to be a member, Mom. In fact, you have a card. I see you use it to get ten percent off groceries at the gourmet market on Tuesdays when they have their senior citizen days." What else am I supposed to say? My shoulders slump and I feel like I'm carrying Steve's ego on them. You try to give a person a compliment and suddenly you're the Antichrist.

Mom scowls, then winces when I say *senior citizen*. "That's different. That's financial optimization."

"No one is insulting you, Marie," Amanda adds. She's been watching this unfold. "And all they're doing is deflecting Shannon from spilling the truth about her date last night."

All three sets of eyes zero in on me. Bing! My brain struggles to keep up with the constant topic shifts. It's like listening to Russell Brand talking about politics after drinking three shots of espresso.

"We kissed! We touched," I confess. "Steve walked in on us kissing and touching. And then the Ice Queen made fun of Steve's penis and bank account, and by the time Declan and I got to the table, they were gone."

"*Who* was gone?" Mom asks.

"Steve and Jessica."

"Back up! Back up!" Amy announces, holding her palm out like she's a cop directing traffic. "Let me understand. You were kissing Declan—your business associate—and your ex-fiance walked in on you?"

"That about sums it up," I say meekly.

A slow smile broadens my sister's beautiful face. "That is the best revenge story I've ever heard." She reaches her palm out to high-five me, and I give it back. Except I miss and go flying across my bed, falling flat on my face as Amy rescues my coffee. A mouthful of high-thread-count Egyptian cotton from my sheets fills my mouth.

Mom just gives me the evil eye, as if I shouldn't still be so out of it. You try absorbing last night and all the permutations and implications and wines and not wake up in the morning with a coordination problem.

"He's dating Jessica Coffin," Amanda says to Mom and Amy, her eyes wide and knowing. The attention is suddenly off me, and I sit up and steal back my coffee.

"Oooooh!" they squeal in unison. Why do they act like I'm supposed to know who she is?

"Jessica is *the* society-pages chick in *Boston Magazine*," Amy explains, eliminating the need for me to ask. "Her family's foundation is doing malaria research in Africa. She goes on these huge expeditions and helps."

"Does she singlehandedly provide air conditioning when they're out in the field? Because that woman is cold as ice. Disney should have cast her instead of Kristen Bell for *Frozen*." They all look at me like I've poured battery acid on top of chocolate mousse. I can take a hint, so I slurp coffee and take deep, knowing breaths.

"I heard she can make or break a new restaurant," Amanda adds, continuing to ignore me, her attention on Amy and Mom. "There was that little Asian fusion place in Wellesley that she went to and a picture of her appeared on The Hub. BAM! Now you can't get a reservation for weeks." Mom, Amy, and Amanda all nod soberly, as if acknowledging Jessica's power.

Pffft. I can go to any restaurant that Consolidated Evalu-shop has a contract for, munch on half a cockroach in a Cobb salad, write up an evaluation, and get the health department to condemn it in forty-eight hours flat. Now who has the power?

"Do you follow her on Twitter?" Amy gasps. Both of them nod—*both*! My mother can't figure out how to juggle two different open windows on a single screen on her MacBook but she has a Twitter account? And follows my ex-boyfriend's snotty girlfriend?

"A tweet that mentions a stylist or a product means insta-success for that person," Mom gasps. "Look at my hands." She holds them out as if we're supposed to admire them. They look like . . . hands.

"Nice moisturizer!" Amanda squeals. They are speaking in Aramaic as far as I am concerned. I am not fluent in spa-speak. I think I am missing the part of my brain that most women are born with, the one that can tell the difference between cerulean and aquamarine, or between beige and taupe. Once they start talking about moisturizers and alpha-hydroxy acid bases and foundation creams, I might as well take a long nap because it's like they're speaking some foreign language I've never even heard of.

"She's a Botoxed Barbie with a superiority complex and no sense of boundaries," I blurt out, looking in desolation at my empty coffee cup. I need more. Nineteen more cups and I'll be closer to human. And I still have to go to work.

Is it seriously only Tuesday? Yesterday feels like it lasted a week. Greg should give me the day off for landing the account. I should call in sick for the level of stomach-churning experiences I faced. I slip my head under the covers and fake-pretend to ignore them all. Like that would ever work.

"Meow!" Amy says. Chuckles looks up and sneers at her like she's an American trying to speak French in Paris.

"What?" I demand, mouth muffled against my comforter. What's catty about what I say? "It's the truth."

"Did she make a pass at Declan?" Mom guesses. Damn. How does she do that?

"No!" They all stare. "Okay . . . yes." Declan. The feel of his jaw against my cheekbone. The way our bodies touched and I could inhale his essence. The push of his hips into mine as our skin tingled with anticipation. I just . . .

"Did he accept it?" Mom asks. Her words say one thing, but her pleading eyes say, *Farmington Country Club wedding.* PoshTots. Beacon Hill in-law apartment.

"He didn't think she was worth one iota of attention," I say, distracted by my own pleasant tactile memories, memories quickly fading away as Mom's question makes me remember the rest of the night. Steve had huffed off, but given me a gesture, using his hand to create an old telephone, held it to his ear, and he'd mouthed, *Call me.*

Bzzzz. We all jump. My phone.

"Jesus—that thing has been buzzing all morning," Amy groans. It's about an inch away from falling off my nightstand.

I come out from under my bed fort and grab my coffee mug, wiggling it in the air between me and Amy. She laughs and grabs it. She really is my new best friend. Amanda can suck it. Whoever brings me coffee gets my loyalty on this fine, post-Declan morning where I am bombarded by meddling people who know more about Jessica Coffin and moisturizer cream performance on veiny hands than they do about the new healthcare law or campaign finance reform.

Twenty-four new text messages. TWENTY-FOUR. Whoa. I am never that popular. Who did I blow last night?

chapter
two

CRINGE. OH, GOD. What if I really did . . . ? Fifteen text messages are from Steve:

How long have you been dating him?
Was this a one-night stand?
Do you miss me?
I miss you.
I miss Chuckles. How is he?
Things ended badly and I think we need to talk.
Jessica was joking about that bank account thing.
I'm not into Jessica at all.
Are you exclusive with him?
How are Marie and Jason? Jason still golf on Saturday mornings?
I forgive you.
I shouldn't have ended things like that.
I've changed.
You haven't changed a bit. And I like that about you.
Please call me.

Seven text messages were from Mom:

Don't forget condoms.

But if you do, there are worse things than getting knocked up by a billionaire. Think of the child support payments.

Your father's having bad gas. Don't marry a man with an irritable bowel.

But a billionaire with an irritable bowel is an exception.

Does Declan have a brother for Amy?

If you get to fly in a helicopter, have sex in it. Mile-High Club. Whee!

I am on my third Lime Rickey and your father says I need to stop thinking about billionaire grandchildren.

One is from Amanda:

Stop thinking about Steve.

One is from Declan:

I'm bringing "both" to your place on Friday. Six o'clock. See you then.

My mind scrambles to remember the day. Tuesday. It's Tuesday. He attaches a picture of strawberries the size of my fist, dipped in chocolate. Dark and milk. But not white, which is a sign from the universe that he is The One, because white chocolate is the jackalope of chocolate.

I read all of these aloud to my pity groupies, who suddenly can't pity poor Shannon with the sad little life. How do you respond to knowing I'm being pursued by Steve the Ladder Climber and Declan the Almost-Billionaire Hot Guy? They look confused.

I want to kill all of them except Declan. When did Chuckles become the good person in my life?

"You guys sent me these texts? Seriously?" I grouse.

Amy rushes back to the bedroom but calls out behind her, "Not me!" The espresso machine begins hissing. So does Chuckles. He gives Mom and Amanda an evil eye that makes old Italian grandmas flinch.

"I was worried about you!" Mom argues.

"You're getting a turkey neck, Mom," I snap.

She shrieks back, "Now you're just being vindictive!" Chuckles lifts his palm like he's giving me a high-five. If my mouth didn't feel like wet sand and my head like a blow-up doll being inflated by a horny, newly released ex-con after serving twenty years, I'd high-five him right back. Then again, that didn't go so well when Amy tried, so . . .

"And texting me about having a billionaire baby when I'm on a business meeting isn't?" If I have to use much more energy to speak I'll need more coffee.

"I was wishing you well."

"You want designer grandchildren."

"Is that so bad?"

Amanda is trying not to laugh, so I pick on her next. "And you! Some best friend. I refuse to hold your hand on those same-sex-marriage mortgage shops next week."

"What the hell did I do wrong? I just told you not to be an idiot and let your squishy inner self go soft on Steve."

"Too late," I mutter. She gives me an eye roll that I take as a warning. A girlfriend lecture is coming soon, the kind where I just say, "I know, I know," over and over and she tries in earnest to get me to realize that I don't have to let him treat me like a doormat. Like the movie *Groundhog Day*, only I never actually learn from my mistakes.

This is why I have sworn off men.

Mom's face goes three shades of pale. "Same sex *what*? Amanda, did you just say *same-sex marriage*? I thought Shannon was dating a billionaire now! A *male* one!" That look of horror Mom had earlier when I made the AARP comment pales in comparison to how she looks now.

Let me explain: for years, Mom assumed I was gay because I didn't like makeup, didn't date men, and because I enjoyed visiting my friends in Northampton, the current lesbian capital of the world.

The only reason she would disapprove of my being gay is that the Farmington Country Club technically has not allowed a gay wedding just yet. Which is why I will never get married there, even if I do marry a billionaire. Not because I'm gay. Because I think everyone, regardless of sexual orientation, should have an equal opportunity to be tortured by their mother into a wedding designed not to celebrate the nuptials of two people in love, but to allow the mother of the bride(s) to prance in all her glory and to scream hot-faced about the ribbons on the table centerpieces being the wrong shade of hot pink and to worry obsessively that Uncle Marty will ask the band to play "Stairway to Heaven" at the reception.

If you can survive that, you are meant for each other for eternity.

"One of the credit unions we do mystery shopping for has a bunch of evaluations where same-sex, legally married couples go into credit unions and apply for mortgages jointly. We're evaluating for discrimination," Amanda explains to Mom.

"With her credit score?" Mom says, pointing and laughing at me. "Shannon's never met a credit card she didn't like."

That is so not true . . . anymore. I had my crazy credit-card spree days and I'm over that now. Loan payments on $50,000 in student debt will do that to you.

"And you have to go in and pretend to be married to each other?" Mom asks, skeptical. She squints one eye like she's sizing us up to be measured for wedding gowns.

"Yes," I say.

She looks at Amanda like I'm not even in the room. "Are you the man or the woman?"

"What?" Amanda and I say in unison.

"You know . . . tops and bottoms. Are you the top or the bottom, Amanda?" Mom looks at us like she's asked whether we prefer pink roses or red roses, as if normal people ask whether hypothetical lesbians have a positioning preference.

"Your mother is so much better than mine," I tell Amanda as I turn and look at her with a *Please make it stop* look. "She can't even say the words 'toilet paper' in public conversation."

"What does she call it?" Mom asks, fascinated.

"By the brand name, whatever she's using," Amanda explains.

"What does toilet paper have to do with lesbians and which one wears the strap-on?" Mom asks.

"OUT!" I bellow. "Get out of my room!"

"Why would you be offended by that, Shannon? Women use sex toys all the time, and I don't mean just the lesbians," Mom says.

I crawl out of bed and sit up, my head trying to secede from the rest of my body. "I really don't want to talk about this," I moan.

"I'll bet if I checked your bedside drawer I'd find a stash," Mom says. Her eyes flick over to my nightstand. I freeze.

"Don't you dare," I hiss.

"Mooooooooom," Amy calls out as she comes back in the room. "That's another nine or ten therapy sessions you have to pay for if you go rifling around in Shannon's drawer looking for rabbits and bullets."

"What do bunnies and guns have to do with sex toys?" Mom looks at Amy like she's crazy.

Amanda is now laughing so hard I think her intestines are twisting.

"You can go with Amanda when she does seven 'marital aids' shops next week," I add, using my fingers for quote marks around "marital aids."

"Why this?" Mom asks, mimicking me. "They *are* marital aids! You try sleeping with the same man for thirty-two years. It gets boring really fast. And there are only so many times you can play 'The Pirate and the Maiden.'"

Amanda stops laughing abruptly.

Mom pats her hand. "I would love to come with you. Do we have to act like lesbians, though? Because if I'm going to walk into a sex-toy store, I'd prefer to come out of there with something Jason would enjoy, too. He's getting adventurous, but a double-headed dildo might make him run screaming from me."

My stomach gurgles in the ensuing silence, turning from a light groan of hunger to a disturbing warning of pending sickness. My sprint to the bathroom makes my head pound, but the cool tile of the floor soothes me, calming me instantly.

That's right. A mother's hand on my clammy forehead should help, but instead she's out there talking about my dad and sex toys while my bathroom floor gives me more comfort.

A few minutes pass and I realize I still have a job. Work calls, and while I could probably text Greg and beg off for the day, I think getting back to work is better. I drag myself into the bedroom and Mom looks me up and down, opening her mouth to say something.

Amy appears to shoo them all into the kitchen for good, the quiet click of my bedroom doorknob giving me assurance.

I don't want to talk about last night.

I want to savor it. Not the Ice Queen part, or the Steve part, but the Declan part.

Okay, a little of the Steve part, because how awesome is it to be found in the most exclusive restaurant in Boston and 1) not be on a mystery shop and choose to eat whatever I want 2) be there with one of Boston's most eligible bachelors and wealthiest men and 3) be found by your smug ex-boyfriend who dumped you for not being able to fit in with people like . . . your date?

Pretty damn awesome.

The vortex of swirling emotion inside me isn't just hangover nausea. It's overwhelm. Emotional overwhelm with a heaping side of disbelief. Declan McCormick wants me. He kissed me. He texted me for a date in four days. With strawberries. And chocolate. And hopefully more kisses, less Steve, and definitely no Jessica.

The only thing better than Steve finding me in Declan's arms would have been having Jessica right next to him.

A plume of jealousy fills the air like a skunk on a spraying spree. I feel like Wolverine and take a sip of coffee to calm myself. If metal claws slid out from under my knuckles right now, I wouldn't be surprised. This kind of jealousy is completely new for me. Uncharted territory. A wash of emotion so tidal-wave-like in its enormity that it makes my chest tighten, my heart stop beating for a split second, and my vision blur a bit.

Or maybe that's still the hangover.

Three deep breaths and two hot sips of coffee later and I can definitely state that nope—that's jealousy.

The memory of her hand on Declan's arm fills me with red rage. It dissipates fast, but the residual shock of being affected like this remains, hotter than my cup of joe and lingering like a bad houseguest.

I don't do jealousy.

Sure you don't, an annoying voice in my head says. *And you don't do revenge fantasies, either.*

My coffee stays down through sheer force of will as a spit-take threatens my duvet cover.

I am not the revenge-fantasy type. Sure, I've daydreamed about Steve having huge regrets for dumping me. In my dreams I'm svelte and have been recently approached as one of the hottest up-and-coming marketing wunderkinds, the type of social media rockstar who has Seth Godin calling her for advice. Steve watches my third TED Talk on YouTube and sobs into his Harvard degree, cursing himself and the heavens for his horrible mistake in letting me go.

But I don't have revenge fantasies. I'm above that.

Last night was so much better than any revenge script I could have written. Hell, better than any romantic comedy scriptwriters could bang out with a huge advance and Nora Ephron's ghost coaching them while Judd Apatow gives them neck massages.

Steve caught me kissing Boston's most eligible billionaire bachelor and—even better—a man sitting at the helm of a company so big and so powerful that Steve would happily become a, well, mystery shopper for them to get some clout. Connection.

Advantage.

Bzzzz.

I look at my phone. Steve. The level of disappointment in me that it is not Declan calling gives me pause. Big pause. Sickening pause.

I've fallen. Bad. Double-plus bad.

"Ignore that," Amanda says as she opens my door and holds a steaming cup of coffee in one hand. Her makeup is all goth-like on this sunny morning and she is wearing work clothes.

"How do you know it's not Declan?" I ask, my words fading with the just-in-time realization that she knows me too well.

"Because you look like a kid who didn't just drop her lolli-pop. She dropped it into an open sewage field and fell in on top of it as well."

"You can tell I'm bummed it's not Declan," I say.

She frowns in a look of confusion. "No. That's what anyone

would look like if they're forced to interact with Steve." She wrinkles her nose in this super-cute way that makes me want to watch her face forever. I know she's doing it out of distaste, but she could seriously patent that and use it to act in commercials. It's such a great encapsulation of how this all feels.

The Steve part, at least.

"Sandra Bullock," she says under her breath, talking to herself.

"Sandra what?"

"She could play you. In a movie."

I'm halfway through a mouthful of latte as she explains, and I spray an impressive fan of coffee all over her arm and my pillow. "Sandra Bullock could not play me in a movie!" I gasp. "Melissa McCarthy? Sure. But not Sandra Bullock!"

"Jesus, Shannon, say it! Don't spray it!" She uses part of the duvet cover to wipe my surprise off her arm.

"Sorry. Your fault, though."

"Mine?" The whites of her eyes seem bigger than usual as she stares me down.

"C'mon. Sandra Bullock? Might as well pick Scarlett Johansson."

Amanda sizes me up. Her eyes linger on my hair, then travel to my neckline. I fell asleep in a weird combination of a tight workout t-shirt and extra-baggy pajama bottoms, pants so big I use an old robe sash to tie them to my waist. My hair must look like something you'd find on Courtney Love, and even in my partly hungover state I realize I smell like fear and happiness.

"Melissa McCarthy. Or Jennifer Lawrence if she put on some weight."

"Thank you for being honest."

"I am always honest." She reaches out to squeeze my hand, a creepy, fake smile on her face. Then she smears the back of her hand against mine, wiping more coffee off.

"You can wear the strap-on, then," I say.

Mom chooses this exact moment to walk in. And then my phone buzzes. She snatches it up before I can get to it.

"Restricted number!" she crows. "It's the billionaire!"

chapter
three

MOM HOLDS MY PHONE up like she's Rafiki from *The Lion King*, presenting baby Simba to the tribe.

"Hakuna matata," Amanda whispers.

"Give it to me!" I snap as Mom refuses to give it to me.

"Marie," Amanda says in a low growl. Damn. She's channeling Musafa. James Earl Jones couldn't do a better job with that growl. I wonder if Amanda could do Darth Vader next.

Mom tosses the phone to me like we're in a game of Hot Potato, and I answer the phone in such a rush I don't give myself the time to feel anxiety or panic or to freak out like I really should because it's *Declan*.

"Hi, Shannon," Declan says. His voice pours over me like warm hot fudge. I imagine his face, all broad planes and narrow intensity, how his jaw is so lickable and his eyes make me smile when he's focused on me. The heady scent of spice and man fills me as I pause, body shivering with the pleasure of knowing he is calling *me*.

He has asked *me* for a date. A non-business date. Not that last night was strictly business. Hah. But this time he's clearly and openly interested in me as a woman. Not as an account or a colleague or a marketing coordinator.

The man bought me a corsage.

And now he's offering chocolate-dipped strawberries and a voice that sounds like hot fudge?

Make me into a Shannon sundae. With a big old banana right in the—

"Hello?" He sounds slightly puzzled, but not unsure. Whatever he's thinking, my craziness doesn't deter him.

"Hi," I say, the word coming out like a happy sigh. I look up to find Mom gawking at me like she can see my ovaries twitching, and Amanda's doing that pretend-quiet thing where she's acting like she's not listening.

Even Chuckles' ears are perked.

This is what it takes to get me to stand up and walk. My feet feel like they're floating as I press the phone to my ear and hear Declan say, "I really enjoyed last night."

All my pain fades. The world seems brighter, suddenly, like there was a layer of fog I couldn't quite see. It's gone, dashed away by Declan. This phone call is the highlight of my day so far.

And if he was serious about coming over on Friday . . .

"What time can I pick you up? And this time, no limo. Though I wouldn't mind watching you split your skirt up nice and high," he murmurs. The words make me hot, a steady pulse forming in my belly, throat, and between my legs. The man could talk me into an orgasm without touching me if he keeps this up.

Chuckles wanders over and begins rubbing against my legs. He's purring. Chuckles doesn't purr. Declan's vocal magic is filling the room with pheromones even neutered cats react to.

How can a mere woman like me resist?

My back is turned to Mom and Amanda, who don't take the hint. I thrash my arm back toward them in a gesture that clearly means *Get out of here and let me have my hot-fudge voice orgasm, you twits*.

"Are you having a seizure?" Mom asks, alarmed.

"I think she wants us to leave, Marie," Amanda says. She's back on my good list. Chuckles closes his eyes and the purring goes up a notch.

"Is this a bad time?" Declan asks, a smile in his voice.

"It's always a bad time when my mother is in the room," I say, my voice definitely not full of chocolate or hot fudge or anything yummy. Mine feels like broken glass and rusty nails as

Mom glares at me, clearly wanting to eavesdrop.

"And don't let her listen outside the door!" I call back as Amanda shuts it. Mom's groan can be heard by Declan, who gives a laugh so sensual it makes my toes curl.

"Now, where were we?" I ask in a voice half an octave lower and, I hope, as sexy as his.

"We were talking about how I want to come over and get to know you better, Shannon. All of you. Right now."

My knees go weak and a buzzing flush fills the skin around them, a wave that crests upward and makes me wet and warm again. How does he do that? I'm trying to imagine him right now. Is he wearing a suit? A t-shirt and jeans? He's so formal and businesslike, hot and sophisticated, that I can't picture it.

"Right now?" I squeak out.

"Not practical, I know," he says, the rumble in his tone like a caress. "Friday?"

"Friday works." I don't want to sound desperate, but I *am* free. Haven't had a date on a Friday night in way too long. "Wear jeans," I add.

I drool—just a little—at the thought of him in well-worn jeans, hiking boots, and a shirt so loved that it molds to all the edges and valleys in that muscled torso and chest of his. Sunglasses and a wicked grin, with a tan that speaks of time outside and . . .

"Are we giving each other wardrobe orders now?" His voice drops down into sultry territory, like his tongue is searching for a register you can only reach naked. "Because I have some preferences in that area, too."

If I were wearing panties right now, they would melt off. Chuckles is making love to my ankles with his fur, and I shake him off. Too much sensation. Too many innuendoes. His purring is disconcerting, because it's almost as if he's . . . happy. Which is impossible. Chuckles' default is misery. Declan would have to be a Time Lord to be that powerful.

"Yes?" I whisper. Preferences? *Mmmmm.*

"Hiking boots. And jeans, for certain. You want to wear layers, and bring something that handles wind." His voice becomes pragmatic. Matter of fact. Friendly and cheerful. The change jolts me.

Wind?

"Wait—what?" This isn't exactly what I thought he meant when he said wardrobe preferences. I am imagining red feather-lined handcuffs and crotchless panties. Not a catalog shoot for REI.

"I'm packing a picnic. There's this great hiking spot in Sudbury I want to share with you."

Chocolate-covered strawberries don't exactly go together with Sudbury, which is a bedroom community outside of Boston best known for producing Chris Evans. Which isn't too bad, I guess. If Captain America can come from there, maybe I can find my own superhero on a nice walk in the woods.

"At night?" Six p.m. doesn't sound like an ideal time for a picnic. Maybe for mosquitoes to dine.

Steve's idea of a "picnic date" involved eating at an outside table at Tavern in the Square in Cambridge, so this would be my first *actual* picnic date. Ever.

"There's a meteor shower on Friday around nine. I thought it might be nice to try to catch some shooting stars."

"That sounds really nice," I say, meaning it. Starbursts behind my eyes would be nice, too.

"It will be," he answers. We both pause. I hear him breathing, a light sound of surety that makes me feel connected. Ten seconds pass and I can feel him smiling. This is so unreal. Declan McCormick isn't really interested in me, right? I'm klutzy Shannon, the woman he met when my hand was inside a toilet. A toilet! Yes, I had a reason for that. A good one. A *professional* one. But still.

Toilet Girl.

He's asking Toilet Girl out on a date. An ominous feeling hits me.

What's wrong with *him*? Maybe he's a creepy stalker type who has a toilet fetish. He made the joke back in the men's room, but if he was projecting his actual sexual kink onto me in a test to see if I'd freak out, and I didn't, then maybe he's got a thing for seeing women put their hands down toilets.

"Shannon?"

I want to ask him. The OCD part of my brain suddenly starts the rollercoaster-on-speed loop-de-loop it does when a new, panicky idea floods my mind. All I can think is "toilet fetish" over and over, and if I don't exorcise this somehow, I'm going to blurt out the question *Do you have a thing for women with their hands in toilets?*

Not because I actually believe it, but because the part of myself that absolutely cannot believe that someone so far out of my league is attracted to me is scrambling to go back to that safe, comfortable place where my best friends are Ben and Jerry and my book boyfriend is Drew from Emma Chase's *Tangled*.

Damn it.

Deep breaths. One. Two. Three.

"Heavy breathing," Declan says, shattering my concentration. "I like it."

Oh, God.

Do you have a thing for women with their hands in toilets?

My mouth opens and I'm certain those words will come out. I imagine him sitting in an old, well-worn, expensive brown leather chair, the kind with brass buttons that dot the seams, and he's holding a brandy snifter full of the finest liquor. Declan's wearing well-worn Levi's and his shirt is pulled out of the waistband just enough to show an inch of perfect, muscled skin right at the navel, a thatch of hair calling out for my hand. His eyes are hooded and have a soft focus to them, the way men get when the blood rushes south and they shift.

They really do. There's a subtle change in them when sensuality takes over, a warm, predatory taste to their words. The air changes, crackling with sparks and fire. It's confusing and heady all at once, because those two states shouldn't be able to coexist.

Yet they do. Yin and yang. Male and female.

Stick and hole.

"What are you wearing?" I blurt out. It's better than *Do you have a thing for women with their hands in toilets?* I smack my forehead, hard, and the dull throbbing from my hangover kicks back into place.

Someone calls my name from the other room but I ignore them. Chuckles stops rubbing against my ankles and goes to the door, pawing the bottom. No way I'm letting him out, yet. If I open the door Mom will tumble over the threshold like something out of a bad sitcom.

"Heavy breathing, and now the *What are you wearing* question?" His voice rolls out like it's on rails, sliding with throaty nonchalance through more innuendoes than I can count. A fun, humorous sound, like we're in on a joke together.

He can't see that I'm dying here, gripped by a set of looping thoughts that race at breakneck speed, driven by a deep fear that this is one big cosmic mistake. I'm torn inside. The reason I mystery shop is that I'm in control. I'm there in secret, watching everyone and everything and—a little bit like a god—the only person whose experience matters in the end. My word is gold, my observations validated, and the whole process is neat. Tidy. Measurable. Documented.

Being felt up and kissed thoroughly in a hallway at a posh restaurant by a man who is so many standard deviations of gorgeous and rich away from me that on a bell curve, he's a million miles away, makes my mind vibrate so hard with uncertainty that it's about to *shatter*.

I make a sound that is supposed to sound like a throaty laugh but sounds more like I'm hacking up a frog's leg.

"Workout clothes, actually," he answers. "No shirt, shorts, and socks and shoes. I just came in from a run. I'm sweaty as hell and sitting on my balcony, feet propped up and drinking a huge bottle of water as I watch the morning sun burn off the clouds over the bay." That's the longest stretch of words I've ever heard from him, and I'm agog.

And drooling.

Shirtless. Sweaty. Burning. A pulsing, throbbing sense pours down, like I'm channeling energy from my pain-filled head to my deeply turned-on nether regions, his casual way of talking about himself and his life making hope take over, dialing down the racing fear inside me, slowing the rollercoaster to a halt and giving it permission to take a rest.

"Oh," is all I can say, the sound half gasp, half surprise. Half hope.

"And you?" His tone is flirty.

"Workout clothes, too." If you count giant penguins all over my oversized flannel bottoms "workout" pants.

"What's your poison?" I know he means what kind of workout do I do, and my brain goes blank. Because I don't. Work out, that is.

Mom's profession comes to the rescue. "Yoga," I say, as if it's the most natural thing in the world.

She's definitely listening in, because I hear a super-loud snort from the other side of the door and she shouts, "The only downward-facing dog Shannon knows is—" and then muffled sounds of indignation.

I really, really do not want to know the end of that sentence.

Bzzz. Someone texts me. I ignore it.

"Six too early for you? Will you be home from work by then?" Declan asks. I finally look at the clock. 9:12 a.m. For a second I think he means today, but he's talking about Friday.

"Yes. It's . . ." My mind is a blur and I can't get my tongue to work properly. "It's perfect."

And then I remember, again, that today is still a work day. Uh oh. Greg doesn't generally hold us to a tight schedule, but it's Tuesday, and that means—

"Weekly meeting!" Amanda shouts as she bangs on my bedroom door. "You have twenty minutes to fit in a shower. Get moving!"

Even Declan heard that. "You need to get wet," he says.

Oh. Well. That did the trick.

"Happy shower, and I'll see you Friday."

Click.

Mom and Amanda barge in. "Well?" Mom says.

"Date. Confirmed. Friday at six. Picnic at the state park in Sudbury. He's bringing dark- and milk-chocolate-covered strawberries," I say. Might as well give them the specifics.

I walk to the bathroom, but before I can get away, Mom says,

"Your mouth is going to have so much fun on that date."

I wince. Amanda frowns.

"You know what I mean!" Mom says in a tight voice. "Quit sexualizing everything. You people have such dirty minds."

"You're the one telling me to get pregnant accidentally by a billionaire to get big child support payments and asking about lesbians and strap-ons," I say, sarcasm dripping from my voice. "I wonder where I could have gotten it!"

"Your father," she says definitively. "The man never met a dirty joke he didn't like."

I roll my eyes and finish my walk to the bathroom. My shower is quick, thoughts of Declan making me anticipate Friday

Tap tap tap. Someone's knocking on the door. "Mom!" I shout. "Can I take a shower in peace?"

"It's Amanda. And Amy."

They open the door. "We need to talk." Steam fills the room as the hot water churns in full force. The scent of coconut and almond fills the bathroom as I shampoo quickly.

"It can't wait until I'm dressed and clean?"

"No." They say it in unison.

"Then what?" I'm really getting sick of the invasion of privacy.

"It's Steve."

"What's he doing?"

"Texting us both," Amy says. "And Mom. He even texted *Dad.*"

"What?" That's the 2014 equivalent of standing outside my bedroom window with a giant boombox over his head playing some old Peter Gabriel song. "He texted *Dad?*"

"Dad forwarded it to me," Amy says, reluctance in her voice. "You need to hear this."

"Go ahead."

"Dear Jason," she reads aloud. "How's the handicap? I miss you and Marie and our dinners out. Shannon and I had a big misunderstanding but I'm hopeful we can sort this out. I would love to catch nine holes with you this week."

"Oh, barf," I sputter.

Silence.

"What else?" I'm distracted, so I accidentally rub conditioner in my armpits instead of shower gel. Yuck.

"He texted me and Amanda and told us we needed to help you get over this unrealistic dream you seemed to have about Declan, and that he saw you desperately throwing yourself at him."

My stomach actually goes concave. It feels that real, like he's kicked me in the gut. "He *said* that?"

"Snake," Amy mutters.

"It's not true, Shannon," Amanda snaps, angry at the very idea. "Don't you dare get down because that asshole is trying to play this to his advantage."

She knows me so well.

Both of them hover around me, their presence both helpful and overbearing. I know they're right. I know it. I do. Really.

So why is it that one cutting comment can undo hundreds of positive ones? Declan just told me he wants to see me. *Likes* me. Desires time with me. He flirted, he joked, he was casual and loose and we talked like people exploring each other. Testing the waters and the edges of who we are, where we intersect.

That's a known. His kiss. His caress. His attraction to me. Whether this goes anywhere beyond Friday, no one can take away the touch of his lips against mine. The slant of his mouth as he eagerly kissed me. The feel of his hands sliding against my skin. The power of his body crushing mine in a fevered embrace.

That's all fact.

Steve's conjecture has a kind of power, though. It's the sneaky power of doubt. And damn if that isn't strong enough to drive out fact, even when it's irrational.

Amanda and Amy look at me like they're dealing with a fragile psych patient.

They kind of are.

Both of them have hive mind and just exit the bathroom as if they telepathically decided it. I finish my shower, dry off, and walk out into the bedroom.

My phone buzzes.

Amanda reaches for it and—

"Snake!" she shouts.

"I can't ignore him forever," I say with a sigh. Something inside tugs at me, a pull I don't like. But it's familiar. Maybe he really has seen the light . . . ?

I think of a door slamming shut. Some self-help book I read last year recommends that when an intrusive thought tries to suck your soul out of you.

In my vision, the door slams.

On Steve's neck.

Ah. That's so much better.

I hit "Talk" and then "End." Closest thing to slamming that door.

chapter
four

WORK TURNS OUT TO be nothing more than a series of details, forms, and paperwork that need to be
dealt with, a ten-minute weekly meeting that mostly
consists of Greg giggling with excitement and saying, "Three
point seven million dollars," over and over, the sum total of
the account we now have with Anterdec, and Josh complaining
about office network protocols in so much detail that I start to
think he's part robot.

We're sitting around the cheap plastic monstrosity that Greg
calls a "conference table," on mismatched office chairs that
look like something from the set of *The Andy Griffith Show*. I'm
slumped as low as you can go, my mind fixated on reliving every
possible moment where my skin touched any part of Declan's
body. This kind of looping I could get used to—it is so much
better than panicked repeat thoughts about whether I remem-
bered to turn off the stove or freakouts that maybe I'd already
been wearing a tampon when I put that new one in.

Near-OCD is a bit like being friends with a sociopath. When
it's on your side, the world is your oyster.

When it's not, everything smells like rotten fish.

"Two words," Greg says as he closes the weekly business
meeting. All four of us are crammed into his tiny little office. It's
2:13 in the afternoon and all I can think about is getting home so
I can veg out and cyber-stalk Declan. I've only made it to page
twenty-three of my Google search. Three more days before our
date, and I feel unprepared.

Greg is standing behind his desk with a look on his face like the cat that got the canary. He's so happy he is scaring us a little. Greg doesn't *do* happy like this.

Something bad is about to happen. The last time he was this happy he landed a bunch of prostate exam stool kit evaluations and poor Josh . . . well, we had to sign a non-disclosure agreement about that set of shops, but let's just say that stool samples and the public health department made Josh constipated from pure performance anxiety for over a week.

Josh freezes in place and his entire body clenches. "What did you do, Greg? Because I am not pooping on a card and taking it to a doctor downtown ever again. EVER. You can't even pay me triple or—"

"How about company cars?" Greg turns around and looks out his window (*he* has a window . . .) and points to a shiny red sports car with a racing logo spray-wrapped all over the entire car, advertising a special tire.

Josh's eyes go wide and his hand instinctively touches the top of one butt cheek. "A company car? For real?"

"For all of you!" Greg morphs into Oprah. "A car for you!" he says as he points to me. "And a car for you!" he says as he points to Amanda. The room explodes into excited shouts and lots of squealing and jumping up and down.

"HOW?" Amanda screams.

Greg takes a deep breath, beaming like a proud dad. He hasn't been this happy since Amanda texted him last night and told him we landed the Anterdec account, and he texted us all a selfie this morning showing him turning the heat up to sixty.

"Consolidated has been chosen as one of only four marketing eval companies to test drive these 'wrapped' ad cars for certain markets. Boston is one of them. We got four cars!"

Josh is ogling the red sports car from the window like Amanda and I look at Chris Evans in a Captain America suit. Actually, Josh looks at him the same way.

"We get *that*?" His arm points like it's detached from his body. He clearly can't believe it.

"Yes!" Greg bellows. "A car for everyone!" Last time I saw

him this excited he got us all free coffee for a year from an account. Free Habanero-flavored coffee from a failed Boston market test run, but enough chocolate powder and cream and it was acceptable. Okay, no—it wasn't. But Greg was so proud.

Amanda, Josh, and I squeal like the kids on *Glee* after winning a sing-off.

After twenty seconds of shouting, we quiet down, and I realize Greg hasn't answered Josh's exact question.

"Greg?"

"You get company cars!" he says again, but this time his face is . . . different. There's a bit of a shadow there, a sheepishness that makes a tiny little tickle form in the place inside me where my hinky meter resides.

"We get that, right?" Amanda says, pointing. "Because that is a very cool wrap. I think of Chris Hemsworth and racing when I see that. Patrick Dempsey."

Josh squeals again. "McDreamy!" We're big *Grey's Anatomy* fans. The entire office. Greg has admitted to having a secret crush on Sandra Oh. We've rearranged business meetings for season finales. We cried when Callie and Arizona got into that car crash.

Greg startles, giving Josh the side eye. But he doesn't confirm.

"Greg," I say, my tone made of steel. Something is off.

"You get *cars*," he explains. "Fully paid by the company. You can use your company cards to charge all gas, all tolls and parking, and all repairs from now on. It's all covered by Consolidated or the client. The contract runs for two years."

"Okay!" Amanda chirps.

"No more mileage reimbursements," Greg says dryly.

"Who cares? Shannon finally has a car that starts with a key!" Amanda adds. She seems starstruck. I think she's just dreaming about a Robert Downey, Jr.-and-Chris Hemsworth-and Amanda sandwich.

"But . . ." I say, skeptical. Josh is frowning. He sees that I am teasing something out of Greg. Details he's reluctant to give.

"But what? You guys have been begging for company-paid cars for years. Now I go and find a client to supply them, and you're giving me the third degree!" Greg's face is red and blustery, but he's not offended or angry.

He's deflecting. You know how there are levels in professional chess playing, like Expert and Master and Grandmaster? Well, the same levels apply in professional deflecting. I am the High Princess Queen Pooh-Bah of it, with a finely tuned radar when others do it.

Greg is setting off all my alarm bells.

"Let's go see the cars, then!" Amanda and Josh rush to the window. "Where are they?" she asks.

"Around the corner," Greg says, reaching in his desk drawer to fish out three sets of keys. Each set is color-coded: dark brown, a rusty auburn, and bright yellow.

M'kay.

Amanda skips down the hall and stairs like she's the lead in a Disney princess movie, while Josh is giving me nonverbal looks and gestures meant to convey something in human semaphore, but I'm clueless. All I know is that Greg isn't giving us the full picture.

"OH MY GOD!" I hear as Amanda shoots through the main doors and peels off to the right, where a bank of cars is parked just behind the building.

Then a bloodcurdling scream of "NOOOOOOOOO!"

Josh and I look at each other and take off at a dead run, bolting through the doors into the blinding sunshine, banking to the right. I'm behind him by a few feet and he stops dead in his tracks. I crash into him, but he's so frozen he might as well be a steel support beam.

And then my eyes register the cars.

I half expect Drew Carey to appear and make that *wha-wha-wha* sound on *The Price is Right*, telling us we lost. Because what I see before me is way worse than my crappy little Saturn. The screwdriver I use to start my car seems like a gold-plated Oscar statue compared to *this*.

"Is that a giant turd on top?" Amanda gasps. "I am not driving a car that has a huge piece of poop as a hat!" Her voice is high and thin, a fluttering, panicked tone seeping in. She sounds like the whiny girl from that movie *The Blair Witch Project*.

I'm starting to think that standing in the corner would be a better fate than what's in store for us right now.

"That's a coffee bean!" Greg protests. My hands and feet have gone numb with shock. The car in question is one of those tiny little Toyota cars, and it's covered in what appears to be an artistic rendering of a latte with that signature leaf pattern that baristas use to mark their specialty drinks. That part isn't so bad, and the coffee chain's logo is fine, but on top of the tiny little car is an enormous brown, textured thing that is about the size of a double kayak and it looks, indeed, like Goliath dropped trou and squeezed out a giant log on top.

It actually makes me imagine I am smelling poop right now, which makes me hold my nose. I look at Josh and realize he's doing it.

The store's motto: *Coffee gets everything moving!*

"I am not driving that!" we say in unison.

"It's a coffee bean!" Greg insists.

"It looks like a giant version of the Baby Ruth from that *Caddyshack* movie!" Josh argues.

Greg studies it and tilts his head, examining it like we're at the Museum of Modern Art. Or . . . ahem . . . the Bromfield Gallery.

"Huh. It kind of does."

An argument begins instantly between me, Amanda, and Josh about who will be stuck with what is quickly named the Turdmobile.

As the two of them duke it out, I extract myself from the argument, because while the Turdmobile was the most graphic of the three cars, now I have a chance to look at the next one, and . . .

Well, let's just say if I were a guy I'd get a rise out of it.

The green one is a huge wrap for a popular drug that helps men with erectile dysfunction. The wrap shows a mature (read: AARP-member age) couple rolling in an intimate embrace in a meadow filled with daisies.

The logo shows two people dancing. The tagline says: *Sometimes you have to be hard to please.*

I make gagging noises when I take a really good look at the couple in the picture, because apparently my mother has been keeping her new career from me.

She's the model.

Amanda and Josh shut up instantly and Greg looks at me like he needs to perform the Heimlich. Josh has met Mom a few times but doesn't see what I see.

Amanda, though . . . Amanda gets my pain.

"Oh! Oh! Marie told me she was working on catalog modeling, but she never . . . Oh, God, Shannon. Josh is just going to have to take this one."

"Josh is WHAT?" Josh screams. "Josh is right here and Josh is not driving a Limpmobile around town. Josh will never have sex again if he drives that!"

"Josh is talking about himself in third person," Greg says slowly, like he's dealing with a mental patient.

"The thought of parking the Limpmobile in my neighborhood in Jamaica Plain makes me do that, you . . ." Josh can't seem to find an insult to hurl at Greg, his eyes skittering between the Turdmobile and the Limpmobile.

In desperation, we all look at car #3.

Wha-wha-wha.

The giant clawed thing on top is the color of rust and red. The actual car is wrapped with the logo for a famous crab shack, and if that was all, it would be fine.

But the industrial designer who created the two-foot-tall, seven-foot-long . . . thing . . . on top of the Smart car had created a masterpiece of a "crab."

It's like they took a baby crab, put it on the Island of Doctor Moreau, fed it nothing but water from Chernobyl, and for good measure handed it off to the *Human Centipede* dude.

"That looks like pubic lice," Amanda says.

We all turn and look at her, mouths agape.

"We studied it in biology class!" she insists.

"Sure," we three say in unison.

But she's right. It looks like the angriest louse ever.

And matched with the store's tagline: *Bring our crabs home tonight and make him dance!*

It just . . . shoot us now.

The three of us get the same idea at the exact same time, and we run around the building to Greg's car.

"Why do you get the cool car?" Amanda thunders. The cheerleader's voice dissolves into Maleficent's vibrant, threatening tones. My balls tighten. Wait—I don't have balls. But if I did, they would tighten.

"That's the car the president of the ad company wanted me to drive," he says weakly.

I think even Chuckles is glaring from my apartment.

"Nuh uh. Nope. I am not driving any of those three cars!" Josh announces.

"My mother is on one of those!" I wail. "For a little pill that makes life harder." Mom's been holding out. I wonder why. She's the type to crow about this kind of thing. Something serious is going on if she's not screaming on the town common about how she's now a "professional model."

"You don't have to drive that one," Greg says.

"So I get to choose between the Turdmobile and the Crabmobile?" I whine.

"I am not driving that piece of crap!" Josh says.

"Which one?"

"Any of them except for yours, Greg!" Josh's voice becomes a baritone, fierce and demanding, with a predator's tone that makes all of us stop and stand a little taller, keenly aware of his manhood.

Josh is about as dominant as an umbrella, so this catches us all unaware. A light breeze pushes clouds in front of the sun and the sky darkens as if he's beckoned some kind of evil force to do his bidding.

Something Wicked This Way Comes. And its name is Turdmobile.

"This is really cruel," Amanda hisses. "Company car!" She snorts. Once you lose the chipper one, all hope is lost. Greg's face reeks of defeat.

"I know," he says as he sits on a picnic table under a tree, the one where all the smokers in the building congregate every hour. "I tried, but trust me—these conversations are taking place at the other three marketing eval companies. It's a joke."

"A joke?" Josh is so angry he sounds like he's about to throw something.

"It's some hyper-ironic campaign designed to drive people to the URLs. There isn't a real chain of coffee shops, or that erection drug, or that crab restaurant. They're fake."

Hope springs eternal.

W AIT, WAIT WAIT," JOSH says, now breathless. "This is a meta-advertising experiment? Like, we are pretending to advertise ridiculously stupid companies and their bullshit products for the sake of a buried advertising campaign to drive internet traffic for a viral campaign?"

Greg looks even more hangdog. "Yes."

Amanda, Josh, and I widen our eyes and stare at the cars. My own gaze can't break away from my mom's face, contorted with pleasure as her man's hand disappears below her waist and is obscured by a bunch of daisies.

Josh and Amanda put their heads together and whisper furiously. I'm just furious. I feel like I'm being lied to by my mom, and Greg, but most of all—

Which is worse? Driving a car I have to start with a screwdriver, or showing up for a date with Declan in a Turdmobile?

It's not exactly a choice anyone ever thinks they'll have to make.

"This is . . ." Josh says, standing up and touching the "coffee bean" on top of the car. His palm caresses it and I flinch. It looks like he's loving on a piece of feces.

"This is," he says again, withdrawing his hand and subconsciously wiping it on his hip, " . . . brilliant!"

"What?" Greg and I exclaim in unison.

"It's so post-hipster! It's like a neo-Warhol post-modern performance art show!" Josh claps his hands like a little kid whose just been told he's going to Disneyland.

I stare dumbly at him. Greg shakes his head slowly and squints, like he's not quite sure we're in the correct dimension.

"A Warhol what?"

Josh waves his hand absent-mindedly and slings his arm around Amanda's shoulders. "Which one is the worst?" he asks her.

"Crabs," they all say simultaneously. Even Greg.

"But the Limpmobile is the worst for me," I say in a tone that would put Veruca Salt to shame.

"Then I shall drive the Limpmobile!" Josh declares.

"I claim the Crabmobile!" Amanda shouts.

"And I get the turd," I say quietly. "Coffee gets everything moving."

"It's a meme!" Amanda says, perky again.

"Huh?"

"You know," she adds, giving me a look that says I'm being obtuse on purpose. But I'm not. I swear. I just don't get it. "You met Declan with your hand down a toilet. Now you'll drive a Turdmobile. It's . . . a meme."

"That's supposed to be encouraging?" I gasp.

"It's a car, Shannon," Greg sighs. "It's a free car, and you also get paid $200 a month on top of your regular salary for driving it more than one thousand miles a month in the greater Boston area."

Josh and Amanda clap at this news. "A raise!" they crow.

"Not a raise," I say. "We're just getting paid extra to humiliate ourselves."

"Pfft," Amanda says. "I humiliate myself for free. It's great to get paid for it!"

"Neo-Warhol post-modern art performance?" I gawk at Josh, who scowls and folds his arms across his chest.

"Shannon, sometimes you have to be hard to please."

"Let me get the keys for you," Greg says, turning back toward the main entrance. He seems looser, less tense. Who wouldn't? He just got a big burden off his chest. And placed it squarely on us.

"I didn't agree to drive that," I hiss. My tone is more

menacing than I want it to be. My head is splitting from caffeine deprivation, and all I can think about is driving around town in a car that looks like an ad for plumbers who unclog toilets the day after Super Bowl Sunday.

Greg comes to a halt at the small picnic table under the oak tree in front of the building's main entrance. Cigarette butts litter the ground around the metal bucket with sand in it. Bright red lipstick encircles every single filter. Louise, the receptionist for the wholesale lamp import firm above ours in the building, must be back to smoking.

"You can't refuse," he says in a calm voice. His eyes meet mine. There is no pleading. He's stating a presumed fact.

"Yes, I can."

"No, you can't."

"Is this a condition of my employment?" The idea of driving a turdmobile around town to do mystery shops, to perform my own personal errands, to shepherd my nephews around, makes my stomach turn into a pretzel.

"Besides," I add, "it's going to make us all huge targets when we do our shops. None of these cars is exactly nondescript." I can't hide the tone of triumph in my voice.

With one slow, drawn-out gesture, Greg points to my car. The paint on the roof and hood is flaking. The passenger-side door is bright red. The rest of the car is black.

"Your car isn't exactly 'nondescript' either."

"It doesn't have a piece of fiberglass poop on top of it!"

My words carry on the light breeze that passes between us just as a long, sleek limousine pulls up in front of the building, not twenty feet from us. The rear window is open and—to my utter shock—the face of Declan McCormick emerges from the shadows.

He looks puzzled. Behind him sits his father with a horrified look on his face. Both men are dressed in suits, Declan's arm reaching out the window to wave me over. Each step I take makes my body tingle. Once I'm close enough, I smell the heady scent of cologne and leather, pushed out by a blast of air-conditioned air.

"Hello, James." I make eye contact and smile, just like I would in any professional setting. "Declan," I add, as if an afterthought, then tear my eyes away from his father and give the younger man my full attention. My body has been giving him every molecule of awareness since the limo pulled into the parking lot. My eyes just need to catch up.

He shoots me a half-smile, the kind where one side of his mouth curls up with sultry amusement. The tingling turns into a full-blown blood blast, making my skin hover a quarter-inch from my body and pushing my sex to a dull throb that needs his touch to recede.

Decidedly unprofessional. But very authentic. My God, the man can set me atwitter with a look. What would a night in bed do?

"Ms. Jacoby," Declan's dad says. "Shannon," he corrects himself, then gives Declan a side eye that I take to mean *What the hell are we doing here?*

Greg comes over and gives an anemic wave. He's clearly as puzzled as James is. Then, suddenly, both of them look at us. Or, at least, I think they look at us. All I know is that I'm looking at Declan and he's staring right back and everyone else fades into a different world where they're important.

But not urgent. The only urgent person in the world is making me his obsession with eyes that won't cut away. I can't breathe, and yet I become air. I can't look away, and yet I see everything in his piercing look. I can't move, and yet I feel connected to every single item in the world, as if I'm one with everyone and every thing.

James clears his throat and taps Declan's shoulder. "The jet is waiting." His words break the spell and Declan turns just enough to cut his eyes away from me. It's like a dimmer switch on the sun has been spun a half-turn.

"The jet can wait longer." Declan's words are cold ice.

"No, son, it cannot. I need to make a series of meetings before yours." James matches Declan's tone. I feel a distinct chill in the air, and it's not the car's A/C.

The black door opens and Declan steps out. The man can

wear a suit like an Armani model on a Milan runway. My mouth waters as he steps out, from classic wingtips on his feet to the heathered lavender tie that is loose around his neck. A crisp white shirt with sterling silver cuff links peeking out under an all-black suit sleeve makes me snap to attention, the top button at his neck undone, his body language tense but his overall look alluring and demanding.

Why is he getting out of the limo?

The car door snaps shut with a resolute tone. Declan's words do, too. "You go ahead, then. I'll catch up."

"How?" James is outraged. "I'm taking the jet."

"Then I'll fly commercial." Declan pulls out his phone and taps into it for a few seconds. "Done. Grace is making arrangements."

"Commercial?" James says the word as if Declan had just announced he'd drive a Flintstones car to London. "Why on earth would you do such a thing?" His expression is tight and he's angry. Deeply furious.

Meanwhile, Declan is closed off. Aloof. Contained, controlled, and in full mastery of whatever emotions must be roiling inside him like a cyclone waiting to strike land.

This is no simple pissing contest. The argument over Declan's detour here—to see me—has roots that go way back.

I'm riveted in place, my hands beginning to sweat. The Turdmobile is a distant memory. A horrid one, but nothing compared to the cataclysm of these two duking it out with every clipped word.

And the many that remain unspoken.

"Fine." James rolls the window up and the limo speeds off.

Declan just shakes his head, eyes narrow and watching me, pointedly ignoring the disappearing car.

"What are you doing?" I ask. My voice is barely above a whisper. I don't even need to turn around to see that Amanda, Josh, and Greg are gone. They're eavesdropping, I'm sure. But they have the decency to give us some privacy.

"I'll survive first class." His face is serious, but I can tell he's making a very dry joke.

I laugh without mirth. A very large, fluffy animal seems to have taken up residence on my chest. My breathing slows, deliberate and careful. The wind lifts loose strands of my hair, and it catches the loose ends of his tie, which flap over his shoulder. He could be a model, like something in *GQ* or *Vogue*, exuding wealth, prestige, confidence, and something timeless. Ancient. Embedded in the way he walks toward me, how his gaze is single-minded and completely aimed at me.

The second his hand reaches for mine I shiver, a delicious stroke of connection that makes my shoulders square. I'm wearing a boring office-drone outfit, casual slacks with old black leather shoes and a long-sleeve cotton wrap shirt that matches his eyes. My hair is a crazy, windswept snarl, and whatever makeup I put on before I dashed out the door this morning has long faded.

"Hi," is all I can think to say.

He leans in and gives me the sweetest kiss on the cheek I've ever received. "Hi. I couldn't stay away."

My heart stops for a few beats. A part of me feels like Carrie, on stage at the prom, seconds before the bucket of pig blood is dumped on her.

This really is too good to be true.

"You're willing to brave TSA agents for little old me?"

His answer is buried in the kiss he gives me, this time most definitely not on the cheek.

The tug of his fingers in my hair, the brush of early afternoon stubble against my lips, the feel of his warm, wet tongue against my teeth all make me moan, a little sound that I have never uttered coming from my throat. Declan clasps me to him harder, fueled by my reaction.

Then he breaks away and says in a voice that makes all the blood rush out of my head, "I knew this was a good idea. I can't stop thinking about you. Friday is too far away and I have to be in New York for the next three days. This was my only chance." His mouth takes mine again, my own hands clinging to him like I'll blow away if I don't hang on. Petals from the blossoms on the trees behind us float on the wind, making me feel like a fairy, as if this were part of an imagined world where magic is real.

Maybe it is.

He pulls back and presses his lips together with a smile that makes those damn hot dimples appear. "I'm willing to brave quite a lot for you, Shannon."

Including the Turdmobile?

All I can do is smile back and keep my hands around his warm waist. His hands are on my shoulders and he's looking me over, searching. Memorizing.

And, I hope, enjoying.

"I also hoped you could spare some time from work," he adds, looking at the concrete block that pretends to be my office building. "All you need is razor wire around the top and it looks like you work in a prison."

"A day in the life of Shannon Denisovich," I joke.

He nuzzles my neck. "A woman who knows her Russian literature," he murmurs. "That's hot."

I pinch myself, because now I know I'm dreaming. Either that, or Amanda's secretly working for some low-rent cable reality television show where hot, successful businessmen make fun of fluffy women with inferiority complexes.

He looks behind me, over my shoulder, and one eyebrow rises high. "Do you have an exterminator in your building?"

That's quite the topic change. From nuzzling my neck to thinking about bugs.

"No—why?" I turn and follow his gaze. Ah.

The Crabmobile.

"Then what . . ." He cocks his head.

Oh boy. How do I explain this?

"It's a promotional thing some company is doing," I say, staying as boring and nonchalant as I can as my fingers play with the rippled muscle of his torso. I could touch him all day. I can't believe he's letting me touch him.

Magic. Seriously.

"So—coffee?" He shrugs. "I don't have a car. Can you drive?"

All the magic disappears in that sentence, replaced by the Eye of Sauron. Staring at me from atop one of the new cars.

"Uh . . ."

"You don't have a car?"

I have two. Neither is acceptable for you to ride in.

"There's a great local coffee shop next door," I say, pointing toward a ubiquitous chain that everyone in the Boston area knows and that is about as far from "great" as I am from "slim."

He laughs and laces his fingers in mine. "How about we just spend a few minutes together."

"You have a plane to catch. Bags to check. Unwashed masses to share germ-laden air with. And you have to get that coveted middle seat between a sumo wrestler and a four-year-old who will insist on unlimited access to your smartphone."

Just then, Greg, Amanda, and Josh all burst through the building's double-doored entrance. All of them have keys in their hands. In rippling-fast motion, my brain processes three things:

1. Declan and I are holding hands in public.

2. I am going to have to take him for a ride in my screwdriver-ignited car.

3. Under no circumstances can I take him anywhere in the Turdmobile.

"Catch!" Greg says, tossing a set of keys at me. As I have the eye-hand coordination of a drunk frat boy going through basic training, I scream like a little girl and flinch.

With flawless precision, the hand Declan's not currently touching me with snaps up and catches the keys.

"Nice," Josh says. As his eyes take in the suited hottie before him, I realize he isn't referring to the catch. Though I know Declan is straight, and I also know I could take Josh down in a cat fight (though he has no hair to grab), I still feel a massive plume of green mist take over my senses.

"Thanks. Declan McCormick," he says, letting go of my hand to reach toward my coworker.

I want to growl.

Declan hands me the car keys. "These are yours?"

Josh's eyes go wide with amusement, and if he could run upstairs to make a big old bowl of popcorn, he would. Explaining my car situation to Declan would have been amusing to me, too, if it weren't, well . . . *me.*

"Yes."

Declan's green eyes are surveying my face, then glancing between Josh and the parking lot. "So you do have a car. Can we go for a drive together?"

I stuff the keys in my front pants pocket. "No."

"Don't worry, Shannon!" Greg says, trying not to laugh. "It's fully insured. You can start driving it right now."

I hate you.

"Company car?"

I nod, miserable. "Yes."

"New cars today!" Amanda adds. She gives Declan a friendly little wave. She gives me a look that says, *You have to face this sometime.*

"I'm not really feeling very coffee-like right now," I say.

"Are you ill?" my coworkers say in unison.

Declan leans in and whispers, "Am I intruding? Because I can leave."

My grip on his arm tightens. "No! It's just . . . the Turdmobile."

"The *what?*"

I pull him by the arm toward the cars and point to my company car.

He reads the tag line. Takes in the car's appearance, his eyes lingering over the roof's distinctive . . . decoration, and finally says, "Is this an ad for civet coffee?"

"Civet what?"

"Civet coffee. It's a delicacy from Indonesia. Collected from coffee berries that cats eat and then excrete."

Josh walks closer and looks at Declan like he's man candy. "Coffee from a cat's ass?" He nudges me and whispers, "Coffee gets everything moving."

I punch his arm hard enough to make him squeak, then pretend I didn't do it.

Declan nods, his face inscrutable. No affect, no crazy attention-seeking demeanor. He's telling the facts. "It's a delicacy.

Sells for well into the hundreds of dollars per pound."

"You feed coffee berries to a cat, collect them out the other end, and people charge hundreds of dollars for the resulting coffee?" I ask, incredulous. My eyes flicker between the top of my new car and Declan.

Chuckles may need a change in diet.

"Have you had this coffee?" Josh asks just as his phone buzzes. He looks at it, eyes wide with alarm, then glances at Amanda, who is a few paces away tucking her phone in her bra.

"Excuse us," Josh adds with a tight tone. "We have to go." I wonder what Amanda said to make him leave like that, and make a mental note to send her my firstborn child as a thank-you for doing it.

"Did I scare them off?" Declan asks, laughing. "Cat-poop coffee too much for them?"

"They've seen worse," I mutter.

Declan's phone buzzes. He reads his text and mutters a curse under his breath. "They added a meeting. Dad's coming right back with the limo." His expression is pained. "I'm sorry. I only have about five more minutes with you."

I can't help myself. I have to say it. "Why me?"

"Why do you keep asking me that?"

"I've only asked once."

He leans against the picnic table, one hip jutting out with a jaunty athleticism that makes his ass muscles tighten. It makes other parts of me clench, too. Yowza.

"You asked over and over on the ride home yesterday, Shannon. You really impressed my driver. Lance said you were the first date he's ever driven who could sing every word of 'Chasing Cars.'"

"I sang Snow Patrol songs in a limo?"

"And then you did an encore of Lady Gaga."

I groan. He's highly amused, and steps forward, scooping me into his arms. I'm caged by him, all heat and want.

"You have no pretense, Shannon. No fake affect, no shield. You're real. Raw. Open. Yourself. I like that." He touches the tip of my nose with his finger, then slowly slides it down my lips, opening my bottom lip a bit. I snatch his finger into my mouth, too timid to go for the overtly sexual gesture.

I just kiss it instead.

"You like it when I'm genuine and just Shannon."

"You're not 'just' anything, Shannon."

Just then, the limo squeals into the parking lot. Declan grabs me in a kiss that bends me back, his arms strong and unyielding, the rushed taking making a flame light up inside that has to last me three days until I see him again.

And with that he breaks the kiss, jogging off to another world.

"Cat-poop coffee," Greg says from behind me. "Dating is nothing like it was twenty years ago. Boy have pick-up lines changed."

chapter

six

FRIDAY. I AM GOING out of my mind now that it is 4:14 p.m. and I have exactly one hour and forty-six minutes to transform myself into a hiking Barbie.

Steve won't stop texting me, though he finally stopped texting Amanda and Amy when they resorted to texting him various pictures off 4chan and Goatse. I'm close to following suit, but that's how I handled our breakup at the very end, and if there's anything worse than being immature, it's being immature in the *exact same way* twice.

I receive a text from Amy with a copy of the last picture she sent to Steve. Who knew that anuses could prolapse? Huh.

My phone actually rings. I know Amanda is next door in Josh's office, talking animatedly to him about simplifying the password policy so we don't need to use three non-standard Arabic characters when we change our monthly passwords, so it can't be her.

Mom is with Dad at an all-day Reiki training, so it must be Carol, my older sister.

I look at the number. Yup. Carol calls for one of three reasons:

1. She needs a babysitter.

2. She needs someone to come over and binge watch *Orange is the New Black* and pick up a pint of ice cream on the way.

3. She needs a babysitter.

"I'm busy tonight," I say as I answer the phone. No preliminaries. Don't need them. Besides, I'm a ticking time bomb right now, with sixteen minutes to go before I can race home and try to turn myself into a nighttime hiking phenomenon.

"You are?" She sounds disappointed. Panicked, really. I hear mayhem in the background. Random animal sounds that are, in fact, just boy sounds. Same thing, really. Until they're ten years old or so, boys are just human versions of beasts.

"Yep."

"Mystery shop?"

"No. Date." The word rolls off my tongue with a delicious fluidity.

She bursts into a long, drawn-out giggle fest. "Good one. Hah! So which shop is it. Donuts? If you ever get another one for the chain of bars where you have to order the filet skewers and two margaritas, let's get Mom to watch the boys!"

I am offended. Why does everyone laugh at the thought of me being romantically involved with someone?

"I have a date. An actual date with the vice president of a company." I want to say more, but I know I'll be skewered if I do. Carol is like a blend of Mom and Amy. Half reasonable and half batshit crazy.

You never know which half you're talking to at any give time.

"Is this the billionaire Mom's been rambling on about? I thought that was some kind of fantasy of hers."

"It is," I mumble.

"So you're not dating a billionaire? She was going on about getting her grandkids into exclusive prep schools like Milton Academy and Buckingham Browne & Nichols—and all kinds of other weird stuff last night."

In the background I hear my seven-year-old nephew, Jeffrey, arguing with his four-year-old brother, Tyler, who only whines in response. Tyler has a speech disorder and the words don't come easily, but he's highly fluent in Whine. My trained ears tell me they're arguing over access to the iPad Mom and Dad got them for Christmas.

"I-duh! I-duh!" Tyler screams.

"Give it to him!" Carol bellows. "When he uses a word right, you have to give it to him."

Jeffrey says something muffled. Carol says something muffled. And then I hear Jeffrey, clear as a bell, shouting, "Eith cream! Eith cream!" Jeffrey has a lisp. Or, as he says, a *lithp*.

"Eye-kee! Eye-kee!" Tyler says, joining in.

"What are you doing?" Carol says, clearly to her oldest. I know that tone. It's the same tone Mom has used on me for twenty-four years. It must be embedded in our DNA. I shudder. Someday I plan to have kids. "Someday" just got kicked back another year.

"If he geth what he wanth by thaying it, why can't I?" Jeffrey moans.

I snort. The kid has a point. Tyler's speech therapist told Carol that in order to reinforce language, she has to walk a fine line. Encourage speech by giving him what he asks for. But after a while, that can lead to problems, so . . .

"Channing Tatum!" Carol shouts. "A million dollars! A free nanny!"

Declan McCormick, I mouth.

Jeffrey giggles. "I want to talk to Thannon!" Shuffling sounds, and then:

"I can fart on command now when you pull my finger," he announces.

"You will be a CEO one day."

"No. I want my own YouTube channel. I'm going to do that inthtead," he says seriously.

"More money in it," I reply.

"Yep. Did you know Tyler peed himself at the dentitht thith morning? It was groth."

"I'll bet." Carol's life is like birth control for me. I absolutely adore Tyler and Jeffrey, but I could do without the pee, poop, farts, vomit, and other nasties from the kids. I mentally add another year between me and motherhood. At this rate I'll start when I'm sixty.

"I need to talk now, honey," Carol says. Jeffrey leaves without saying goodbye.

"You live a life of luxury," I say. It's now 4:23. Carol gets exactly seven minutes of my attention.

"Speaking of luxury, I got an actual child support check today!"

Of all the words I expect ever to hear from Carol's mouth, these are not it.

"WHAT?" Her ex, Todd, ditched her and the boys three years ago. He's played "Daddy for a Day" here and there. More there than here. It's been seven months since anyone has seen him.

He has never paid her a dime in child support. Tyler never even learned to say the word "Dada" or anything close to it. He occasionally says "Puh-puh" for Papa, which is what Jeffrey calls my dad.

I just get a big old smile. When you have a speech disorder and you're four years old, "Shannon" isn't exactly top on your list of easy words. A smile and hug is close enough to my name.

"I know!" Carol exclaims, then lowers her voice. She doesn't speak ill of Todd in front of the boys. Ever. I give her huge credit for that, because I don't know if I could stay that classy in her shoes. "An actual check from the state."

"That means he got a job working over the table!" Carol has a child support order. Todd owes close to five figures in unpaid support. He refuses to get jobs on the books, and never files taxes. She'll never see that money.

"Something like that," she says, her voice hiding something.

"How much was the check?"

She pauses, then says with a laugh, "Eleven dollars and sixty-one cents."

I snort again. "Don't spend it all on one place."

"I spent ten dollars on my birth-control pill copay and the rest on Pokemon stickers for the boys." Again, that pause. I hear her gulp something quickly and then Tyler's distinct whine.

"I'll get water for you, honey! Just a minute!" Carol tells him. She says quietly into the phone, "He's incarcerated. The pay is from his wages at a prison in Ohio."

"WHAT? Does Mom know?" For years Mom has made jokes about Todd finding his way to prison, but we all wrote her off as just being angry.

"Not yet. I've barely found a way to manage all this filthy lu-
cre. Let me breathe a few times before tackling Mom and Dad's
reaction."

"Don't run out hiring financial planners just yet," I crack.

Her bitter laugh makes me cringe. "Yeah. Right. Now his
back support obligation is reduced!"

"Eleven dollars? Oh, Carol. That won't even buy a pack of
diapers." Mom and Dad help her as much as possible, but . . .

"That's why I need to get Tyler toilet trained," she says with
a resigned tone.

I feel myself weighed down by the weight of her weariness.
Suddenly my date with Declan feels trivial. A bit flighty and selfish. I want to tell Carol I'll help her.

"I can't babysit tonight," I tell her. "I'm so sorry." It feels
icky, like I'm rubbing her nose in my happiness and romantic
promise.

"No, no, Shannon, don't feel bad!" she protests. "You should
go out with him! What's he like? Does he have a helicopter?"

What is it with the women in my family and their obsession
with men who ride in helicopters? "He's hot," I whisper.

"Hot Guy!" Amanda shouts from behind me.

"Hey!" I shriek. "Josh is the one who does that to people!"

"Hot Guy!" he says in a falsetto, standing right next to
Amanda when I turn around, heart thudding out of my chest.
Assholes. Maybe they're both part vampire. And not the hot,
sparkly kind.

"I am having a *private* conversation," I say archly.

"About Hot Guy," Greg says, poking his head in my doorway.
Now all three of them are staring at me.

"Hey!" Who knew *private* was code for *everyone flood
Shannon's office and turn into MI5 spies*?

Carol is laughing hysterically on the phone.

"You can talk about Hot Guy whenever you want on company time, Ms. Three Point Seven Million," Greg croons. Eww.
It was so much better when he made us reuse plastic silverware
and groaned about toner ink costs.

"What does he mean, three point . . . huh?" Carol asks as I wave Josh and Amanda off like they're evil spirits. Greg hovers. I pull a tampon out of my purse and he scurries off like a vampire walking past an Italian restaurant in Boston's North End.

That trick works *every* time.

Carol's words sink in. Discomfort slams me with full force. "Oh, uh . . . Declan's company gave our company a multimillion-dollar account."

"Because you *slept* with him?" Carol gasps.

"I did not sleep with him!" I shout.

"Good girl," Greg calls back.

"Did you seriously just call her a 'girl'?" Amanda says. I hear hushed arguments through the thin walls as Carol emits a long stream of words that sound like my mother, minus the rabid need for billionaire grandbabies named Thayer Spotterheim "Scoochy" Mayflower Vanderbilt Kennedy III.

"—and you don't need to give it up for a business colleague just to land an account!" Carol finishes.

"You take after Dad," I mutter. "Because Mom seems to think I should give it up so she can have her Farmington Country Club wedding."

Carol snorts. "She didn't like the fact that I eloped with Todd."

"'Eloped' sounds so elegant. You ran off to Vegas and got married by a transgendered Elvis impersonator who moonlights as Elvira. Those pictures were . . . um . . ."

"I know," she sighs. "Thank God you and Amy haven't been as stupid. Yet." She sounds so beaten down that a wave of guilt hits me, even as I stare at the clock. 4:29 p.m. Should I be a good, supportive little sister or fake another call so I can get her off the phone and rip out of here to get home and look better for Declan?

Amanda solves that dilemma for me. "Is Carol *still* on the phone? And talking about her wedding?" she shrieks as she walks up behind me. "The word 'Elvira' must mean yes."

"Yes."

"Then tell her you have to go for your hot date! You have a billionaire to boink." She makes a shooing gesture toward my door. Carol and Amanda adore each other. They have a mutual interest in mocking me endlessly whenever they're together. I'm so glad I help people bond.

"Go! Boink! I'll call Amanda and trick her into babysitting for me," Carol says.

"Ooooh, good one!" I hang up before Carol changes her mind, and grab my purse. Amanda's phone is ringing before the outer door closes behind me. I walk down the concrete hall bathed in blinking fluorescent lights and look toward the main door's blast of sunlight through the window, the way a tiny vegetable shoot searches for the sun after it breaks through the outer shell of a seed.

And then—

I'm free.

My stomach flips like it's an Olympic diver, and my eagerness drains as I reach my car because . . . this is real. Serious. I have a date with a man who wouldn't have noticed me if he hadn't found me hiding in a men's-room stall with my hand down a toilet.

And yet . . . he's an intelligent, respected, gorgeous man with eyes that go hot when he looks at . . . me? I steady my breathing and let the rush of warmth fill me.

Even as I thrust the screwdriver into the lock and turn the car on, the burst of excitement that comes from knowing that he really wants to get to know me better turns into a tingling anticipation.

Because.

Because.

I'm free.

chapter
seven

'M NOT FIVE MINUTES into driving home when my phone buzzes with a text. A few months ago I decided not to answer my phone while driving, so I ignore it like Simon Cowell at a preschool holiday choir festival. Driving with a cell phone pressed to your ear isn't illegal—yet—in Massachusetts, but I can't climb into a limo without ripping my skirt, or walk across a room in heels taller than a grasshopper, so should I really try to manage a two-ton vehicle and a mobile call at the same time?

My hands feel like bricks—white-knuckled bricks—by the time I pull into my parking spot and ding a plastic trash can as I slam the car into park and grab the phone. Three messages.

All from Steve.

"Blah," I say, tossing the phone back in my purse. As if I have time to even think about Steve right now. Somehow, in under an hour, I have to go from an ogre to a princess. And I'm no Cameron Diaz. No amount of effort is going to transform me from Plain Old Shannon to Imaginary Perfect Woman when it comes to this date with Declan.

Deep breath.

My mind seems to know this. I am enough. I—*as I am*—can have a wonderful time with a man a few years older than me, considerably more sophisticated, excessively more successful, and I can go toe to toe with him in the boardroom and the bedroom.

My entire body tightens. And not in the good way.

Can I?

Twelve deep breaths. That throat-tightening feeling, the rib-cage that is a little too small, the spacey eyeball-floating thing—all of it recedes a bit. I am freaking out in my crappy car with minutes ticking away before Declan will show up, and somehow the only thoughts I can experience are those that undermine me. Ridicule me.

Invalidate me.

Who do I want to be? *This?* Quivering Shannon with insecurity issues, stuck in some kind of purgatory from Steve and filled with his ideas about who I am? Goofy Shannon with a hovermother and two sisters who view me as comedic relief?

How about I start seeing myself as Declan sees me. But what, exactly, does that mean? He's funny, intense, handsome, accomplished, and interesting. The only way to know what he thinks about me is to spend more time with him and to experience it. Tonight I will do exactly that. We'll talk, we'll walk, we'll dance that careful dance that crosses boundaries between our distinct selves as we perform a ritual.

For millennia men have pursued women with varying signals and women have responded with a plethora of replies. We're just a man and a woman with a spark between us. Whether it lights something on fire depends entirely on how strong that connection really is.

Or whether we can rub something hard enough to light a blaze.

Bzzzz.

Steve again. I smack my forehead with a quietly-muttered "Aha!", because that's my answer. I keep asking myself what on earth makes Declan want to date me.

And Steve, of all the people in the world, is the key.

Mr. Invalidator is undermining me by simply communicating with me. It's not even *intentional*. The content of what he's trying to communicate doesn't matter. Our shared past means that even being *bzzzz'd* by him carries an emotional message.

I snatch up the phone and, without reading his texts, delete them all. Then I delete Steve as a contact from my phone.

It feels like flushing a deeply clogged toilet after working for hours with a plunger and a snake to reach the goal. *Whoosh!*

Should have done that last year, but I couldn't. It felt like cutting off the stump of an amputated limb.

I close my eyes and feel. *Feel.* The air goes in as I inhale and I imagine breathing with Declan, our air mingling, intentions and suppositions and hopes and interest all swirling before us in an atmosphere of mutual enjoyment.

My eyelids flutter and as my eyes drift around I can see him, casual and smiling, laughing and quiet, nuzzling against me, my view obscured by the soft wave of his hair, by the layout of his eyelashes against his cheek, the look of light stubble across an iron jaw.

I inhale deeply and remember his scent, the mix of citrus and spice and something deeper, fragrant and infused with promise. The taste of wine on his lips, how fire and grapes mixed in our kisses to make a kind of ambrosia I want to experience again. And again.

And then I run my fingers lightly across my arm and remember the weight of his hot skin against mine. His arms claiming me, hands hungry to touch more of me, to combine our flesh and to revel in the nuance and the carnal.

How it felt like finding my way to a home I never knew I had.

Tap tap tap. I turn to look toward the sound and there's my mother's face pressed up against the window, her makeup smearing the glass as she leaves a bright red kiss on my already-dirty window. The fact that it's off center annoys me even more.

"Hi, honey! We're here to make sure you go on your date looking good!" She lifts up her makeup bag. It's bigger than most NHL player duffel bags. Pink with silver buckles, that thing has more chemicals in it than a Monsanto pesticide lab.

"And my new mascara came. Four layers of color!" she squeals.

Four layers of torture and doom.

"Great," I say weakly, grabbing my purse and climbing out of the car. "My eyelashes will cross into three states."

Four days ago I was walking down the same apartment stairs

I'm now walking up. I wore an elegant black dress, my mother embarrassed me thoroughly, I split my skirt, and I rode to one of the finest restaurants in Boston with a man I'd met just twelve hours earlier in a men's bathroom.

And now here I am . . . getting dolled up again for a date with the same guy. My eyeball has barely recovered from Mom's game of Pin the Eyeshadow on the Donkey on Monday.

She yammers a steady stream of words about Dad, yoga class, something involving the words "vaginal ultrasound" and "banana" and "online condom site." Because none of those words should ever be uttered in sequence, I have to block it all out. My dreams, though, will be vivid tonight, because the subconscious is like Chuckles.

Eventually you pay the price for simply existing.

I walk in my front door and a lovely surprise greets me. Chuckles is smiling—smiling!—with his eyes closed and ears tucked back, sitting in my dad's lap.

"Dad!" I shout, rushing to him. He stands and dumps Chuckles on the floor. The look Chuckles gives me convinces me that he has Feline Borderline Personality Disorder, and a chill runs through me. I'm about to be the target of one hell of a character attack.

Too bad, kitty, I think. *Daddy's little girl always prevails.* I glare back at him over my dad's shoulder as we hug and Chuckles slinks away. Ha. Score one for Shannon.

Pretty bad when the highlight of my day is beating my cat at being loved by my own father.

Dad looks . . . different. He's two years older than Mom, and has that middle-age paunch all the fathers of my friends have, except for Mort Jergenson, who runs ironman triathlons and makes my dad mutter about "showoffs" and how "only a trust fund baby could do that marathon shit" under his breath.

He conveniently ignores the fact that Amy does that *marathon shit,* too. She didn't qualify for the Boston Marathon last year, and everyone was sad for her when she got the news. Mom, however, was a sobbing mess on race day when the bombings happened, and for two hours no one could locate Amy, who had been in the city along the race path to cheer friends on. Fortunately, she was fine and back at mile twenty in the crowd.

This year she did run. And Dad couldn't be prouder.

If there's one thing my family has taught me, it's that being a hypocrite is nothing to be ashamed of. In fact, some people polish their badges and wear them like an award.

"Dad, what did you change?" I scrutinize him as we stand in the living room. He's beaming at me and Mom scowls.

"Look closely," he urges. Mom says nothing. That, alone, sends chills down my spine.

I frown and squint. Something about his face has changed. The clothes are the same—old jeans and a faded blue polo shirt. The same scuffed brown boat shoes he's owned since I've been alive. His hair is squirrelly and full of tight auburn curls, as always. Eyes are warm brown and hooded slightly by sagging eyelids that all my friends' parents seem to be getting. Except for the mothers who can afford lid tucks. Then they just look REALLY EXCITED ABOUT EVERYTHING. You can tell them the tag on their shirt is showing and THEY ARE JUST SO JAZZED.

It's like looking at a meerkat nonstop.

He rubs his chin. Then I see it. "You have a goatee!" I peer closer. "And it's *red*."

"Red" doesn't quite describe it. Dad's had a scruffy beard on and off for years. Gray took over at least since I was in third grade. This is a young man's color, a vibrant red that almost belongs on a punk skateboarder.

"He did it himself," Mom spits out, as if she were shooting a hocker ten feet in a contest. "Tell her what you used, Jason."

"Kool-Aid!" Dad says, crowing. He plants his thick, callused hands on his hips and beams at me, proud and glowing. It dawns on me that he only comes over to our apartment when something is broken or when Amy and I invited him and Mom over for dinner. Dad doesn't just drop in like Mom does.

"Kool-Aid?" I eye the clock on my coffee maker. 5:17 p.m. Damn. I want to talk, but . . .

"Yep! It looks great. Jeffrey says I'm the hippest grandpa

around. And Amy agrees. Said I look like a hipster a decade ahead of my time."

"Dad, I don't think that was a compliment."

He looks like I slapped him. "Why not?" The sudden look of insecurity on his face makes me feel so bad, like the day I took the car cigarette lighter to the new leather seats in his Mustang to make pretty circles. It was his first brand-new car. I was five then and didn't know better. But now . . .

Mom touches his arm gently, with a great deal of pity, too. "Because 'hipster' means you're trying too hard."

"How would you know?" he growls at Mom, his eyebrows burrowing together into one big semi-gray caterpillar. He's hurt. Why does this stuff mean so much to him? To me? Why do we change ourselves in an effort to get approval from other people? And when we don't—or, worse, when we're mocked—why does it trigger so much pain?

I look at the clock. *5:20.*

Why am I analyzing deep philosophical questions when I have a billionaire to dry hump in forty minutes?

"Amy's called me a 'hipster' more times than I can count," Mom says. "Especially when I showed up for Parents Weekend at her college freshman year in an outfit from Hot Topic."

That snaps me back to reality. "You didn't!" Poor Amy. She never told me that story. Probably repressed it.

Dad gets a hungry look in his eyes as he combs over Mom's body from toe to head. "She sure did. You looked like a sex kitten. Like a blonde Adrienne Barbeau. Sophia Loren. Raquel Welch." His hand reaches for her and she steps in toward him. His palm lands on her ass. I turn away.

"Jason," Mom coos.

Chuckles starts to gag. He's back on the chair where Dad was sitting with him.

"See? Even Chuckles can't stand it when his parents do this," I mutter.

And then Chuckles vomits all over my recliner. Half a mouse's body emerges.

"Oh, gross!" I shriek. Chuckles looks up and squints, like he's asking me what the hell is wrong with me for not being grateful for the offering. If Clint Eastwood were a cat, he'd be Chuckles.

Go ahead. Make my day.

"Don't you feed that poor cat?" Mom asks. Her hand is on my dad's ass now, too, and they're both massaging each other like asses are an endangered species and the only way to keep them alive is to rub them.

"I have a date," I choke out. "In less than forty minutes. And if I have to watch you two making love to each other with your hands, I am going to join a convent and never touch another man for the rest of my life. But before I do that, I'll take Chuckles' lead and vomit."

"We're grown adults with a healthy sexual appetite," Mom chides. Dad just gives her a look that makes Larry the Lounge Lizard seem prim.

But they stop touching each other. Whew.

"You're my parents," I snap back. "You have three kids. That means you had sex three times with a sheet covering you with a hole in it as far as I'm concerned. I can't have images of you being all squishy and touchy-feely in my head when I'm kissing Declan!"

Dad has that insecure look on his face again.

Damn.

"Declan," he chokes out. "Declan's the new guy? The one your mother thinks will get her that wedding at Farmington?"

"You just don't want to lose the bet," Mom says. She pulls out a hand towel, shakes it out, smoothes every wrinkle, and starts unloading makeup from her kit. It's like watching a surgeon get ready for a heart transplant. Her precision and focus is startling.

"What bet?" The words are out of my mouth before I realize I've just given her an opening the size of Rob Ford's nostrils to talk about whatever calamity this bet involves.

"We have a bet," Dad says with a sigh. At least he's gone back to looking like my dad and not like a horny teenager.

"About me?"

"About Farmington Country Club. I bet your mother than

none of you three kids will ever get married there."

"What's the wager?" I am really, really afraid to ask.

Mom is holding what looks like a giant pizza-oven paddle in her hand. She reaches into the bag and pulls out a jar of pancake makeup. Oh, crap.

"Your father gets to try something I've never let him do in more than thirty years of our being together."

Amy happens to walk in just as Mom is explaining and asks, "Anal?"

chapter
eight

DAD'S EYES BUG OUT. Mine stretch so far across the room I think they're going to fall out a window. Only Mom stays calm and waves the hand with the makeup paddle in it. "Oh, no, honey. We already—"

"MARIE!" Dad bellows. He glares at Amy like she's a complete stranger who just accosted him. "And Amelia Langstrom Jacoby, what do you think you're doing talking about . . . well . . . *that* around us?"

"She's the one who lent me those *Fifty Shades* books, Jason," Mom says in a *sotto voce*. As if we can't hear her. My apartment is so small that Chuckles can hear her from the roof.

"Oh." There are moments in our family where poor Dad has to deal with being the only testicle owner in a field of ovaries. Having the toilet seat down nonstop for thirty-plus years is one of those issues. Learning where to park at the mall to get that perfect balance between being close to an entrance but out of our teen girlfriends' sight is another. Dealing with four periods at different times took a kind of engineer's calibration to get just right. And a lot of mad rushes to the grocery store to get the perfect ice cream to make our Medusa heads behave.

And this is another one—hearing his now-adult daughter, his baby, talk about anal sex. And having his wife join right in.

I—I have a ton of sympathy for him, because I. Do. Not. Want. To. Hear. About. This. At all. Ever. I could go my entire life without thinking about anal sex itself (or *mostly* not think-ing about it . . .), but the thought of my parents reading my sister's borrowed copy of *Fifty Shades of Grey* and then using that as some kind of blueprint to try out—

This is how desire dies. My formerly warm-for-his-form nether regions can't think about Declan now without imagining Mom and Dad in a Red Room of Pain. No wonder Mom's asking about helicopters and billionaires.

"Why are you talking about anal sex when Shannon's date will be here in twenty-three minutes?" Amy asks.

Dad turns a shade of red that perfectly matches his beard. Whoa. Didn't know that vasodilation could produce that color.

"I wasn't talking about it! You started it!" he sputters.

Mom approaches me with a mascara wand that looks like she used it as a dipstick in a sixty-year-old tractor on a farm. "We need to do those eyes!" She sniffs the air around my neck. "Did you shower this morning?"

"Yes."

"Hmmph. You wouldn't know it." She glances at the clock. "No time for a shower. Maybe you should just douche."

All of the color drains out of Dad's face. Now he looks like he has Ronald McDonald's hair plastered on his chin, like he just experienced the McDonald's version of the Donner Party.

"Nobody douches nowadays, Mom!" Amy protests. "What guy wants a mouthful of petrochemicals and perfume?"

Dad turns the color of cheap photocopy paper.

"You need a chair, Dad?" I'm worried he's about to faint, and I cannot have anyone fainting in my apartment a mere nineteen minutes before I need to sprint out the door and engage in professionally inappropriate groping with my client.

"Actually, yes," Dad mutters.

He sits down right on top of Chuckles' mouse victim.

"You ever have that 'not so fresh feeling'?" Amy asks Dad.

"Oh, God," he groans. His brows connect again and he places his hands on the arms of the chair. My eye catches the glint of sunlight off his gold watch and a second of unreality pours through me. Watch. What's it like to wear a watch?

He pushes up and hovers, frozen in place, his butt in the air.

I don't like to think about my father's butt.

"JASON!" Mom screams. "I can't believe you sat on a dead mouse!"

Tap tap tap.

All four of us spin toward the sound. I look at the clock—5:53—before turning toward the inevitable.

Declan McCormick is the kind of guy who shows up just a little early.

A little *too* early.

Dad stands up all the way. Mom bum-rushes me and bodily forces me into my bedroom. Amy runs her fingers through her hair and I see her checking herself in the steely reflection of the stove's backsplash. A flash of jealousy roars up in me, like it did with Jessica back at the restaurant.

"You need to clean yourself up now! Jason will keep him occupied and Amy can keep him happy."

Now I'm seeing green. "Amy will most certainly NOT keep Declan happy!" I say in a sound that can only be described as slightly panther-like, including the baring of fangs I did not know I possess.

Mom is ripping a vent brush through my hair and shoving a pair of clear, red-thing underwear my way. "Here."

"What's this? A scrunchie?"

"No. Your sister's underpants."

"You want me to wear Amy's thong?"

"Shannon," she says, exasperated as she pulls my hair into a braid, "fashion designers do make underwear smaller than a semaphore flag, you know? Men love butt floss."

She snaps my braid against my back and the screech screech of metal hangers against the closet bar tell me she's in my wardrobe, trying to find something perfect. I can't see her because I'm pulling off my shirt, but then I stop when I realize my bedroom door is still open.

I peek out. Dad is crossing the room and now he's shaking Declan's hand. The back of Dad's jeans are disgusting. The half-dead mouse is stuck to the mess.

And then—plop.

It falls to the ground and bounces between his legs, right into the space between him and Declan.

Mom mercifully closes the door as I whimper.

"It will be fine," she soothes, pulling my shirt over my head. Her threaded brows nearly cross. "My God, Shannon, when did you last buy a new bra? Before iPhones were invented?"

"Nothing wrong with it. It's comfortable."

She laughs. "Comfort has nothing to do with dating!" I look on my bed. She's laid out a hot-pink spaghetti-strap top, a short tan skirt, and a pashmina. Plus heels that have to be Amy's, because if I walk on those I'll look like one of the misfit toys from *Toy Story*.

"We're going on a picnic. In the woods. On a hiking trail," I say slowly.

"I know. I aimed for a practical look."

"You missed. It's like you aimed for New York City and hit Hawaii instead."

"I have impeccable fashion taste!"

"For decorating Russian email order brides." Red g-string, hot-pink top, tan miniskirt that shows whether I used a hedge trimmer or not, and *come-hump-me-and-give-my-mom-billionaire-grandbabies* pumps.

"Shannon!" Desperation shines in her eyes. Or maybe that's just the new colored contacts she got to add some mystery. They're a shade of violet that could only be made in a New Jersey chemical plant.

"I am wearing hiking boots, jeans, a long-sleeved shirt, and very little makeup."

Mom reaches for her heart like she's having palpitations. "You can't!" She looks like that old dude from the '70s sitcom Mom and Dad watch on cable. The guy who works at a junkyard and shouts, "I'm coming, Elizabeth!" and fakes a heart attack whenever he doesn't like something his son says.

I think those TV writers knew my mom.

"I will!" I really won't, but right now I have a really amazing guy I'd like to have ask me out again, but my dad is offering up half-digested rodents from his ass. At this rate, I'll be lucky to get second-hand email forwards from Declan's assistant.

"Why would you *do* that?" she cries, trying to block me from my own dresser and closet.

In full panic mode as the swirl of everything threatens to take over, I reach into my top drawer and pull out a pair of faded light blue underpants. They're so old the cloth has worn away in parts, leaving bare elastic.

"Step away from my closet or I'll wear *these*!"

"Noooooo!" she screams. It's loud. So loud my dad bursts through the door two seconds later.

I'm standing in my ancient bra and work pants, holding a pair of underwear that really shouldn't be allowed to be used as rags for washing the car. My hair is in a gorgeous braid, but Mom is holding a giant can of Aqua Net now and the nozzle is pointed right at me.

"Whatever's going on, don't blind the poor girl, Marie!" Dad shouts.

Declan is standing just close enough to Amy to make me want to claw her eyes out, and the two lean toward each other as they peer into my bedroom. Eyebrows shoot up to hairlines—one auburn, one dark—and a familiar expression crosses Declan's face.

Yet again, I've embarrassed the crap out of myself and he's amused.

This is getting old. Fast.

"Get in here, Jason!" Mom mumbles, grabbing his arm. "You have dead mouse cooties all over you."

"I can't change, Marie," he says, holding his hands up in a gesture of helplessness. "I don't have a spare set of clothes anywhere."

"Shannon must have a pair of sweatpants that fit you."

Dad is six feet two and about 240 pounds. I'm a good five inches shorter and don't weigh as much. His belly is right where my waist is. There is no way I own a pair of pants that will fit him, and I tell Mom this. In the language of Dog Whistle.

"Get your *special* sweats for your dad. You have a pair," she says in a tough-as-nails voice.

"Special what?"

"For that time of the month."

"We're supposed to wear special pants when we're bleeding? I thought that was a Jewish ritual or something."

Mom sighs heavily. "For when you're bloated."

"For when I'm—oooohhhh," I mutter. Now I get it. I hate when she's right. I march over to my dresser and reach into the top. My XXL flannel jammy bottoms are like stretching a hot-air balloon over a blimp.

And four to five days a month, I live in them. A few pints of ice cream and a lot of salt 'n' vinegar potato chips do, too.

Dates start out in many ways. Most begin with the first meet-up. Your place, his, the bar, the restaurant. Whatever. The specifics aren't important—the simple joining of two bodies into one shared space is, though.

I'll bet that in the expanse of time, space, and millions—billions!—of dates throughout history, none of them started with cat puke on a father's ass and ended with him wearing his daughter's period sweats.

"You want me to wear *what*?" Dad roars. *Roars!* My father is many things—warm, kind, unfailingly patient (because you have to be in order to stay married to my mother)—but "dominant male" is the lowest thing on his list of attributes. His shoulders seem to expand and muscles in his neck pop out, like he's becoming the Hulk.

"Anything is better than dead mouse," Mom says with a sigh. She doesn't seem to see the massive transformation in Dad.

"Wearing my daughter's . . ." He can't say "period."

Tap tap tap.

chapter
nine

'M STILL WEARING JUST a bra and work pants. A flush of panic chills my skin as I remember that Declan is just a handful of feet away, waiting for me, and probably hearing every word of my parents' argument over my menstrual wardrobe.

"Shannon?" Amy says through the door. Her voice is hushed, but I can make out her words. "You might want to get moving. Declan's here."

"I know he's here," I say back. "I saw you talking to him." My voice sounds like that pea-soup-spewing chick from *The Exorcist*.

"I am also cleaning up the cat mess," she says through what sounds like clenched teeth.

I'm struck dumb. Dumb. I can't believe Declan just witnessed that. Welcome to my apartment!

Welcome to my crazy life.

"Thank you," I whisper back with genuine emotion. "I appreciate that."

"You owe me."

"I owe everyone."

"Including me," Mom adds, "because we are going to make you beautiful." She has four—four!—tubes of mascara lined up and I swear she's mixing joint compound into the under-eye concealer.

"Shannon doesn't need any of that," Dad says to Mom, reaching for her hand. "She's beautiful right now. Look at her." And then he realizes I'm not wearing a shirt, tearing his eyes away and turning his back to me.

"Dad, please," I say. "Wear my jammy pants." He takes them from my bed and walks slowly to the door, completely silent. The gentle click of the door closing after he leaves feels like a rebuke.

I throw on the shirt I'd planned to wear all along, kick off my shoes, peel off my stockings, and shimmy out of my pants. Mom turns away, but flings the red thong at me. It lands on my head like a deranged spider.

Ignoring it, I grab a pair of simple bikini underwear and my well-worn jeans, and I finish getting dressed. Then I take care of basic hygiene with deodorant, and tuck my shirt in. If it's chilly tonight, a sweater would work. Mom watches with the preying eyes of a hawk.

A hawk with an eyelash curler clutched in her talons.

My lightweight v-neck made from a blend of silk and cashmere is perfect, so I tie it around my waist. I can't run to the bathroom without having Declan see me, so I do what I can with my own makeup at my vanity on top of my dresser, ignoring Mom, whose silence has turned lethal.

Aside from needing to brush my teeth before putting on lipstick, the Shannon looking back at me from the mirror looks pretty good. Brown hair pulled back in a lovely braid, I have that fresh-faced, naturally athletic look, with my skin clear and a light layer of makeup applied to make it look outdoorsy. Brown eyes framed by a little mascara and a hint of eyeliner look more excited than scared. My nose is exactly where it's always been, and my cheeks are flushed with a mix of applied color and organic arousal.

"You look like a fifteen-year-old going on her first date, Shannon. Like one of those athletic types."

"We're going hiking, so that's perfect!"

"You're not going hiking. You're going on a charm mission."

"A what?" What the hell is a charm mission? I have visions of debutantes wearing handguns on their thighs and rappelling down glass skyscrapers in Jimmy Choo heels.

Mom smoothes the wrinkles at my shoulders and tucks a loose wave of hair behind my ear, tweaking my look with little ministrations that used to annoy me when I was younger. These days, they make me feel loved.

"Charm mission. You're auditioning, Shannon." She lets a huge rush of air come out in one big whoosh. "Don't you see that?" Her voice changes from exasperated to concerned, as if it dawns on her, mid-breath, that I really don't view this situation through the same lens that she does.

"It's a date. Not an audition. There's no *role* I'm trying out for."

Her laugh is a little too cynical for my poor anxious self, because the sound of it pouring out of her makes all the hair on my arms stand up.

"Oh, honey, yes you are. You're too naïve to see it." She shakes her head and takes a deep breath, her words coming out as she exhales. "Men like Declan McCormick require a certain kind of woman."

"Steve required a certain kind of woman. See how well that went?" I just hope it's not the same *certain kind of woman*. A mental image of Jessica Coffin chooses that exact moment to invade my brain. I shove it away and replace it with one involving Declan's hands, my ass, and a kiss that crowds everything else out.

Her eyes go troubled on my behalf. Or maybe she's actually reflecting on my words. Then she says: "Steve and Declan are nothing alike."

"Because Declan comes from money?" Steve wasn't born into it. He scraped and clawed his way up. Declan's family—according to Amanda's research—has been rich longer than the United States has existed. Something about shipping and mining. Her words trickle trough my subconscious as Mom continues.

"No—not because Declan has more money. Because Steve is a scrabbler. Always has been, and always will be. His sense of self depends entirely on whether his ambition is being filled. If he feels like he's making progress, then his identity feels secure. If he's standing still or falling back, then he loses who he is."

She's gone wistful, and Mom doesn't *do* wistful. I am acutely aware of the ticking of time, and of Declan's presence behind that door, and yet I'm riveted. I've never heard my mother wax rhapsodic about anything other than new spring colors in the latest lululemon fashion campaign.

"Honey," she says, her hands on my shoulders. Our faces are a foot from each other and her eyes shimmer under something that isn't quite tears. "Declan knows who he is. There's a quiet confidence that men from his kind of family possess. It's easy to be with someone like that when you know who you are."

She frowns. "But if you don't—if the deep core of Shannon isn't anchored—then being with him can feel like you're lost. The world around you will insist that you're standing on solid ground, and then one day you'll realize you're just balanced really well atop an enormous piece of driftwood in the middle of the ocean."

A prickly heat begins where my heart lives. She's not talking about me and Declan. She's talking about *her*.

And someone other than my dad.

"How do you know this, Mom?" I whisper. Nothing else matters right now. Her eyes are filled with pain and memory, and she opens her mouth to respond, time moving slower than normal.

Tap tap tap. "Shannon?" It's Declan's voice now.

Damn. "Almost ready!" I say so brightly I could light Los Angeles at night through sheer cheeriness.

Mom's face goes back to neutral. What just passed between us feels too important not to talk about, and yet . . .

I grab my purse and check for everything I need. Wallet, cash, makeup, EpiPen—

"You have your EpiPens?" she asks, as if reading my mind.

I pull both of them out of my purse and wave them like magic wands. Which they kind of are.

"Yep. One in case and one as backup."

Worry flickers in her eyes. "Don't stray too far from a path. You know what happened last time you were stung."

I'm highly allergic, as we learned in kindergarten when I stepped on a bee and my foot blew up. I've been stung twice since then, and the last time the anaphylactic reaction was bad enough to cause throat swelling.

"It'll be dusk soon. Not much chance."

"But still." Her voice shifts to a register that makes my heart ache. I remember how terrified she was for the two bee stings she was there for. The third happened three years ago when I was still in college, and while the paramedics were fast and acted effectively, it was harrowing and horrifying.

I'm careful, though. Determined, methodical, and I know exactly what to do down to the letter. If stung, call 911. Then swallow Benadryl. Inject myself with an EpiPen. Get to safety quickly. Receive medical attention. That's it.

Oh. And pray.

I've been trained on EpiPen use. I take first-aid classes and CPR classes every year. I've watched videos over and over on treating anaphylactic reactions to bee stings, and I've been lectured by countless doctors. Mom and Dad had a 504 plan for me in school—like a special plan for kids with medical issues that might interfere with schooling—and while life doesn't offer adults 504 plans, I have had to develop one in my own mind.

"I am fine, Mom."

"You've never been the outdoorsy type. I don't understand why he can't just take you to that lovely restaurant at the top of Prudential building."

I do not confess that I haven't told Declan about my allergies. Who throws that out after being asked on a date? Third date. Deadly allergies are definitely third-date material.

"I'll be fine." My voice has an edge. I can feel it as the words come out. It's threatening to cut me. I have to get out of here.

Alarm speeds through her face as she looks at me. Really looks at me. "Of course you will." She straightens her shoulders. "You'll be fine. It's your father I have to worry about. Do you have any idea what he must be going through out there, talking to a billionaire while wearing flannel pajama pants with penguins all over them?"

Bzzzzz. My phone and Mom's phone buzz at the exact same time with a text.

It's Steve's *mother's* phone, which is still in my contacts list. "I know that's not Monica, because Monica can barely dial a mobile phone, much less figure out how to text. Leave me alone, Steve!" I mutter.

I read the text:

Dinner. Tomorrow night. You and me. I'm buying. :) Steve

"Say yes," Mom says. I look up, expecting her to be reading over my shoulder, but she's looking at her own phone. Then I realize Steve has copied my MOM into the same text message.

"He invited you, too?"

"No. He started looping me in to your texts to make sure I tell you to answer him."

I have seven thousand ways to respond to that, most of which involve throwing something at his smug face. But then I realize that if I don't see him, this will never end. It's easier to have a farewell dinner than to keep ignoring him.

Fine. I text back. *Make reservations at the same restaurant we were at yesterday. Seven. KTHXBYE!*

I do that for two reasons. 1) He hates to spend money. Too bad. 2) He hates textspeak.

Okay, maybe for a third . . . because a part of me does want to see him.

"Shannon," Declan says from behind the door. "If this is a bad night . . ."

I grab the doorknob like it's a life preserver and yank it open.

There's Dad, wearing my penguin pants, looking about as comfortable as Steve at a monster truck pull. Declan is the picture of calm and cool, unruffled and in the moment, though he seems primed, ready to move on and get the hell out of here.

Me too. Not the calm part, but the leaving part.

I pull Dad aside. "May I have a word?" Declan's eyes scan my body as I try to catch his gaze to communicate that I'm happy to see him and that I'll be with him in a minute. I fail because Declan's too busy staring at my ass. Then my boobs. Back to my ass.

Men.

"Earlier in the week, when I went out with Declan, she shouted about prom and kissing through the open window.

Please don't let her do that when we leave. Please." I keep my voice low. Declan leaves a decent distance between us, but I think he can hear.

I'm trying not to snicker at my dad's outfit. He can tell.

"I promise," Dad says, but he's uncertain. Then his eyes light up. "I could keep her distracted, though."

"Yes!"

"But . . ." He waggles his eyebrows like there's a bug crawling on them. It's weird enough that I cock my head and study him.

"Are you having a stroke?" I ask. I've read that people over fifty are more prone to get them.

"No!"

"Then what's this?" I imitate him.

He bursts out laughing, tipping his head back. Declan looks at me with a quizzical look. I shake my head lightly and mouth, *I'll tell you later.*

"That's an old man trying to tell you I could distract your mother by attacking her," Dad explains.

"Ewww." I look at my open bedroom door. "Just do it on Amy's couch, okay?" I want to be able to sleep in my bed without having to call a priest to do a sexorcism.

He pulls his head back as if struck, then says sternly, "We would never have sex in your or Amy's bed!"

"Good."

"Only on your kitchen table," Mom calls out.

"MOM!" Amy shouts.

"I kid!" Mom shudders. "I would never touch your father with dead mouse germs all over him." She eyes him, leaning against my kitchen counter, two penguins trapped under his hip as he sips a cup of coffee. "Then again, he's kind of cute in those jammy bottoms."

chapter
ten

ECLAN'S EYES LOCK WITH mine. My mind goes quiet. The shift is so fast that it leaves a sort of ringing in my consciousness, like there's an echo of the hustle-bustle of the craziness that just came to an abrupt halt. Like ringing a gong and hearing the lingering peal minutes later. It can't be real, yet your mind invents it.

The clarity feels false, even though it isn't. His eyes, though, tell me that it's very much real. He smiles when he sees me, the grin a full expression of pleasure. There's no leer, nothing suggestive, and it's not one bit sultry.

It's the smile of a guy who is happy to see me.

"You're clothed," he points out. "You look nice."

"And she doesn't look nice unclothed?" Mom asks with a tone of offense in her voice.

I blink rapidly. "I know what he means, Mom. He saw me with just my bra—" I say, rushing to fill the awkwardness.

Declan cuts me off, his words overpowering mine with a steady firmness that makes me go silent even though I've not been asked. "She looks beautiful all the time." His tone makes Mom pause and blush, as if she's the one in the wrong. Commanding and absolutely certain of his own words, Declan is poised, confident, strong—

And wearing jeans and a t-shirt. Faded Levi's that look like he was poured into them, with a silky cotton t-shirt the color of soft moss. Like me, he has a shirt tied around his waist, except his is a flannel tartan plaid. He's wearing hiking boots that look well-used.

L.L. Bean could put him in a catalog and see a spike in sales. Women would lick the pages. Rugged sensuality oozes off him as he stares at me, though his words were for Mom.

Even Dad stands still with anticipation, waiting for Declan's cue.

Mom clears her throat, thinking she should speak. "Of course she is."

"You two need to get going," Dad says. I realize the washing machine is on. He must be washing his jeans. "We'll be here for a while."

Mom's just staring at Declan. He is focused on me. Chuckles is staring at the trash can, where Amy set the half-devoured mouse corpse on top of a precariously full pile of garbage.

"Let's go," I declare, grabbing Declan's hand. It's warm and soft and as his fingers squeeze mine a rush of heat fills me from head to toe.

But mostly right smack in my center.

I pull him down my front steps, which are so much easier to navigate in hiking boots, then stop. The only car that could possibly be his is a gleaming black SUV with a hood ornament that is code for luxury.

"This is mine. Climb on in," he says, reluctantly letting go of my hand and unlocking the vehicle. The aroma of his cologne and well-kept leather waft out as I open the door, and when I slide into the passenger seat it's like riding on a stick of soft butter. Why can't they make panties out of this kind of upholstery?

"Nice," I say, meaning it. The dashboard looks like something out of the movie *Serenity*, with more gadgets than I knew existed.

Declan catches me gawking and says, "It gets me where I need to go."

"What's your other car? The TARDIS?"

He laughs. That was a test. Any man who doesn't know his basic *Doctor Who* lingo isn't getting to first base with me.

Oh. Wait. He already has . . .

He starts the car, puts it in reverse, then pauses. Putting it back in park, he turns to me, his strong hand moving from the gearshift to my shoulder. Warm eyes meet mine and he says:

"Your dad was interesting. Is having a dead mouse drop in between us like that some sort of sign? Is it your family's version of a horse head in my bed?"

I can't laugh. Can't scream, can't cry, can't *anything*. "That's a mating ritual," I finally squeak out.

He cocks one eyebrow and my lady parts all faint from sheer overwhelm.

"Did I pass?" His slow smile makes me melt.

"My cat coughed up the mouse right before you arrived," I confess.

"Your sister told me." He laughs. "I seem to bring some kind of trouble whenever I'm around you."

My turn to raise an eyebrow, because—huh? *He's* taking this on? *I'm* the one who has a dark cloud of surreal weirdness hovering over her. And I don't mean my mother.

"It's not you. It's me," I say.

"Don't you need to save that line for when we break up?"

"We're not together—" He cuts me off with a kiss that makes the world stop, then pulls back, his palm caressing my jaw, thumb rubbing against the exact spot where my pulse was jamming like a reggae band.

"Let's go drink wine in the woods and gorge on chocolate-covered strawberries," he says, pulling away. He throws the car in reverse and begins to pull out of the spot.

"Are you sure you're not part female?" I joke.

His eyes are dark and smoky, with a possessiveness I now know I'm not imagining. A raw attraction makes the air between us seem electrified. The car comes to a halt and he's on me, mouth and hands everywhere, the interior space of the SUV narrowing to a pinprick, as if all time and space were in his palms, the soft skin of his mouth, the eager need of his tongue. My hands sink into his hair, roam down his neck and over his shoulders, our mouths and arms and legs searching for some truth we need to take a *lot* of time to find.

"Apparently I have something to prove," he says, breathing

hard against my ear, my fingers pausing at his waist, wanting to pull his shirt up so I can touch his hot skin. His chest rises and falls, pushing into my own yielding flesh as I burn with need for him. If I weren't sitting in the passenger seat of a car my legs would wrap around his waist of their own volition and I'd violate public indecency laws right here in my own driveway, stripping us both naked and steaming the windows.

"You do?" is all I can manage to say.

"I'm all man, Shannon. Let's make sure you know it by the time the night is over." His eyes bore into mine. He is the only thing in the world right now. A thin sheen of sweat covers me, making his body slide against mine, our shirts tangled along with our limbs. My nipples tingle and I feel a direct line between every molecule in the space between us and my giant, throbbing self.

I can feel how much man he is. Again.

I reach for him, pulling his head to mine, my own boldness a swift surprise. He doesn't need to prove one damn thing to me.

"Just kiss me like that again," I whisper.

He doesn't answer with words.

shopping
for a
billionaire

#3

chapter
one

THE STATE PARK HE choses is really close to my apartment, but might as well be a world away. Large tracts of
land dot the landscape as we tear down winding roads, bit-
tersweet vines choking off large oak trees, the road dictated by
old-growth trees as wide as cars. Omnipresent pines fill in the
spaces between the oaks and maples, and the ground is covered
with ivies ranging from the poisonous to the benign, invasively
taking over much of the land.

An insect buzzes by and I jump. Not a bee. Whew.

Cracked trees still bear scars from the massive ice storm that
hit this area nearly six years ago, the orange and beige colors
dotting the view as we get out of the SUV and look around. The
parking lot is small, bordered by large rocks that a few little kids
are climbing on. A park sign and map aren't important to us,
because Declan seems to know the way.

"How have I lived here for a year and not come here?" I wonder aloud. Three tree stumps sit side by side. The middle one is
taller and has a rustic chess board hammered onto it, the outer
stumps serving as stools.

"Maybe you need to take more risks and try new things," he
says with a smile.

It's not quite dusk, so the sky still lights up the woods, but
an ethereal quality infuses the air. Declan pops the trunk and it
opens electronically, a slow ascent that seems too measured.

He pulls out a small backpack, a thick plaid blanket with wa-
terproofing on one side, and another backpack, this one with a

flat bottom. I grab my purse and sling it around my neck and under my arm, reaching for one of his cases.

"I've got them," he says.

"Let me carry something." He shrugs and I take the blanket. There is one wide path to the left, splitting the woods. It looks like an old road, but there is no sign of asphalt. The pale grey sky is a broad stripe above us on the walkway. The path curves up ahead, like a rolling strip of dirt ribbon.

"You come here often?" I ask as we start the walk.

"Now there's a pickup line."

I laugh, the air filling my lungs and making me chuckle far longer than I need to. I'm nervous. I should be. He reaches for my hand and his skin is warm and dry. He interlaces our fingers and we fit. Our bodies are aligned just so. We shift quietly into a walking pattern and he tips his head up to admire the sky.

"I don't think I need to find icebreakers with you," I say, turning to admire him. He looks back at me with a smile that lights my whole being.

His face goes serious, dimples gone, eyes searching. "That's what I like about you, Shannon. I don't need to find anything when I'm with you. You just are. And being with you feels like living in real time. Moment by moment. Like I . . ." He dips his head down. Our shoulders are touching, and the strap from one of the backpacks slips a little.

The pause feels eternal.

"Go on," I say, giving him a gentle nudge. His hand in mine feels like a lifeline. Men don't talk about me this way. Men don't talk *to* me this way.

I want more.

He stops right in the middle of the trail and sets down the slipping backpack. His hand never leaves mine. Dusk is peeking through the clouds, the air a hair cooler than it was even a few minutes ago. The sound of the little kids playing at the parking lot fades, followed by the distant thumps of car doors closing. An engine starts.

Those green eyes look so genuine. Young and eager, nothing like the shut-off, shut-down man who argued with his father earlier this week, or who turned cold at our first business meeting the day we met. Declan opens himself up to me right here, right now, and I can't stop meeting his eyes. What I see in them is such a mirror of what I feel deep in my core that I go still with the possibility that everything I've tried to convince myself was impossible exists.

That makes Declan a dangerous man.

But I can't stop looking.

"Dating is so ridiculous," he says, his neck tight as he swallows. I can tell he's trying to hide his emotions, and a part of me screams inside for him to keep the curtain pulled back. To call off the masons he's mustering to quickly rebuild that wall that separates him from the rest of the world.

The rest of the world includes me, and right now I want to be next to him, holding hands like this, hearts beating together and bodies relaxing with the relief of not having to be on guard.

"Yes." The less I say, the better.

He takes my other hand, and now we face each other, hands clasped. He's a head above me and I have no high heels, no oak-paneled walls, no dimly lit hallway as a refuge or a prop. We're a guy and a girl in the woods trying to figure each other out.

Trying to figure ourselves out.

"Women want to date me because I have money. Because I'm a McCormick. Because they can get something out of me, or gain some social or career advantage." His eyes flash and his voice goes bitter, but he never strays from my gaze. I will myself to maintain the look now, because I don't want to make him think I'm one of those women. I'm not. He could be a street musician who busks for a living and who has twenty-seven different recipes for ramen noodles and I'd fall for him like this.

That certainty slams into my heart like someone dropped a brick on it.

"But not you," he adds. "You had no idea who I was when we met." There's a lift in his voice at the end, not quite a question, but not quite a flat statement, either.

"No, I didn't. And it wouldn't have mattered."

He arches one eyebrow and takes a step closer. Our jeans rub together, thighs mingling. "Really?"

"I'm having more fun right now than I ever did Monday night," I reply, struggling to convey a feeling. It comes out wrong. When we just look at each other my intent is clearly communicated. Why do words have to make everything so complicated?

"Then I have to remedy that, because I can think of quite a few moments on Monday night that were way more fun than anything we've done so far." His grin has a lust-filled curl to it.

"I . . . Declan?" I have to say this. Have to.

"Yes?" He presses his forehead against mine. I look up.

"I don't want your money. I don't care about your money. In fact, I'm worried you're after mine."

He laughs.

And then I add: "But before we go any further, I do have something I want to ask."

"Go on."

"*Do* you have a toilet fetish?"

"Now you're just deflecting," he murmurs against my neck, then steals my mouth for a kiss that makes the world go light and dark, all at once, entirely through the connection of our bodies.

I break the kiss and look over his shoulder, back at the parking lot. "We've walked no more than a hundred yards."

"I guess we should actually hike on a hiking date." He picks up the backpack and we walk at a reasonable pace, our legs synchronized. For a few minutes silence is all we need. The crunch of old leaves on the path makes the air seem to have a soundtrack. Chirping birds and woodland creatures add to the sounds.

No one else is here.

"There's a clearing about half a mile ahead where we can set up," he explains. The path right now is straight but it goes up an incline, jagged rocks dotting the ground. I have to use a little effort to walk, and we let go of each other's hands to navigate.

I haven't felt this present, this in the moment, in . . . ever.

With Steve there was always something to say, some mission to accomplish, some goal involved in whatever we did together. From going to the "right" movie to keep up on current trends to making sure we dined at a "fashionable" restaurant to be seen or to converse about the food at work parties, every minute we spent together had to be in service to some larger goal of helping him meet the next layer of life in the ladder of achievement.

Here I am, hiking up a rugged path with a guy who is so many levels higher in business success than Steve, and all we're doing is walking among the trees to go sit and drink wine and eat strawberries under a meteor shower.

Wow.

And I wouldn't be anywhere else right now. Even my mind grasps that. It's leaving me alone, letting me soak in Declan and the sense of peace and greatness that comes from his attention.

We walk quietly until a small trail leads off. Darkness is hinting now, dusk making its entrance, and the newly sprouting leaves in the tall trees cast more of a shadow than they did even fifteen minutes ago. I'm guessing we're close to the trail. My legs don't hurt, but they're definitely noticing we've walked farther than the distance from my car to my office.

It feels great.

The trees clear quite rapidly until the full grey sky is open and brighter without the cover of tree limbs and buds. A wide stretch of matted weeds spreads out before us, clearly old farmland that hasn't been used for that purpose in decades. Because it's spring, the growth has a raggedy aspect to it, a mix of early yellow flowers, clover, and dead straw still hanging out from last year.

"Here," Declan declares. He stops just after we walk down a slight incline and reach a small spot of even ground. The optimal size for a big blanket. I'm tingling with anticipation and I take a second to remind myself to breathe. He's so gorgeous, and being out here in nature in a scene out of a National Geographic special (and not the kind on the mating habits of the albino rhinoceros) gives me a kind of thrill I can't quite describe.

Something fiery and settled, exciting and comforting.

Distracted, I open the blanket and shake it out, gently spreading the perfect square on the grass.

A warm breeze hits us, belying the chilling air. "Make up your mind, New England," I say. "Is it winter or spring?"

He laughs. "And you say you've lived here your whole life? Remember the two feet of snow we got in '97? Or the inch that came in May back in 2002? Watch out. Mother Nature may be playing a trick on us with this balmy fifty-seven degrees."

"Every school kid remembers the April Fools' Day blizzard! That was awesome! No school for days!" My answer makes his smile deepen.

"You were what—eight?" he asks, bending down to sit on the blanket, digging in one of the backpacks to pull out a bottle of Chardonnay and a small white container of what I assume are the strawberries. My mouth waters. Not at the food. At the sight of his strong, muscled legs stretched out before him as he works a corkscrew on the bottle.

"Yep. That made you . . ." I do quick math. "Twelve?"

"Eleven. My birthday is in August. Sixth grade."

"Third for me."

I reach for the container and open it. Yep. Strawberries.

A loud *POP* announces the uncorking of the wine, and I rummage through the backpack to help find the wine glasses.

"Here," Declan says, reaching into the second pack.

He hands me coffee travel mugs.

"Huh?"

"Look closely." The tumblers are made of clear plastic with black tops, like coffee travel mugs. But when I look closely I see it—plastic pretend wine glasses built into the coffee mugs.

My laughter fills the night. "These are perfect!"

"Sippy cups for grownups. Grace highly recommends them."

"Then give Grace my thanks."

He unscrews the tops off the wine "glasses" and pours us each a healthy amount of white wine. Each movement is deliberate, careful, firmly in control. He puts the tops back on and hands me mine. We're sitting together, hips touching, knees up and braced. I'm comfortable like this. March was an unusually wet month and April wasn't much better for the first week. The ground is springy but not wet, the verdant greenery of the new plants poking out with sweet hope. A fly buzzes by my ear and I ignore it.

The view is gorgeous, as farmland and fields roll with glacier-made hills and valleys before us. A ring of thick woods surrounds the view, and it's a welcome relief from the chatter of the city just a few miles away. Route 9 is an endless string of mini-malls, regular malls, grocery stores, and chains, all buttressed by the city or Route 495 and its business belt. We're sandwiched between the suburbs, the city, and massive interstates, but in this quiet, reflective spot we could be anyone, anywhere, at any time.

I gulp the first half of my wine. A fruity flavor with just enough sweetness to make it easy to drink but dry enough to be enjoyable. I compliment him on the choice.

"Grace, again, I must admit," he confesses. No embarrassment. Just the gentlemanly acknowledgement.

"Then to Grace," I say, raising my tumbler for a toast.

"To Toilet Girl," he says with a playful smile.

chapter
two

"**T**O HOT GUY." WE drink. We kiss. We sigh. He reaches for my now nearly empty tumbler and picks up a giant strawberry covered in dark chocolate.

"To first dates," he says as he hands it to me. My mouth fills with the second-best-tasting thing this evening, the first being him.

"This is our second date," I say around a mouth full of divine fruit and chocolate.

"It is?" He seems genuinely surprised. "I thought Monday was a business meeting."

He's playing me. I swallow quickly and grab my wine to finish it off and clear my mouth.

"If Monday was a 'business meeting,' I can only imagine how you define a 'merger,' Mr. McCormick."

"Is that a request for a demonstration, Ms. Jacoby?" His mouth is on mine before I can answer, tasting like fruit and happiness. His tongue parts my lips and this time he's more insistent, the earnest sweetness swept aside by a familiarity that grows between us. His hands envelop my waist and pull me to him as he reclines back on the blanket.

We're lying down now, his legs stretched out along my own, one knee pushing between my thighs as his heat seeks mine. He smells so good and tastes even better as his tongue runs along the edges of my teeth, hands in my hair, then down my back, caressing me like he owns me.

Or wants to.

My own hands can't get enough, and I shift, feeling his hardness against my belly. Knowing that he's hard for *me* sends an electric zing through my entire body, making me wet and needy. I've never felt such all-consuming want for someone else, a lust that threatens to wipe clean my common sense, to eradicate my inhibitions, to make me move and react from a place of primal desire.

His hand slides under the waistband of my jeans, hot skin against the small of my back, and I moan, that small sound of pleasure driving him to explore. His other hand slips over my breast, cupping it, and I take his touch as permission to see what I can discover on him.

This is a lovely game of I Spy. Except we're using our hands.

He fills his palms with my ass, his own throat letting out a low growling sound that makes me wetter. The wind makes the field undulate as the sun peeks out from behind clouds, making a final, desperate attempt to shine before its day ends. All I can do is feel. My sex begins to throb, breasts swollen and plaintively wanting more of his body, his fingers, his touch.

His wanting me is the most erotic turn-on ever. Knowing he's hot for me, feeling his response to *my* presence, *my* mouth, *my* touch.

Me.

"Shannon," he whispers. Just my name. I understand, because his name zooms through my mind a million times a minute right now, trying to embed itself in deep grooves, to make it the only word I can think even when my mind is completely gone and I am nothing but sensation.

Declan.

This feels so good. So achingly good to have our hands and skin and lips and tongues all working together to get acquainted. He kisses my neck and one hand runs a long, luscious line up from my ass over my ribs to cup a breast from underneath, his thumb tweaking one nipple until it's rock hard.

I gasp. I want so much more. The movement pulls my shirt out completely from my waistband and I wiggle, primed for him. In addition to throwing EpiPens in my purse, I've added a handful of condoms because you really never know. Splendor in the grass . . .

"You are so lush," he whispers as he pulls away, my mouth raw and burning from so much kissing. I like it.

"You're amazing," I say as he pulls me on top of him, his erection pressing into my abs, my leg falling between his, thigh pinned between two powerhouses of muscled legs. I'm crushing him and he doesn't care, his caresses insistent and making it very clear that this could go as far as we want it to, all the way, and the Shannon that normally would demur is most definitely not the one in charge right now.

As he flips me over effortlessly, Declan's mouth crashes into mine with a roughness that I like more than I would imagine. He's covering me, the push of tight legs and his hardness on my inner thigh, his hand under my bra now, teasing and stroking until I'm throbbing. Nudging my legs apart, he continues to sweep my mouth with his tongue, leaving me breathless and intoxicated.

And not from the wine.

A fly buzzes near my ear and rushes off. Then a second. My shirt lifts up under his controlled hands and he works the clasp of my bra, freeing my breasts.

"You are so beautiful," he whispers as my shirt pulls up and he slides both hands over my swollen bosom, my breath catching in my throat, body completely vibrating for him.

Gently, he pulls me to the ground again until we're on our sides, hands exploring, mouths catching and releasing, my mind a blurred tornado of arousal. His hip nudges against mine and my hands go to his jeans, dipping down the front just enough to—

His groan gives me permission.

Apparently, my touch grants him a certain leeway as well, because his hands work the button of my jeans. Normally, I would pause. Date number two (or one? I'm not sure, and math isn't exactly on my mind right now) is a bit rushed for this, but I don't care. It feels right. It feels *so damn right*.

Freeing the front of our jeans simultaneously, we both go

slowly, the curve of his lips on mine changing in its slope, our warm, wet exploration delicious and inviting, unwinding slowly as if we both recognize that time and space are ours.

His torso is like warm marble peppered with a sprinkling of hair, his hitched breath as I slide down that final half-inch deeply gratifying.

Cupid's arrow hits its mark just as he reaches my core and I gasp.

No—really. Cupid's arrow just stung my back.

"OW!" I shout, jolting up, my hand that just brushed against his thick rod now scrabbling across my rib. My bra is loose around my chest and a deep, intense burning is centered right on a specific spot on my back.

"What? What's wrong? Did I hurt you?"

I climb away from Declan and sit on the ground, filled with pain and insta-worry that I've ruined the moment.

"No, no, not you." A freakish dread fills me as a fly buzzes in my ear again. And then one bites me on my back again.

That's not a fly.

"Oh my GOD!" I scream. "Get it away from me!"

Declan looks at me with alarm, his face drowsy with desire and the intimacy we'd just been in the thick of.

"I didn't mean to push too hard or to ask you to do anything you didn't want to," he says in a rough voice. The look he gives me is confused and multilayered, open and closed at the same time.

I can't process it because my entire body is throbbing. Blood and adrenaline and venom pulse through me, a blind cloud of panic descending.

Then I kind of get it.

"Not THAT!" I shriek. "THAT can come near me any time!" I point in the general direction of his unzipped jeans. "I mean the bee!" Three lazy, floating bee bodies hover over us like un-manned drones centering in on a target.

"What?" he chokes out.

"Call 911!" I scramble for my purse, which is under the backpack. Throwing items randomly in the air, I realize time is precious. At best, I have a handful of minutes.

He frowns, then his entire face changes with dawning recognition. "You're *allergic*?" Something more than standard surprise fills his voice, but I can't parse it out right now, as my body begins to swell. His phone is out with breakneck speed and he's dialing before I can answer.

My vision starts to blur. Unadulterated terror sets in. The list of steps to contain the sting escapes me, all drowned out by the mental chant of OMIGOD OMIGOD OMIGOD that won't stop looping.

I lose track of time. Declan is speaking to someone and describing our location. Then he's off the phone and I find my purse. He fishes through his back pocket, pants loose around his upper thighs, and he takes a moment to pull them up, snap, zip.

Then his hands are on me and he's holding his wallet. Two condoms poke out.

"Seriously? Now is NOT the time," I say. My voice is raspy and distant, like someone's scratching a cardboard tube shoved up against my ear.

"Not *that*—here." He hands me a foil packet of Benadryl, already torn open. I take the capsules and dry swallow them. I grab the tumbler of wine and, without any other option, I take a big swallow to make sure the pills go down.

"EpiPen?" he asks sharply. I recoil, even as my vision starts to pinprick.

"How do you know? And where did you get the Benadryl?"

"My brother Andrew is highly allergic, too. Wasps, in his case." He's tossing my tampons and old cough drops and receipts and makeup out of my purse with military precision and laser focus until he finds the EpiPen and hands it to me.

I pop the top off, but before I inject, another bee floats over. Looking down, I see the issue: we're near a nest of ground bees. The blanket is literally on top of them. Leave it to me to make out with Hot Guy on top of a Nest of Death.

Declan follows my gaze and realizes it, too. He reaches around me just as I tighten my grip on the pen and slam it as hard as I can into my hip, but he nudges me and my aim falters as I bring my forearm down as hard as I can so the needle goes deep in me to administer the epinephrine I need and—

I inject him in the groin.

"God DAMN!" he shouts, springing to his feet and inhaling so deeply I fear he'll pass out. One of us has to stay conscious, and at this rate it won't be me. A sound like rushing water fills my ears.

The Benadryl isn't helping, and that dose of epinephrine is the only thing keeping me from anaphylactic shock as I feel my breathing speed up, but my throat starts to narrow, as if Darth Vader has me in his grip and won't let go. Declan is limping and huffing, taking deep breaths and making grunting sounds as he comes toward me like Wolverine on the attack.

I fumble for my purse and keep trying to say "I'm sorry," but all that comes out is a strangled whooping noise. Declan grabs the purse from me and I can see the veins in his neck bulging, can watch his pulse throb in front of me as he pulls the cap off the second EpiPen, rolls me onto my stomach, pins me in place, and pulls my jeans down to expose my ass—

"What are you doing?" I rasp.

—and then slams the needle so hard into my butt cheek that the wind is knocked out of me.

The world goes dark, then light again as he scoops me up and begins running down the path toward the cars. He's favoring the hip near where I injected him, but still moves with remarkable speed and agility. My head feels so heavy, and my arms and legs flop, even though I know I should be surging from the EpiPen's contents. Maybe it's the wine. Maybe it's overwhelm. Maybe it's impending death.

"I'll get you there," Declan says. "C'mon, Shannon. Stay awake." That's an order, the hard grit in his voice like being barked at during basic military training, but his voice strains with fear and a gentleness that tells me I have to listen to him.

"I'm here," I mumble. He's running hard and I can hear his heart pounding against my ear, pressed against his sweaty shirt. We're more than half a mile from the parking lot and I hear a horrible wheezing sound. My weight isn't a small number, and I feel embarrassed that he's struggling so hard to breathe through carrying me. Yet he cradles me, mumbling something as he runs. All I can sense is the tumbling of air against his lungs and ribs.

If I could just move, I could stand and walk back to the lot. I start to resist, to try to help.

Then I realize the wheezing is coming from me. Not him.

He's moving swiftly and with great power, and my throat stops swelling. This is how the EpiPen always works, like slamming the brakes on a car going a hundred miles an hour. For me, the relief comes in waves. First, the swelling stops, but it doesn't recede. It just doesn't get worse.

That's what has happened now. I'm so tired, though. Exhausted and depleted, and it takes everything in me to stay upright in his arms so Declan can carry me. The ground becomes bumpy and he slows down, carefully navigating down a slope on the wider part of the trail. It's dark, and insects buzz in my ear.

"Bees?" I mumble.

"No," he says, his panting heavy from exertion. "Flies. But the two bees that stung you—" He's huffing through a final sprint and I can make out a red flashing light in the distance.

Two. Oh. That's it. I've never been stung *twice* like this. My eyelids feel like quilts covering my vision, and my lips tingle and balloon out. If only I could lift an arm and give him some help. I will it to move but it doesn't. Nothing does.

I'm sorry, I want to say. Maybe I do. It's hard to tell.

And then I fade out completely, remembering nothing more than the steady sound of Declan's breath as he races me to safety.

" **I** S HIS PENIS GOING to fall off?" Mom's voice floats into my awareness as a big, bright light blinds me. Am I in heaven? Hell? Somewhere in between? If Mom's here, that narrows this down considerably. I'm either alive or in purgatory.

"Whose penis?" I mumble. "What did you do to Dad this time?" Someone squeezes my hand and I open my eyes slowly. They feel like wet wool blankets coated with glass shards, but I open them all the way anyhow.

Amy is the one holding my hand, and she looks so scared. "Not Dad. And don't worry."

My mouth tastes like dry pencil shavings that have been sitting in Death Valley for a thousand years. "Where am I?"

She names a local hospital.

"Why am I here?" My mind feels like dry pencil shavings, too. I'm cold suddenly, and my legs begin to shake. I have no control over this, and soon my chin chatters.

Mom grabs a stack of blankets and starts covering me in them, in layers up and down my body. The thick, heavy warmth cocoons me.

"You were stung by a bee, honey," Dad whispers, taking my other hand. I turn to look at him and his eyes are red-rimmed. Crying?

"Two, actually," Mom says.

"Daddy, don't cry," I mumble. "I'm sorry."

That makes Amy start to sob. "You don't have to apologize

for something you can't control, Shannon," she says. "And thank goodness you're a paranoid freak," she adds.

"It comes in handy sometimes," I mutter, unsure what she means.

"You really scared us," Carol says. Carol! Carol's here, with a frightened-looking Jeffrey, who can't seem to look at me. Geez. Why is my seven-year-old nephew here? Haven't seen him in, what—a month? He's getting so big, with those long eyelashes and—has he been crying?

"Hi, Jeffrey," I croak out. He gives me an uncertain wave. I try to wave back, but a sharp stab of pain in my hand halts me.

An older female doctor with more salt than pepper in her hair strides into the room. It's not really a room, I see—there's just a curtain between me and another bed, where I hear two men talking in hushed voices.

The doctor looks at my chart and flips through pages, jotting notes. Her white jacket has little gold pins all over the lapel and she smells like freshly bathed dogs. Her face is tight. She looks up and realizes I'm awake.

"Shannon, that was close," she says in a clipped British accent. "I'm Dr. Porter." She sounds like Judi Dench playing an older female doctor in a *Doctor Who* episode, because there are so many tubes and bright flashing lights in the room that I feel like I'm surrounded by Daleks that have taken over the TARDIS. "Good work by you and your date, though his aim was remarkably better than yours."

"Thank you," says a deep, familiar male voice from behind the curtain. "I agree one hundred percent. And Shannon, I'll never go target practicing with you. Ever."

Huh?

"And no, Marie, all my equipment is in place and intact. She got my *thigh*," the voice adds in a tone that makes it clear there is no follow-up discussion.

"Thank goodness!" Mom chirps. "Can't have grandbabies if it falls off," she whispers.

Maybe I'm the Dalek, because all I want to do now is scream EX-TER-MIN-ATE at her.

"I am five feet away and can hear every word," he growls. The curtain whips back in one smooth movement and there's Declan, alone, buttoning his jeans.

The memory floods me instantly. Wine. Hiking. Making out. Sex (almost . . .). Bees. EpiPen.

"I didn't break your penis, did I?" I rasp through vocal cords that feel like painful ribbons. Because that would be the Epic Fail of Dates. I would have to become a nun if I broke a man's penis. My name would become part of Urban Dictionary, like Lorena Bobbit. *"Why'd you stop dating Jill?" "Because she tried to Shannon Jacoby me." "No way, dude . . ."*

"What, exactly, were you doing out there?" the doctor asks, one eyebrow arched perfectly. She sounds so disapproving and snobbish, the way only a British person can, the accent so intelligent. "And no, you broke nothing. You're fortunate the denim on Declan's jeans helped to reduce the injury from the injection."

I try to hate her but don't really have the energy. Mom's words break through some of my angry confusion, but they leave me stunned and overwhelmed.

"No one broke anything, and I think everyone should go so I can take care of my daughter." She looks so defeated. Where's the sarcasm? The over-the-top exuberance and social cluelessness? The inappropriate oversharing?

Mom's eyes are swollen and hollow at the same time, and my throat closes again, except this time not from being stung.

I look at Declan, and he's looking back with so much concern that I close my eyes, unable to process anything.

"I was stung?" I murmur.

Mom scooches Amy over and takes my hand. Carol's holding Jeffrey's hand, with little Tyler perched on one hip, his eyes zeroed in on the television, which is set to Cartoon Network without sound. Jeffrey looks a lot calmer now, and he's watching Declan with narrowed eyes, like he's studying him.

Poor boy. His own dad never comes around, so maybe he's just checking out the Daddy crowd. Not that Declan's a daddy. Or is he? My head really hurts.

Amy and Declan share an inscrutable look. "Twice, honey."

She slows her speech down, her eyes watching me carefully. All her makeup is gone and the hand that grabs mine is shaking.

They've all been crying. How bad was I?

"Did I die?"

Declan's face shifts to a quick expression of shock and he swallows, hard. He looks like he's about seventeen suddenly, wide-eyed and frozen.

Dad stands up and points to him. "No. But only because of him." Everyone turns and looks at Declan.

Steve would have smiled and taken all the credit if I'd been stung and he'd carried me out of there to an ambulance. As my brain starts to clear, I remember that Steve was there the previous time I was stung, back at UMass. That had happened on campus, and Steve had screamed like a little kid and run away, leaving me with my phone and my purse, digging furiously for the EpiPen.

He'd only come back after the paramedics arrived and I'd nearly passed out.

What Declan did was heroic in every sense of the word.

"We were half a mile—" I say. The rest of my sentence is choked off by my dry mouth.

Reading my mind, Declan grabs the pitcher of water on the tray above me and pours a glass that has a straw sticking in it. He hands it to Mom, who ministers it to me like I'm on my deathbed.

Am I?

"Early spring bees. Who knew they'd be out?" Dad says.

"That was my fault, sir," Declan says in a low voice. Contrite, even. "I chose the picnic spot and didn't think to clear the ground for bees' nests." He sounds angry. He should be. It was my fault for not telling him.

"Who would in April in Massachusetts?" the doctor snaps. I've never seen Declan like this, furious at himself, sheepish and so young looking, like he thinks he deserves to be upbraided for something that was completely out of his control.

"I should have." He looks at Mom and Dad. "My brother is highly allergic to wasps, and—" His face shuts down as he caps his emotions. My entire body aches, like someone is stabbing kitchen knives into my thighs, my butt, my neck and upper arms, but none of that pain compares to what my heart feels watching his reaction.

"No," I croak out. "You did everything right. You didn't know. I should have said something, but it's never been a big issue."

Mom snorts. "Shannon," she says in a chiding voice. Whether it's a "big issue" or not has been a bone of contention between us ever since I was first stung.

Then she squeezes my hand and looks between him and me. "You did everything perfectly, Declan." She lets go of my hand and stands, grabbing him for an embrace. "You did everything perfectly, and thank you for saving my daughter's life."

My eyes start to water and two tears trickle down each side of my face, rolling into my ears. It itches. A tightness in my throat triggers panic in me. Too close to what I felt after the bee stings. My breathing becomes labored and the doctor checks my pulse.

"Slow breaths, Shannon," she says in a soothing tone. "The adrenaline is still in you and it will be a while before you're okay."

I nod, following her instructions. Mom's arm is thrown casually around Declan and they look like they've been best friends for years. It freaks me out and warms me at the same time.

Jeffrey clears his throat and opens his mouth. I see two white nubs along his gum line, the permanent teeth poking through. His nose is big and sunburnt and his cheeks have freckles on them.

"Yes?" I ask, giving him permission to speak in a crowd of scary grownups who tower over him.

It's Declan he turns to. "Did you break your penith?"

Oh, that lisp.

Suppressed snickers fill the room. We sound like a bunch of taste testers for canned baked beans after a new product line rollout. *Futt-futt-futt* . . .

"No, buddy, my penith—penis—is just fine." Declan reaches

down and ruffles his hair. Jeffrey leans into the touch like a cat cozying up for some petting.

"Good." Jeffrey tugs on Declan's shirt. Declan bends down, but what comes out of Jeffrey's mouth can be heard by everyone.

"Jutht tho you know, you thouldn't play with your penith anywhere exthept in your bedroom. The penith is a private plathe."

Declan's eyes widen. Dad's hand flies to his mouth to cover a grin. Even the British doctor chick is trying not to laugh.

"Thanks," Declan says with a stage whisper. "I'll remember that *forever*."

Jeffrey's on fire now. A room of grownups paying attention, and a dad (in his mind, Declan's a dad, because all men over twenty-five are "dads") who is riveted by what he's saying.

"And you know what elth?" Jeffrey is king at court. He makes eye contact with every grownup as he takes roll.

"Yeah?" Declan is amused. He's confident and fine with a room full of adults making fun of his penith.

"You thouldn't let Auntie Thannon touch your penith. It's a private plathe and no one hath the right to touch it without your permithon. "

Oh, I had permission, bud. I can't, of course, say that, and the room is now filled with giggles and people biting their lips so hard they are causing de facto piercings.

Carol lunges for him. "Let's go get ice cream!" She mouths *I'm sorry* to Declan, who waves it off and gives Jeffrey a high-five as she scurries out the door with her boys.

Then Declan turns and faces the crowd. "You no longer have permithon to even *talk* about my penith."

"She needs her rest, anyhow, and I've had quite my fill of 'penith' jokes at this point," the doctor tells Mom and Dad. Declan shakes Dad's hand. My father pulls him into a manly hug and claps him twice on the back. It's a macho thing that would make me laugh if I had the energy.

Declan whispers something I can't hear to them while Amy kisses my cheek and squeezes my hand before letting go. "He ran with you the entire way to the car. The *entire* way." Her eyes rake over Declan's body in a way that makes me tingle with jealousy. Or maybe that's just my catheter shifting a little. Why do I have a catheter? How long have I been unconscious? "Even after you stabbed him in the crotch."

I snort. It hurts. Everything hurts. My eyes feel like slits in a slab of organ meat.

"How long have I been here?"

"About fifteen hours." She looks at her phone to check, and nods. "It's morning now."

"Jesus." I swallow. "Why does my throat hurt so much?"

"They had to put a tube down your throat to keep you breathing." She can barely say the words.

"Oh." I look at Declan, who is quietly talking to my mom. They keep looking at me with worried expressions.

"Not only do you manage to catch a billionaire, you catch Captain America," Amy adds.

I try to laugh again but it comes out as a choke. She slowly lets go of my hand, trailing off, and follows Mom and Dad out as the doctor explains something to them about my care.

Declan and I are alone. And all I can do is start to cry. Big, messy tears that would devolve into a true ugly sobbing if I had the airway to spare. Instead, the fat teardrops just pour into my outer ear and collect there with a maddening itch.

"Why are you crying?" he asks with a tenderness in his voice that makes me cry even more. In seconds, he's across the room and stroking my hand.

"Because I almost destroyed your penith!"

The deep, booming laughter is so unexpected, like a sudden thunderclap on a clear moonlit night, that the sound shocks me and makes me gasp another apology.

He sits on the bed next to me and strokes my hair, tucking a long strand behind my wet ear. "Shannon, that was my fault. I moved and shoved your arm and you—"

"You're taking a lot of blame for what happened," I whisper.

He sighs, his neck and shoulders relaxing. "I do that when I think the woman I'm falling for is about to—" Declan swallows, his eyes boring into mine. Feeling his arm shake, his voice husky and low with worry, drains me of all my energy.

"It was that bad?"

"Let's just say I never, ever want to go through that again."

"Good. Because you're allowed to have a toilet girl fetish, but not a bee sting fetish," I whisper.

The room goes still as he smiles with his eyes. No laugh, no chuckle. Then I realize what he's just said.

"Falling for me?" I ask.

Without answering, he climbs on the bed beside me.

"I, uh, I don't want to get pee on you."

"Isn't it a little early in our relationship for golden showers?"

I sputter, then gag, then cough for too long. I think I damn near fill the bag. "No, I mean . . ." I gesture to my pee bag.

"Oh. That." With a flick of his wrist he moves a tube just so. I'm on my side, so we spoon, and whatever he did makes it all work somehow. His hot thighs press against my backside, arm reaching over my waist and pulling me in. His touch is tender and careful, gentle and safe.

"Or do you have a hospital bed sex fetish?" I ask, yawning. I mean, really—hot, rich guy who saved my life and he's cuddling with me while I have a tube shoved up my urethra and I'm peeing in front of him? Only real in Fantasyland. Or Fetishland.

He lets out a low sound of amusement. "Believe me, of all the fetishes I could have, this is the last one on earth I'd want right now." I must have given him my yawn, because he joins in.

"You must be exhausted, too," I whisper. "I pumped you full of epinephrine when I injected you. I'm so sorry."

He hugs me tighter. "It was an accident. And it's been, what—most of a day now."

How can he be so forgiving? Steve would have ranted for days about my injuring him, as if it had been a character flaw of mine. Declan takes my klutzy mistake in stride.

I pull away and half-turn to face him. "Accident or no accident, I put you in danger." I feel stupid and confused. The bed is small but his warmth feels so good.

"All I have to do is process out some extra adrenaline. My organs can take it. *You* came damn close to . . ." He won't say the word, so I do.

"Dying."

Tension fills his entire body from knees to hands. "Yes. Andrew came close when we were kids after a wasp sting. The whole family carries extra Benadryl at all times, and he has two EpiPens, too. It's not something you take lightly, and if I'd have known about your allergy, I never would have . . ." He sighs. "I would have made different decisions."

"That's my fault." My voice cracks. "I don't like to let it limit my life, and when you asked me for an outdoor date I didn't want to be—" I pause and yawn again. The room is getting dimmer and I hear the beeping from various machines down the hall. Machines that monitor heart rates and IV flow, that keep people safe and alive.

"What?" he asks gently.

"*That* girl. That weird girl who is sensitive and who lives a restricted life. Who imposes that on you." It occurs to me that maybe Steve didn't like picnics because of my bee allergy. That makes me frown. Perhaps he thought about me with more care than I realized. I seize inside, even though I do not have the energy for any of this.

Why am I thinking about Steve as Declan's scent fills me like the perfect prescription for healing?

"You wouldn't impose anything on me. I'm a grown man who can make his own choices." His voice is gruff. I don't feel vulnerable, though. This is an open give-and-take. I'm his equal. His very tired equal.

I yawn again. "Then I guess I was worried I'd give you one more reason not to choose me." I squeeze his hand and he squeezes right back.

"Why?"

"Because this is unreal."

He shifts against me, the rough denim of his jeans sliding against my bare legs. Sinking into the comfort of him, I sigh, a long, luxurious sound that feels like an endless exhale. As if I've been holding my breath for a year and can finally let it go. If you can't tell someone how you feel right after they've saved your life, when can you? Besides, if he doesn't return the feelings I can blame delirium for my confession.

"It is for me, too, Shannon," he says softly, his breath sending strands of hair against my cheek.

Oh! He's joining in. This is new territory.

He continues. "I can't believe that I found someone like you. And that you see something in me that makes you want to be with me." He swallows, and I can feel the movement on my shoulder. "I've spent years just chasing arm candy and bedmates." He's confessing to me, baring his soul.

I freeze, taken out of the comfort zone and into wishful-thinking territory.

"I'm not arm candy?" I try to sound lighthearted but instead I just feel raw.

"You're a chocolate-covered strawberry. A dozen of them. On top of a chocolate mousse cake." He nuzzles my neck, his smile imprinted under my ear.

"Do you really mean it?" I try not to sound as pathetic as I feel. Hope rises inside my chest, crawling out of a cave near my heart, shielding its face against the first shaft of sunlight it's seen in a long time.

He gets what I'm really saying. "Do *you?*"

"Do I feel the same way?" I break free from our spooning and very carefully turn over to face him. He's vulnerable and wanting, his eyes open and watching me carefully. No pretense. No shields. No walls.

"Yes." He's inventorying me.

"I can't believe you want to be with me. I'm . . . nobody."

"You're everybody," he says with a firm passion. His hand slides along my jaw and under the nape of my neck. "And watching you today, after those bees . . . I can't lose you."

"You won't." I reach forward, the IV pulling on my arm, a sharp, needling pain making me wince. He pulls the tangled tube away from its knot with such care I want to cry from the joy of being treated like this.

"How about we both just stop right here."

My heart squeezes. "What do you mean?"

"This is what we both feel. It's real. It's *real*," he says with urgency. His lips press against mine and the kiss is so sweet that tears spring to my eyes. His body moves toward me and stops. He pulls back and closes his eyes. "And it's so real that we need to let down our walls and let reality guide whatever comes next."

"I have always lived in Realityland. I'm the mayor of it. It's the rest of the world that doesn't cooperate."

He smiles.

"No, seriously. Have you met my mother?"

Now he just shakes his head with amusement. We both yawn at the same time, slow, lion-like sounds. I turn back around and he snuggles up.

"Are you allowed to nap with me?" I ask. I think half the words disappear as I fade off to sleep.

"It's better to ask forgiveness than permission," he says, the vibration of his words against my neck a cozy feeling. A feeling I could get used to experiencing every day of my life. "Besides, the nurses take pity on me. They're also a little jealous of you."

"Jealous?"

"When I had to strip down to show them the EpiPen puncture, they got an eyeful."

My laughter is quieter than I want it to be. I'm so tired.

"Is this the weirdest date you've ever been on?" I mumble as sleep overtakes me.

"Probably." A long pause, and then he adds, "The EpiPen was definitely the most inventive sex toy a woman has ever used with me."

I'm in a state of exhausted bliss, and as I float off, a thought occurs to me.

"Declan?"

"Mmm?" He's breathing slowly, his voice muted in the tiny room. I almost feel bad interrupting him, but I have to know. The thought won't go away.

"How did your mother die?"

His breathing halts, the warm muscles behind me solid and tense like granite. Then he relaxes, as if by will. The monitors ping on.

"It's not important. Go to sleep, honey."

"You called me 'honey,'" I whisper, my eyes filling with tears. He can't see me, and that's good.

"I'm just so, so grateful you're going to be okay." His hand rests on my hip with a possession and a familiarity I like. I like it very much, but I'm so, so tired.

"Thanks to you," I mumble, and then that's all there is.

chapter
four

THE FIRST DATE I have after I get out of the hospital feels like a combination of a bad *Girls* episode and sealing myself to the bathtub during an unfortunate do-it-yourself waxing session.

What? Why do you think my mother insists on making me go with her to the spa? She let me get out of it this week because of billionaires and bees and that whole Shannon-almost-died thing, but I know it's coming soon.

This bad date, though—it turns out it's going to be a doozy. The kind of night where you go on Truu Confessions and skewer the person, then it becomes a BuzzFeed article and the next thing you know you have a podcast that propels you to a cable show and then—

"I wish I had been there, Shannon," Steve says in a low murmur. That's right. I'm on a date with *Steve*.

Not Declan.

Declan is off in New Zealand slaying Orcs or whatever you do "on business" in New Zealand. He almost offered to bring me, but the whole IV-in-the-arm thing and my mom's screams about New Zealand bees killing her daughter put a stop to that. "Bad timing" will be etched on my gravestone, I swear.

Plus I have a backlog of shops to do, including two podiatrist offices (checking fungal safety protocols), one cigar shop (to see if there's clerk bias against women), one massage company (hallelujah!), and fourteen fast food restaurants testing out a new Caesar salad.

Fortunately, I like anchovies. Amanda's allergic to them (she says . . .), so I know what I'll be eating for lunch for the next three weeks.

Last night I got into a lovely sexting session with Declan that ended in some pictures of him and a few pictures of me and let's just say thank God for the fact that pictures you take on Snapchat all get deleted within a few minutes, because if this relationship goes south there would be pictures of me in compromising positions way more embarrassing than a hand in the toilet.

Steve is, instead, my "date." He keeps calling it a date, and I keep calling it, well, *nothing*. We're at a local Mexican joint where all the food is homemade and delicious, but coated with cilantro the way my mother puts on mascara. Three layers deep and with a ruthless efficiency few can master. At least none of the cooks poked my eye out while applying it.

"If you'd been there it would have been awkward, Steve," I say in a no-nonsense voice, though I reach forward and pat his hand. That's such a patented Marie Jacoby gesture that I freeze and snatch my fingers away as if I'd been burned. They say you turn into your mother as you age. Kill me now.

Weird. It's so weird to realize how much of your parents seeps into you unconsciously. Pretty soon I, too, will wear nothing but yoga pants and use push powder to fluff up my thinning hair while talking incessantly about Farmington Country Club weddings and my dildo collection.

And if I had married Steve, that pretty much would have summed up the next three decades. I shudder again and shove a fried tortilla chip in my mouth to stifle a groan.

"Why would it have been awkward?" he asks, one corner of his mouth turned up in what I assume is an attempt to give me a seductive smile. He looks like the Joker, minus makeup.

I chew fast and swallow hard. "Because Declan and I were on a date." Do I really need to spell out the obvious?

"Got a problem with two men at once?" he says in a guttural tone I've never heard from him.

"What the hell is wrong with you?" I bark. "And ewwww,

who wants two men at the same time?" One is hard enough to handle. If I want two men at the same time then one of them can change my oil while I have sex with the other one. Now there's a fantasy.

Steve just laughs and says, "I thought you two weren't dating." He uses both hands to pick up his drink, which is a strawberry margarita the size of a bucket. You could host a pool party for toddlers in there.

I cock one eyebrow and try not to sigh. "You caught us kissing at the restaurant two weeks ago. We're *dating*." My voice is firm and kind of flat, the way you talk to a pollster during a presidential campaign. Like you want to be nice and do your duty, but c'mon—let's get this over with so you can go off and spin this conversation to your advantage in the most sociopathic way ever.

"That doesn't mean you're dating." He takes three enormous swallows of his drink and sets it down, salt coating his thin upper lip. Steve then unrolls the silverware from the yellow cloth napkin and shakes the cloth onto his lap. His hands are steady but something is off. Why am I here again?

Whatever ambiguity I felt when Declan and I dined with Steve and Jessica is gone. Long gone, and now replaced by apathy. Something even less than apathy, though. A growing annoyance that makes me see Steve is part of my past. Not my future.

The clarity makes me ache for Declan right now. Of all the times to be in New Zealand, frolicking with Hobbits. Hobbits have nasty feet. My mind drifts to the podiatrist visits I have to complete later this week.

"I don't routinely shove my tongue down the throat of people I'm not dating." The words slip out before I even deliberate whether to say them. If Amanda were here she'd be cheering. A few weeks ago I'd have never challenged Steve like this, but a few weeks can change *everything*.

He pauses in mid-movement, nostrils flaring, then he's the one who sighs. "I'm not sure I know that for a fact, Shannon." His eyes snap up and catch mine. The look he gives me is hard and accusatory.

"What is that supposed to mean?"

"I think you're dating him to make me jealous."

Thunk. That's the sound of my jaw falling through the earth's crust, magma, core, and splashing into Declan's lap in New Zealand.

"You think I'm—"

"It's brilliant!" He takes a long draw off his drink. "Seriously. Making sure you pick the same restaurant where I'm with Jessica. Using Jessica's online presence to help boost your profile—"

"What?" Where does he get that from? I want to be tweeted about by Jessica Coffin about as much as I want to suck on Steve's toes. "You think I'm jealous of you and Jessica and I'm dating Declan McCormick to . . . to . . . what?"

"Get me back."

A deeply wheezy sound emerges from my throat as the tortilla chip I shoved in there lodges itself in the worst way possible. I'm not in danger of choking to death. Just gagging in pain until the offending object moves out of the way.

Hmmm. That kind of describes Steve, actually.

The tortilla chip cracks and goes down (and no, that doesn't describe *me*), and with a big swig of my water glass I finally look at him with tears in my eyes from having my throat lacerated by a completely innocent piece of food.

"You think I want you back?"

He takes a big chip, dips it in the salsa, bites off half, and double dips. That's right. He just offended Jerry Seinfeld and the crew with one bite.

"Of course you do. It's been a year, you're still single, and you're here. With me. On a date. So—it worked." He spreads his hands magnanimously, as if accepting defeat for some battle I didn't know existed. "You win."

"I win *what?*"

"You win *me.*"

"I don't want to win you! I never win anything! If I'm going to win something, it should be an all-expenses paid trip to Puerto Vallarta or a Kia Optima, not an all-access pass to be the slobbering, under-appreciated girlfriend to an over-important fleshbag who thinks I'm inadequate and who has an ego bigger than his penith!"

Well, now. Who knew that was in me? He doesn't seem offended, though. More worried that other people heard me, but not actually upset by the content and meaning of my words.

"You're not the woman I thought I knew."

"You mean the woman you *rejected*." I reach for my own bucket of sugar and alcohol and take a few gulps of liquid courage. Mine is a cranberry margarita, which sounded way better when I read it on the menu. It tastes like a cough drop mixed with Love's Baby Soft perfume.

"'Rejected' is such a harsh word." Steve splays his massive hands across the table and stretches forward, as if he wants me to hold hands. Nope.

"No kidding it is. It *hurts*."

Our eyes lock and I realize that just like I don't understand why I'm here, *he* has no idea why he is here. For the past week since I got out of the hospital he's hounded me to get together, and now he's got me. All my attention, all my focus. But he has no idea what to do with me.

"And that's why you don't reject a woman like Shannon. Ever."

The growling voice comes from behind me and I literally jump in my seat about three inches, falling back down onto the hard wood with a jolt that spreads up from my tailbone and through my eyeballs. Which are currently locked on Steve's shocked face.

He is staring at a point behind me, above my head.

I whip around, knowing that voice, and my breath catches in my throat. Declan's standing there, a day's worth of stubble peppering that strong chin, his business shirt unbuttoned at the top, no tie, and he's delightfully rumpled, his grey suit wrinkled in all the right places, pants tight and tailored to fit like a glove. He looks like he just spent the entire day in motion, and as my eyes take him in he looks at me greedily.

His hand slides along the bones of my shoulder, cupping the

soft skin at the back of my neck, and his lips find mine for a gentle, polite kiss that makes me throb everywhere. Sexting last night wasn't enough. Never enough. I swallow hard as he pulls back, the scent of him full of sweat and cologne and soap and *home*.

"Hi," he says to me, eyes claiming mine. Steve clears his throat. *Steve who?*

"Good to see you, Declan." Steve stands and offers his hand. Declan completely ignores him, his eyes boring into mine, hand on my neck like he's drowning and touching me is the only way to breathe.

"Hey," Declan finally says in Steve's general direction.

"We were just talking about—" Steve starts to say, but Declan interrupts him.

"How you rejected Shannon." Declan's words are granite. Iron. Platinum. Take the hardest element and multiply it by every time Steve told me I wasn't good enough and you come close to Declan's voice.

I feel like I'm in a bubble. My skin is tingling and burning with exposure. People don't talk to each other like this in my world. We aren't direct and clear with our boundaries like this. We don't make declarations like Declan, firm "no" statements that Steve is flat out wrong for trying to shame me—rather than *me* being wrong for whatever he's trying to shame me over.

That invalidation is the greatest sin.

I've been taught to joke my way through discomfort. To let people cross my internal lines because that's fine—they love me, and besides, maybe it's okay. No big deal. *Ha ha*, laugh off that feeling in the pit of your stomach that says this is wrong. *Hee hee*, go along with the joke at your expense because pointing out the truth will make everyone *else* uncomfortable.

With Steve, I kept thinking all those years that if I could "just" change enough to stop his newest criticism, then I'd be perfect. If I could "just" be on edge all the time and try to guess what my next misstep would be in his eyes and stop myself before I transgressed, then he would be happy with me.

If I could "just" learn to live life according to mixed signals and constantly shifting expectations . . . which meant I would never, ever be good enough.

Ever.

A jumble inside me feels like shattered glass being moved and realigned with great care, like reassembling a broken mosaic to put it back in place with the least damage possible. Declan has armor I cannot imagine wearing. He has a core that knows who he is and what he wants without the reflection of others. No mirrors pointed back at him telling him to internalize what everyone else thinks of him.

If I hadn't touched him, kissed him, joked and teased and played with him, I would think he was a god. But no . . . he's flesh and bone and real and authentic and . . .

Mine.

And I am enough for him. Enough as is.

More than enough.

And that is true even without Declan.

"I—" Steve is speechless. Declan's godlike status just went up a notch, because Steve's bloviating is hard to stop, like trying to prevent Mom from getting up at 2:30 a.m. on Black Friday to stand in line at a big-box store and come home with a television bigger than the height of our house because "It was only $39.97! And they gave me a free coffee!"

"Come here," Declan says, pulling on my hand. He's crossed oceans for me. Cut meetings short. Slept in airplane seats designed for children who aren't tall enough to ride rollercoasters. His pull leaves no question, no opportunity to argue. I'm going with him, and Steve's nostrils flare.

"What are you doing?" Steve asks. He doesn't ask, though— the words come out in a livid monotone. Years of dating and he'd never shown jealousy toward any other guy, even when we'd been at nightclubs and someone grabbed my ass. No protectiveness, no possessiveness, no sense that he was upset that I was someone else's hand candy, objectified and easy for a grab that meant nothing and everything at the same time.

All those years of being his . . . *what*? What was I to him?

"I'm taking Shannon," Declan says in a tone that is the

mirror opposite of Steve's—full of passion and infused with feeling. His words are measured but the meaning behind them isn't.

She's mine. You fucked up. Go away.

Wait. Those were the meanings behind *my* words, actually.

Declan pulls a wallet out of his back pocket, his other hand firmly holding my elbow with a grip that is not unpleasant. He tosses two twenties on the table and with a gentle nudge turns me away from Steve, who sits there, impotent, staring gapemouthed at the cash.

Declan's steps eat the floor between where I'd been sitting and the main door, my legs like tingling rubber bands as I work to match him. The way he just treated Steve makes my brain buzz. It was so . . . rude. So . . . macho.

So . . . *right*.

chapter
five

"THANK YOU," I SAY as he pushes the door open and a burst of sunset explodes before my eyes, feeling returning to my legs, my lips, my body. As the steps take me away from a man who had never cherished me, never seen me as anything more than a tool, I feel my body fill in.

Like a paint-by-numbers project, here comes my dignity in a lovely shade of purple. Blue stands for confidence. Rich red for clarity. A sedate adobe represents patience, and green is the color of hope.

Declan's eyes.

"For what?" he asks as he holds the car door open for the (of course) waiting limo outside the restaurant.

"For that." I thumb toward the restaurant, half expecting to see Steve's distorted face pressed against the plate-glass window. "Um, how much did you hear?"

"You mean the part about his tiny penith and his huge ego? Because that was great." A half-grin and hearty laugh follow. "'Penith' will never not be funny."

Declan's hand is on the limo handle when I realize—my car!

"Wait. I drove here," I explain, a sinking feeling hitting me at once. Practical Shannon. How would I get home if Price Charming sweeps me away on his mechanical steed?

"Turdmobile?" he asks. A passerby gives him a funny look, staring at the limo with one eyebrow cocked.

"Yep." I look over at the parking lot where I stashed the damn thing. Even mixed in with a bunch of late-'90s junkers, the car stands out like my mom at a Submissive Wives conference.

"I'll bring you back," he says, opening the door. Declan slides in next to me, shutting the door with a sound that sends a thrill through me. We are hermetically sealed in the cool leather, the divider firmly up so that all we are is a man, a woman, and a bunch of alcohol in the back of a car bigger than most dorm rooms.

"Thank you again."

"That was nothing."

"That was *everything*."

The ferocious, feral nature of the kiss he gives me before I can finish saying the final word tears away at any restraint I pretend to have. As his mouth devours mine, his hand slides up under the thin cotton skirt I'm wearing.

"Mmmm, skirt," he says against my lips. Apparently my flesh has the ability to make him lose entire grades of vocabulary. Who knew? His fingers take advantage and slide right up my quivering thigh. He's not teasing.

He's very, very serious.

Today is not supposed to be the day. *That day* is supposed to be carefully planned, with roses and good food and wine and a carefully manicured Shannon. *That day* should involve a giant full-body waxing session, a few pokes in the eye with Mom's mascara wand, and a trip to a lingerie shop filled with self-loathing and best-friend reassurance that spending $200 on pieces of silk Declan will tear off my body in seconds is totally worth it.

Right now? Here? I have leg stubble that is coarser than snapped pine trees after an ice storm. My lady place hasn't been trimmed in so long it looks like Malcolm Gladwell's hair. Small woodland creatures probably make their home in there, and while I did (thank God) shower this morning, it's not like I thought my cobwebs would need to be cleaned out today.

Of all days.

He's breathing slowly against me, body curled up and over mine, hovering and so . . . male. Being wanted like this by a man who is the undisputed leader in any given room full of penises is a turn-on, and my mind shuts off as the body takes over, his fingers making that all too easy as he finds my throbbing center.

Oh, he really is a god after all.

The way he strokes me, slow and deliberate, as his tongue works in concert with his fingers, my mouth and sex both wet and wild, brings me to the edge so fast. I'm so ready.

I want him so much.

The car pulls away from the curb and I giggle as we lurch, his erection pressing into my hip. His face is dark with want. I'm wet with need. We're a match made in limo.

I undo his pants and reach in to grip him, the sharp hiss of air sucked in through his teeth my reward. I pull his pants down enough to look and see what I never got a chance to gaze at before we were so rudely interrupted by the Bees That Nearly Killed Shannon.

He's beautiful. Thick and veiny and big, skin soft and vulnerable.

"I didn't break your penis after all," I say. I can see a tiny puncture mark with a fading bruise, though, just an inch or so away from the base of him. If I'd been just slightly off . . .

"No, you didn't. But maybe you will tonight. In the best of ways." His hands roam over my back, skimming the surface of my skin, then pressing with more urgency.

I laugh, a sound of anticipation.

"Are you evaluating me? Am I aesthetically pleasing?" he asks in a throaty chuckle. "Do you have your app ready to write up your review?"

My answer is to release him and push him back against the seat. I throw one leg over his lap and straddle him, settling over his unleashed self, the thin cotton triangle of my panties the only thing keeping us apart.

"You're part of a new project. The Shopping for a Billionaire Project." I wiggle just enough to make him groan.

His hands slide under my shirt, cupping my breasts, and with a grace that makes me moan he unclasps my bra and wraps those big, strong palms around my breasts.

"How am I doing so far?"

I make a noise of contemplation. "Eh. Six out of ten."

He arches one eyebrow, clearly displeased. "Six? I don't *do* six."

I move against him, the shaft sliding along my nub, making my next words come out with a quaking tone. "No, you're no six." I close one eye and slide up, shivering. "Maybe seven?"

His abs tighten, shaft lifting just enough to make little light bursts appear, somehow making an entrance in my open-eyed vision.

"Six? Let's go for ten," he insists. The snap of my panties registers for a second as a sharp, cutting pain against one hip as he rips them off me. All that separates us now is something deeper than decency.

Declan senses it, too, and shifts just enough, reaching into his back pocket for his wallet. The condom appears and he puts it on as I watch his hands, his face, marveling at the unreality of the moment.

Yet it feels more real than anything I can fathom.

He guides me back into his lap and I settle my thighs around his hips, his tip at my entrance like a beacon, mutual throbbing making a pulse that joins two rhythms.

And then he's in me, kissing my neck, pulling my shirt up over my head, bra hanging from a door handle and he thrusts up into me, thumbs on my nipples, my body burning for more.

More more more.

The thrill of his fullness in me, of the movements as he kisses me, with slow, languid kisses so lush and patient. The kind of kiss you give someone when you mean it. When you want to be with them.

When they're enough.

More than enough.

"I have wanted you since the first time we met," he says, serious and breathing hard, his hands on either side of my face, eyes lasered in on mine. A shock of hair falls over his forehead and the day's beard gives him a rakish look, even as he's tender and loving.

"You rivet me, Shannon. You make me want you more than I want to be in control, and no woman has ever done that. I abandoned a merger negotiation in New Zealand because I kept looking at our text stream and wondering why the fuck I was settling for pictures of you when I could be inside you."

Oh!

I don't have any words. He hammers his point home and I gasp, tightening.

He groans, breaking our gaze, pulling me in for a kiss that tastes like promises and desire.

"I needed you. Need you. Need this," he says, pulling his hips back, clenching his abs, then sliding back up, making me pitch my head back, the sensation too immense to take in just through one part of me. My arms, my face, my flushed skin, it all feels like it's part of Declan, and he's part of me, and we're both part of the sky, the clouds, part of everything.

"I need you, too, Declan," I say as I tip my head back down and unbutton his shirt. The feel of his hot skin as I skim my palms across his pecs makes me wetter, the heat from our coupling like my own star, bright and radiant. "I can't quite believe this is happening. That you're with me. That we're here."

"You're hot and warm and tight," he groans. I pull in, making my core strong, and he utters a primal sound that is both threatening and satisfying. I made him do that. *Me.* His thumbs caress my hips and I surge for a second, shivering with a quick tingle. A moment of self-consciousness kicks in as his hand caresses my belly under my skirt, thumb pad stroking down again to find the spot I want him to touch the most.

But the palm across my belly makes me think about my curves. My abundant flesh. My . . . extra. My *too much.*

He frowns, watching my face. "What's wrong?"

"Nothing." The word comes out breathy and forced, like a cheerleader whose leg fell off but she's in denial, still completing her program. *Damn it. Don't do this, Shannon. Don't ruin it.* You would think I'd have felt this way when we were at the park, or the first time we kissed, or the times he's touched me intimately, and yet—no. It takes being in a limo, surrounded by the trappings of wealth and status for me to feel this sense of inadequacy, quite suddenly.

I know exactly why, and it sucks.

The first time Steve ever hinted that I might not be good enough was, of course, in a limo. My junior year in college and we were on our way to some business networking event. He'd evaluated me from top to bottom and found the cut of my dress "a bit outdated" and asked whether I'd been exercising enough lately.

I ate a small salad for dinner that night.

Declan cocks his head and stares me down, thumb stroking until I move involuntarily, the self-consciousness replaced by a growing wave inside.

"Tell me," he murmurs.

"No—really." The slow circles he traces in my most private flesh are like a language he's transmitting through these maddening finger presses.

"Tell me," he says again in a voice that makes it clear I can't escape.

"It's . . . my body." As sunset descends, the shadows outside pass by like a crowd in motion, except we're the ones moving. The limo glides left, then right, and Declan and I float with it, micro-movements sending waves of grinding want through me as the pressure of his fullness in me touches little fragmented spots that send my body thrills I didn't know I could feel.

"Your body is . . ." His voice drifts away as his eyes rake over me, methodical and appreciative. I'm not used to this. Sex is frantic groping in the dark, where I'm glad for the cover of the obscurity of darkness. What Steve or other lovers felt when they touched my skin was so much easier to handle than imagining them looking at me. When they touched me under covers or in the grey night, I could just feel and enjoy.

I'm watching Declan look at me and feel my self-consciousness melt away, like a layer of skin that sheds gently. His eyes are hooded, filled with craving, and as his gaze lands on my breasts I can almost feel him, his eyes like fingertips searching for truth and love.

"Your body is beautiful," he says gruffly, as if contradicting someone who said otherwise. And, actually, he is. All the voices who tell me I'm imperfect. The moments when Steve looked at rail-thin women in public, or the *harumph* of telling a store clerk I needed a size sixteen.

The internalized, yappy-dog chatterer that has taken up residence behind my ear and that lets loose a steady stream of thoughts and feelings about my loose skin on my belly, the lush breasts that never fit quite right in my bra cups, the pants that don't smooth neatly across my waistband, the thick, muscular calves that rub against the finely tailored wool of his pants.

That voice.

"Beautiful," he says with a tender thrust upward, pulling me down for a kiss. His tongue slides between my lips and he's telling me again how beautiful I am, except this time with the topography of his mouth. Yearning pours through me like molten lava and I'm fused to him, inside and out, as a wellspring of emotion overwhelms me.

"Who told you otherwise?" The sad tone that escapes between his lips isn't sad for me. Carrying a distinct sound of disapproval, he's correcting the distant critic who put it out there, the one who planted the seed of inadequacy inside me.

The guy who made me feel like I wasn't enough—because I was a little too much.

"They were *wrong*." The emphasis on the last word makes me shudder.

"Perfect and ripe and warm," he whispers, making me melt more.

The feel of his tanned skin under my own palms, how his eyes seem so interested and captivated, the play of his words on those lips as he misses me and says more that I can't really understand because oh—*oh!*—now he moves in a pattern that takes me to places where words are mere formalities.

Where sensation is the language of choice.

One finger trails a line between my breasts and he plants a kiss in the valley. "You're everything I want," he whispers, tension in his voice stretching his words out as he begins his own tipping point. He takes one pebbled nipple in his mouth and the rush of warm wetness makes me clench, which in turn makes him groan.

No words. The leather seat presses against my knees and he brushes my hair away from my face, tucking it behind an ear with such precision as he tongues my breast and makes me stop. Stop thinking, stop wiggling, stop the world—stop *time*, because I am everything and nothing in his arms.

My own body moves in long, even strokes against his, and then without warning he's above me, out of me, leaving me with a hollow ache that cries out for more. Declan's arm wraps around my waist and he spins me effortlessly under him, the limo seat so wide we can fit comfortably, our thighs slick with sweat and more, his face filled with passion and a tantalizing seriousness that brings back a handful of words.

"You're beautiful, too," I whisper, looking up at him as anticipation is poised between us in that timeless moment before we break through the invisible wall. The wall that separates every couple before they knowingly—*willfully*—breach it to connect two separate beings, making one flesh, one desire, one need.

One climax. Giving yourself to another person is one thing. Truly letting go as you lose yourself in them is quite another.

"I didn't know there were men like you out there," I add, reaching up to push a lock of hair out of his face. He's so intense, so purely centered on me, eyes alive and fully in the moment. We're on a threshold, and I have so much bursting inside me that I want to say.

"You make me feel like it's okay to be me, Declan. No one's ever done that before." Our breath mingles in the small space between us, my legs tightening around him, my body and heart wanting to be as close as possible. I'd have to crawl inside him to be any closer, and I'm shaking with an all-consuming force that is so much more than anything I've felt before.

"I wouldn't want you to be anyone else, Shannon."

I smile wide as he drives home inside me, his face dipped down to kiss me, his mouth fire and ice as he thrusts, my body filled with a kind of madness that makes me seek release at the same time that I can't help but cling to him.

His hands rest on my waist as he tightens, his face hot over mine, our bodies half clothed. This feels so illicit, so naughty, and as the limo comes to a pause at a stoplight a massive plume of boldness blooms in me.

This is who I am. Declan is who I want. His face shifts as he pushes over and over, my legs shaking and my hands seeking whatever skin he has exposed, the connection morphing into something so illicitly primal.

And when he leans down, still in control, his hand between my legs and giving the slightest butterfly touch where I need it most, I utter his name in a fevered moan, my climax hitting without reservation, all restraint gone, my mouth full of whispers and groans, my fingers digging into his shoulders as he tells me to come, to come, to *come*.

I do.

He joins me, torso and chest tense and hands digging into the leather seat on either side of me, my legs wrapped around his waist, his murmurs in my ear like a song as he bites the lobe and shudders like he's captivated by a series of prayers to a god I can believe in. The air around us is hot and spicy, like woman and man mingling together, the scent of sex and sweat and perfume and cologne burning into my brain.

This is the scent of mind-blowing sex. Yankee Candle needs to patent it.

"You," he says with a hiss, pulling out of me and turning around. He ties off the condom and throws it discreetly in a small trash can with a little swish lid that makes me laugh. I don't know why. The giggles descend on me and I cannot stop.

"That's a first," he says.

"Sex in a limo?" I gasp between chuckles.

He gets a surprisingly sheepish look on his face. "Uh, no," he says slowly. But not apologetically.

If this awkward turn of conversation is supposed to spoil the mood, it doesn't. I just laugh even more. Absurdity makes me laugh. Having sex for the first time in a year makes me giggle. Fucking Declan in the back of a limo makes me sputter.

"What's a first, then?"

"A woman overcome with giggles after sleeping with me.

Most don't find it so . . . comedic."

"I just had sex in a limo," I explain.

"You know what comes next?" he says as he pulls up his pants and snaps and zips up. I realize I am completely naked from the waist up and scramble to find my shirt, unable to think. Naked! In a limo! With Hot Guy! Laughing!

"What?" I ask as I shove my arms into my sleeves and pull the shirt over my head. Wait. Where's my bra? Oh. There it is. Hanging on the door handle, one strap wrapped around the gleaming metal, the other on the neck of a crystal decanter of something amber, lounging lazily.

"Love in a helicopter."

chapter

six

"**I**S THAT A PROMISE or a threat?" I ask as my head shoots through the neck of my shirt, my hair caught under it. I'm sweaty and feel like I've just climbed Mt. Declan, legs aching and body buzzing. But *ahhh*, the summit was damn nice, and the view . . .

"Both." He laughs and rides his hand up over my thigh.

"I like both." I close my eyes, trying not to cringe as I feel him brush against my decidedly not-smooth leg.

He senses the change in me and caresses my jaw with his fingers, turning my eyes to him. "What is it?"

This is the moment when every woman balances between saying "fine" and telling the truth. I'm sitting in a limousine with a man who holds more power than two hundred of me combined, and all I can think about are my stubbly shins.

The divided mind turns me in two distinct directions:

He's different. Real and genuine. Go with it.

and

He's about as interested in the truth as he is in going to CVS to buy you a pack of tampons.

I go for the former, because the cocky grin he's giving me right now is so authentic that it feels right to be honest and open, vulnerable and real, and to stop worrying about what I think he's thinking.

How about I try just saying what I think?

Deep breath. Deep breath. The car lurches forward and his hand tightens on my thigh, his other arm snaking around me protectively. I nestle in and say:

"I wasn't exactly prepared for a date." I run my own hand against my thighs and say, *"Skritch skritch skritch."* And then I close my eyes and wish for a tornado to appear and take me away so I can wake up and realize this is all a dream. Plus the ruby shoes would be a nice addition to my wardrobe.

I can't believe I just said that. Skritch? What am I, an animated character from *Ice Age*?

"Sound effects?" His booming laugh fills the car. Bright lights dot the horizon as the sun nearly finishes setting, and I realize we're at a small airport. "You're giving me sound effects?"

He runs his hand along my leg and up between my legs. A rush of heat, and yet more arousal fills me. How can I want more?

"I like sound effects," he adds, "but the ones you made a few minutes ago were far superior."

"I—" My lips turn to liquid, like he just shot me with ten times my weight in Novocaine.

"If I want a smooth woman, I'll put you in my clawfoot tub at home and shave you myself," he says.

Blink.

"I'll run you a hot bath, undress you with my own hands, soap you up and make you com—" He licks his lips and looks me up and down, then continues. "—fortable. And that's a promise," he adds, leaning down for a deep kiss. I can imagine the scene; his eyes show it to me.

The car comes to a slow stop and the engine goes silent. I can't speak. Can't move. Can't think. I'm one big, throbbing hormone.

Declan pulls away and points out the window to a helicopter. A sleek black machine that looks like something out of a movie, like the insect version of a Transformer.

"What are you, Batman?" I ask as words return to me, marveling at all this. A headphoned pilot is at the controls, and the blades aren't moving. Lights blink and Declan steps out of the limo, waving to the driver, who climbs back in the front seat.

I step out on legs that feel strong and well used. The copter blades start a slow circle and sound revs up.

"I wish. But you'll have to settle for plain old Declan," he shouts.

"You're anything but 'plain,'" I call back.

Cupping a hand over his ear, he shakes his head. He didn't hear me. That's okay, though, because he doesn't need to.

The ground feels springy under my feet as I hold my hair in one hand to keep it from whipping around my face as the helicopter blades rotate faster. The wind the machine creates is magical, the contraption about to elevate us into the air, high above the city. I have no idea where Declan is taking me and I don't care. My body throbs and I'm sore from that amazing encounter in the limo, but I get the distinct sense that *that*?

That was only the beginning.

Love in a helicopter? No way. The pilot gives me a sharp nod, the engines roaring so loud I can't hear a thing. Declan offers me headphones and I put them on, muting the *chuk chuk chuk* sound.

"Welcome aboard, Ms. Jacoby," says a new-to-me voice. The pilot raises his hand with a wave.

"That's Joel," Declan's voice explains, crackling over a static-y connection. He points to a little knob on his own headset and I realize it's the volume control. I fiddle with mine and get the sound to the right level. Speaking in a normal voice is all that's needed.

Joel speaks a bunch of Flight Language to some sort of tower personnel. He might as well be casting a spell or getting directions to Hogwarts. The words and numbers make no sense to me, but I'm in awe of it anyhow. That a human being can learn how to successfully navigate a machine like this, not only through space but through three-dimensional space, is amazing.

Driving a car on the ground is hard enough, but to know which direction you're going and to keep track of where you are vertically? It's like rubbing your tummy, patting your head, and playing Farmville while singing "The Star-Spangled Banner" at the same time.

And this is why I never became a pilot. That, and failing Physics 101. Pesky detail.

Declan's speaking in code with Joel, his hip digging deep into mine as we cram next to each other on the helicopter. He closes the door and the sound of the blades changes. It's like someone shoved a feather pillow over them. The helicopter begins to jostle and I dig my fingers into his thigh.

He smiles at me, all stubble and dimples and bright irises. A reassuring arm wraps around me. "Takeoff is always hardest," he says.

"I'll bet you say that to all the girls."

Joel makes a snorting sound, then cuts his mic. Declan shoots him an annoyed look, but returns his attention to me. "I've never taken a woman in my chopper before. Not on a date."

"Is that what you call this?" I can't stop touching him. My hand goes to the collar of his shirt, where a smattering of dark hair covers his collarbone. I want to lick him. Taste him. Nestle my cheek against his chest and hear his heartbeat. I want him in me again, the feel of his release, of his trust to give in to me.

Divergence is turning my life into something unrecognizable. A few weeks ago I knew what to expect from your average day. No, I couldn't plan it meticulously, no matter how hard I tried, but a certain contentment made each week pretty predictable. Settled. Relatively comfortable, if a bit lonely. Get up, have coffee, go to work, do mystery shops, prepare presentations, come home to Chuckles, hang with Amy and Amanda.

Lather, rinse, repeat.

Drive my junky car. Have dinner at Mom and Dad's. Overthink and overplan everything, then obsess about my tendency to overthink and overplan.

A billionaire player like Declan was, most definitely, not part of any plan. Not even part of my fantasies, which had taken a bizarre turn toward the superhero realm. If you can't have a superman, you might as well get off on dreams of threesomes with Iron Man and Loki.

My Batman joke really was just a joke, though.

Declan is better than the Avengers and the X-Men combined.

As I stroke the fine weave of his wool suit pants, his thigh shifts under my measured touch. Rippled steel bands react under my palm, the soft inner thigh flesh yielding the tiniest bit as I grasp him, feel his response. He inhales slowly and rests his chin on the top of my head, closing his eyes.

He's enjoying this. Letting me explore him, confirming he's real and under my inventory. Here's his forearm. There's his biceps. And the chest is right here. The scruff on his cheek makes contact with my cheekbone and I soften into him. Our bodies fit beautifully together. We fit together.

We.

We can't say a word to each other right now unless we want the pilot to hear, so we sit in silence. His hands mimic mine, soon finding my curves and valleys, swells and peaks. The way he touches me makes me feel desired. Appreciated. Not just wanted, because anyone can be wanted.

He makes me feel *cherished*.

"Check out the Red Sox game," he says, pointing to the well-lit Fenway Park. It's an early game for the season. Everyone seems so tiny, so insignificant, and yet thousands—tens of thousands—of people are all congregated to watch the game, to party, to be one with the energy of the crowd.

For a split second, I wish Amanda were here. Sex in a limo with a near-billionaire! And a hot man who looks like a *Men's Health* cover model. Watching a Red Sox game from above, flying over the gleaming city lights.

Me—*Shannon*—with Declan McCormick.

And then . . . my own mind does a 180-degree turn. Sometimes the clearest moments come when you least expect them, and this is one of those times.

You can't believe it because you won't let yourself believe it. Let go of your own self as an obstacle and imagine how much more you could do and be.

And be cherished.

Tears threaten the inner corners of my eyes. My throat aches with a sickly, bitter taste. I lean in to Declan and press my ear against his heart, the fine cloth of his shirt cool until my face warms it. A tear mars the perfect whiteness of his shirt and I don't care.

Thu-thump. Thu-thump. Thu-thump. Steady and strong, his heart continues at its regular pace. I wonder if he's always like this. So calm, so confident. Without being smarmy or a blowhard, Declan manages to embody so many qualities I've wanted in a man, but thought were mythical.

He's nothing like my own father, who is a sweet, non-judgmental man. But Dad isn't the dominant type. I've never seen him move through life making split-second decisions and assessments of character and behavior and filtering a person in or out based on their response. Dad doesn't walk into a room with a feeling of command. He's many wonderful things, but Jason Jacoby is anything but the leader of a pack.

And that's okay. Really. Because I can love my dad but want a man for myself who is completely different.

"We're almost there," Declan says, pointing through the window at the scattered lights below. I'm so deep in my thoughts that somehow I manage to forget to look outside, to see the show unfolding beneath us. Complete darkness has descended over the city; it's a moonless night, so up here in the sky, the air has a whiff of intrigue to it. Without the bright white orb in the sky to shepherd us, the chopper's movements feel more than a little surreal, like riding Space Mountain at Disney, except there is no enclosed building, no track, no line.

We move down, more of the city rolling out before our eyes. A long patch of nothingness spills into view suddenly. The copter shifts downward and we're flying fast over water. Declan kisses my ear and I see the white caps of waves cresting, my body drained. I'm tired and spent, yet wired and excited. It's not from the copter ride.

It's from knowing there're so much more to come.

Joel says a bunch of numbers and phrases again, then suddenly we're hovering a few feet above the ground on a tiny island, a tall building brightly lit right next to us. The flight itself was fast, so fast we must be on one of the Boston Harbor islands. I can't tell which one. The tall, lit building is a lighthouse, the old kind. The lighthouse's beacon faces out to sea and a small golf cart is parked next to the structure.

"Powering down," Joel explains. I sit in place, the copter's vibrations making my skin tingle. I'm parched, and just as the last *snick* sound from the blades' rotation makes its final sigh, my stomach growls louder than a zombie bear that stumbled across a bunch of fresh raccoon brains.

"Hungry?"

"Starving."

Declan has a satisfied look on his face, as if he's hiding something he's quite proud of. "Good. You'll like what's coming next."

As long as it's me, I think. He gives me a look that says he's read my mind.

I'm about as graceful as a three-legged elephant with arthritis as I climb out of the helicopter, managing somehow to step on Declan's foot and elbow him in the abs as he helps me down. Joel gives us a thumbs-up and walks away as Declan takes my arm and escorts me to a small door at the base of the lighthouse.

"I assume we're still in the United States?" I ask. "Because I left my passport at home."

"Glad to hear you have one," he says as he opens the tattered wood door, the paint worn down, the old dark oak underneath poking through white paint as faded as old bones left out in the sun for too many summers. A narrow set of stairs, all made of concrete from a time when I imagine Puritans hand-mixed it, curls up to the sky in a dizzying spiral. I inhale the scent of sea salt and centuries.

His words warm me, though. Where could we go? Where would he take me? Not that it matters, as long as I'm with him. He hinted about New Zealand last week, but I thought he'd been joking.

I guess not. My neck hurts from staring straight up, the lighthouse's peak blocked by a ceiling.

"What is this place?" I ask. I can see the stairs curve up at the top and stop.

"I wanted to take you somewhere you've never been. Finding

a restaurant that a mystery shopper has never eaten in or evaluated is a daunting task. But I think I've risen to the occasion." His hand on the small of my back pushes gently so that I go inside, my shoes scraping against old stone.

The main door clicks shut and echoes up, the sound carrying to the heavens.

"I think you've succeeded," I whisper. My voice reverberates. I shiver involuntarily, and Declan's arm is around me instantly, pulling me to his warmth.

"You scared?" He's amused.

"No," I protest. "It's just a little cold. And dark." Flickering gas lamps dot the path upwards, like something out of a Gothic novel. Declan clearly has a thing for these sorts of places. The walls remind me of a mausoleum without the names and dates etched in the front-facing stones.

"Don't worry," he says, pulling back and gesturing for me to go first up the stairs. "The manacles in the torture chamber are lined with a nice, thick sherpa fleece."

HALT SO FAST his front slams into my ass. I can feel *exactly* how he's risen to the occasion.

"Huh?"

"That was a joke."

I turn and face him. His lips are twitching around a poorly contained look of amusement.

"Look here, buddy," I say, poking my finger against his perfect chest. "This isn't like one of those books where the billionaire steals the poor, underpaid intern away from her horrible life and they discover a mutually beneficial BDSM lifestyle, m'kay?"

He pretends to be crestfallen. "Oh. Okay. Then I'll just call Joel and we'll take you home." He reaches into his back pocket for his phone and fake dials. I can see he's actually on ESPN and checking scores. The Red Sox are playing at Fenway right now. I know that because we flew over them, and that fact makes the entire night seem so surreal.

Seem? It *is* surreal. Magical. A little too perfect.

My stomach growls in protest. "What about dinner?" I ignore him and start walking up the stairs. There's no railing, so I cling to the stones with splayed palms, thanking God I'm not wearing high heels.

"Nice view," he says, suspiciously close behind me. A warm hand slides up between my thighs. "Here, let me lend you a hand."

"That hand isn't helping." His fingers slide under my already-soaked panties and he gives me the slightest touch against my wetness. We pause and I cling to the wall with even weaker legs.

"Really?" he murmurs against the back of my neck. "It seems to be making things much . . . smoother."

"You're slick."

"Actually," he says, "you're the one who's slick." As tantalizing as being felt up on the stairs is, there's a very real danger that we will roll down the stone steps and end up in the hospital again and I, for one, cannot emotionally handle two dates in a row ending with an Explanation of Benefits form and an ER co-pay.

"Let's get upstairs and see what you have for me."

He takes my hand and puts it on his fly.

"That's not quite what I meant, Declan."

He glides past me, making sure to press every inch of his chiseled self against my own soft curves, taking the steps up carefully until his ass is in my face. It's a fabulous view.

"Normally I'd say 'ladies first,' but right now you're procrastinating, so—"

"You're groping me on the stairs and making it so I can't even walk! How is that procrastinating?" I'm talking to air, though, because by the time I say that, he's halfway to the top, bounding up like this is part of *The Amazing Race* and he's on the annoying team that's always way ahead of everyone else because they're in good shape and all that unfair crap.

So I trek my way up, one frightening stair at a time. My hand brushes against something soft on the stones and I scream.

"What's wrong?" he calls down.

If I confess, he'll just make fun of me. Or, worse, come back here and drive me wild with those fingers and we'll tumble down the stairs to our deaths. No one would find us for days. We would be the lead story on New England Cable News for weeks.

Billionaire Meets Death with Klutzy Woman. News at eleven.

I force myself to take the stairs at a faster clip. By the time I climb the equivalent of three stories, my quads are screaming.

Screaming to be wrapped around his hips.

The most delicious scent tickles my nose as I make the final turn up to the top of the stairs, Declan standing there, holding open a small door. I have to duck to enter. Oregano and rosemary and something else fill the air, and as I come to a full standing position I'm greeted by a scene out of a dream.

Tall, sculpted windows arc high toward a flat ceiling, with the ocean surrounding us in a 360-degree spin that is beyond breathtaking. The room is just beneath what I assume is the lighthouse's warning light, because an arch of glow comes from above at regular intervals, making this room ethereal and supernatural, as if Declan had conjured it with magic.

The actual room has a small soapstone stove with a fire burning in it, which helps, because the air is chilled this high up and far out into the harbor. Two large L-shaped sofas ring the wood stove, and a series of blown-glass lamps dangle from the ceiling in muted earth tones and adobe. Thick Persian rugs cover the well-worn wood of the floor, wide pine flooring hearkening back to a very different time.

And a small table for two with candles in large crab buckets filled with seashells is the source of the incredible smell that makes my mouth water and my stomach beg for mercy.

Declan has that effect on me, too, but right now I am all about the meal. I need some calories. Sustenance. Protein, because one of those sofas is so big and covered with a small Matterhorn of pillows, and the entire room is like a woman's idea of the perfect sex den.

Which it is.

His arm sweeping out in a welcoming gesture, he invites me to sit at the table. I see a plate full of chocolate-covered strawberries, cheese, and a bottle of white wine.

"You know me well."

"I want to know you better." Declan pulls out the chair and I sit, scooching in, my hand reaching for one of the strawberries without thinking. The bite is sweet and juicy, the chocolate smooth and creamy, and this time, there are no bees to ruin my mouthgasm.

Declan sits across from me and leans back, his hands at his navel, eyes piercing. "You come here often?" he asks.

"Nice pickup line," I mumble through a mouth full of awesome. I swallow and look right back at him. "But you should know I'm a sure thing."

His throaty laugh makes me tingle in all the right places. Again? *Again?* Confession time: I've never had sex twice in one night with a guy. Given a blow job and had sex? Yes. But actual *sex* sex twice in the same night? Nope. I'm at a loss here, frankly. We, um, did the deed. Now we're eating dinner. This sumptuous room is designed for nothing but rolling in the sheets.

Or lack of sheets. Naked on that soft, velvety couch. Or the rug. Or just . . . naked. Anywhere. My eyes drift to the glass walls facing the ocean, the sound of waves lapping against the island's shores like the blood pounding through me. Imagine making love while looking out into the expansiveness of—

"You're deep in thought." Declan's pouring two glasses of wine and I didn't even notice him stand and uncork the bottle. It's getting hot in here. I finish my strawberry and smile at him, reaching for the wine.

Which I promptly drink in a series of gulps that would make any NBA player on a time-out proud.

"This is unbelievable, Declan," I say, looking around. "How did you find this? Is it a restaurant? It doesn't look like one."

"It's ours for tonight."

"That's it? C'mon. Explain."

He smiles. "Okay. I donate money to a historical preservation society that works on buying and restoring lighthouses. This one isn't in danger, but plenty of others are. I know someone who knows someone who sacrificed a few small animals to give me access to this place. It's the only lighthouse within a short helicopter ride from Boston. I hired a few people to outfit the place to my specifications and . . . here we are."

"I think that's the most you've ever said to me in one breath."

He shrugs. "You insisted."

"Why?"

"Why did you insist?"

"No. I mean, why all this?" I throw my hands up. "This. You didn't need to do this for me."

"I didn't need to. I want to."

"Why?"

"For the same reason you're here."

Letting go of this nagging "why me" voice is harder than I thought. I imagine Chuckles looking at me with disapproval, shaking his head. The man just made love to me in a limo, for goodness' sake. Of course he wants me. Of course he likes me. At the rate I'm going, I'll ruin this, so—

Let

It

Go

Great. Now I have the theme song from *Frozen* stuck in my head forever. Yeah. Sure. Try making love with that pinging through your brain. Disney characters are only aphrodisiacs for people who troll FetLife.

Declan's eyes have narrowed and he's watching me. "You really do wear your emotions on your face."

"And in my hands," I add, flailing them. He's been wearing his suit jacket this whole time—even when we were doing the nasty back in the limo—and now he slips out of it, stretching the fabric across the back of a cloth-covered dining chair that's primly tied with a neat bow.

His shoulder muscles ripple with movement under his shirt and I realize I've never seen him naked. Never even seen him shirtless. My breath comes in sudden halts as it hits me that I'm really here. Mr. Grey Suit is in front of me in an intimate, romantic setting he created for me, and this is my real life.

He unbuttons the cuffs of his shirt and rolls them up. I'm hypnotized. I can't stop watching as his deft fingers go through the motions like a performance, his eyes tilted down and watching what he's doing, making himself comfortable.

He's spent so much time thinking about my comfort. Focused on me. My eyes eat him up, enjoying not just the view but the intimacy of this moment. So simple. So ordinary. Just a man on a date in a new relationship, rolling up his sleeves after a long day at the office, waiting to sink into a lovely dinner and some nice sexy time.

Except he's flown across countless time zones, interrupted my pseudo-date with my ignorant ex, had his way with me in a limo, flown me in a helicopter to a remote island, and now he has me (voluntarily) trapped on a remote island where anything could happen.

So not ordinary.

"Enjoying yourself?" His voice is warm milk and burnt sugar and rum-soaked ladyfingers with hot fudge sauce and an invitation to spend a weekend on Martha's Vineyard on the beach without clothes or other people.

"I really like what I see." It helps that I just felt his abs underneath me and they roll like Ben Wa balls, sleek, sexy and hypnotically solid.

"Me, too." He reaches for my hand and takes a long, slow sip of his wine. My own gulp earlier is kicking in, loosening me, making me want to run my legs against silk sheets and the soft strands of his leg hair, imagining his naked body and his own happy trail leading down . . .

I don't have to imagine it, though, do I? I'm about to live it.

Without comment or affect, Declan lifts the covers off our plates, revealing lobster and steak. "I hope you're not allergic to shellfish," he says dryly.

"No, thank God. I love lobster." We smile at each other, and something's different. I face it head on.

"Speaking of allergies, thank you. I didn't know about your brother."

"Of course you didn't. But now you do." He picks up his silverware with hands that are steady. Mine are shaking like a four-year-old with a pogo stick on Christmas morning.

"Good for me, then, that you came prepared."

He pauses mid-bite. "Yes," is all he says, then continues eating. The lights above us go round and round, giving the room a hypnotic glow.

"How does Andrew handle it?" I take a bite and let my words hang there. Declan's quiet, finishing his food, and I get the sense that he doesn't want to talk about this, but I do. There's no way I'm going to act like it never happened.

"Handle being so allergic?"

"No, handle being the Green Lantern."

He smiles. "Touché. Okay, he handles it by carefully orchestrating a life where he's never near a wasp."

I laugh. Declan pours another glass of wine for me. I nod my thanks and he sets the bottle down, conspicuously not filling his own glass.

"Impossible."

His eyebrows go up in mirth. "No, it's quite possible. He has drivers who meet him in underground parking garages, flies only at night in the cooler temperatures for that twenty-foot walk on private tarmacs to the company jet, and exercises indoors."

"He must be paler than a vampire." Then again, so's my belly. It hasn't seen sunlight since Kristen Stewart smiled.

"Tanning booths and vitamin D supplements cover that."

I'm chewing a glorious piece of lobster as his words sink in. "You're joking."

He swallows his own bite and finishes his wine. "I'm completely serious. It's how he copes."

I'm stunned. The allergists over the years have cautioned me to take measures that reduce my risk, but no one's ever suggested such extremes. "Were his stings that bad?"

"He's only been stung once."

"Once?"

"And his throat closed up."

"Oof. That's really rare. You don't normally have a reaction that bad for the first time you're stung."

"Bad enough that he lost consciousness. We got him to the ER in time." I can tell he really, really doesn't want to talk about this, but it's calming me. Centering me. Hearing him talk about his own experiences and his brother's allergies makes me feel less like an oddity.

"Your mother and father must have freaked."

"Mom was dead by then." His face is a stone mask. My heart squeezes.

"Oh." What the hell can I say after that? Shoving a mouthful of perfectly done filet is the only way to respond. Declan pours himself another glass of wine, filling it within a half-inch of the rim, then empties the rest of the bottle into my glass.

Neither of us has to drive, so why not?

He studies me, taking liberal sips of his wine, then puts the glass down and reaches for my free hand. I'm slowing down, full of delectable food, wired and aroused.

"You're worried I can't handle the bee thing." It's not a question. And he's mostly right.

I take a moment to think about this before answering. "No. Not quite." He gives me a skeptical look. "It's more that you handled it so well. Precisely perfect. The last time I was stung I was with Steve, who ran away in a panic and screamed so much the EMTs who arrived after I called 911 thought he was the bee sting victim. Delayed my treatment."

Declan's face goes tight and angry. "Not only is he an asshole, he's a dangerous little shit. Leaving you in a medical crisis." With a hand so tight I'm afraid he'll shatter his wine goblet, he grabs the wine and drinks it all down in a series of fast gulps that make his neck stretch, muscles on display.

"You learn a lot about people in a crisis."

chapter
eight

MY WORDS HANG THERE as he stares at me a few beats longer than normal. My heart is throbbing about two feet lower on my body, our eyes connecting for seconds longer than they should, the air warm and charged.

"You learn everything you need to know," he declares.

"Then you now know that I will turn you into a Viagra eater in a crisis."

He wants to laugh but doesn't let himself. "I think, in a true emergency, that you click out of this insecure mode you live in and the core person inside picks up."

I lean forward on my elbow, pushing my plate away, and reach for my wine. Two sips later and I ask, "Tell me more about this core." My actual core pulses from down below, wanting him to touch it. I could give him GPS coordinates at this point. Hell, I could take my leftover food on my plate and create a food sculpture map to help him.

"You first. Tell me what you think about me." What guy does this? HUH?

"What I think about you? You're a superman, Declan. You're Hot Guy. I'm Toilet Girl. I'm wondering why"—I gesture around the room—"you picked me."

"*Tsk tsk*," he chides. "That's not what I asked."

"Okay, what I think about you."

"What you think about me. Not what you think about 'Declan McCormick.'" Yes, he uses finger quotes. "What you think about *me*." His eyes are soulful. Serious. Contemplative and evaluative. He's asking a very different question in those eyes than he's saying with his mouth.

"You. Just . . . you. Not the image. The man."

His lids close and he lets out a long sigh. "Yes."

"I think you're an enigma because I don't know you that well." His eyes fly open. "And yet I feel like I've known you forever." He reaches for my hand and I grasp his, hard.

"I feel the closest I've ever felt to being *myself* when I'm with you. Whoever that is. You don't judge me. You don't shame me or act like I'm the outsider in everything. You don't use sarcasm like it's a tool or a weapon, and you speak so plainly and clearly it's like you've invented a new language."

The room goes still. The lighthouse light stops. We're lit by candle and the flicker makes shadows shimmer across his face in a pattern that burns into my memory as it unfolds. I will never forget this moment until the day I die, which will hopefully be when we are in our nineties, in bed after making love, and holding hands.

"You're this bad-boy billionaire—" He starts to protest and I hold up a hand, brushing my fingers against his lips. "That's what your image says. Billionaire. You're the jet-setting Boston Magazine society pages poster boy whose father built a crazy-massive empire. You're one of the Bachelor Brothers everyone talks about. You and Andrew and Terrance are all over the local blogs, the free grocery-store newspapers, the *Boston Globe*, all the magazines. Women like Jessica Coffin want to marry you and have posh little babies and host Beacon Hill ballroom parties in your townhomes with the warped eighteenth century glass windows. The ones the rest of us only see from the outside in the summer when we can scrape together enough money to afford to take a long ride on a Duck Tour."

He chuckles against my hand, then kisses my palm, pressing it against his face.

"Go on."

"You want more?"

"Hell yes, I want more."

"No." His eyes widen a bit with surprise. I've challenged him.

He doesn't smile, but the eyes stay intrigued. "Your turn," I add.

A long pause. Too long. The room feels so small, so warm as I'm under his scrutiny, my request feeling like a gauntlet thrown on the ground too hard.

And then:

"You make me think about my life beyond the date, the kiss, the sex, the ride home."

He stands abruptly, eyes filled with more emotion that I can't interpret. In a flash, I'm in his arms, his mouth on mine, the taste of wine on his lips, his tongue, making my head spin even more. My hands slip around his waist and untuck his shirt, reaching up to feel his bare skin.

Declan pulls back, our mouths an inch from each other. "When I look at you I can see my future roll out in one long laugh, like a red carpet of fun and intelligence and hope. A ripple of joy that stretches into the horizon until it disappears. Not because it ceases to exist, but because it's infinite."

My heart presses directly against his, and the two beat in sync. Our foreheads touch and his eyes blur as my vision goes hazy. I close my eyes, his words, oh, those words . . .

"I know who I am in the world, Shannon. I don't need you to define me. What I need from you is what I can't find on my own. And right here"—he lifts my chin, his eyes loving and warm—"right here." His hand slides between us and settles on my heart. "Is where you redefine me."

He kisses me gently.

A slow shake of his head makes me blink over and over, signals confusing and overwhelming. My knees tingle and his arms are the only thing pinning me to earth. "I don't talk like this with the women I date. I'm not even quite sure where these words are coming from." He smiles like he's asking me to translate, but my heart is on edge, waiting for me. "My heart, I guess."

Mine stands up like it's doing the wave in a giant stadium filled with all the heartbreak I've experienced until now. And yes, it feels like it fills a stadium.

"I don't feel this way with the women I date. But you're nothing like the typical women in my life, and this is anything but a typical relationship."

Our kiss deepens and I reach down, cupping his tight ass. Which buzzes suddenly. I jump and move my hand away.

He sighs. "I've been ignoring that for the past twenty minutes, but . . ."

I pull the phone out of his back pocket and give him an extra squeeze. He groans. I shrug. He looks at his phone and groans extra loud.

"Damn it. I have to call Grace."

"I understand. She's the 'Other Woman.'" My turn to use finger quotes. They feel as stupid as they seem.

He cocks one eyebrow and stares me down.

"I'm joking."

"I know you are, because Grace is old enough to be my grandmother and is married to a rugby player."

I laugh. "He'd kill you if you made a move."

"She."

"She what?"

"Grace's wife. Seventy-three-year-old female rugby player."

Leaving me with that interesting tidbit, he turns away and speaks into the phone. I take the opportunity to check my own phone.

Twenty-seven messages. Nine from Steve:

What the hell, Shannon?

He's such an asshole.

Are you safe?

I think he's an emotional abuser.

Your car's still here.

Should I call the police?

I texted your mother.

Thank him for paying.

Ask him what he thinks about Canford Industries and whether it's a good stock buy.

Delete. I repeat it nine times. Go ahead, Steve. Call the police. The fact that you texted my mother means . . .

Yep.

Nine messages from her:

You ditched Steve for Declan? Good girl. Aim higher. Shall I start booking a spring 2015 spot at Farmington?

I don't even read the other eight. Delete times nine.

Eight from Amanda:

Your mother is texting me. You ditched Steve?

Is Declan being emotionally abusive? Steve's saying yes.

Steve is on Twitter creating hashtags about you.

Huh? I stop reading and call her, furious.

"What the hell is going on?" I hiss into the phone. Declan's back is still turned, his shirt tail hanging out over that hot, tight ass I just had in my hands. Now I'm spewing invective at my best friend about my arrogant ex. Something is very wrong with this picture. The candles still burn, the room is still filled with sex and promise, and I'm—venting about *Steve*?

"Steve's been calling and texting your mom and me about how Declan appeared and made you leave. How scared and vulnerable you looked. How he thinks you're being emotionally abused."

I just had the most mind-blowing sex of my life while straddling Declan in a limo and I have to deal with an ex who is acting like a middle school gossip girl?

"He WHAT?" I ask. A little too loudly, too, because Declan frowns and walks toward me.

"What's wrong?" Declan asks. I can't wiggle out of this one.

"Nothing," I say with a chirp. I'm turning into Amanda. There's no way I'm telling her what Declan just said to me, his heartfelt confession, because I can't even wrap my head and heart around the words. He said everything I feel, except with clarity. When I think the same words they just come out like unintelligible babble. "Just a . . . work problem."

"Not with an Anterdec property?"

"No, no . . . just a pest control issue," I hiss. I motion for him to go back to his call and suddenly, the room feels cold. Broken. Lost.

Or maybe it's just me.

I hear a decidedly masculine voice on the other end of Declan's call, the dissonance between my assumption it was

Grace and the male voice confusing. "Declan?" the voice says. "Just because you don't like what I have to say about her doesn't mean you should ignore me."

I know that voice. It's James, his father.

Declan frowns at his screen and shows me his back. Hmmm. *Her?* Does his father not like me? Or are they talking about some other woman? Of course they are. I'm being silly and self-centered. Why would James McCormick 1) not like me? That's akin to not liking a golden retriever. I'm the epitome of nice and 2) even bother with me. He only noticed me because Declan pointed me out in that business meeting a few weeks ago, and almost bailed on a business trip to swing by my office, and saved my life . . .

Hmmm.

"Steve's crazy, Shannon, and we know it. Don't worry. Your mom thinks you're a feminist hero, though, for going on one date and leaving with another guy." Amanda's voice slices through my rapid-fire thoughts.

"I wasn't on a date with Steve! I'd rather get a Brazilian wax with battery acid."

"Ouch," she says in unison with Declan, who is now off the phone and behind me, all heat and muscle bearing down, moving with a slight rhythm that tells me exactly what—and who—is coming next.

"Gotta go, Amanda. We're in a lighthouse in the harbor and Declan's about to—"

Click.

"About to . . . ?" He kisses my shoulder, taking the phone out of my hand as his thumb presses the "Power" button. His chest is hot against my back and as he leans around me to set down my phone on the table, I realize his shirt's unbuttoned. Bare skin warms my cotton shirt and he turns me to face him.

I look at the L-shaped couches across the room, the flicker of fire in the glass door of the wood stove making the velvet seem so soft, so welcoming.

Like Declan's hands as he lifts my shirt for what feels like the umpteenth time this evening.

"You," he says with a growl as he reveals my bra, "are so hot."

"I'm Toilet Girl."

"You're Hot Girl."

"That's *your* title."

"I'm Hot Girl?" He takes my hand and puts it at his waistband as he undoes his belt. He has a point.

"I retract that statement."

"This isn't a newspaper article. You're not a reporter." His voice holds a smile. "Unless you're undercover and investigating me."

"I'm only dating you for the account," I joke. "Nothing more. No Woodward and Bernstein. No deep cover."

"If you're only dating me for the account, then you nailed it two dates ago," he whispers as he unclasps my bra. The shiver that runs through me vibrates into the scarred wood floor, carrying out into the ocean's waves, triggering a tsunami somewhere in the Azores islands.

"Then why am I here?"

His mouth stops me from saying more, slanting against mine, his arms strong and lifting me to tiptoes. My bare breasts press against the heat of his pecs and the push of his abs against my belly makes me feel more intimate than when he was inside me, in the limo.

"Let me show you exactly why you're here, Shannon."

And he does.

" Y OUR MEDICAL EMERGENCY MADE the local Patch news!" Mom shouts from the kitchen. Mom begged and begged and begged and guilted and blackmailed me into coming to one of her yoga classes, and then she snuck into my phone and texted Declan, pretending to be me, and he's here.

Here. Standing in my childhood home drinking orange spice tea and wearing workout clothes that make me feel feral.

"Great. Just what we need. Notoriety from a news site that covers misspelled store signs and duck crossings with as much space as they cover fatal car accidents and government corruption," Declan mutters.

"What did they say, Mom?" I ask, forcing myself to be polite. I'm drinking chamomile tea and it's not relaxing me. You could pump Zen Tea into me via IV and it wouldn't work. My heart is the sound of one hand clapping, flailing in the wind, trying to find something to rest against.

Watching Declan sit on our sunken sofa, perched with perfect posture and powerful legs encased in Lycra stretch fabric, confuses the hell out of the wiring in my brain.

"And Jessica Coffin mentioned you!"

Declan groans, then covers it with a sip. His eyes take in the room. Mom has a thing for thrift shopping, even though Dad complains that we can afford to buy new, as long as it's at a discount warehouse. Born and raised in New England, Mom's Yankee sensibilities tell her she can't dare to buy a new dresser even though she spends $60 a week on mani-pedis. The incongruity has been long pointed out to her, like explaining that driving seventeen miles to go to a different grocery store to save $1.70 on apples isn't worth it.

"She says, 'Buzz buzz sting sting run run stupid stupid.'"

"What, no 'oink oink'?" I joke.

Declan smacks my knee, hard, and gives me a glare that says, *You're ridiculous* and *Stop it* and then his look says *I want to make love right here on the couch in front of your mother.*

And then he kisses me so hard even Mom goes silent.

"So," she interrupts, her voice high and reedy, "we need to get going. Downward Facing Dog is for yoga class, not on my nice Bauhaus sofa."

Declan ignores her and smiles against my mouth. Aha. I'm sensing a trend. He loves to smile while kissing me while defying the people most interested in controlling me. Hmmm. I should think that one through, but the flutter of his fingers against my breast makes me think I'm about to pop my Bauhaus sofa cherry and then my sex starts doing jumping jacks and shouting, *Control me! Control me!*

"I'm going to class! Need to be there early!" Mom's shaky voice carries through the room at a distance.

Declan's hand leaves my breast and he waves silently, mouth a bit busy. I hear the click of the front door as it shuts and he pulls away, smile intact.

"Mission accomplished."

My face falls. *"That* was your mission? To drive my mom away? I can do that by pretending to be a Republican."

His face becomes a stone mask. *"I'm* a Republican."

I punch his shoulder lightly and laugh. "You almost had me there."

The expression doesn't change.

Oh, hell no. Even Steve was a Democrat. Most of the time.

"What are you?" he asks.

"I'm a Stewartarian."

"You worship *The Daily Show*?"

"It's like my daily mass." My heart is hammering. I hate

politics. I don't even really have a party. In Massachusetts almost everyone I know is a Democrat, and if they're not, they're originally from New Hampshire or Maine. So . . .

"Are you one of those screechy liberals who crams your morals down other people's throats because you view the world through a rigid ideological lens and can't bear to see other people making different choices?" he asks.

"You sound like Rush Limbaugh!" I squeak.

He's laughing, though. "Replace 'liberals' with 'conservatives' and you get the same end." He chuckles quietly, then caresses my face. "I don't care what you believe, as long as I can have a rational conversation with you."

"The only topic where reason goes out the window is cilantro."

"Cilantro?"

"Tastes like soap."

"Same here."

"Oh my God! It's true love!" I clap my hand over my mouth as if that will shove the words back in.

The grin he gives me changes as his eyes shift to something behind me. The clock. "We're going to be late."

Breathe, Shannon. Breathe. Let respiration restart so you don't pass out on top of blurting out that you're in love with him already. It's only been a month. Who falls in love in a month? People on LastShot.com, where you openly confess to having STD lesions, and gamers, that's who.

"And," he says as we stand, stopping me from grabbing a kitchen knife and carving out my vocal cords, "nothing says true love like Mexican food that tastes like laundry detergent."

ONE OF MOM'S FRIENDS from college moved in a few towns over and took an old chicken coop on her property and turned it into a yoga studio. Yep—chicken coop. Except this is like a chicken spa, and if any actual chickens ever set foot in here I think they'd face twenty-five screaming women all searching for their pillow-sized Vera Bradley bags to bash the poor creatures to death.

Declan and I arrive and immediately change the demographics in the room:

1. We lower the average age by a mere two years, but hey, we're outnumbered . . .

2. Declan alone increases the average income by five figures.

3. He adds a male to the group. The only male in the group.

Mom urges us to get in the front row, and I scout it out carefully. Yoga freaks have this thing about their space. No one actually, officially, claims a space, but they do in their *minds,* and no matter how much yoga is supposed to be about awareness and acceptance and detachment and flow, so help you bloody GOD if you take a yoga freak's spot in class.

Namaste, motherf—

"I am so glad you're here!" Mom squeals as Declan rolls out his mat. We're barefoot and I can't stop peeking at his feet. For a guy, they're remarkably nice and athletic and groomed. "Metrosexual" is not the word I'd use to describe Declan, but his feet scream *manscaped!* I imagine them sliding up and down my calves . . .

He starts to stretch and smiles at me, beckoning with his eyes to join him. I bend down to unroll my mat and a popcorn popper goes off.

Wait. That's just my joints.

And twenty old ladies' necks all turning at once when they realize there's a man in the room, and he's not on Viagra.

(At least, I assume he's not. And it's no thanks to me. One inch in the wrong direction with that EpiPen and . . .)

I shudder and he reaches over to give me an affectionate caress. "You cold?"

Twenty sighs fill the air. Mom appears up front, setting up her blocks and yoga mat. This is Restorative Yoga, which means everyone in the room pays $17 each to lie around on a foam mat and fall asleep. How Mom ever got into this business is still a mystery to me, but anyone who can get paid to make her customers zone out and snore and be *praised wildly* is pretty freaking brilliant as far as I'm concerned.

He leans over for a kiss.

Twenty moans rise up behind us.

And then—scuffling sounds.

"You know Marie will have us do Downward Dog and Cow," someone hisses. A chorus of voices all say "Ooooooh," followed by a whispered frenzy. Those are yoga positions where you shove your butt in the air.

Hold on a second . . .

"I'll pay your class fee if you give me the spot," says Agnes. I only know her name because the last time I was here all the other women were gossiping about her because allegedly she's a bit of a loose woman. How you label a ninety-year-old woman "loose" is beyond me, but all I can think is *GO AGNES.*

When I'm ninety I hope I'm still doing yoga and that my libido cries out for a piece of a man, Viagra or no Viagra. The clitoris does not have an expiration date. The hard part must be finding a man with similar interests, a similar life timeframe, and one who isn't in a lovely white cardboard box on someone's mantle.

"You think you can always get everything you want, Agnes," one of the other women hisses. "Not everything has a price."

"Some views are priceless," another woman sighs. "I'll pay for two classes if you—"

As I turn to watch the brewing fight behind us, Declan's lips are twitching. He leans over and says, "Ten dollars says Agnes ends up leading a Senior WWF brawl back there."

"MMA is more her style."

"Corrine, I swear!" Agnes shouts. "You can stand there like a mule all you want and refuse to budge, but I know about your bone density levels." Her voice carries an ominous tone.

"You wouldn't!" Corrine cries out. She's seventy-something going on fifty, with a wig from Farrah Fawcett's day. She looks like she's in a wind tunnel. Oh—no. That's just really bad plastic surgery.

"I'll nudge you just enough to fall and you have a hip that's more fragile than Putin's ego."

Wait a minute here. These old ladies are threatening bodily

harm and broken bones so they can sit behind my boyfriend and ogle his ass?

I crane around behind him and take a good look.

Yep.

Totally worth it.

"Ladies! Ladies!" Declan stands up without using his hands to even touch the ground, displaying ab and core strength that makes everyone freeze, drool, and sigh at once. Someone back there might even have farted.

He holds his hands in the air, palms out, to get the group to pay even more attention to him. "Let's make it a bit more fun, shall we?"

Mom stops her preparations, her finger about to push the button to start the sonorous soundtrack.

"If one of you can guess how Shannon and I met, you can win the—"

Twenty women shriek, "TOILET GIRL!"

"MOM!" I howl.

"Don't shake her hand," Agnes whispers to Corrine, who stares resolutely ahead and doesn't give Agnes a millimeter as my mom comes over to me and Declan with an *Oh, shit* look on her face.

"It's such a charming story!" she says in a stage voice. "My daughter being a professional at the top of her game in business, meeting the billionaire son of James McCormick—"

"The Silver Wolf," Corrine gasps, giving Declan the once-over with eyes like a Terminator robot from one of those movies, evaluating him for specific fleshy characteristics that meet her mission's criteria, which I suspect involve twisting her body against his in non-standard yoga positions. "You look like him."

"My father has a *nickname*?" he mutters, then mumbles quietly to me, "A sexy nickname? Gross."

"Your father is a gorgeous hunk," someone calls out.

"Dad doesn't date anyone over thirty," he says under his breath.

"Oh, goody. My timer doesn't pop for six more years," I hiss.

He flinches, and I can't tell if it's from the radioactive sarcasm in my voice or from the idea of my dating his father. Hopefully, it's both.

This is *not* restorative.

"Ladies! We're running out of time!" Mom calls out, now back in place at her mat. She gives me a fake helpless look and mouths *What can I do?*

More therapy, I mouth back.

She gives me a hearty thumbs-up, then leads the class through a series of warm-up poses that leave me sweatier than Mom during the height of menopause. Declan hasn't broken a sweat. Six women are trying to share one yoga mat behind him, though.

Soon we're all on our backs, stretched out on the floor, listening to Pink Floyd. If they handed out little LSD stamps before class, this part would be even better. Instead, I hear light snoring, the high-pitched whine of someone's uncalibrated hearing aid, and the sound of Every. Single. Woman getting up at least once during full-body relaxation mode to pee.

The bladder does not acknowledge Restorative Yoga. It's an anarchist when it comes to Savasana pose. *No snooze for you!*

In the dark, "Comfortably Numb" comes on, and I feel something brush against my hip. Declan's hand finds mine and he interlaces our fingers. I relax immediately at his touch, layers of tight muscle giving way, and as his warm palm reminds me that he's there—really there—I wonder if it is true love when you finally find someone else who thinks cilantro tastes like detergent.

His hand, fingers woven into mine like a web, goes slack, too. We're shedding layers through touch, and maybe there's something to this whole Restorative Yoga thing, I think, as a warm cloud of deep bliss surrounds me. Declan shifts his arm so slightly, his palm sliding against mine, and I can feel him smiling.

Sinking deeper, the world fades out and all I am is my hand, touching him, and it's so much more than enough that I dissolve into a state of harmony that slips into a peaceful darkness.

chapter
ten

" **I** HOPE YOU TWO die just like that." Mom's words
make my eyes snap open. She's standing over me, the
yoga studio's lights on full blaze, and there are about ten
other sets of eyes boring down on me.

Us. Me and Declan. I turn my head, confused and fuzzy now
as I come out of my slumber, and see he's out cold, still. A big
patch of drool covers one side of my mouth and even my hair is
a bit soaked at the jaw line.

"You hope we—what?" Instinct tells me to sit up, to run
away, to escape from being the focus of the yoga version of Ray
Bradbury's *The Crowd*.

"I hope you die just like you are, right now. So cute." All eleven
women stare at us like we're part of some modern art exhibit
and sigh in unison.

Declan's right eyebrow shoots up and he says nothing.

"You want me to *die*?" I ask, incredulous. "In your yoga
class?" He squeezes my hand and I try not to laugh.

"No, I mean, you know, in sixty or seventy years. That you
two die after a long, happy marriage and plenty of kids and
you're peaceful old people who die just like that." Mom's elabo-
ration doesn't help.

"I wanted that, too," Agnes says. "But my husband, Jerry,
had other plans."

"How did he die?" Mom asks. But she asks as if she knows
the answer already.

Agnes looks at me. "He got his hand stuck in a toilet and

couldn't get out. I was on a tour of Niagara Falls with my church group for three days and he starved to death."

Declan groans, his body curling in a bit. He's trying not to laugh, and he shakes, abs rippling against his tight Lycra shirt, his ass tightening.

"Ooooh, keep it up. Nice glutes," someone says. That just makes him laugh harder. Now I sit up and let go of his hand. For some reason, I'm jealous—jealous!—and don't like all these people eyeing my man candy.

He's mine.

"Your husband didn't really die like that, did he?" I'm cynical enough to think there's no way that story is true, but just gullible enough to worry that if I assume it's a joke, and it isn't, that I'll destroy an old woman's feelings.

"No. He died porking a retail clerk at the mall. They were on the elevator. He was a security guard. Heart attack. The man didn't touch me for seven years and then he goes and sticks it to the pretzel stand girl."

That makes me bark with laughter as Mom waves her hands behind Agnes and mouths It's true.

Oh, hell. I can't win.

"I hope I die in the arms of someone I love," Mom announces. Declan's laughter comes to an abrupt halt, the change so distinct it makes the hair on my arms prickle. Something in Mom's declaration hit a nerve with him, and it makes me see how little I really know about him.

He stands, fluid and graceful, then yawns. This is no normal yawn, though. It's a lion's roar, with arms stretched nice and high, his belly button exposed as he reaches for the sky, stretching and extending his muscles and joints. The body on display for us all is, decidedly, the nicest eye candy ever. Fine, Swiss eye candy. Candy made from slave-free, ninety-percent cacao farmed by happy rural cooperative workers working to save the whales.

"Can I just touch him, once?" someone asks. "It's like all those Nike ads with the sweaty, hot men come to life, within reach. I thought they were all done with trick photography.

This—this is like learning Bigfoot is real."

A green wave of mist covers my vision. What is wrong with me? I'm jealous of women who haven't needed to use birth control since the moon landing.

But yes—I am.

"Bigfoot is real, Irene," Agnes says to the owner of the disembodied voice. "I saw it on the Discovery Channel last week."

"You're so naïve, Agnes. That show is just trick photography and some guy with too much hair on his body. My Dave was that way. The man could go around the house without a shirt on and you swore he was wearing a mohair sweater. That's all Bigfoot is."

The two descend into bickering as Mom shoos the crowd out, thanking them for coming and talking about seeing them next week.

Declan snuggles up to me. "You like what you see?"

"Mmmm, eye candy. Zero calories and better than licking a lollipop."

"I've got a lollipop you can lick."

Mom, of course, happens to walk over to us just as he says that, and she pretends to be shocked, then pretends she heard nothing.

"So, Declan, did Shannon invite you over for Easter dinner?"

Huh? We never discussed this. Why is Mom acting like I—

"No, Marie, she didn't," he says slowly, not making eye contact with either of us, his body bent in half as he rolls up his yoga mat. We're greeted with the mighty fine view of his ass, and we sigh in unison.

I elbow Mom—hard.

"I can't help it!" she hisses.

"You better help it. It's icky."

"You're right! You're right." She appears to take me seriously. "It is icky. I'll stop right now." She gives me a look that's genuinely contrite.

"Well," Mom says loudly as Declan turns and faces us, "even if Shannon didn't invite you, I'm inviting you."

His eyes travel slowly from my face to Mom's. "When is Easter?" he finally asks.

"This Sunday!" she sputters. "In three days." With a frown, she says, "But I'm sure you have plans with your family."

"We haven't celebrated Easter in more than ten years," he says in a matter-of-fact tone.

"How awful!" Mom exclaims, grabbing his arm. Her eyes almost glisten with tears, and she's truly shocked. She pauses. "Are you Jewish? Is that why?"

"No."

The lack of additional information unsettles both me and Mom. Declan has this way of being shut off. He's not cold, exactly. It's more like talking with a lawyer who isn't going to give one single additional bit of information than is necessary in court.

Except we're not in the middle of a legal proceeding. We're in my mother's yoga studio, talking about a holiday where the Easter bunny and a giant ham prevail. What's up with him?

"Mom, if he were Jewish he wouldn't have celebrated before. He just said it's been more than ten years since . . ." I turn to him. "Since your mom died?"

He nods. But nothing more. He's so . . . wound, suddenly.

"Will you be there?" Mom asks, her smile so sweet and warm. "We have a loud, crazy family and I'm the queen of it all. And I make a killer ham."

"You buy it from the ham place down the street," I say. "The kind with the crusted sugar on the edge, all spiral sliced, and then she makes the sweet potatoes with little marshmallows . . ." My stomach growls.

He thaws. "Who can pass that up?" Eyes that were green tundra seconds ago warm up, and his body loosens. "Thank you, Marie. What time?"

"Two for dinner, and at three we do the Easter egg hunt." Mom looks happier than Martha Stewart being told that Gordon Ramsay's coming for dinner.

"What can I bring?"

"Your helicopter." She is practically jumping out of her skin with excitement.

"Um, I was thinking more like a bottle of wine, Marie." Declan wraps his arm around my waist and presses an absent-minded kiss against my temple. He smells like sweat and comfort, spices and safety.

"Okay, fine. But the helicopter would be one hell of an entrance." She just doesn't know when to stop.

"Where would he land it, Mom? In Dad's garden?"

"Why not? He hasn't planted anything in there this season yet."

"How about I arrive in my own SUV, wearing something other than a suit, and I bring suitable Easter egg hunt items and a bottle of wine?"

"And your Batman costume," I add with a smirk at Mom.

"Leave our sex life out of this," he stage whispers.

Mom turns pink and stammers. "I—I'm so glad you'll be there!" She skitters off to the office.

I hit Declan in the pec. My fingers crack. "Why did you say that?"

"Because I like to beat her at her own game." His smile is so impish I stand on tiptoes and give him a grateful kiss.

"You'll never win," I say, sighing.

"Never say never."

"YOU NEED TO PEE," Tyler says as Declan walks in the front door of my parents' house on Easter afternoon. It's two o'clock and my boyfriend (that still gives me shivers to say it) is punctual. And, as promised, he drove his SUV, is wearing a long-sleeved, blue button-down with the sleeves rolled up to the elbows and jeans that fit him achingly well, and holds a lovely bottle of wine.

Declan bends down to be at eye level with my four-year-old nephew, who has his standard, serious look on his face. Tyler has little bow-tie lips, short brown hair, and brown eyes fringed by eyelashes so long they reach the ceiling.

"Thanks, buddy, but I don't need to pee."

"You need to pee!" Tyler insists as Carol comes running from the kitchen and whisks him away to the bathroom.

I get a questioning look from Declan and try to explain. "Potty training. And Tyler has a language disorder, so right now he confuses 'you' and 'I.'"

The lights go on for Declan. "I see. So he was saying 'I need to pee.'" He laughs. "I hope he made it."

Carol starts clapping and cheering from afar.

"I'll take that as a yes." Declan's kiss is polite and brief, so routine it warms my heart. That is the kind of kiss you give someone you're becoming very comfortable with, and I love it.

Love him.

"Declan! You're here!" Mom comes barreling out of the kitchen wearing a red apron that says "Will Cook for Sex." She gives him a warm, motherly hug. He's a head taller than her and yet she's the one enveloping him. He closes his eyes and surrenders to the embrace. A tiny corner of my heart grows a little more.

"Wine, as promised," he tells her, handing off a bottle of something white. Looking artfully around the empty front room, he says with some care in a whisper, "And I have a bunch of plastic eggs stuffed with candy and toys out in my car. Where should I put them?"

Mom's grin splits her happy face and she gives him a big kiss on the cheek. "You sweetie! When we're ready for the egg hunt we'll just grab them and hide them." She holds the bottle away from her, squinting to read the label. "Jason! Come see Declan and take this chilled bottle out of here!"

Dad walks down the hall and joins us. He's wearing a matching apron, khakis, and no shoes or socks. I think Dad is allergic to socks and shoes.

"Declan!" They shake hands enthusiastically. "Good to see you." Mom hands Dad the bottle.

"White!" she chirps.

"Thank you," Dad says to Declan. "Want a beer?"

"What about the wine, Jason?" Mom screeches, scandalized.

Declan and Dad ignore her, like they planned it in advance.

Dad shoots me a wink.

"Sure. Whatcha got?"

"You like stouts? I've got some microbrew from this little place in Framingham . . ." Declan walks away, following Dad, and just like that, he's integrated into the household.

I stand in my own childhood home and look around the living room. Everyone's congregated in the tiny kitchen and I overhear Amy telling Carol about running in the marathon. Mom and Dad could buy a five-thousand-square-foot mansion in Osterville with an enormous living room and everyone would still cram into the kitchen to talk and taste and hang out.

Declan breezed into the house, was told he needed to pee by a child, offered up a bottle of wine, and boom! Dad takes him to his Man Cave in the backyard like we're married and have been together forever.

I'm sensing a trend here.

This might actually happen. Me and Declan.

Carol walks into the living room, rubbing vanilla-scented lotion on her hands. She stares at me for a second, eyebrows raised. "You okay?"

"Dad just took Declan to the Man Cave."

"He's being accepted into the tribe."

"Is that good or bad?" I give her a helpless look and sink down onto the couch. The springs are shot, so I literally sink down, my feet flying off the floor. I bury my head in my hands.

Carol stands over me and finishes rubbing the lotion. "I think you're afraid of success."

"What? No. No, I'm not. I never had a problem with Dad taking Steve into the Land of Grunts and Farts." Dad has a little hundred-square-foot shed that he winterized a while ago. It's got a television, ancient lounge chairs Mom tried to throw away years ago, and all his old sci-fi paperbacks he's been collecting since the 1960s, lined on homemade shelves.

He illegally piped a wood stove in there, and has an old milk jug I suspect doubles as a toilet in a pinch. Sometimes he and Mom have fights so intense he sleeps out there. Just for one night, though. The Man Cave smells like male sweat, Old Spice, and onions. Seriously. There's a minor methane crisis in there. Jeffrey says it smells like Grandpa.

"Dad only took him back there to be nice to you. He hated Steve."

"I know." Once Steve dumped me they allllll came out of the woodwork to tell me what an ass Steve was, and Dad led the charge. He was like a pressure cooker. Once you popped the seal on the lid, more steam than you knew existed came pouring out.

Enough to burn if you weren't careful.

"'Pearls after swine' was the exact phrase he used all the time," she adds.

"He said that about you and Todd, too."

"I know."

"No, like, at your wedding. And when Jeffrey was born. And then Tyler, and—"

"Got it. Don't need my nose rubbed in it."

Silence hangs between us for a second. I look like a hybrid of Mom and Dad. Carol, though, looks most like Mom. Lighter blonde hair, blue eyes, a round face with dimples, and plump cheeks that make her look perennially cheerful, even when she's not smiling. She's the oldest, and life hasn't been easy these past few years.

"Any luck with jobs?" I ask. She's the one who got me into mystery shopping. Back when I was hired on full-time she had a great full-time job. Then Tyler began having huge behavioral problems, Todd dropped off the face of the earth, and she was laid off. Mom and Dad have helped. Carol mystery shops with the kids when she can, and she's living on unemployment and some vague government assistance I don't quite understand. She has a degree, and loads of determination, but not a lot of time or hope.

"I have an interview with a call center. Night shift. Mom says she and Dad can help with babysitting." Defeat oozes in her voice.

"Minimum wage?"

"No, actually. More like a standard three-to-eleven shift. I'd have to rely on Mom and Dad too much. It's not fair to them."

"They love Jeffrey and Tyler," I protest.

"I know. It's just . . . you don't have kids. You don't understand." Her eyes shift down and she looks like a very serious, contemplative version of our mother. The dissonance is hard to reconcile. I don't think I've ever seen Mom look . . . reflective.

"No, you're right. I don't." I do want kids someday. Watching Carol struggle the way she has definitely made me extend "someday" by a few years, though. Tyler and Jeffrey are the best kids ever (I'm biased), but they haven't been easy to raise without help.

"And you're dating a hot billionaire."

I roll my eyes and she smirks. Ah. Now she looks like Mom again.

Hot Billionaire chooses that moment to walk in, overhearing Carol's comment "You're dating another guy named Hot Billionaire?" His easy touch as he wraps an arm around my waist just adds to her embarrassment. I remember when she brought Todd home, when I was thirteen, and I thought he was so hot. Jealousy poured through me then, as Todd would give her hugs and kisses and little love pats. *That* was love, I thought. Back then, before Todd turned out to be pond scum.

Declan's not Todd.

Carol turns bright pink. It looks like she poured a bottle of Pepto-Bismol all over her face. "We thought you were in the Man Cave, grunting and eating roast meat off a stick," she says.

"We were, until the little boys found us, and now your dad is playing horsey with them and he sent me in here for a rescue team."

Carol laughs and takes the chance to escape. "I'll rescue him!"

"Dinner's soon! Declan, can you help set the table?" Mom comes out of the kitchen, her hair so thoroughly sprayed and set in stone by some chemical that will likely be proven in ten years to cause cancer, but by God keeps her hair in place even as she cooks.

"Sure." He winks at me and walks toward Mom. "Where's

the dining room?"

Mom leads him through the kitchen into the formal dining room, the sanctuary of Good Food and the room we use exactly three times a year: Easter, Thanksgiving, and Christmas. When not in use for a holiday, the dining table doubles as a storage facility for junk mail, LEGO toys Mom finds while vacuuming, and random light bulbs Dad needs to remember to replace with LEDs but never does.

Mom's really pulled out all the stops, with a pale blue linen tablecloth and matching napkins. I wonder which thrift store she got that deal from, and then I see the glasses. Matching crystal glasses at each seat, the tops edged with gold.

"Like my table?" she asks proudly.

"Where'd you get it all?" I ask, definitely admiring. Mom and I have a shared love for "thrifting" and yard-saling.

"Savers!" she exclaims, then catches Declan's confused look. "What's Savers?"

Amy happened to come into the room and is halfway to greeting me and Declan, arms stretched out for a hug, when she stops cold at Declan's words. "You don't know what Savers is?"

"Get me some smelling salts," Mom jokes, "because I'm about to faint. Declan, we have to take you thrifting!"

"Thrifting?" He seems amused.

"Shopping at thrift shops. Yard sales. Estate sales. That sort of thing. And Savers is a chain of thrift shops."

"Used items?" He still seems confused. "So you only buy used items? Like antiques?"

Mom's turn to look confused. "Declan, you've never bought something used?"

"An antique. Sure. Dad buys them all the time for the office and his house. But otherwise . . . no."

"You just shop in regular stores for everything?"

"I have shoppers who do that for me. Unless it's clothing. Then I just go to a tailor."

"Oh," Mom says quietly. An awkward pause fills the air.

"I would love to go 'thrifting' with you, Marie," he says with a smile. "It sounds like fun."

He is officially the Best Billionaire Boyfriend I have ever had.

Mom relaxes and points to the fridge. "Can you get the butter lamb, Declan? It's time to get the food on the table."

His face goes slack, the friendliness replaced by a kind of tempered shock he's obviously trying to hide. "Butter lamb?"

I laugh, trying to get him to chill out. "A few generations back, Dad's family was from the Buffalo area. Polish. There's this tradition where you—"

"Where you have a pound of butter that's pressed and formed into the shape of a lamb, and you put it out on the table at Easter," he says.

Everyone freezes. Jaws drop. Eyes open wide.

"You know about the butter lamb?"

His hands are shaking, just a tad, as he shoves them in the front pockets of his jeans. "Um, sure. My mom was from that area. We had one every year." He swallows so hard we can all hear the click in his throat, and his face is uncertain, eyes blinking rapidly. "I haven't seen once since . . ."

"Since she died?" I ask gently, my hand reaching out to his forearm for reassurance. He doesn't move, doesn't flinch, doesn't change his stance. I want to ask him again how his mother died, but this really isn't the time.

Nod.

"Then wonderful!" Mom gushes. "Not wonderful that your mother died, but wonderful that you can reconnect with an old family tradition." She reaches for his shoulders and directs him to the fridge, then walks past him to the stove to stir something. A timer goes off and she mutters to herself.

Declan sets the yellow lamb on the table and looks out the back sliding doors toward the yard, where Dad is pushing Tyler on the swing set.

"Can we go outside?" he asks in a ragged voice.

"Of course." We head toward the door and I pause with my hand on it. "If this is too much, we can leave. Go somewhere quiet and—"

He takes both my hands in his and smiles at me with troubled eyes. "It's more than enough, but not too much. I want to stay. Your family is lovely."

"My family is crazy."

"Crazy can be lovely."

chapter
eleven

B Y THE TIME DINNER and the Easter egg hunt are over, everyone has turned into a human potato bug, round and grey, a series of roly-polies stuffed silly. Conversation has devolved into exclamations of how good all the food was and groans about how our stomachs are about to explode.

"Can I see your childhood bedroom?" Declan asks. He's relaxed considerably since he first arrived.

"Want to examine my Barbies?" I stand and reach out for his hand, leading him up the stairs. Jeffrey and Tyler are in the backyard shrieking and chasing Amy with little toy guns, shooting foam bullets at her. They miss every single time.

Dad has actually undone his belt and the top button of his khakis, and rests in a lounge chair like Al Bundy, one hand tucked in his waistband.

Mom's in the kitchen fussing over the leftovers. There's enough food to feed an army.

"My room isn't anything special," I explain as we walk up the carpeted stairs. When Amy turned sixteen Mom finally got her wish—cream carpet—and even now, more than five years later, it feels weird to me. I went away to college and the house had industrial green, flat carpet and came home to a *Better Homes and Gardens* spread.

"It's special because it's yours."

We're greeted, first, by the giant head of Justin Bieber on my bedroom door.

"Nice. You were a Belieber?"

"That's a sick, sick joke from Amy."

I open the door and Justin steps aside. "Voilà!" I sweep my arm around the room. White furniture, all of it "thrifted" and refinished by Dad. Simple sheer curtains. An entire wall of cork squares with push-pinned articles and pictures from teen magazines. A ton of shells from vacations to Cape Cod.

Nothing amazing. The amazing part, actually, is that Mom hasn't made me clear it out yet. She claimed Carol's old bedroom as a yoga studio a few years ago. My time is likely ticking.

Declan's hands are all over me suddenly, his lips on my shoulder, caresses in places that tell me exactly what he's thinking, and he's not thinking about Justin Bieber.

At least, I hope not.

"We can't have sex in here!" I hiss. Jeffrey and Tyler are thumping up and down the carpeted stairs now, with Jeffrey calling out numbers. An impromptu game of Hide and Go Seek is afoot, and I don't want the kids to catch us hiding something of Declan inside Auntie Shannon.

"Why not?"

"For one, my twin bed is so small you'll poke my eye out before you hit the target—"

"Is *this* the target?"

I struggle to speak as electric jolts shoot through me like I'm mainlining a battery. The heat pouring out of his rock-solid chest and hips that press into my own belly makes my knees go weak. Teenage Shannon who spent many fitful nights dreaming about this moment is clashing with Responsible Shannon.

"And for two, I don't want anyone in my family to hear!"

As if on cue, Jeffrey shouts, "Ready or not, here I come!"

"I want to hear *you* say that," Declan whispers as he bites my earlobe.

"You—I—what are you—oh my God," I gasp as he slips his hands under my waistband and does unspeakable things.

"Then let's go have sex in your car."

"We can't have sex in my *car!*" Teenage Shannon is, like, totally grossed out by the idea of finally having sex in her parents' house but doing it in a car that looks like it should be sprayed down with bleach and scrubbed with a toilet brush is even worse. All the Shannons agree on this point, even the pulsing little Shannon in my pants, the one that keeps screaming Yes yes yes even though she doesn't have a mouth.

"Why not? We already had sex in mine, so fair is fair. Your turn."

"I drive a car with a *turd* on top of it."

"Maybe that's my real fetish."

"Oh, toilets aren't enough?"

"I'll show you a fetish or two."

A rush of warm electricity fires out from my core through every single pore on my body, and I'm about to agree to whatever he wants and throw in a few of my own requests as well, when—

"SHANNON!" Dad's voice is joyful and blessedly ingenuous. "Let's get ready for ice cream."

"Ice cream?" Declan murmurs, fingers sliding up to find my throbbing point that makes me inhale so sharply a strand of hair gets caught in my nostril.

"It's trad"—my voice hitches with arousal and groaning need—"ition. We stuff ourselves silly and then go out for chocolate-dipped cones. The local ice cream joint opens today. Then we go to the movies."

"Ice cream and the movies on Easter? I love your family."

"I love your fingers."

"I have other long bits of me you might love, too."

"THANNON AND DECLAN!" Jeffrey screams, right outside my door. Oh, no. Did I lock it? Did Declan? "It ith time for eyth cream!"

"I love eyth cream," Declan says as he kisses me, his tongue probing deep, wet, and luscious. This is the kind of kiss a man gives a woman when there are no preliminaries, where you go right for the marrow and the soul, because all those surface layers peel away with a single touch.

The kind of kiss you can enjoy and treasure for the rest of your life without ever experiencing any other kind.

"Hey, Shannon, are you guys—" Amy barges through the

door the same way she did when we were kids and living at home. Hell, the same way she does in our shared apartment *now*.

Declan smiles against my lips, pulling his hands out of my pants, leaving me frantic and disassembled.

"Oh, you two are having a different kind of dessert," she mumbles, pulling back and closing the door, but not quite fast enough.

"Auntie Thannon! Declan! Eyth cream time!" Jeffrey bursts into the room and slides between us, wrapping his little arms around my waist. "Group hug!"

Amy snickers.

"Group hug?" Declan ruffles his hair anyhow, but the disappointment and skepticism in his voice makes me snicker, too.

"Ice cream and the newest Pixar movie will have to be a poor substitute."

A spreading grin lights up his face. "No. A great substitute."

I smack his shoulder. "Hey!"

"We have all the time in the world," he adds, pressing a kiss against my cheek.

"Groth," Jeffrey mutters, pulling on my hand. "Eyth cream!"

"You owe me a double, kid," I say as we all head downstairs to the waiting crew.

chapter
twelve

"YOU ARE THE WORST wife *ever*," I hiss to Amanda as we get out of the Turdmobile. We've parked a few blocks away from the credit union and she's nattering on about strategy in between grilling me about my relationship with Declan. A quick glance at my car and the light bounces off a bunch of little sparkly things littering my floor. The Easter Bunny was good to Jeffrey and Tyler. A little too good. Plus, Mom still insists on giving her own kids a basket, so I have enough chocolate egg foil wrappers on the floor of my car to build three disco balls.

I kill the engine and climb out of the car. A kid on a skateboard who looks like he's about twelve, with a Justin Bieber haircut and a Minecraft t-shirt, waves as he skates past and says, "Your car's a piece of shit." His laughter trails off.

So does my self-confidence.

"Ignore him. Focus on me. Tell me every detail about Declan. Your bedroom after Easter dinner?" We have both been so busy for the past two weeks. Amanda was at a big mystery shopper's convention in Kansas City last week, and this is the first chance we've had to talk in person. It figures: I live a dull, boring life for freaking *ever*, and just when it gets good she's not around. And now we can catch up, but we're about to pretend to be married.

While I describe my sex life.

Hmmm.

"No—Jeffrey stopped us."

She frowns. "Did you seriously have sex in a limo, on a

helicopter, and in a lighthouse?"

"Yes."

"You can do it in a car. You can do it in a bar. You can do it with long hair. You can do it in the air. You can do it in a limo, you can do it—you're a bimbo!"

"Hey!"

"You can do it in a lighthouse. You can . . ." Her voice trails off. "What rhymes with lighthouse?"

"Winehouse?"

She shudders, then laughs. "Day-um!" She stretches the word out like it's taffy. "Declan has the refractory period of a seventeen-year-old boy if you had that much sex in one night."

I blush.

"In a *helicopter*?" she squeaks. Squinting, she rolls her eyes up, as if trying to imagine it. "How did you not fall out a door or something?"

"It was, um . . . one-sided." My face is as red as her painted lips.

"A one-sided helicopter?"

"A one-sided sex act. On the way home."

"You gave him a—oh. Got it." She gives me a high-five. I smack her palm back and feel a roiling sense of doom in my gut. Are we seriously talking about all the ways I had sex with a man—a very, very attractive man—while walking to a mystery shop in which we have to pretend to be married?

"So . . . I am guessing you didn't go back to that Mexican joint to collect Steve. "

I snort. "No. Though Declan was shocked on Easter when Mom gave him a big old stuffed bunny and his own basket that contained half of the Walgreen's candy aisle."

She nudges me. "It's getting serious if Marie's making Declan a basket."

"And you'll be proud to know I deleted Steve's eleventy billion texts. He's such an ass. Why did I ever date him?" Between her comment about Declan and Mom and my own feeling of detachment about Steve, I think I might be moving on. Finally.

She uses her hands to make it clear she agrees. "We've all

been asking that question for years!"

"All?"

"Me. Josh. Greg. Amy. Your dad. Hell, even Chuckles would agree if he could talk."

"Chuckles is an equal-opportunity hater, so his contempt for Steve isn't surprising."

"He was on Twitter and Facebook chasing you down. It was pathetic."

"Chuckles?"

She makes a face. "Steve."

I saw the tags and tweets briefly before he deleted them. I'm guessing someone got to him and convinced him that starting hashtags like #freeShannon and #billionaireaggression wasn't exactly good for his business prospects. I'm too aglow with the newly emerging relationship with Declan, from yoga to butter lambs, to care.

"I know." The air is crisp and clean after a morning downpour. A cold front came in and swept out a bunch of oppressive humidity, leaving this spring day for sunshine and that damp-around-the-edges kind of world that feels like its just been baptized.

"You really like Declan." Amanda pauses and looks closely at me. My heart soars and sinks at the same time. She's looking *at* me. Not through me. Open-minded and non-judgmental, my bestie is trying to tell me something.

"I do." How can I explain how much he affects me, the longing inside even when I just saw him twelve hours ago at Easter? The sour taste of Steve's "date" with me is washed away by the rain. Whatever bitterness I've been clinging to has dissipated these last few weeks. Steve is a non-entity in my life now. He let me loose.

I should thank him, in fact, because I would never have broken up with him, and if he hadn't set me free I would never have met Declan. Never have succumbed to this attractive man. Never made love in a limo or basked in the afterglow in a lighthouse on the harbor. Never had Declan over for Easter, or had second dessert at his apartment long after the kids' movie ended . . .

Never been Toilet Girl.

She squeezes my shoulder. "I'm really happy for you." Amanda pauses, then mumbles, "Would a lesbian wear this shade of lavender?" Her hair is still black, lips bright red, and she's wearing a conservative suit. It makes her look like something out of a 1980s music video. Her question throws me out of my thoughts.

"Would you stop asking me what lesbians do?" I throw my hands in the air and lower my voice as passersby start to stare. "How would I know?"

She seems chastened. "Fine. I just don't want to blow our cover."

"We're pretending to be two women married to each other so we can apply for a mortgage using joint income. I don't think Greg could find a more boring mystery shop if he tried." The shop requirements were clear. The day after I came out of the hospital last week, Amanda and Josh had gone to a different branch of the credit union and posed as a married heterosexual couple. They were treated according to the institution's protocol. Now the question is: will the bank officers treat a gay couple differently?

"Remember the vacuum cleaner secret shops?" she says in a voice laced with indignance.

I flinch. "Okay . . . so he could find something more boring." Thirty minutes with a canister vacuum cleaner salesman demonstrating dual-level suckage action had the potential to be nice and porny, but instead it was like bad sex.

You just want to grab your things and get out of there as fast as possible and avoid having your feet sucked on.

My phone buzzes. "Let me guess," Amanda says, closing her eyes and touching her head with her envelope, like some old talk show skit. "It's Steve."

I check. She's right.

We should do dinner again. Without being rudely interrupted, he texts.

Okay, I write back, then indulge in a giant wave of

self-loathing. Why did I say "okay"? What else should I say? This is the umpteenth text from him about that night in the Mexican place. Declan's timely appearance and deliciously engaging pseudo-kidnapping makes my toes tingle right now, my body on fire with the memory. Like a cat in a hot spot of sunshine, all I want to do is stretch and purr.

Steve makes me want to hiss and claw something. And yet I still say "okay" when he doesn't get the hint. Maybe my idea of a hint isn't strong enough.

I haven't told Amanda everything about Declan. How he seemed jealous, so possessive, coming straight from New Zealand and tracking me down, taking me by limo to his helicopter, then riding around the city until we landed on the island. How he was so charming and controlled at Mom's yoga. The way he emotionally disarms her, but without being rude. The way he makes me feel so secure in just being true to myself.

I slow my pace a bit, wondering if I'm walking funny. I should be. More tingles. I share everything with Amanda, so this is new. Keeping it all to myself makes it have more meaning. Savoring what Declan and I have, and our combined desire to have so much more of it going forward, isn't so much a secret as it is private.

Personal.

Ours.

Mine and Declan's, something we share with no one else. I want to hang on to that for just a little longer, before Mom starts booking reception halls and ordering roses dipped in dye that matches some obscure bra strap Kate Middleton wore at her third polo game with the future king.

"Why are you seeing Steve at all?" Amanda asks.

"Masochism." It's an old joke, but that doesn't mean it's not true.

She speeds up until we're walking at a fast clip and almost at the main door to the credit union. The building looks like every other brick business building with white trim, and a discreet white sign with the name is centered above a bank of glass doors. Warnings dot the entrance:

Remove all sunglasses, hats and hoods. You are being recorded.

Sometimes I think about flashing my boobies for the poor schmuck whose job it is to sit in front of a bank of security cameras and keep an eye out for danger. A little light in a dreary job, you know? I made the mistake of saying this to Mom once. She did it.

Turns out my cousin Vito is a mall cop and was nearly blinded by the sight of Aunt Marie's tatas. He still calls her Aunt Antiviagra. She thinks he's speaking an Italian endearment.

"Don't flash the cameras," Amanda hisses as we walk in. She really does know me too well.

"I won't."

Grabbing my arm, Amanda pauses in the foyer. "You okay?" The way she peers intently into my eyes makes me realize she's really asking whether I've recovered from the bee stings. From the enormity of everything with Declan.

"Yes."

"You came back to work kind of fast."

"I needed to. You ever been bed-ridden with my mom taking care of you?"

"I thought Declan came by every day!"

"He did." I smile at the thought. Mom was practically feeding me chewed-up food from her own mouth and giving me water from an eyedropper. That whole "Oh, my poor baby almost died" stuff required a rescuer. Declan had fit the bill. Except for his time in New Zealand on that business trip, he'd been by my side each day.

And then he'd swooped in on my dinner with Steve and taught me how much fun helicopters can be. I shiver with the memory.

"True love means having your boyfriend watch the *The Sapphires* and *The Heat* three nights in a row with you," Amanda says with a sigh.

True love means being made love to above the city lights, I think, but of course I can't say that. Or in his apartment, which smells like fine cologne, pine, and a special soap. Someone in a suit steps through the doors and ignores us. Then I realize what

Amanda just said.

"What boyfriend?" I ask.

She looks confused. "Declan. What other boyfriend do you have other than that electronic bedside-table monstrosity you call Edward Cullen?" Her face scrunches up. "And it's about as old as him, too."

I grab her hand and lace my fingers through hers. "You're the only boyfriend I need, sweetie." Standing on tiptoes, I kiss her cheek.

She jumps back like I've poked her with a cattle prod. "Greg better give us a bonus for this one."

"He has to come with Josh and do the male-male shop, so I don't think there will be any bonuses."

"Poor Josh. They'll look like a bear and a twink."

My turn to jump like I've been electro-shocked. "Huh? What's that mean?"

The receptionist is giving us nervous looks. Amanda nudges me. "Never mind. You really don't watch enough cable television."

"What does that have to do with—"

She puts her arm around me and pushes us both through the main door into the cool, marble-floored bank, the scent of money filling the air. "Let's get this done and over with."

"I agree. I can't be married to you longer than one hour."

Within ten minutes we're ushered into a glass-walled room with no real door, filled with dark oak furniture, brightly patterned carpeted floors, and a no-nonsense balding man who looks like he eats entire rolls of antacids for fun.

Jim Purlman is the senior mortgage officer for the credit union and asks us how we met.

Amanda and I exchange confused looks. "You mean, like, how we were in the same class in third grade?" she blurts out.

Jim looks like he's half Irish and half something else, with a beet-red nose and eyebrows that haven't been tamed since 1977. The skin under his eyes is paper thin and baggy, and what hair he has is grey, grown in a comb-over style I haven't seen anywhere other than in old square photographs from the 1960s in my mom's photo albums. The physical kind that smell like old cigarette smoke and liver spot cream.

But he breaks out into a kind grin and says, "What a wonderful love story. Sweethearts since you were little. Found your soul mate young. You two have kids?" He leans his forearms against the glass-topped desk and waits in anticipation for our answer.

I'm struck mute. We'd been told this set of evaluations came at the request of the credit union's board, a reaction to complaints. Jim's response is absolutely not what we were expecting.

Amanda saves the day, reaching for my hand and stroking my wrist with her thumb. A tingling shoots through my body, and it's not the last remnants of the EpiPen's contents. Her eyes meet mine and holy smokes, ladies and gentlemen, we have some acting.

At least, I hope it's acting. Because I am completely into Declan.

"Fate brought us together on the playground and we're hoping it will be kind to us in the kids department." She smiles so sweetly at me that my pulse races and my cheeks flush. There's a settled passion in the way she carries herself, and Jim hunches slightly in his chair, as if relaxing from approval.

"I'm sure you'll find the right man—" He shakes his head slightly. "Er, sorry. The right *path* to have the family you deserve."

Amanda lets go of my hand and puts hers on my knee. Thoughts of Declan set my core on fire. Being touched at all like this, in a partner kind of way, seems to set my screwy wiring into ablaze mode.

"You look like you're about to cry," Jim says.

I reach up and wipe a watery eye. "We're still overjoyed we were allowed to be married," I answer.

"When was that?"

"Two weeks ago, at our town's courthouse."

"So you have a marriage certificate?" he asks.

"Do you need to see it?" To Jim, Amanda's shift in personality can't be noticed, but I get what she's doing now. Legally married heterosexual couples don't need to show a marriage certificate to apply for joint income mortgages, so if he asks, we must note it on the evaluation.

"Oh, no!" he exclaims. "I just meant it must be great to know you can be married and have all those legal protections."

And just then, someone taps on the glass. I turn toward the sound and my entire body goes cold, frozen like a popsicle.

Standing before me is Monica Raleigh.

Steve's *mother*.

"Shannon!" she exclaims. Thankfully, I've used my real first name on the application here for the mystery shop. But I absolutely cannot break my disguise, and therefore Monica can't know we're here on an evaluation. Absolutely not. No failed shop for this one.

Even if it kills me.

I STAND ON SHAKY legs and she gives me a half-hug, the kind where you can't tell whether the other person has a pulse or not. A cloud of Cinnabar perfume fills my nose and the back of my throat, the taste like rancid cinnamon.

"I haven't seen you in so long," she adds. It's been a year, yes. But Monica never liked me. Ever. Not one bit. Her fakery should be lauded, because she put on a surface act about me. Doing the bare minimum was her form of liking me. A familiar, low-grade shaking begins inside my body, as if my bones were starting to rattle from the first signs of an earthquake.

She looks like a shrunken version of Steve, with the same slightly negative set to her jaw, as if the world has to prove that any shred of positivity is possible. Her default is suspicion and pessimism.

I used to think that was a sign of intelligence, as if being pessimistic meant you just had figured out The Truth long before everyone else did. Now I think it's a nice cover for being a bit of an asshole and not knowing how to find your way out.

She looks like Steve, except she's a bird. All that's missing are wings. Her waist is thicker than her breast, her legs are scrawny, her feet splay out, and her resemblance to a bird wouldn't be so sharply distinctive if she didn't henpeck everyone.

She also has eyebrows that lift perpetually, making me think she's questioning everything I say.

"Amelia!" she exclaims as she turns to Amanda, who leaps

up and practically curtseys. Monica does that to some people. She has the air of a queen and the snootiness of a social climber. Steve and I dated for how many years and the woman doesn't remember my best friend's name?

Amanda doesn't correct her. It would be like trying to correct King Joffrey. You'd be beheaded in seconds.

"What are you two doing here?" she asks.

"Hello, Monica," Jim says, standing and coming around the desk. He looks like he's part wolf, predator eyes devouring her. Monica's wearing something stylish from one of the boutiques near Neiman Marcus in the Natick Mall—oh, excuse me, the Natick *Collection*. Can't call it a mall. Every other town calls their enclosed shopping center a mall, but Natick's developers appear to wish they were designing Rodeo Drive.

And Monica acts like she lives on it, even though she's really a suburban mom.

"Why, Jim!" she exclaims, like Scarlett O'Hara in *Gone With the Wind*. I half expect to hear *fiddle-dee-dee* come out of her mouth and for South Boston to burst into flames. Have the Red Sox lose in the seventh game of the World Series and that might actually happen.

"Amanda and Shannon are here to apply for a mortgage," Jim explains.

Amanda and I share a look of horror and professionalism, tenuously balanced at the half-and-half point.

"A mortgage? You're buying property?" Monica's eyes light up. "How ambitious of you, Shannon. I thought you'd stay in that dead-end job forever and never show any chutzpah. Steve taught you some good skills, didn't he? I'm sure you appreciate everything he did for you all those years."

Screech. Stop the merry-go-round, because someone needs to get knocked off her high horse.

I can't let Jim know that I used to date Steve. Not, at least, until Amanda and I finish this evaluation from hell. I know I'm in hell because Monica is the queen here. She could marry Hades and have him whipped in no time.

Amanda's all too aware of the predicament, but can also see

smoke coming out of my ears, so she steps between me and Monica, opening her mouth, just as Jim says:

"The newlyweds are here to buy their first house together. Isn't that something?"

You date a guy for a few years and you get to know his mother fairly well, even if she has a stick up her butt so long she could pick oranges with it. Monica won't leave now because she's a bulldog with her teeth in my calf, and the charade has to be held up. Blowing our cover means alienating Consolidated Evalushop's other major client. Greg has held on to this long-standing contract for years, and while we all joke about how boring evaluations for banks, credit unions, lending companies, and insurance can be, it pays the bills and keeps the marketing company where I work afloat.

When a steady contract is at stake, I'm willing to leverage my (not so big) sense of dignity to keep the client happy.

Unfortunately, I took the same approach with Monica all those years, letting her digs and condescension chip away at me for the sake of Steve.

"You've gotten married?" she gasps, craning her neck around the credit union, looking for an obvious suspect. "Where is he?"

Amanda reaches for my hand and pulls me close, her shoulder banging against mine as she bends down and kisses my cheek. "He is she. Me. We're the newlyweds."

Monica's social mask doesn't just crack. It shatters. "You're, you're . . ." Her mouth twists like she's accidentally eaten a live gecko. "Lesbians?" The word emerges like that goopy, growling head from John Hurt's stomach in *Alien*.

Amanda looks at her watch and doesn't answer the question while I do my best imitation of a twelve-pound sea bass being pulled onto a ship with a hook in its eye and mouth opening and closing, unaware of its pending slow, painful death.

"We both have an appointment in thirty minutes, so could we move on?" Amanda says to Jim in a *don't you dare say no* voice. Powerful and commanding, she's also casual in an enviable way. I almost want to date her. Wait. I'm married to her. I can't date her.

Jim rallies. "Of course, of course! Monica, so good to see you," he says as he reaches to shake her hand. She snatches it away, and instead those demon eyes glare like twin rubies, pointed at me.

"You're a lesbian? A married lesbian?" Her tone is that of a preschool teacher explaining that there are seven continents to a group of three-year-olds, as if I don't know what I am saying and she's correcting me. She sounds unhinged.

She sounds like Jessica Coffin "explaining" the Bromfield art gallery to me.

"Yes," I say in an out-breath, the word floating off on the air like a fart. She flinches.

Then her entire face morphs. Jim goes back to his desk and mutters something about getting the paperwork in place. One claw-like hand reaches for my upper arm and pulls me a few feet away from him, and now her words come out in a hurried hiss.

Amanda follows us, still holding my hand and grinning like a Disney character. If Monica is an evil queen, then Amanda has somehow turned into Dopey in seconds.

"You like women."

"I love women!" I chirp.

Her frown deepens, eyes flickering left and right as if retrieving memories to process. My hand starts to sweat and Amanda lets go of it, wiping it on her skirt. She shoots me a pleading look, as if to say there's nothing we can do about this.

You know those news reports about people who have cars suddenly plunge through plate glass windows into storefronts and houses?

I now consider them lucky. *Oh please God, send one now.*

But no. Instead, Monica says, tapping a manicured index finger on her peach-coated lips, "It all makes much more sense now."

"What is that supposed to mean?" Amanda and I say at the exact same time in the exact same WTF? tone.

Monica's face transforms as she thinks, the locked jaw softening as seconds pass. "Oh, dear. No wonder you and Steve didn't work out. You were looking for a Boston Wife and he was looking for a wife in Boston."

A Boston Wife. I've heard the term before. Antiquated phrase used to mean lesbianism long before it was socially acceptable to say *lesbian*.

"I dated Steve and loved Steve and he rejected me," I say, a red cloud of fury growing over my head, ready to unleash a torrent of poison on Monica.

Jim clears his throat. Did he overhear that?

"Can you blame my son?" Monica is clutching imaginary pearls so hard I think she's giving herself a tracheotomy. "He sensed it. He's intelligent, and he's a man. A red-blooded, masculine man with needs. You clearly couldn't give him what he needed, so he left." She sniffs the air. The gesture is so snobby it makes me bark with laughter. Dame Maggie Smith could take lessons on aristocratic pretension from Monica.

"We are talking about the same Steve, right?" Amanda asks me. "The same guy who wore his socks during sex and who insisted on making you buy all the Japanese tentacle erotica on your ereader book account so it was never traced back to him?"

"Some things are meant to be private," Monica whispers in a scathing voice.

"Monica, he buys old Japanese prints from the Meiji period and puts them on his bedroom walls. Haven't you ever taken a good look at what's going on in those paintings? The octopus hanging on to the woman's half-naked body isn't there to be cuddled," I add.

Eyes widening, Monica looks like she might pass out. I start to feel guilty. I could really grind the knife in right now, but I don't.

"Your red-blooded, masculine man has some really weird Hentai fantasies," Amanda says flatly.

"Wait," Monica says, eyes clouded with confusion. She pulls out her phone and taps into what looks like her text message screen, then reads something. "Steve told me you're dating Declan McCormick now." Low whistle. "Impressive." Her eyes flicker to Amanda. "You accept the fact that Shannon is . . . bisexual?" That word seems easier for her to say than *lesbian*, but it still manages to come out sounding like she's accidentally bitten into a piece of chocolate-covered poop.

I freeze. Amanda does, too. What can we say? How do I explain to my fake wife that I have a real billionaire boyfriend?

Amanda laughs. "That's just business."

Monica's eyebrow shoots to the sky. "You're pretending to date Declan McCormick? Even Jessica Coffin made a comment about you two as a couple."

Amanda grimaces. I know she follows Jessica on Twitter. This is a mess. Certified, Grade A, failed-shop mess. If I admit I'm dating Declan, the entire mystery shop falls apart. If I don't, Monica will start up the rumor mill into a DEFCON 1 level, complete with whooping sirens and fainting blue bloods.

I'd rather have my hand stuck in a toilet while eating hazelnut-flavored horseradish.

Amanda is cutting her eyes over to Jim so sharply she looks like she works for Wüsthof, and she squeezes me with more affection than a three-year-old meeting her first creation from Build-A-Bear. "Right, honey? You're just dating Declan to make a solid business deal even better."

Monica is eyeing me like my mom eyes a seventy-five-percent-off sale at Gaiam. "That's right." Fake smile. "I'm working on being more aggressive in business."

"Steve would be proud," his mom mutters. "He tried so hard to help you develop that killer instinct."

I open my mouth to say something, and Amanda presses her finger against my lips in what looks like an affectionate gesture.

"So you're really, truly not dating Declan McCormick for his looks? His charm? His money?" Monica persists.

"For his company's money," I say, instantly hating the words in my mouth. Trying not to blow my cover means I'm about to blow chunks. Amanda squeezes my hand and nestles closer. I feel green. I'm Kermit the Frog right now.

"Everyone's so much happier now, aren't we? Steve certainly is." Amanda's words make Monica back down. She reaches into her purse and fiddles with something on her phone, then looks up at the wall clock.

Tight smiles all around. We look like the "After" picture from a two-for-one coupon for plastic surgery.

"Your mother must be very happy to have one of her girls married off." She pauses. "Again, I mean. I know Carol's divorced."

Oh, no.

"It was a simple, civil ceremony," I shoot back. "Not an actual wedding." I squeeze Amanda. "We're holding a wedding and reception quite soon."

"Really? Where?"

"At Farmington," Amanda blurts out.

Amanda doesn't realize that Monica is on the board of directors for Farmington Country Club.

"You *can't*." Monica's voice becomes low and roaring.

Jim happens to wander over at this exact moment. "Can't what?" He's holding a stack of printouts. I see a mortgage disclosure statement thicker than a thirteenth-century French stone castle wall in his beefy hands.

"Can't have a wedding at Farmington Country Club," Monica says in hushed tones.

His expression is bemused. "Why not?"

Monica blanches. "Because it's not done."

"Weddings are done all the time there." His eyes narrow and his jaw tightens. Go Jim! You're getting one hell of an evaluation. At least, after I go puke in a trash can and take four Xanax.

Monica stiffens. "Of course." Smile so tight she could slice cheese with it. "We'll see about that," which, when translated from Bitchspeak, is actually *Oh hell no they won't*.

Jim gives me a searching look, then grants Amanda one as well. "Shall we?" He holds up the stack of papers. "You newlyweds have a home and a life to start building." He gives Monica a cold look. "Right this instant."

She frowns and pretends to answer her phone, her exit remarkably anti-climatic.

"Sorry about that," Jim says as we settle in. I'm guessing another half hour or so of paperwork and then we can leave. If only my credit score were higher than my bra size.

"No problem. It happens," Amanda says. Her tone is neutral but I know she's testing Jim. My body is about to supernova with anger and parts of me will turn into ribbons of flesh that stretch into the parking lot and strangle Monica, so I stay silent and just brood.

"The truth is all over Shannon's face," Jim points out.

"The truth?"

He looks pointedly toward where Monica just exited, sighs, and pulls out the first paper from the stack, clicking a ballpoint pen. "Some people would rather hide behind a mask than be vulnerable and real." His eyes are open and respectful, but something darker passes through them.

And with that, Jim just got the highest score possible on this mystery shop.

And I lost everything important to me because I couldn't ditch my mask.

chapter
fourteen

THE FIRST PERSON TO message me is my sister, who does it to my face.

"Oh MY GOD," Amy screams as she crashes through my doorway, nearly flattening the cheap hollow-core door. Her hair springs to life around her like Medusa's snakes as her neck snaps up and down between freaking out at whatever's on her phone screen and making eye contact with me that reminds me of the women in *The Handmaid's Tale* when they are sent off to their assignments.

"What did Mom do now?" I ask. Note to self: get deadbolt for bedroom door. Especially if I plan to have overnight guests.

Which I do.

"It's not Mom. This time. For once." She paces, her hair like a lady in waiting. I run my hand through my own locks and find a rat's nest of limp, stringy hair. How does she manage to look like a cross between Merida and Christina Hendricks while I look like a drunk Cameron Diaz in *Bad Teacher* combined with Melissa McCarthy after that unfortunate diarrhea scene in *Bridesmaids*?

Genetics.

"Then who?" I reach for my phone to check messages from Declan. He was working late last night and then had a board of directors meeting for some big charity organization. We're meeting tonight at my place for drinks. As in, he'll drink me and I'll drink him and eventually we'll cave in to basic sustenance needs and order Thai takeout.

"Jessica!"

"Jessica . . . who?" I'm rubbing my eyes, trying to wake up. Before being so rudely interrupted I was in the middle of a dream where Declan and I were in a cabana on a beach on some tropical island, naked and tanned and drinking something fruity and delightful out of a half coconut . . .

"Coffin!"

"Jessica Coffin." I say the name slowly, then open my messaging app.

157 messages.

Say wha?

"Why do I have 157 messages? Steve isn't THAT crazy!" I shout.

Amy throws her hands in the air in exasperation. It just makes her look cuter. If I do it, I look like I'm swatting flies. "That's what I'm trying to tell you!" Her eyes are filled with panic and pity. "Your life blew up last night in cyberspace." She pauses. "And, soon, real life. Have you heard from Billionaire Boy?"

"What the hell does Declan have to do with anything?"

The front door opens and someone shouts "Hello—oh, Jesus! Leave me alone! Those are new shoes!"

"Chuckles!" Amy and I shout at the same time. The cat had his balls hacked off forever ago but sometimes he still marks his territory, especially on shoes with laces that go up the ankle. As Amanda stumbles into my room shaking her foot, I see I'm right.

"Why are you wearing gladiator sandals in my place? You know Chuckles pees on them."

"Forgive me for forgetting that you have a cat with a lace fetish," she says back, fuming. "They're in style right now." She grabs a towel draped across the back of a chair and starts wiping her foot, cursing under her breath as she teeters off to the bathroom. The faucet turns on just as Amy zeroes in on me.

I cut her off. "Coffee? I can't handle a crisis before I've had three cups."

"Tough luck, sis, because the crisis is here whether you're caffeinated or not."

"And what, exactly, is the crisis?"

She points to my phone.

157 messages.

"Read those while I make you a double espresso. You're going to need it." Her ominous warning makes me frown, and Chuckles wanders in with a disapproving look that makes me scan the room for laces of any kind.

Fortunately, I have a taste in shoes that veers pretty close to that of a skateboarder, so I'm safe.

He sniffs the air, narrows his eyes, and looks at the phone in my hand. *Go ahead,* he seems to say. *Make my day.*

Now my cat is giving me Dirty Harry lines. This is worse than I thought.

"But before you read your messages, you need to read Jessica Coffin's Twitter feed," Amanda explains as she comes out of the bathroom shoeless. "It's . . . well, honey," she says with a compassion that makes my heart race. "Honey, you need to have that coffee in you."

'Honey' is what Declan calls me, I almost cry out. It sounds pathetic and ominous when Amanda does it.

"How bad can some frozen woman's Twitter feed be? What does it have to do with my life?" They're scaring me. She's just some woman Steve dated. Some woman who wanted Declan.

"Remember yesterday at the credit union?"

"How could I forget?"

"How we ran into Steve's mom?"

"Get to the point." Amy brings me a coffee and I take a sip, burning my tongue. The coffee could peel paint, it's so strong, but that appears to be intentional.

Oh, boy.

"Monica must have said something to Steve who said something to Jessica." Amanda and Amy share a look that makes my blood run cold. Chuckles smiles. I should rent him out as an interrogator for the Russian mob.

Oh, this is bad. Really bad.

"And Jessica—what? Mentioned me on her Twitter feed?" I make a huffy laughing sound. Ludicrous. What's a Tweet going to do to me? Hurt my Klout score? Ouch. You hurt my fake internet feelings.

They look at me with alarm. "Yes," they say in unison.

I glare at Amanda. "I knew that tentacle porn comment would bring us nothing but trouble."

I reach for my phone in slow motion, like something out of *The Matrix*, except instead of feeling like I'm part of some kickass save-the-world moment, I feel like an insect that is two seconds away from being crushed by the windshield of a Mini Cooper.

Amanda holds her phone out to me as Amy stares at her and whispers, "Tentacle porn? Do I even want to ask?"

@jesscoffN says: *Lesbians who date billionaires to make big business deals. Sounds like a reality TV show or a trashy romance novel*

"That's it?" I laugh. "No one cares."

"Look at the stream that follows," Amy says in a voice you'd use to tell someone they've walked around in front of the CEO of their corporation with their skirt shoved in the waistband of their pantyhose.

@bigdealmkr: *Let me guess. SJ? Unbelievable*

"SJ? Shannon Jacoby? What? People talking about me online using my initials? C'mon, guys, this is . . ." My voice disappears as I read the rest. Bigdealmkr is Steve. I remember the day he picked his username.

@jesscoffN: *@bigdealmkr I guess some people are so desperate they'll stoop to anything, even cheating on their wife to make a business deal*

"What? What?" I scream with laughter. "This is fucking hilarious!"

"Keep reading," Amanda urges, nudging my elbow so I'll drink more coffee. I suck down half the now-cooler cup and my eyes scan the page as I scroll through.

About twenty people asking Jessica to "dish" or "spill." Obviously scheduled tweets from Jessica for places to eat or shop.

"This is nothing!" I insist. And while a creepy, cold electric feeling is growing in my gut, I stand by that. I mean it. This is just stupid online social media crap that doesn't affect me in real life. Right?

"Look at the one that Tweets Declan."

"Declan?" That cold electric feeling sparks like someone's flipped a breaker.

@jesscoffN @anterdec2 *How's business?*

"That's no big deal." But my voice is shaking. I'm quivering, the vibrations deep inside, like a flock of birds has been scared by a distant gunshot and needs to flee, flying straight up without a plan or a pattern. Just panicking and needing to move.

Thousands of birds inside me begin their sudden migration, but there's no way out. They bang into my bones, my skin, my muscles.

"He never responds," Amy says quickly, eyes wide and so blue I want to swim in them.

"Why would he? He knows it's bullshit." But that's the problem, I fear: does he? When you don't know what people are saying about you to others behind your back, all you're left with is your own crazy imagination. And I have a penchant for self-torture that is so strong I should headline at a masochists' convention.

"Check your messages. Maybe he texted or called."

My fingers feel like icicles as I fumble with my phone. No voice mail. A quick scan of my email shows a few communications with mystery shoppers who encountered problems, a couple who lost receipts, and a ton of junk mail.

157 text messages.

I open the app with a finger that feels like I'm pushing the nuclear war button.

I'm getting tweets from people in high school who didn't bother to acknowledge I existed back then. People who openly mocked me. And is that my former orthodontist? Christ. Who's next? My gynecolo—

Yep. @openwide123—that's the gynecologist, not the ortho.

Most of the messages, though, are gibberish from people I don't know, all from Twitter. I opened an account a few years ago but barely use it. Did someone loop me into the @jesscoffN conversation?

Amy explains. "Steve did it. He referenced you. You can see it in his feed."

"We can explain this to Declan," Amanda whispers as I groan.

I ignore her, searching my messages. Nothing from Declan. Nothing. Not a word. Silence is worse than outrage.

Much worse.

"We have a meeting today with him," Amanda adds.

"Who?" My voice sounds like it's coming from the end of a very long tunnel.

"Declan. We're meeting with Anterdec today."

chapter
fifteen

"**O**H, GOD." I PULL the covers over my head like it will accomplish something. Inside my white, billowy pretend cloud of escape, I wish I could go back to being five years old, when the worst thing that could happen to me was to have to wear the wrong colored ribbon.

Amy comes back in. "Shannon? Come out from under there," she insists. I pop my head out like a turtle checking it out after an atom bomb's been dropped.

In my panic I hadn't noticed she took my empty coffee cup and now she's returning with a full one. When did she become so servile? Ever since I met Declan she's been waiting on me. Not that I mind—coffee in bed is best served by a naked man who smells like sex, but a close second is, well . . . *anyone* delivering hot coffee in bed.

I reach for the cup, grateful. "Thanks."

"No text from Declan?" she asks, pointing to my phone.

"Nope."

"You're sure? With a bazillion messages you might have missed one."

"Go ahead." I point my chin at my own smartphone. "See for yourself. Or," I add, taking a long sip of coffee, "*don't see.* There's nothing to see. He's dumped me, hasn't he?"

A big, tight wave of pain and lust billows through me. It's the feeling of tidal waves pulling back from shore, exposing all the starfish and hermit crabs to the sun and air, helpless and at the mercy of a force of nature so much stronger.

Jessica Twitterhead Coffin.

"That Tweet wasn't so bad."

"It's pretty incriminating," I mumble. I can't believe my life has imploded because of comments made in 140 characters or less. If brevity is the soul of wit, then Twitter is the steaming pile of manure at the end of the horse. Yeah, I know that comparison made no sense, but I'm sitting here in bed with 157 text messages, most of them from people with Twitter handles like @lebronsux4ever and @mygunmyheart and I'm supposed to have a cogent reaction?

And not one damn message from Declan or @anterdec2 or . . .

"Wait." I snap my neck up at Amanda, who, I realize, is now a redhead. Her hair is the exact same color as Amy's. I narrow my eyes. "You said we have a meeting with Declan today?"

"And James and . . . Andrew." I can see long strands of drool coming out of her bright-red-painted mouth when she says that last word. Great. Now my best friend wants to hump my boyfriend's brother. This could be a sitcom.

Except a good sitcom needs a crazy mother to invade at just the right moment. I pause, because if ever there were a time for Mom to appear, it would be now. I close my eyes, cross my legs, and just . . . wait.

Chuckles climbs on my bed and settles into my lap. This must be worse than I thought if he's offering me comfort. You know how those nature shows on cable TV talk about how animals have a preternatural instinct to sniff out natural disasters like tornadoes and earthquakes before they happen?

Uh oh.

"Why did you just go blank?" Amy asks. She keeps wandering in and out of the room and I see why. Her hair is pulled up now in a perfect up-do, one long, springy curl cascading down around each ear. Her work suit is cut to fit her curves and she's inserting a simple pearl earring into one creamy lobe.

"Why do you look like a young Chelsea Clinton?"

She beams. "Do I? Because she worked for venture capital firms, too, and now she makes six hundred grand a year!" My inadvertent compliment makes me forget, for a split second, the mess in cyberspace I apparently need to deal with in real life. At Anterdec.

Today.

"I think that six hundred grand has something to do with her last name, Amy."

"Whatever." Amy fluffs her hair. "If I can make half that I don't need to chase billionaires."

Ouch. Chuckles leaps off my lap and gives her ankles a rub. Too bad she's not wearing laces. His head twitches around and our eyes lock, as if my damn cat read my mind.

"What time is the meeting?" I ask Amanda.

"One o'clock. But Greg wants to have a strategy session before we go."

"Strategy session?"

"James McCormick wants us to start evaluating his high-end properties immediately. They've experienced a significant financial loss over the past two quarters at their major hotels, specifically." She claps her hands with joy, like Pee Wee Herman. "We're gonna shop The Fort! We're gonna shop The Fort."

All I can manage is a scowl. "One o'clock." Can I wait that long?

My damn mind-reading friend says, "Text him. Call him."

"He didn't text or call me!"

"Maybe he's just busy."

"Amanda, he was sexting nonstop after our last date, and then he goes cold." I hold up a finger to get her to pause. She's sliding her shoes back on, and I want to warn her, but . . .

I type *Please call me* and click send, hoping he replies.

She watches me, and when I'm done Amanda says, "Maybe he lost his phone in a toilet?"

I throw a pillow at her. Chuckles chases after it, then stops at her foot. I open my mouth to say something but it's too late.

"Jesus Christ!" she screams as a thin stream of yellow pee hits her foot. She limps back into the bathroom, whimpering something that sounds close to a Scottish curse you'd hear Geillis Duncan mutter in one of the *Outlander* books.

Chuckles looks back and me and I swear he winks.

"Bad kitty," I mutter through a smile.

"Did you train him to do that? Why does he pee on laces and gladiator shoes, of all things?"

"Your kink is not my kink," Amy says as she slings her leather bag over her shoulder. She really does look like a commanding businesswoman, ready to take on a boardroom full of investors, cat-pee-free and blissfully unencumbered by Twitter rumors about her sociopathic use of a bad-boy billionaire to clinch a business deal while cheating on her lesbian wife.

Say that five times fast.

"What does that even mean?" Amanda shouts from the other room. "I don't have a kink. I'm vanilla."

"Nobody's truly vanilla," Amy scoffs. She gives me a mischievous look, playing Amanda. "You have to have a kink. Getting golden showers from Grumpy Cat, for instance."

"Golden *what*?"

Amy frowns at me. "And *she's* the one who gets to do sexy toy store evaluations?" She shakes her head sadly but, thankfully, does not elaborate.

"No, but Mom offered to go with her on those."

Amy's face twists with agony. "Poor Amanda."

"Right. Mom has a kink or two she can lend."

"I don't need a kink!" Amanda insists, walking into my bedroom smelling like the orange air freshener spray we keep in there.

"Everyone needs a kink," Amy and I say in unison.

And it was like saying *Beetlejuice, Beetlejuice, Beetlejuice*, because my front door opens and in walks my mom.

"You summoned her!" Amanda hisses. She's holding her sandals again, and turns to my closet just as Mom walks into the scene. "You better have some nice shoes I can borrow."

Mom looks at Amanda's shoes and immediately whips around to look at Chuckles, who is staring into the mirror on the back of my bedroom door and hissing at that strange cat.

"You wore shoes with long laces around him?" Mom giggles and shakes her head slowly. "I'm so sorry."

"Why are *you* sorry?" I ask.

"That's my fault. Um . . ." Her brow furrows. "Actually, it's your father's fault. He wore that gladiator outfit that one time we got into this little role play where I pretended to be tied up for the Kraken to come and take me, and Chuckles panicked. He peed all over Jason's feet and I haven't been able to wear a pair of sandals with ankle laces ever since."

Amy freezes in the doorway.

"But Marie, the Kraken . . . why would you use that in a bedroom role play?" Amanda's muted voice calls back. She's buried in my closet. I see her ass poking out and I want to kick it.

"Don't provoke her! I don't want to hear!" Amy dashes out the door. I hear the apartment door slam. My fingers are in my ears as I say "tra-la-la-la-la" as loudly as I can to drown out whatever depravity-laden story Mom is oversharing.

Amanda's distinctly paling face tells me I need to keep up my verbal assault. Even Chuckles looks a shade or two lighter than usual.

"Shannon! Shannon! You can pull your fingers out of your ears," she says with exasperation, as if I am the transgressor.

Amanda mouths *Be careful*.

I pull my fingers out and Mom says, "You're coming to my yoga class on Friday." It's Tuesday, so I have three days to agree and then come up with a really lame excuse to back out. Agnes might rough me up in the alley if I show my face without Declan's ass.

"Okay," I say.

"And no excuses! Chuckles did not have a leg amputated, like you said last month to get out of coming."

Damn. Chuckles examines his front paw with a distinct expression of relief. Great. I'm going to come home to find he's used my jelly bean stash as a litter box, aren't I?

"Sorry, bud," I whisper to him from across the room. "I'll bring home some catnip. Please don't eat the computer cords again."

Amanda and I share one of those looks where a series of weird, covert gestures and eyebrow movements somehow translates into facial semaphore code. *Does Mom know about me and Declan and the Twitter mess?* is my basic question.

Seventy-two twitches and grimaces later, the answer is *no*.

Whew.

"Marie, we're very late for work," Amanda says. "How about I make us a coffee while Shannon showers?"

Mom's eyes narrow to black-smudged triangles. Whenever any of her daughters are too nice to her, she's suspicious, and Amanda's her fourth kid in her mind.

"Is Declan in the bedroom?" she says with glee. "Is that why you're acting so weird?"

I wish.

"If he were?" Amanda says. Ouch. Shoot me through the heart, but I see her point. Mom starts to back out slowly. It's not technically a lie, right?

Then she stops and looks at Amanda, hard. "If he's here, why are *you* in the bedroom?"

Amanda slowly, exquisitely, arches one eyebrow and stares Mom down. It's like Laura Prepon in *That '70s Show* and *Orange is the New Black* with a heaping dose of Angelina Jolie thrown in.

Mom's look of horror is beyond perfect. "I, um, uh, I have to go," she says quickly. We hear the apartment door slam and Chuckles gives Amanda an admiring look and lifts his front paw toward her like a high-five.

"I can't believe you implied we're having a threesome," I squeak out. But hot damn, it worked! I need to file that little strategy away next time Mom comes over and wants me to get a Brazilian or those pedicures where the fish eat all the dead skin.

"I can't believe some role play kink between her and your dad makes your cat piss all over my shoes."

"Touché."

Tears threaten to push through and I can't quite catch my breath. What if it's over before we really got started? So much is there with Declan, and I—

Amanda's steady hand presses into my shoulder. "If it's any consolation, the early reports are coming in from the credit unions and there is clear discrimination going on in at least two branches. The LGBT mortgage program will help weed that out. You might want a divorce, but—"

I stick my tongue out at her.

"—but we made a difference."

That makes me cry, finally. "Great. Can't even wallow in self-pity," I sniff. "I may have screwed up my one chance at happiness with a great guy, but we also made a difference and helped people."

"Don't look so glum."

I sigh. "I know. It's just . . . I don't regret doing the shop, but at the same time, let me feel what I feel. Okay? I can feel two conflicting emotions at the same time. It's called being human."

A few beats of silence stretch between us. And a handful of sniffles.

"Get your butt in the shower and let's go see Declan and figure this all out. The longer you cower in the bed, the stupider this gets. Don't let a Tweet dictate your life," she counsels.

"When did you become a philosopher?" I stalk off to the bathroom without waiting to hear her answer.

"When your cat turned my foot into a litter box." She taps Chuckles' extended paw and I swear he separates his little toes and gives a "peace out" sign.

"What if he . . . what if I . . . oh, God." My hands shake and my heart feels like it wants to run away and bury its head in a giant vat of double-chocolate brownie ice cream.

Amanda's sympathetic face comes into view through the hair curtain I have covering me. "The only way to know what Declan is thinking or feeling is to go see him."

"What if I've blown it?"

"You don't know that you did."

"Easter was so special."

"Then you have nothing to worry about," she declares. "No guy shows up for a holiday with the family and then ditches a woman because of a stupid tweet."

"Really?"

She shrugs. "I don't know. That sounded like a supportive thing to say."

"Too much honesty is not a good thing."

"No kidding." She sighs. "Why do you think I'm still single?"

I blink back my tears. "But not enough honesty gets you tweets from a woman who looks like something out of Madame Tussaud's wax museum."

My phone buzzes.

We both freeze.

It's Declan.

shopping
for a
billionaire

#4

chapter
one

DECLAN'S TEXT SAYS:
We'll talk

"That's it?" I gasp, Amanda closing her eyes slowly, as if someone reached over with fingertips and shut them, like on a corpse. It is apt; it feels like someone just died. I'm supposed to hop in the shower and get ready for work, but how do you do that when your entire life is imploding?

"He answered, at least." She reaches in behind the shower curtain and turns on the water for me. A part of me feels infantilized. I can turn on my own damn water. I don't need help. I know how to use a shower.

Another part of me is helpless and racked with a kind of cryogenic emotional freeze that renders me useless. She leaves the room and gently points to the phone.

"Answer back."

The door shuts like her eyelids did just a moment ago, though Chuckles manages to slip in through the inch-sized crack as Amanda leaves. Didn't cats accompany the pharaohs in ancient times as they were laid to rest in their burial crypts?

Something's dying right now, and as he snuggles up against my ankles without meowing, his presence calm and serene, I feel a deep disturbance inside. Chuckles is being nice to me?

This is *bad*.

Tremors fill my fingers as I pick up my phone and stare at his sparse text. Two words. I get two measly words? No replies until now, no acknowledgement of the cyber-mess that has made real life an emotional land mine for me.

Just . . . *We'll talk.*

I type back:

Okay. See you soon.

I hit Send with fingers vibrating so much they could be used as a sex toy prototype.

By the time I finish going through the motions and cleaning my hair and body, he's had plenty of opportunity to answer.

Nope. No text.

I'm all cried out and numb now, wondering how we could go from talking about finding each other and enjoying so much together to this coldness, this arctic freeze that doesn't even have an explanation. Not even a pseudo-explanation. We're dancing on broken glass and denying that it hurts. Ignoring the river of blood that lubricates the pain. Only maybe I'm the one feeling all the pain. Perhaps this is nothing to him. A blip. I'm someone he used to sleep with and all that's left is the final "It's not you . . ." conversation where he walks away and I disintegrate into a thousand shards of glass.

That he walks all over with bloody feet.

It's not that I really think he's that cold. In fact, the opposite: the man I have gotten to know over the past month isn't the man who is doing this right now. Two different men. Or—two different sides of the same man? Why do I have this long history of being surprised when people show a different side of themselves?

You would think I'd stop being so naïve, so childlike, being shocked when someone changes. I guess it's because I don't change. I am who I am (whoever that is . . .) and I'm what Josh calls a WYSIWYG—What You See Is What You Get. No hidden subtext.

Maybe, though, for Declan I'm a WYSINWYW—What You See Is Not What You Want.

I need to pull him aside and call it all out, to say what isn't being said. How do you do that when you don't even know what the other person is thinking? I'm no mind reader. I definitely don't want to be one, either, because *eww*. Can you imagine how quickly you'd learn how perverted everyone in the world really is?

And how judgmental?

I get plenty of perversion and judgment from my mom, thanks. I don't need more. If I get to have a superpower, mind-reading isn't what I want. I'd prefer a clitoris inside my vagina, thankyouverymuch.

Now *that's* a superpower.

Yet when I ask Declan what's going on, I get *We'll talk*? The sudden sub-zero temperature change from him is starting to look like the North Atlantic current being shut down.

Men. Can't live with them, can't shove an EpiPen in their groin and keep them.

"You ready?" Amanda calls out as I towel off my hair.

"You're still here?"

"I figured I'd drive you to the meeting."

"Because you think I can't drive?"

"Because I think this is going to be hard."

I stew over that one for a second, wondering why everyone thinks I'm a fragile porcelain doll. Then I realize I am. Right now, at least.

"Okay," I call out. "But we're taking your car. If I'm about to be dumped, it won't be while driving the Turdmobile."

"A girl's gotta have standards," she shouts back with a laugh.

IT'S AN ICEHOUSE IN here.

And the air conditioning isn't even on.

Unfortunately, Declan never responded to my text message, and he was also not anywhere near the hallway where I lingered like a seventh grader hoping to bump into her crush outside the band room instrument storage closet.

(What? Like you never did that . . .)

The players are the same, but the game has changed. James and Andrew sit on one side of the table, a glass of water in front of a third, empty chair. Amanda, Greg, and I are on the other side. No tension; James and Greg are in cordial conversation when Amanda and I join them. Greg came first to settle some details, and now the entire show begins.

Without Declan.

Andrew's giving me inscrutable looks. I seriously cannot tell whether he knows about the Jessica Asshat Coffin mess, and if he does, what he thinks. He looks like a slightly lighter version of Declan, with the same bone structure, a jaw that can go hard and resolute with anger or firmness as well as it can go soft and sweet with a smile.

But they're both impassive when it comes to expressing emotion in a business setting, and I suspect Andrew's like his dad in that respect as well. James just looks kind of dismayed with the world all the time. Like everyone is going to disappoint him anyhow, so why bother?

As if I said that aloud, the elder McCormick cuts his eyes my way and gives me a long look. His eyes narrow to triangles, so much like Declan's that I feel that strange tightness in my chest. Not anaphylactic shock, but something close to it. I think it's the feeling of having my organs removed from my body by my own stupidity.

Starting with my heart.

James calls the meeting to order. Amanda and I share frantic looks meant to convey one singular question:

Did I sleep with a billionaire in a limo only to have it all ruined by pretending to be gay and running into my ex's mother, who turned to a social media whore in an attempt to reclaim her son's balls?

And the answer:

Pretty much.

Time machines are *soooooo* underrated. If I had one and was given one chance to go back in time and fix anything I wanted, I would go back to the moment Greg announced those gay prejudice credit union shops and say *no*.

(Yes, I know I'm supposed to say I'd go back in time and kill Hitler or stop the burning of Joan d'Arc, but I'm kind of shallow right now.)

No time machine. No giant sinkhole to swallow me up. Not even a psychotic cat who can pee on James' foot and give me a reason to escape. Only—

Declan.

He walks into the meeting and gives everyone a gracious smile with frozen eyes so cold you could use them in a camp cooler for a long weekend and still have cold beer.

"I apologize for being late. I was detained."

"You make it sound like you had no choice, son," James says with a low chuckle. Andrew and Declan share a look that reminds me of Amanda and me, minus the lip biting and grimaces.

"It felt like it," Declan growls.

James leans back, clearly in the catbird seat, and it's dick-waving time now. "If you're going to run the entire marketing department for an international corporation, you have to accept that some cultures handle the standard business lunch quite differently." He shoots Greg a knowing wink.

Greg winks back like a drag queen with a stuck eyelash. "Quite differently." He's trying to fit in, and I know that, but my sympathy lies with the women whose faces are pressed flat against the corporate glass ceiling, with a stripper's pastie-covered nipples smashed on the other side of the glass as we all try to pretend there's nothing to see here, folks.

"Is this 'business lunch' an issue that all marketing professionals need to deal with?" I keep my voice as even as possible, but even I detect the officiousness in it. Amanda gives me a sharp look, while Greg rubs his mouth like there's something in there. His foot, maybe.

Declan's in the middle of pulling files from his briefcase, but as my voice fills the air he moves more slowly, lips twitching. Aha. I nailed it. I'm not jealous—whatever "standard business lunch" and "some cultures" are code for doesn't matter. I'm imagining strippers as a side dish along with sixteen-ounce medium-rare tenderloins and the dripping butter sauce for their lobster being poured over augmented breasts on a stage.

James and Declan share a long look. Declan gives a nudge of his head, in deference or—perhaps—to allow the old man to make a fool of himself.

Either way, it's about to get real.

And it just got a lot colder in here.

"I would say that all vice presidents of marketing who work with a variety of international clients will eventually be taken on a more . . . salacious expedition at least once or twice in a career." James' cocky smile looks like a caricature of Declan's. "The higher you fly, the greater the lengths you go to please a client and close the deal."

Greg looks a bit sick. *I'm* his closer. What does this mean? Do I need to cultivate a taste for pole dancing?

"What about a female vice president? Would she be expected to attend a . . ." I bite my words off carefully and spit them out in slow, snappy chunks. " . . . sa-la-cious 'standard business lunch' experience, which, I assume, means hookers and blow?"

Andrew is taking a drink of water and does a spit take like something out of a Jimmy Fallon clip. Most of the water in his mouth lands on Amanda's cleavage across the table, which makes her jump to her feet.

It is so much easier to take on the client's asshattery than to deal with the subtext in the room, and James is giving me fabulous fodder for my self-righteous streak. Way easier than dealing with that tight-chest feeling about losing Declan, who has managed to avoid eye contact with me.

"I hardly think you're in a position to comment on salacity and business relations, Ms. Jacoby." James' eyes are those of a hawk, coming in for the kill. "How *was* that helicopter ride, son?" He doesn't look at Declan. His eyes are entirely on me.

I have a choice as all the oxygen in the room disappears, along with any hope of a relationship with Declan, or of an ongoing career for me in the bigger Boston corporations. I can back off and go home and cry and eat pint after pint of ice cream and suck down Hot 'n Sour soup like it's about to be banned like Sriracha sauce, or I can stand up to the big bad CEO who decided I'm an ant and his words are a magnifying glass in a nice patch of sunlight.

"Dad." One word. Declan's single word is a nuclear bomb.

The heat coming from Declan's anger can keep a small village in Greenland warm for the winter.

"Oh, please, Dec. The driver and the pilot told me. It's not as if she's *really* the lesbian that people on that Twiterlicious thing are saying."

Andrew's wiping his face with a handkerchief and offers one to Amanda while giving her a speculative look that I'd normally pay way more attention to, but I'm in the middle of soul death, so I'm kind of distracted. Where's my Mom with a good butt plug story about now? I'd even welcome Agnes and Corrine's nonagenarian cat fights.

"Good play, Ms. Jacoby." He leans forward on the table. "I know from Declan's glowing descriptions of you that you're about as gay as I am poor. That tells me you held on to your assumed identity quite thoroughly so that you could perform the function assigned to you by the client."

"What does that have to do with anything?" Declan's voice could cut diamonds.

"It means she's the perfect candidate for corporate espionage."

chapter
two

G REG'S TURN TO DO a spit take. "Is that business
guru speak for mystery shopping these days?"

James laughs. How can the man laugh when he's
managed to alienate and/or piss off every person in the room
except for Andrew, who appears to be trying to decide whether
to be alienated, pissed off, or to ogle Amanda's low-ish-cut silk
blouse?

For the record, his penis appears to win.

Family trait.

Wait a minute. James knows I slept with Declan in the limo
and in the helicopter, and what the hell, let's throw in the lighthouse part, too. He knows about the credit union mystery shop
and me and Amanda. He knows about Jessica's Twittergate
mess. What the hell *doesn't* this man know?

"No, Greg. Corporate espionage means I'd like for Ms.
Jacoby to be assigned to evaluate The Fort—"

Amanda's sharp intake of horrified breath makes Andrew
perk up as her chest lifts.

"—and also Le Chateau."

Now she shrieks. It's a fairly professional-sounding shriek,
but still. "Le Chateau is your competitor! Why would she mystery shop—oh . . ." She closes down to neutral as fast as she
ramped up to livid. It's impressive, and I'd appreciate it more if
Declan weren't shredding my heart.

Scribbling furiously, her next words come out like machine
gun bullets. "By having the same person evaluate both high-end

properties, you get an even sense of the failings and mastery in each."

"Indeed. And we need someone who can hold their cover," James says with a cordial tone that makes me question my sanity. Wasn't he just being an asshole? How am I supposed to keep track of the villain in here if he keeps changing his personality?

"*I* held my cover," Amanda mutters. Greg gives her a dirty look. Amanda gives him double back. He blanches.

"Yes, you did," James notes. "And after Shannon successfully finishes both properties, you can be the next evaluator in three months' time. Your own mastery did not go unnoticed."

"But *you're* not really gay, right?" Andrew blurts out, his eyes on Amanda's breasts.

Awkward.

James rolls his eyes. "My sons need to retake their sexual harassment training, I see."

"It's not sexual harassment," Declan and I say in unison.

Oh, thank God. He understands. He understands! I close my eyes and inhale slowly, then open them to give him a big, friendly, warm, loving grin.

He stares back with green ice cubes.

Uh.

"The mess is unconventional, I'll admit," James adds, pushing contracts to Greg. "But Ms. Jacoby isn't a known entity in the circles we inhabit—"

Translation: I'm a nobody, so he doesn't have to worry that I'll be recognized at a competitor's luxury property even though Jessica has been tweeting about me to all the cyberspace rubberneckers in Boston.

"—and I trust the evaluations will give us valuable insight into gaining a competitive edge."

"In other words, you're giving me more responsibility, and expanding the contract with Consolidated Evalu-shop?" I ask, and this time it's my eyes that are on Declan while asking James the question.

"Yes," Declan answers me. Not James. "You're very good at living a double life and are quick on your feet when it comes to lying." He cuts his eyes away. "That will suit you well in business."

No. *No no no no no.*

Amanda pivots and coughs, the strain getting to her. Andrew's eyes ping between me, Declan, her chest, and his dad. Greg just looks constipated, eyebrows bunched like a caterpillar in heat as he reviews contracts that have been read so many times they might as well be the Bible.

"And," James adds, stuffing folders into his briefcase, clearly done, "how's business?"

The spear aimed from an icy stretch of glacier that is his heart right now hits its target with pinpoint precision. That's what Jessica tweeted to Declan.

"May I speak with you in the hallway?" I hiss at Declan, grabbing his forearm. He turns into a marble statue, though emotion flickers in his eyes. His Adam's apple bobs as he swallows, and his stiff muscles radiate mixed signals.

"If you wish." He shakes off my hand, though not with an angry movement. More with a cold precision that somehow is worse.

"We'll finish negotiations," James says, eyes twinkling, as if he's accomplished something. "And it's good to see you walking around, Ms. Jacoby. Last I heard from Declan, you were bed bound."

Another sex joke? Are you kidding me? My tongue loosens in my mouth, ready to lash him, when even the venerable James McCormick has the decency to turn red with embarrassment and backtrack.

"I meant your allergic reaction to the stings. That you were in the hospital. In a hospital bed," he stammers. "My son was very worried."

"Your son was the only reason I'm here," I say gently. The amusement is gone from his expression, replaced by a kind of sad intrigue, his body uptight and loose at the same time as if it can't make up its mind.

But control and authority prevail as his mask reappears and he turns away from me with a dismissive wave. "I'm glad

Declan could do what he needed to do in a crisis. That proves he's matured."

Andrew's neck snaps toward his dad, a red fury pouring into his skin so fast it seems he'll burst. I turn toward Declan to find him in the threshold, one hand curled into a gripping claw on the door's trim, close to snapping the wood in half.

What the hell is going on? This conversation suddenly has nothing to do with me and Declan, or with Twitterhead Coffin, or with my credit union shop. There's a subtext here I don't understand, and it stings.

Declan lets go of the door with a loud smack of his palm against the wood and slowly, with a little too much control, moves out. I can't even admire the undulating grace of his anger or ask him why he and his dad are speaking in Angry Man Code, a language that seems designed to neuter the other man and stuff his balls down his throat.

But this isn't just macho bullcrap. James' comment about Declan and crises and maturing resonates somewhere inside Declan, but he's wound so tight, and I'm skating on thin ice already.

There's no way to be open and just ask what's going on.

He spins around so abruptly that I stagger and fall against the wall, banging my hip on a piece of trim. "What do we need to discuss?"

How could the same man who told me I was beautiful, who put his mouth in places where only speculums have gone, look at me like I'm a gnat that should be swatted out of existence?

"Can we have coffee and talk?" I can't think of what else to say.

He just blinks. No answer. I stare back, unyielding, even as my mind screams in childlike sadness. Something is broken, and it's not just me. I didn't break it. He's not telling me something and it's between us, without shape or form, taking up all the known room, and yet it has no name.

"Coffee?" He makes a strangled huffing sound. "How about at one of my stores?" His voice is acid. "I hear we're testing a new peppermint mocha with wasabi syrup. Oh, wait—you would know better than I do."

I actually flinch and pull back as if he's slapped me. If he had, it would be easier. "I-I-I just want to talk. About the pretending to be gay thing, and the Jessica Coffin thing, and—"

"I know you're not gay." His voice carries a bit as he punches that sentence out with a tongue made of steel, his face so tight you could turn it into a drum.

"I guessed as much. It shouldn't have been hard to figure out."

He makes a sour face and glances at an imaginary watch he isn't wearing. Either he really does have another meeting or he's in a hurry to be done with me, and the latter feels like ice picks in my gut.

"Shannon, I don't know what your game is. Maybe the other night was all acting—"

"No! I swear! No game!" An ominous layer of straight-up terror begins to cover me like a blanket that brings no comfort.

"You're paid to act," he says viciously. "*Act*. You're paid to pretend, right? To go into a business setting and pretend to be something you aren't, all while observing every nuance, every detail. You're a chameleon who changes to meet the expectations of the people in that setting, with the ruthless efficiency of an international spy." His breath is heavy and full of anger. "You're quite proud of it."

"But not with *you*," I plead. "Never with you."

"How am I supposed to know? You're a bit like the boy who cried wolf, honey."

My head ricochets back. Honey. That's what he called me in the hospital.

"You told that blowhard's mother you're just dating me to close a deal. Well, you did." He motions toward the closed door. "My dad just gave you a plum new assignment. Your company makes more money, we get a crack corporate spy, and everyone goes home happy and satisfied."

He's baring his teeth now in a smile that is so ferociously barren of compassion or caring that it mesmerizes me. I can't turn away, but at the same time I want to curl up into a ball and cry.

"You really think that about me?" I whisper quietly. Mercifully, the tears are behind a wall of summoned self-righteousness. I need it right now. I know every word he says is dead on in its own twisted way, but I can't let it be true, because there's a larger Truth with a capital T right next to his smaller truth.

"What else am I supposed to think? You told me yourself in the lighthouse that you're 'shopping for a billionaire.' You told your ex-boyfriend's mother that you're dating me to close a business deal, and some screwed-up game of grown-up telephone ends on Twitter with a high-society wannabe trying to embarrass me on a social media platform so silly it uses bird metaphors."

I snort nervously.

Pity fills his eyes. Oh, no. This is end game. I know this look, because it's the same expression Steve had when he dumped me. *No. No. No.*

"I can't do this, Shannon."

No. Please.

"You're just too . . . much."

Great. So he lied to me about loving my abundant body.

"Too many layers to tease through, too many what-ifs, too many half-truths and un-truths—"

Wait! He's not slamming my curves. He's slamming my integrity! Hold on there, buddy. You can make fun of my fat (which he didn't), but—

"That is bull," I thunder back. A receptionist at a desk at the end of the hall cranes her neck forward, peering at us. Like a turtle, she snaps it back, hidden.

When Steve dumped me I just sniffled and took it, curled into myself on a park bench near my apartment, sitting on the lawn of a local college. No way am I cowering now. If this is over, it'll be over on my terms. Or, at least, I won't go down without a defense. A fight.

Words.

"There's bull here, all right." He's breathing hard, and if this were a sitcom or a Nora Ephron movie this is the part where we'd shout at each other and then he'd grab my face, hard, and kiss me like I've never been kissed before, until my muffled protests are drained out of me by the sudden clarity that only hot lips can provide.

"You spend your life trying to get everyone else to believe you're something you're not, Shannon. And when you're not play-acting, you're begging for validation. You change yourself to become whatever it is you think everyone wants you to be." He runs an angry hand through his thick hair, the dark waves spreading across his forehead as pained eyes finally show me a tiny bit of the tempest inside him.

A mail clerk trundles by with a squeaky cart. We're blocking the hall. He stops and waits, staring dumbly at us, one finger in the air like he's about to interrupt in the geekiest way possible. He reminds me of Mark J., and that? THAT fact is the one that makes the tears almost pour out, because it reminds me of the day I met Declan, of how Mr. Sex in a Suit looked that morning, so crisp and unknown, and how in the short expanse of one month I could go from hot, liquid lust for a guy I don't know to this.

Arguing in a hallway at work about whether I'm sincere or not.

"You don't know me." It's the only sentence I can form right now.

"You didn't give me a chance! I took a chance on you, and you just—" Some primal emotion without name blinds me. "Which Shannon am I supposed to date—the one lying in the men's room, the one lying at the credit union, the one lying about her allergy?" His voice breaks.

Screech. The mail dude nudges the cart, then jumps, like he's scared himself.

I scooch out of the way and the squeaky cart rolls on by.

"I didn't lie about my allergy! And what the hell do you mean you 'took a chance' on me?" I can think of *plenty* of ways to interpret that remark, and not a single one is good.

His voice feels like a sharp blade being dragged just

gently enough across my throat to leave a scrape. "You lied by omission."

Declan's lips are tight and his eyes are anywhere but on me. There's nothing I can say, is there? He's decided in his own rat brain that he's done with me. All this "which Shannon are you?" crap is just that—crap. He's hiding something, and it's pretty damn obvious. To me.

I was good for a screw in the limo and the lighthouse and . . . well, for that, but I'm not good enough to date in front of Daddy. He's just like Steve, only the stakes, and dollar signs, are bigger.

Did I mess up? Sure. But his reaction is so utterly out of proportion with the facts.

Plus—I'm done. Done explaining myself to irrational people who seem to care only about proving they're right. If who I really am doesn't fit into his image of who I am, then he can go suck it.

"I can't make you believe me," I say with a voice that is surprisingly even. "I don't want to."

That makes him look at me. *Really* look at me. The first sign of hesitation flashes in his eyes.

"In fact, if you can't even listen to me try to explain what's happened over the past day, then we never had one iota of what you claimed we had."

His eyes soften.

"You said a lot of things to me, too, Declan. And I remember every one of them. And you know what I'm remembering most of all?"

He just stares at me.

"When we were kissing at the restaurant that first night, you said: *He has no power over you. He discarded you. Don't give him that power back. You are worth so much more.*"

Declan's turn to look like he's been slapped.

My own eyes narrow into tight bands as I take my time, letting his own words thrown back at him sink in. His jaw grinds but he says nothing, though his eyes are so conflicted.

"You know what? I *am* worth so much more. You don't want

to hear me out? Too bad. Coffee offer rescinded. Deal off and over. Everything's off the table. Good day, Declan. Have a nice life."

"Shannon," he says as if making an involuntary sound. It's not a groan or a growl or even a question. Just a statement.

"I'm either authentic and real or I'm fake and cunning. I'm one or the other. You don't even get to choose anymore, Declan. You took that choice away from yourself."

I turn on my heel to leave, and then casually throw my final words over my shoulder.

"You can't have *both*."

"I don't want both. I want the real Shannon. And since *you* don't know who that is . . ."

A tingling red ball of rage takes over. Steve dumped me because I wouldn't turn myself into a pretzel and *stop* being myself. Declan insists that the "real" me, whatever that is, isn't enough either. I can't win.

So I'm done playing.

"You know what, Declan?"

Silence from him. Just that cold, green resolve in eyes that used to smile on me.

"Go validate yourself." It takes everything in me not to give him the bird as I walk away.

chapter
three

"THIS IS THE PART where I'm supposed to say he's an asshole and she's so much better off without him," Amy whispers to Amanda as I go through my seventh tissue in five minutes, "but I can't honestly say that."

I am on my bed, wearing an old pair of velour pants that I think my grandma left at Mom's house before she died. My torn pink shirt—the same one I wore the day I met Declan—is technically *on* my body, but I've been wearing it for three days straight now. It could animate of its own accord and walk away. Can bacteria become sentient? If so, my shirt has become a form of artificial intelligence.

And I smell like bacon and cookie dough. Don't ask.

"Whoever said breakups are a time for honesty?" Amanda whispers back.

"But I can't even lie about Declan!" Amy insists. "The guy's really perfect."

Amanda murmurs something in agreement.

"I can hear you!" I wail. "And you're right! That's why this hurts so much!"

Amanda rushes over with the half-melted pint of ice cream. I can't even bring myself to take a bite. That's how bad this is—a breakup where I don't eat myself into oblivion.

It's the Breakupocalypse.

"Get it away from me," I mutter. Chuckles comforts me by settling in my lap and rubbing his puckered asshole up and down my arm. Nice. Not only have I not showered in two days, and I can't touch ice cream, but now I smell like cat butt.

I wonder if I feed him coffee cherries if I could make cat poop coffee from it and—

Then I remember Declan is the one who told me about cat poop coffee. I can't even look at Chuckles' butt without being reminded of the biggest mistake I ever made.

I make another mistake by saying that aloud. "Chuckles' butt reminds me of Declan." I sniff.

"She's turning into our mother," Amy whispers to Amanda without moving her lips.

"So it's bad enough I lose Declan, now I'm turning into *Mooooooooom*," I wail. "That's like learning your dog died and you have a bot fly larva growing on your labia."

Amanda peels my laptop out of my fingers. "Someone's been watching way too many zit-popping videos on YouTube today," she mutters.

"She's been holed up in here all weekend, logging in to work and doing reports. She says she doesn't need to step outside for anything for at least nine days because of a batch of new, over-eager mystery shoppers who will do all the in-person work for her and she just has to manage paperwork," Amy tells Amanda.

"When did you get a penis?" I ask my sister.

All the eyebrows in the room except mine hit the ceiling. "When did I what?" Amy asks.

"You mansplained that perfectly. Over-explaining something that didn't need to be over-explained, with just enough conde-scension to make me hate you. Perfecto!"

"She's losing it," Amanda murmurs out of one corner of her mouth.

"I already lost it. Lost him. Lost my dignity. Lost . . . every-thing." I lean forward in a slumping motion. A cloud of fleas bounces around me.

I really am ripe.

Or Chuckles is infested.

"He's a shallow asshole!" Amanda says with about as much sincerity as Mom telling me she really liked my hair when I dyed it purple in eleventh grade.

"He's not. He's so damn amazing, and I—he—we . . ." I snatch my laptop back from Amanda and pop it open. "I just don't know what the hell happened. None of it makes any sense. All I know is it's all Jessica Coffin's fault."

I navigate to a zit video that features a man who appears to have a white-nippled breast growing out of his love handle. A woman bearing a heated pair of tweezers and wearing purple latex gloves performs backyard surgery while a group of relatives sit around a picnic table eating ambrosia salad.

My people. These are my people. This video will be—

"AUGH! GROSS! TURN THAT CRAP OFF!" Amy screams. Chuckles gets up and sits on my keyboard, making the video fast forward with no sound, then pause. No satisfying mashed potato goo coming out of the skin of people who view pus as entertainment.

People like . . . *me.*

"What have I become?" I moan. "I'm one of those weirdos who watches zit videos."

"You're a woman who doesn't understand why her asshole ex did what he did," Amy soothes.

"And a weirdo," Amanda adds.

"That was last year. That was Steve. How can this happen to me again? How? Something is wrong with me. I'm damaged somehow. Invisibly damaged. I'm doomed to never understand why men flee from me. Why I'm not good enough. What the fatal flaw inside me is that drives men away."

"It might be the lack of showers," Amanda says softly.

I throw Chuckles at her and walk away.

"That was not supportive," Amy hisses.

"I was about to shove Vicks VapoRub up my nostrils."

"So it wasn't just me?" Amy sounds relieved.

"I CAN HEAR YOU!"

"Then go shower!" they say in unison.

"A few more emails," I mutter. A batch of new mystery shopper applications has come in. I routinely process them. It's a formality, just a series of emails I have to open and read because—

"Marie Jacoby?" I shout. Does one of the emails really say

my mother's name on it?

Amanda presses her lips together to hide a smirk.

"Mom is now a registered mystery shopper with Consolidated Evalu-shop? What the hell?"

"She wanted to do the marital aid shops, and some others, so I walked her through the steps for certification." In order to get the really good mystery shopping jobs, you have to take an online certification course. It's not hard, but it's no cake walk, either.

Pay a fee, take a test and boom—certified for a year.

"Mom did all that? It's bad enough Carol does some of my shops, but MOM?"

"She said that if the company's paying for her to try out new warming gels, sign her up."

"I refuse to be her supervisor," I say flatly.

Amanda looks alarmed, and then we both find the answer. "Josh!"

"Josh is a techie," Amy says.

"He handles overflow," I explain.

"Josh is so cute."

"He's gay."

"I know!"

"So Josh can take over with Mom," I say, forwarding her info to him. There is no way in hell I am mystery shopping nipple clamps with my mother. The sad part is, she'd be better at those shops than anyone else I know.

Sad.

"Quit stalling and get in the shower." Amanda takes the laptop from me and shuts it firmly.

"I showered regularly for Declan!" I protest. "That's not why he dumped me." The steam rises from the shower head as I strip down. Amy and Amanda are in the threshold, like I'm on some sort of watch I don't know about. Are they worried I'll harm myself? The worst damage I could inflict would be eating two entire packages of peanut-butter-stuffed Oreos, and if they think their presence will prevent that, well . . .

Too late.

"Jessica Coffin has some blame here," Amy says in an ominous voice. "Poking him on Twitter."

"He never cared about Twitter," I call out. The rhythm and flow of cleansing myself helps. Lather, rinse, lather, rinse, conditioner, leave it on. Soap and clean the filth off me. Rinse. It's a ritual cleansing. Normally I'd cry in the shower, but my sister and best friend are outside sharing theories about Why Declan Dumped Shannon, and while there's plenty of fodder for material, the way they're talking is such a relief.

Because they're just as perplexed as I am.

The lesbian thing? He knows I'm not. His fury at thinking I'd been using him to climb the corporate ladder and land a big client? C'mon. Couldn't he tell by how my body, my heart, my lips, and hands responded to him that I was—am—sincerely falling for him?

Is he a commitmentphobe? Am I just a fat chick he decided to bone because he could? Does he harbor the same snotty pretense that Steve has about wanting a more refined woman? Did my bee allergy turn him off? *What what what?*

My mind is my own worst enemy, looping frantically through every possible scenario to understand what my heart already knows:

He's gone.

But why?

And if I can't have him back, then how can I get through the minutes that become hours, the hours that become days, and the days that roll out and on and on without sharing a look with him? A hug or a kiss, or a casual wink that holds so much promise?

Who else on the planet could I meet with my hands down a toilet and have them ask me out on a date?

(One without a toilet fetish, I mean. There are 588 people on FetLife looking for women who put their hands in toilets. That's not an imaginary number—I checked.)

I turn on the waterproof radio Amy uses when she showers. "Ain't No Sunshine" pours loud and proud through the tiny bathroom, and *that?*

That gives me permission to cry in the shower. Big, fat, ugly tears of pain and abandon. Of promises that just died, of hope that was murdered, of the sound of his name rushing in to fill all the cracks in my mind.

Declan.

How do you drive away the very thing you once welcomed so eagerly just weeks ago?

You start by letting it leak out through your eyes.

I hear the door close quietly and I cry under the hot water for as long as I have tears. My mouth is so dry it should have sand in it. Maybe this is how I try to block out the last few days: death by intentional dehydration via tears.

A soft knock on the door shocks me. "What? You don't barge in on me anymore? Oh, dear sweet Jesus, am I that bad off that you're walking on eggshells around me?"

"Mom called," Amy says.

"And?" I shout, turning the water off.

"She wants you to go to her yoga class tonight, after you're done with work. Says it will be good for you."

As I dry off, I groan. "All those old ladies will ask where Declan is!"

"Think of it as a Golden Girls gripefest."

"That's not helping."

"Mom will take you out for ice cream afterwards."

"Not helping either." I am sliding my underwear on over my hips and it appears they have shrunk.

"It's really bad," Amy says to Amanda.

"I can hear you through the door, you know! Those cheap hollow core pieces of crap Dad's always complaining about are about as effective at hiding your comments as Mom is at being tactful."

"Yoga. 7:15. That's the message."

"Fine!" I choke out, talking to the steam. "I'll meet her! But I'm getting toffee *allllll* over my double chocolate chip ice cream and she has to tolerate the crunching!" I shout.

"I'll text her for you so she can bring ear plugs."

I make a sound of disgust so deep in my throat I think I've

inherited a hairball from Chuckles.

"Amanda and I are leaving now," Amy declares.

"But I'll be back tomorrow!" Amanda shouts.

"Of course you will," I call back. "You have to deconstruct my failure."

"With pad Thai! My treat!" she shouts back. I hear the front door close.

Yoga class, huh?

An image of Declan's tight, muscled ass in workout clothes at the only yoga class he attended makes my heart race, my mouth feel like sandpaper, and parts farther south get moist. Moister than they are from the shower. And then the tears return.

One of the hardest parts about breaking up with someone is that moment when you realize they will never, ever touch you again. Not once. Not one stroke, one love pat, one kiss, one lick, one thrust—nothing. Dry and barren defines your new relationship, and the deep intensity, the push and pull, the dance that was all-consuming in getting to know them and defining and redefining boundaries, it's all . . . gone.

Just gone.

All done.

Over and out.

Forever.

I'm never going to have Declan lace his fingers through mine. *Never* rest his palm on my ass and squeeze. *Never* thread his fingers through my hair and tug gently as he kisses me with such urgency you'd think we had to make love before the house stopped burning.

Never.

Never is a long time.

Never makes me cry again.

Never is the loneliest word.

Never.

chapter
four

W HEN I ARRIVE AT Mom's yoga class, the room is at
capacity. Packed. Sixty women and one older man are
in the room. I do a double take at the man.

"Fire marshal," Mom explains. I jump and make a little
sound of surprise, because she's like a vampire. So swift I didn't
realize she was there.

"Fire marshal?"

"There might be too many people in the room. Someone
called him in."

"What's going on? Is Sting here or something? Willem
Dafoe? Alec Baldwin's wife?"

"Ha ha. Hilaria Baldwin. She's a famous yoga instructor, but
nope! None of those people are the reason." Mom beams at me
and looks around behind me. "Where's Declan?"

Ah. Now I get it. Hoo boy. Mom has a thousand-dollar yoga
class and I get to be the bearer of bad news. What a great way to
get restoration.

"He's not here."

"Running late?"

"No. Not coming. We broke up." Oh, those last words. They
feel, literally, like last words. Someone should shake some holy
water on me and I'll just go into Savasana and everything can
slip away.

Not really. No guy is worth that.

"You broke up with a billionaire? Are you insane? They don't
grow on trees!"

The image of Declan hanging from a branch, sweet and ripe and ready to be plucked, isn't helping.

"I'm . . . sorry? I'm not sure what to say." Tears threaten the edges of my eyes. *No no no.* Can't cry in front of a group of women drooling to stare at my ex-boyfriend's butt.

"Oh, honey!" Mom's trying to be supportive at the same time that she's freaking out on the inside, because Declan was obviously her Big Draw.

"I'm not leaving!" I hear Agnes shout to the poor fire marshal, who looks a bit panicked.

"No one has to leave, ma'am," he says. The guy looks just enough like Dad to make me look again. "But I do need to ask that the class be capped at seventy people, and that the two exits remain open at all times."

"Who called him?" I cock a suspicious eyebrow at Agnes as I try to change the subject.

"Probably Agnes. I'll bet she hoped he'd clear the room and she could sneak in to get the prime spot behind Declan. She's offering an entire unlimited class card for two months if people will back off."

"Who knew a billionaire's butt was so valuable," I crack, and then . . . I really crack. A tight ball of sorrow fills my throat and my ears burn. The tears come now and Mom's arms are around me, one hand smoothing my hair, messing up the ponytail.

"Oh, Shannon, it's going to be okay. It will. I don't know what to say right now," she adds, twisting her head and looking helplessly around the room.

"I know. I didn't want to tell you, but—"

"I want to know the rest. Really. I want to know the entire story, but right now . . ."

I wipe the tears off my face with a little yoga towel. "Gotcha." I sniff and compose myself.

And then:

"SHANNON!" Jesus, Agnes has some strong lungs for a woman who looks like a desiccated Hobbit. "Where's Declan?" The leer on her face as she says his name takes three decades off her.

"He's not here. Sorry," I peep.

Silence. All shuffling and whispers and movement halts.

"Not here. Running late?"

Good God.

"No," I say, extending the word with a tone of contrition. "He's just not coming. Sorry."

"Why are you sorry?" Corrine asks. "You're not him. You have nothing to be sorry about."

And that makes the waterworks come pouring out.

A sudden rush of women surround me, hands patting my back, wrapped around my shoulders, soothing me. Out of the corner of my eye I see a few women scowl and trickle out of the room.

The fire marshal is noticeably relieved.

Mom is in the middle of the group. Their hands and throaty sounds of comfort are so kind that I can't hold back. Grief and fear and reproach and regret pour out of me in a string of sobs so disjointed they sound like a new modern music composition.

And then the questions begin. Oh, the questions.

"Did he cheat on you? I read an article in *Science News* about how men with higher status cheat on their mates more than men with lower social status and income. So maybe you need to aim lower."

Aim lower?

Corrine jostles Agnes hard enough for the two to look like bone-thin weeble-wobbles, frantically grasping at each other to avoid falling. Two other women in the group help them to stay upright.

"That's silly," Corrine grouses. "I've known men who were gas station attendants making minimum wage who were cheaters. You don't need to be a billionaire."

"He didn't cheat on me," I say, sighing. Every attempt to catch Mom's eye is met with the careful avoidance Mom has honed with the care of a neurosurgeon removing a tumor with tendrils that spread out like the Flying Spaghetti Monster.

"Bad in bed?" Agnes asks. Every eyebrow is arched now. All breathing has paused. Enraptured, the crowd slowly closes in as if I'm about to spill the salacious details.

"Uh, no."

One big exhale. "Good. Last thing I need is to have that fantasy destroyed."

What?

"If you're going to date a hot, rich man he'd better be good in bed, too. Otherwise, the myth is as boring as sleeping with a guy who thinks taking out the garbage for you is foreplay and whose idea of cuddling is to reach over you afterward to grab the *TV Guide*."

"Ladies!" Mom claps her hands. It's the sound of rescue. "Time to get started." She looks like a blonde Michelle Bachmann teaching pre-schoolers. Crazy eyes and big smiles abound.

"Wait, Marie," Agnes shouts. She's wearing magenta Lycra bike shorts and a t-shirt that says [insert funny saying].

Seriously—that's what it says. Just the brackets and "insert funny saying." I like Agnes more and more every time I see her. "We need to know more about Declan. Why did you two break up?"

Mom ignores her. "Some of you have already met her, but this is my middle daughter, Shannon. She's the one who dated a billionaire and then she pretended to be a lesbian for her job and got outed."

Oh. My. God.

The old woman next to me pats my hand. "It gets better, dear."

"Lesbians?" another old woman sniffs. "We didn't have those when I was younger."

"Oh, she's not really gay. She just acts like it when she has to do mystery shops. And when she ruins her life." Mom fluffs her hair and turns to her iPod, poking the screen. Languid music fills the air, but it's not enough to stop the lambs from screaming in my head.

Corrine's face lights up. "If he thinks you're a lesbian, then here's your solution: call your wife and call Declan and offer him a threesome."

Disturbing murmurs of assent fill the air. Even the fire marshal is listening now.

Especially the fire marshal.

"Every man wants two women at once," Agnes adds.

"We tried that once," Mom says. The entire crowd turns its focus to her. While it's a relief to be out from under scrutiny, having Mom talk about her and Dad getting it on with another woman is about as much fun as going to a feminist rally with Robin Thicke.

"You did?" someone asks. The fire marshal is now leaning against the wall. Pretty soon I expect to see him smoking a cigarette and talking about how this was the best capacity check he's ever had.

"We were going to go to one of those meet-up things where you find other people online who have the same, uh . . . tastes." Mom makes actual eye contact with me for a second and it appears—sweet Jesus!—even she has an oversharing limit.

"What happened?" I ask, turning the tables.

"Jason chickened out." *Not you?* I want to ask.

"Not you?" Agnes asks. If I were standing closer to her I'd give her a fist bump.

"I . . . well, anyhow," she says, weirdly avoiding the question. "We just bought one of those 'real dolls' and had at it."

The entire room is struck dumb.

"You had sex with a doll?" Agnes finally asks.

"This alone is worth the seventeen dollar class fee," Corrine whispers to a group of shocked women.

"*I* didn't have sex with it. But . . ."

"Dad did?" I squeak. Brain bleach. Brain bleach. You cannot un-hear that.

She claps her hands twice. "Topic change! Let's start out in Child's Pose."

"You can't just cut us off in the middle of something that salacious! How many of us here have had husbands who humped a woman-shaped version of water wings?" Corrine shouts.

Three women raise their hands.

Kink is the new black.

"This is supposed to be restorative yoga!" I hiss to the group, eyes blazing and on Mom. "I did not come here under duress to listen to people talk about their partners humping plastic sex dolls."

"Well, dear," Agnes huffs, "we didn't come here to listen to you tell us how you destroyed a fantastic relationship with a billionaire with an ass so sweet you could hang it on a wall at the Museum of Fine Arts."

More murmurs of assent.

"So no one is getting what they want today!" Mom says in a too-cheerful voice. "Let's forget about kinky sex and settle in to taking a nice, meditative breathing session."

Groans of dissent.

As we crawl on our mats, Agnes leans over and says in a scratchy voice, "Make sure the next boyfriend is eye candy, too, and I'll buy you a new pair of yoga pants.'

"The poor woman lost Boston's hottest eligible bachelor, Agnes. We should buy her a consolation prize."

"A vibrator that smells like money?"

That was Corrine. I just . . . I can't sit here and talk about sex toys with a woman who looks like my second grade teacher. Can't.

Won't.

"And now we relax," Mom intones as deep chime tones fills the air.

Yeah.

Right.

chapter
five

"**Y**OU *DID* LOSE A billionaire," Mom says as she joins me, sitting at the booth at the local ice cream parlor, my spoon digging into a puddle of caramel and marshmallow sauce that is about as viscous as any salacious fluid I've ever put in my mouth before (and considerably tastier). "It takes a certain kind of skill to drive a man like that away."

"I love you, too, Mom," I mumble after shoving the chocolate-chip-caramel-marshmallow love in my mouth. That's right—love. I can buy a giant glass full of sugared love. The proof fills my tongue with a sweet coating of love, the cold chocolate bliss biting into my teeth and gums, my stomach groaning with anticipatory pleasure as my six dollars buys me a gustatory hug, kiss, and if you add in the peanut butter sauce in the ramekin on the side—maybe even an ass grab.

"I don't mean to rub salt in the wound, honey."

"Then why are you standing there with a brick of Himalayan salt the size of my head and beating me with it?"

She purses her lips in what looks like a Chuckles' butt imitation, then softens. "I'm sorry. You're right."

I freeze, and not from an ice cream headache. I go completely still.

"Say what?" I choke out.

Mom rolls her eyes. "I can admit when I'm wrong." Her own glass full of love is perched in front of her, a bunch of berry-flavored nonsense covered in more berries, with whipped cream on top. This is how I know we cannot possibly be related, because my mother only eats berry-flavored ice cream. No chocolate sauce, no caramel-y gooey joy. She won't touch cookie dough ice cream, nor butter pecan, nor anything with chunks of chocolate in it.

That's just . . . it's like she's a poor imitation of someone who possesses XX chromosomes. Like she's a Stepford Wife. The only thing worse would be to hate ice cream, and if I ever meet someone who does I'll have to pull out the microchip embedded in their neck and scream, "POD PERSON!"

I just stare at her. I feel so hollow. I'm so empty the ice cream on my spoon starts to drip back in the sundae glass.

Her lips snap shut and she gives me a look of compassion so deep and authentic it makes tears well in my eyes.

"You're really hurting, honey."

All I can do is nod.

"I wish I could make it better."

"You said the same thing when Steve dumped me, Mom."

"I meant it then, too." She's a little disheveled after yoga, a little less done today, makeup lighter, her hair perfectly in place and hairsprayed so well it would take a Category 4 hurricane to blow a single strand out of place, but she's more . . . Mom. More of the woman who tucked me in bed with a nighttime story, the mother who catered to me when I was sick, the one who taught me how to use an EpiPen by injecting herself in the thigh seventeen times before I got it right.

The mom who just is *there*. A steady presence. We joke and she needles (pun intended) and is overbearing and judgmental, but she's Mom no matter what. She'll love me no matter what. She will invade my apartment and respect boundaries about as well as Vladimir Putin and chime a wine glass to get me to kiss a billionaire client and over-babble about her sex life with Dad, but by God, she's got my back.

And right now I need her more desperately than I need a shower.

And that is saying *a lot*.

Using her Mommy Sense, which is like Spidey Sense but

with more judgment, she stands, walks to my side of the booth, moves closer to me, and just opens her arms. A whiff of something floral and spicy fills the air between us and then I'm in her warm embrace, crying so hard I will probably leave a salt lick on her shoulder, and I get to fade away for a few precious minutes and stop being Shannon, stop being the stupid woman who blew it with the best guy ever, stop being the feminist career woman who can't believe Declan is such an ass, and—

I can just cry and be held by my mommy.

Who is murmuring something unintelligible in my ear, but it sounds like she's saying, "Like father, like son."

"Huh?" I pull back. The steel blue of her lightweight rayon jacket has a brow-shaped wet spot on it.

"Like father, like son," she says, a scowl making her crow's feet emerge.

"What do you mean?"

"James." She says his name like it's a curse word.

"What about James?"

Silence. Mom doesn't do silence. The hair on my arms starts to stand on end.

"Mom?"

She shifts uncomfortably in her seat, spooning the perfect ratio of whipped cream, berry ice cream, and fresh berries onto a spoon. Then she stuffs the entire concoction in her mouth so she can't talk.

"When you swallow, the truth is coming out."

"That's what *he* said," are the first words out of her mouth.

"What does that even mean?"

"I was making a joke. You know. He. Swallow. Um . . ."

"Joke fail."

Her eyes narrow. "It's never, *ever* not funny to joke about swallowing."

I regard my marshmallow cream in a whole new light and drop my spoon. "Thanks, Mom. You just ruined my chocolate comfort."

"It's not like you need the sugar."

"Since when do you criticize my eating habits? That's like Paula Deen telling Dr. Oz how to eat."

She frowns. "Let's talk about Declan."

"Let's not. Let's talk about James. His dad. Who you . . . know?"

She turns the same shade of pink as her ice cream. "I don't know how to talk about him."

My mind races to do the math. "You can't possibly know him from anywhere. He's at least ten years older than you."

"Seven."

My turn to narrow my eyes. I feel like a snake, ready to hiss, or hug her to death. "Spill it."

She bats her eyelashes innocently. "Spill what?"

"Two seconds ago you were doing heavy-duty mother-daughter bonding over what an ass Declan and his father are—"

"Not Declan. Just his father."

"Spill it!" I shout, slamming my fist on the tabletop. She flinches.

Anger feels so much better than depression.

"We dated."

My turn to flinch.

"Oh, God. We're both sampling from the same male gene pool?"

She frowns. "This is a bad time to make a swallow joke, isn't it?"

I shove my ice cream away and start to gag. Maybe another hairball from Chuckles.

Mom primly wipes her mouth and sighs, leaning forward conspiratorially. "I dated James very briefly when I was young and single and working in Boston as a stripper."

"WHAT? When were you a stripper? Does Dad know?" I knew Mom worked as an artist's assistant years ago and had memorized her stories about living in abandoned warehouses in the scummier parts of the city, but this?

"That's right," she says calmly. "When I stripped the canvases for the—"

"A paint stripper," I say, relieved.

She looks confused. "What did you think I meant—oh, dear!" Her laughter sounds like bells tinkling. "You thought I meant I took off my clothes for money?"

"That's the generally accepted definition of 'stripper,' Mom."

"When I take my clothes off for a man, I don't expect to get paid for it."

I just blink.

"Okay, maybe dinner and a movie . . ."

"You're just prolonging the inevitable here, Mom. You dated my boyfriend's father?"

"Ex-boyfriend. Ex-boyfriend, dear."

"You rang?" says a familiar voice.

No. Not Declan. This story would be so much better if it were, but . . .

It's Steve.

chapter
six

"YOU HAVE THE MOST interesting conversations, Marie," Steve says with an unctuous tone so slick you could dip focaccia bread in it.

"And you have the uncanny ability to appear in the most unusual places," I mumble.

"Like a fairy godfather," he says with a disarmingly sweet smile.

"Like a psycho stalker," I retort. My mouth goes dry. I can't stop looking at his eyes. He seems almost . . . appealing. But that voice. It's like he's being warm and sweet at the same time he's convincing me to invest in a Bernie Madoff scheme.

"I like my answer better," he challenges, the sweetness gone suddenly. I sigh with relief, because the dissonance was too hard.

"That's because you're a bit unhinged," I say. Loudly, as I reach for my sundae and shove more chocolate goo in my mouth. "Go away, Steve."

He cackles. It sounds like Dr. Evil, high on NyQuil. "*I'm* the unhinged one? You pretend to be a lesbian and double-cross your billionaire ex and *I'm* unhinged?"

"Double-cross?" Mom asks, curling her arm around her ice cream protectively. "Shannon double-crossed someone?"

He pauses and stands awkwardly. If Mom asks him to join us, all bets are off.

"She cozied up to Declan McCormick and slept with him to get some big accounts for her company. All while pretending to be a lesbian," he declares. He's wearing a simple white button-down shirt, khakis, and Crocs. Steve is the only man I know who insists that Crocs count as business casual wear. Sure. For nurses.

"How do you know she was pretending?" Mom asks. The catch in her voice makes the tops of my ears go hot. She's up to something. I wish Chuckles were here, because I could read his frowns to understand better what Mom's ulterior motive is. I'm on my own, though. No Kitty Radar in an ice cream shop.

"Because I dated her for years and I would know if I had slept with a lesbian," he replies, voice dripping with sarcasm thicker than the impenetrable layer of ego that he wraps himself in, like a forcefield of arrogance everyone else knows is invisible, but he thinks is Kevlar.

"How would you know if you slept with a lesbian?" Mom asks again. "Is a lesbian's vagina a different texture? Do they use a code word during sex? Do they bring a U-Haul on the first date? Do they refuse to perform blow jobs on you?"

Steve's jaw drops a little and he starts breathing through his mouth.

I keep mine shut and sit back, ready to watch Mom in all her glory. It's kind of nice to watch her turn this on someone other than me.

"Uh, I, uh . . ." he says.

She turns to me with a pseudo-accusatory look on her face. "Shannon, is that why Steve was always so uptight? You wouldn't play the flesh flute?"

Marshmallow cream comes flying out my nostrils as I choke to death. It's a hell of a way to go. I imagine the Stay Puft Marshmallow Man greets you in heaven on a white cloud of fluff.

She points at me and grasps Steve's arm. "See? She can do it with ice cream. I'd imagine that marshmallow cream tastes better than—"

"Mom!" I cough. I'm not rescuing Steve. I'm preserving my nasal passages, because if she makes another comment about fellatio I'm going to shoot hot fudge so far into my sinus cavity I'll have yeast infections in my brain.

"My sex life is none of your business," Steve says in a cold voice.

"I did," I tell Mom, pretending Steve's not here. "But let's just say it wasn't an even trade."

Steve's eyes fly so far open his irises look like they're swimming in a bowl of cream. Marshmallow cream.

"You can't talk about blow jobs with your mother! That's . . . private," he insists.

"Like feeding Jessica Coffin stories to tweet is private?" I say sweetly.

"So you went up the elevator but you wouldn't go down," Mom needles Steve.

"I . . . what? No, it's not . . . I didn't . . . you don't . . ." *Give up*, I want to tell him. You're just digging the hole deeper, and that's just more rope Mom needs to get to lower the bucket of lotion to you.

She turns to me and pats my hand. "Poor thing. No wonder you didn't fight him when he dumped you. It was a blessing. Being with a selfish, egotistical blowhard is one thing. But a selfish, egotistical blowhard who is bad in bed isn't ever worth it."

Steve looks like someone just removed his voice box with a corkscrew. His mouth opens and closes, his eyes jumping like little fleas trying to find a safe place to land. He's struggling to think and speak and react and I get the distinct impression that this conversation is not going as planned.

"I did not say a word to Jessica," he argues, eyes shrinking to tiny, piggish triangles. Ah—so he's going to address that and ignore the giant sucking chest wound that Mom just gave him over his, well . . . giant suckage as a sex partner.

He's hovering over us, shifting his weight from one hip to the other, and leaning down. A veritable tower of terror, I tell you. I am afraid for his dignity, which is about as likely to remain intact as a rock star's t-shirt in a mosh pit.

"*Someone* fed her the story," I retort.

"I'm not that someone."

"Then it was Monica."

He snorts. It makes him sound like a manatee. "My mother

and Jessica aren't close."

"Monica isn't capable of being close to anyone," Mom says. "It would ruin her varnish."

Steve frowns. "That's my mother you're insulting."

"Yes," Mom says. "It is."

"Why did I even come over here?" he asks the air, waving his hands around as if he has an audience. Every single person in the store ignores him, because in the battle for attention between Steve and a giant peanut butter fudge sundae, he's losing. Big time.

"We were wondering the same thing," Mom and I say in unison.

"Maybe to apologize for being so selfish in bed with Shannon?" Mom adds in a voice that carries through the ice cream parlor at the exact moment the satellite radio station pauses between songs. Now Steve's got all the attention he wants. And he clearly doesn't want it.

"Dude," says a college student, a guy sleeved with tattoos. "That's sad," he says as he walks out carrying a loaded ice cream cone the size of my cat's head.

"Would you please tell your mother," Steve hisses, bending down to whisper in my ear, "that I was not . . . that I . . . that she's . . ."

This is the part where, for all those years, I anticipated what he wanted me to say and played puppy dog to whatever he wanted. I used to wag my tail and eagerly jump up and do what he wanted, including fetching the same stick 127 times in a row.

I got accustomed to being in a state of panic when my man was being challenged by someone else, especially when he was a douchebag who would take it out on me emotionally, later, when all the people who had a deep core that was strong enough to call him on his bull were gone. Conditioned to becoming the peacemaker, the neutralizer, she-who-must-appease-the-overin-flated-ego-in-a-skinbag, I felt the cold flush of fear that he was going to overreact.

But that was then. And *then* is long gone.

I let my heart beat once. Twice, Three times. Ten. The

silence between beats is excruciating. It feels like an eternity, with Mom watching Steve with shrewd eyes that are zeroed in on him now that he's maimed, and she's waiting for him to bleed out enough to go in for the kill.

And then another space between beats. Another. One more, all with Steve giving me that *look*. The one that holds expectations—thousands of them, carefully cultivated over years together, his well-worn reflex of knowing I'll jump right in and—what?

Save him?

Silence. Heartbeats. Spaces between.

I need to save *me*.

I look him in the eye and say the exact same words he used on me, more than a year ago, when he broke up with me.

"I'm sorry, Steve. It's just that you were never really up to par for what I need."

One corner of Mom's mouth tips up and her fingers twitch. She wants to high-five me, and the muscles in her neck tighten. She wants to say something but breathes through her nose instead, captivated but uncharacteristically quiet.

Steve has this expression of patience that melts into disbelief, as if his brain is on a three-second delay. He's finally realizing that I'm not going to rescue him. Coddle him. Prop up the mythology that says he's the center of the universe, that his emotional core is radioactive and therefore must be protected from exposure at all costs. He's trained me to believe that it's my responsibility to buy into his idea that he's above criticism, and anyone who dares to confront him is ignorant and worthy only of derision.

Silence and non-movement are my weapons now. And while I'm clumsy and unskilled, I'm using them to protect my core.

Finally.

This is what Declan meant about Steve. Not letting him make me feel inferior. Except Declan was wrong.

Dead wrong.

It wasn't that I let Steve make me feel lesser.

It was that I let him convince me that the order of the world demanded that I *am* lesser.

And I'm seeing now that the way the world works isn't some pre-defined set of rules that other people get to make and impose on me.

Steve finds his voice. "I'm done." And he just walks away with fisted hands and a tight jaw.

"So am I," I say in a clear, but calm voice, pushing the ice cream away.

Mom's speechless.

Which means I won in so many more ways.

chapter
seven

THE SLIDE OF HIS hands, soft palms with squared fingernails moving out of my vision as he cradles my face, makes
me inhale slowly, devouring the taste of his breath. We're
in bed, nude, skin against skin and heat against heat, the combination turning us into a fireball of sensual desire.

Desire that will soon convert and combust into a licking
flame.

I've waited so long for this, the press of his fingertips into
my belly, the slow crawl of his mouth over my breast, the warm
wetness of his mouth, his tongue tracing circles that make me
taut with a craving for his taste. My body is a landscape for
him to explore and I sink my hands into Declan's hair, the long
strands a surprise. He's growing it out, a stark contrast to his
short, clipped look, and when he catches my eye with a jaunty
grin, one half-curl pops over his eyebrow and makes me fall in
love all over again.

Again.

As if there could be more.

The space between us is so small you can't fit a heart in
there, much less two. We'll have to share one that beats enough
for us both as his mouth finds mine and says, "I'm here." The
next kiss says that he's here to stay, and then that turns out to be
a tiny white lie as he travels the valley to the sweet, supple parts
of me that are so achingly ready for his mouth, his fingers, his
throbbing flesh, our pounding need.

He's back, in my bed, and it's like he never left. Bright green eyes with tiny flecks of brown and topaz at the edge of the pupils are so close that I can read the colors. If I had the gift of second sight I could tell you what his orbs tell the world about all the dimensions of love we share, but I'm woefully incapacitated as he captures my red nub, enticing and teasing, mouth exploring where I tremor with anticipation.

"Beautiful," he murmurs in a voice I know so well, using words I've heard before, in the limo, on a lighthouse floor, in my own bed.

My own bed, where I am right now.

With him.

"I've missed you. Missed—" My breath hitches, the words broken in half as he splits me with an expert touch that does exactly what he wants, that draws all the blood from my inner self to the surface, giving him a wonderful playland to use as he pleases, for pleasure and joy.

"Missed me?" Declan pulls up, then murmurs in my ear, tongue loose and leisurely on my neck, the gentle kisses he peppers down the side turning into fiercer love bites. I'll have marks in the morning, little notes that play the melody of these minutes, hours in bed together.

A relief map of sorts. A cartographer's plot, charting the way to join me in ecstasy.

And yet . . . a chart for one and only one man to follow.

Ever.

"You never need to miss me again, Shannon. Never." His kiss makes me clench, the friction of belly against abs like he's already in me, touching deep and unleashing a release so strong I can't hold back.

"I love you so much, Declan," I whisper.

My own hands become greedy, needing to accumulate more memory of his hot skin, wanting to memorize the contours of his marbled back, his muscled thighs, the soft skin where leg becomes sex. In the inner curve of his hip I find a place only I can excite, one that he reserves for me—and *only* me—and his next word echoes my own thoughts.

"Mine. You're mine, Shannon. Forever. Don't ever doubt

me, please. Trust me. Give over to me. Let me love you. Let me show you how much I love you."

Declan's eyes have gone dark green with desire, the color of emerald velvet, like a cape spread out on a mossy hill in Ireland for two lovers to enjoy an afternoon frolic in the sun, the coast and the rush of the ocean surrounding us. He's all sea air and crash and rolling hills, dotted with the sunshine of homecoming and love everlasting.

In a flash, I'm on my back and he's over me, poised to claim me, my legs opening of their own will, my body so primed. So ready. So—

Beep beep beep.

My heart pounding, my hands fisting the sheets, and a puddle under me the size of Lake Chargoggagoggmanchauggagoggchaubunagungamaugg (yes, it's a real lake in Massachusetts), I wake up mid-climax, thrashing a bit and shaking myself out of what is, disappointingly, just a dream.

Another damn dream.

Third one in three days.

All my pink bits are hot and wet, all my other bits are cold and tingly, and my brain bits are embarrassed as hell that I can have the female equivalent of wet dreams against my will by thinking about a man who will never touch me again.

Never.

There's that word again.

I am covered in a sheen of sweat, and oh, if only you could sweat disappointment and unrequited love out of your pores. I'd live in a sauna for a month if it could exorcise the demon of heartbreak that lives inside me, teasing me with subconscious fantasies of reunion, of unconscious motives that make me google Declan, follow him on Twitter, wish for one brush with him so we can talk it out and reunite.

I'd take a drug to make the pain go away. So far, copious amounts of chocolate have done nothing but make the pudge around my waist a little softer. If only I could drive the pain out with a master cleanse. Someone should make a protein shake and market it.

The Breakup Smoothie.

Declan's taste is in my mouth. The touch of his lips is between my breasts, so real I reach up my shirt to chase his fingers. The lingering sense that he really was here, that he really did travel across my skin and give himself to me in my curves and hollows, makes me feel haunted.

Haunted.

As the cool morning air fills in the space between dream and reality, it chases all the vestiges of my Dream Declan away, leaving me bereft.

Chilled.

Unmoored.

I grab my phone and shut off the alarm, then check my calendar. I have a mystery shop today, one in person about two hours away.

Two hours? That's a rare one. Why would I—

Oh.

Yeah.

That one.

The sex toy shop. We're being paid travel time plus our mileage to handle a series of sex toy shops, to make sure they're not selling pornographic materials to minors. And if they have a tobacco license, we're checking on cigarette sales to minors, too.

As my lady parts stop their Gangnam Style dance imitation and I catch my breath, I remember the worst part:

Mom is my partner on these.

Thoughts of Mom and a naked Declan doing unmentionably delightful things to me do not mix. It's like Baileys Irish Cream and sloe gin: warning! Warning, Will Robinson!

You throw up when you combine the two.

Chuckles climbs on my bed, sniffs my crotch, and gives me a mildly disgusted look. It's not rivetingly disgusted, though, which is alarming.

That means he's come to expect to be disappointed in me.

Or I need a shower.

Either way, even my cat thinks that my dreams are deviant.

And you can't sink much lower than that.

Or so I thought.

"I THOUGHT AMANDA WAS doing this shop with me. Not you!" Mom grouses as we pull into the parking garage in downtown Northampton. I love the rare mystery shop that brings me into this college town, where the coffee shops are fabulous, you can find the best smoothies anywhere, and street buskers are as conversant about American foreign policy as they are about the best vegan restaurants in town.

But I don't relish the idea of comparison shopping vibrators with my mother. That's up there with looking forward to getting a pap smear, a root canal, and a colonoscopy at the same time.

Which I'd prefer over this.

"Me too, but she tricked me." *Tricked* is a tiny confabulation. Okay, a huge one. She offered to spend a few hours snooping on my behalf and getting some dirt on Declan if I took Mom on this sex toy mystery shop.

No bleeping way.

"Fine, then," Amanda had said. "If you don't take the sex toy shop with Marie, I'll tell her the truth about that taping of Rachael Ray."

"You wouldn't!"

"Try me."

My mother is the biggest Rachael Ray fan EVER. I had a chance to go for a customer service evaluation last year, and Mom had begged, pleaded, and cajoled, but I'd stood firm.

Okay. I *lied* and told her my Rachael Ray shop was cancelled. Being embarrassed is one thing, but on television?

I have to draw a line somewhere.

And that line brought me here to Northampton to a nearby sex toy store with my mother.

Being humiliated on the Rachael Ray show suddenly looks so much more appealing. Amanda stood her ground, and here I am . . .

"I can't believe they put a sex toy shop here," Mom says as

we get out of the car.

"Here?" I look around at the quaint brick buildings, eyes catching the glint of sunlight off the large display window for an art gallery. "Oh, no. Not here. We're just in the parking lot to grab a good cup of coffee."

She rolls her eyes but smiles and links her arm through mine as we walk across the bridge from the car park to the shopping mall building. "You and your coffee. Why not just stop and get an iced coffee from—"

I stop her before she names a ubiquitous coffee and donut shop. I also shudder. "That's what you drink when you have no choice."

"No, Shannon—that's what you drink when you mystery shop for a living."

Twenty minutes later, good lattes secured, we pull out of the lot and head toward Smith College along Route 9, a slightly scenic route to our destination. I'm driving slowly, as traffic is thicker than usual, when the long, slim, swanlike body of a tall blonde catches the corner of my eye. I slow the Turdmobile down, and a guy hauling trash on a bike—a trailer full of actual garbage cans, five or so in a straight line—makes his way past me with effort.

"Nice piece of crap," he calls out in a jocular tone. Mom waves and says something friendly.

My eyes are locked on what turns out to be Jessica Coffin. "Yep. She sure is," I say.

A group of pedestrians clogs a zebra-striped crosswalk and I'm forced to stop, my eyes eating up the scene. It's definitely her. Without a doubt. She looks over and her eyes fix on a spot above my head, her nose wrinkling in distaste. She's seen the coffee bean on the hood of my car and correctly determined it looks more like a piece of—

Her.

My impulse to give her the finger remains firmly suppressed, though what's the harm? She can't possibly realize it's me, right?

"What are you staring at?" Mom asks.

"Jessica Coffin."

"JESSICA COFFIN?" Mom screams. And by "scream," I mean bellows like a foghorn being amplified by a Gillette Stadium sound system.

Blonde hair down in a white curtain around hips slimmer than my thigh, she shimmers as she turns and her eyes narrow. Eyes on me (or my car, or maybe my mother, who is wildly waving her arms and screaming, "Jessica! I love your tweets!"), Jessica slips her hand through the kinked elbow of a man standing with his back to the road. She leans in to his ear, whispers something, and then clings to him like a lover with casual access to her man.

In profile, the two look like something out of a *Vogue* article. A giant banner across the courtyard between the buildings announces the opening of some new children's wing near an art museum. Or a botanical garden.

The man turns just enough for me to see that it's Declan McCormick.

Maybe that new children's wing is in hell.

Cars behind me honk as I sit here, frozen, going out of my mind. Jessica and—

"DECLAN!" Mom squeals. "SO GOOD TO SEE YOU!" She's half out the window, and if I push the button and slowly close it on her, maybe she'll snap in two, ass remaining in the car with me and screaming head rolling down the street, scooped up by the next bicyclist carrying away the trash.

Speaking of trash, I look at Jessica once more, and a white wall of rage takes over my vision.

BEEP.

Mom pulls her body back in the car as someone behind me screams profanities about my feces-topped car. I hit the gas and thud into something, just hard enough for me to realize I've made a terrible error in the heat of furious passion.

A barrel of garbage goes flying up in the air, lands on the top of my car and rolls down, spewing food waste of every kind imaginable, then chunks of used tampons, and finally a thick batch of slime-coated paper.

And Mom's window is open. Wide open.

By some miracle of divine intervention (for Mom) or crap-tastic luck (for me), the open end of the trash can is on my side. I get an armful of what smells like composted marijuana mixed into about four cups of semen. Fermented semen, that is.

Sprouted, fair-trade, organic, non-soy spooge.

Or maybe it's just vanilla pudding. I should be reasonable here.

Jessica's derisive laugh can be heard over the screaming ban-shees in my head, and a thousand cars all start honking at me in unison. The people-powered garbage dude is apologizing pro-fusely. It turns out the trash can popped out of his cart just as I hit the accelerator and it's actually not my fault.

Finally. Something's not my fault.

I fling my arm repeatedly in varying rotations of horror in an attempt to get the worst of *whateverthehell* that stuff is on my skin, while Declan gives me a pitying look that makes the white wall of rage come back. If small children didn't dot the crowd around Jessica and Declan I'd ram the car into them, pinning her in place and shoving the garbage can on that perfect curtain of hair while doing some revenge-type thing of undetermined specificity to Declan.

"Shannon?" Mom gasps. "Shannon, honey, you're saying the F-word over and over again and I think we need to get going."

BEEP times a thousand plus composted garbage delivered by guys who only eat paleo diets and who think mashed dates in coconut milk are "dessert" is a kind of math problem that makes me shut down. Completely.

Ignoring the mess, ignoring the honks, and flipping off the car behind me and—did she really?—Jessica and Declan, Mom storms out of her side of the car, pulls me out of the driver's seat, throws a towel she found in the back seat over the driver's side, plunks herself down, and waits for me to move all zom-bie-like into the passenger's side.

I'm covered in just enough slime to feel like Carrie, on stage at her prom. There's a thought. My fingers on the door handle, I stop, the sound of ten thousand horns like Buddhist gongs being struck in unison. Eyes on the building next to Jessica, I will it to crumble and crush her to death. Or a manhole cover to split her in half. An intake vent to suck in her hair and scalp her.

Thirty seconds of trying and all I get is a cloud of fruit flies in my eye. And when I go to wipe it, I get ganja-scented goo up my nose.

"Get in the car, Shannon! We have sex toys to visit!"

I am so done.

chapter
eight

P AD THAI BROUGHT OVER to your bedroom by your best friend after a long day of listening to mystery shoppers give excuse after excuse for late field reports is the nectar of the gods.

Amanda shoves a piece of chicken satay in her mouth and mumbles around the meat. "That's it? He's seriously just . . . done? He dumped you because you pretended to be a lesbian?" We're reviewing the past week's events because we're all still in WTF mode over how my relationship fell apart.

"No, he dumped me because he thinks I dated him just to get business deals." Like that's so much better.

"And because you swing the wrong way." Amy declares this around a piece of shrimp so big it could choke her.

"I don't swing the wrong way!"

"There was that girl in college . . ." Amanda adds, making Amy's eyes go wide, either from shock or maybe she really is choking.

"One kiss! Everyone experiments at least once." I told Amanda that story in confidence.

Amanda and Amy shake their heads no.

"Seriously?" Now I have to add *this* to my ever-growing list of Shannon faux pas?

"I thought you were a little too good at the credit union," Amanda says with an arched tone.

"C'mon . . . well, anyhow, I'm not gay and Declan knows I'm not gay. He's not upset about it. That's a red herring. Mom keeps thinking it's why he broke up with me and she's wrong."

"Then . . . why does he think you were only with him for the accounts?"

I retell his version of why he thinks that. By the time I'm done, Amy looks horror-stricken and Amanda is patiently picking lint balls off her cotton socks.

"Oh," they say in unison.

"Ouch," Amanda adds.

"Yep." What else can I say? Other than confessing my need to throw myself into a bottomless pit and enjoy the ride forever while thoughts of Declan torment me, there isn't much more I can explain.

"And then you saw him with Jessica Coffin at Smith College. Touching each other," Amy says.

Amanda waves a piece of chicken in the air and says, "But we figured that out. They're both part of that charity. Her father and his father donated more than a year's tuition at Smith to the project, so they're just there."

"Together," I groan.

"But not *together* together," Amanda insists.

"They watched me run into a garbage can and cover myself with slime."

"There are worse things," Amy says.

"Like what?"

"Being caught with your hand in a toilet in the men's room?"

I hit her. Hard. With a piece of shrimp.

"That can't be all there is," Amy insists. She's in her running clothes, tight knee-length Lycra pants and a tank top with a built-in shelf bra, two other sports bras underneath. The Jacoby girls aren't just well endowed. We have so much breast tissue that if left unleashed, one good sudden turn to the right and we could knock out a small village.

She stretches. I reach for my ice cream. Both involve moving muscles, right? So I'm exercising right now, too. Hand, wrist, tongue, taste buds, sorrow-filled heart . . .

"So the whole Twitter thing happens," Amanda says in a contemplative voice. "Declan claims that he understands the lesbian thing was for work. But he says you told him in the light-house that you were only dating him for the account—"

"That was a *joke!*"

Amy holds up one hand to get me to pause. Amanda is deep in thought, eyes on the windowsill, staring so intently at a small basil plant that it might spontaneously turn into pesto sauce.

"—and he quoted Jessica, and then something about Steve's mother?"

Ouch. "What I said to Monica about only dating Declan for money got back to him."

"*I* said that!" Amanda protests.

"I confirmed it." A sick wave of horror pours through me. Even at the time, when I said it, I had a premonition it was a bad idea.

Now I know it. And I can't let it go. Over and over, the memories of everything I ever said to Declan that might make him think I was manipulative and not earnest in my intimate moments makes me cry.

I couldn't just own up to the truth and blow the mystery shop, could I? Most people would. Instead, I tap-danced to please all the different people I thought I needed to please.

And in the end I lost the one I wanted to please the most.

"Still doesn't make sense," Amanda says, brooding. "He's not *that* shallow."

"He's *that* accustomed to being used by women for his money and connections, though," I wail. "He told me I was special because I wasn't trying to use him." The memory of his vulnerability during that conversation makes me feel like I'm two inches tall and covered in excrement. He thinks I violated that. Violated his trust.

That is what hurts the most.

Amanda's still shaking her head slowly. "I still don't buy it. You guys weren't together for that long—"

"A month." I wish it could have been forever.

"—but he's an eminently reasonable guy. You're a reasonable woman. He should have heard you out. Should have listened."

"He's overreacting," Amy concurs. "And he was kind of weird at Easter. Uptight and shy. Mom said the butter lamb freaked him out. Maybe he has a dairy phobia?"

I snort. "No. It reminded him of his mother."

"Hmmm," Amanda says, stroking chin hairs she doesn't have. "Perhaps that's part of this."

"Huh?"

"Nothing. Let me think this through."

I'm kind of done with this conversation and now am absent-mindedly reading work email. It's the kind of day where I can get away with working from home. I don't have any mystery shops today. Just 115 emails from the people I manage.

As I open emails and scan quickly, I see we have three new approved mystery shoppers. Amanda and Amy take over the Declan analysis, trying to understand his motives, while I check out. I've worried and wondered and analyzed this issue to death, and can only come to one conclusion:

When you date a billionaire and something goes wrong, it's always your fault.

The next twenty minutes go by in a blur as I sit on the couch and process email, Chuckles eats a ficus leaf and then hairballs it up, and Amy and Amanda ignore us while strategizing.

"Earth to Shannon!" Amanda says.

"What?"

"How did Declan's mom die?"

I halt. "I . . . I don't know. I asked him twice and he never answered."

All six eyebrows in the room shoot up. Eight, if cats have eyebrows.

Amanda snatches the computer from me and types furiously. And then she gasps in shock.

"Oh, Shannon. Oh my God."

"What?"

"Read."

The obituary Amanda pulled up on the computer screen has

a breathtakingly lovely older woman's photo front and center, a thick chain of pearls around her neck, her hair pulled back in a smooth updo. Lively, friendly green eyes so familiar my heart tugs at me stare back.

Elena Montgomery McCormick.

Declan's mother.

Born in 1956. Died in 2004. She had him when she was older, and that makes James in his late fifties, which makes sense. My eyes race over the words to get them all in, and then I come to a dead stop.

Stung by the words in front of me.

The obituary is tasteful, mentioning her three kids—Terrance, Declan and Andrew—and her loving husband, James.

It's the link under it, though, that makes me hold my breath. Makes time stand still. Makes the air go thick.

The headline for a *Boston Globe* story reads:

Local business leader's wife dead from wasp sting.

Oh my God.

Amanda's hands are gentle on my shoulder as my eyes race across the page. "I can't find more about it, yet," she explains. "There isn't a major news story to explain how it happened."

"His brother had a bad incident around the same time," I tell her, brain reeling. Declan's mother died from a sting? *Died?*

"I guess this explains why he knew exactly what to do with you," Amy whispers, eyes glistening. My own throat goes salty and tight as tears I didn't know I had in me spring to the surface. The memory of that picnic, how Declan was so calm and steady yet swift and immediate, reacting with perfectly orchestrated steps, how he ran with me in his arms so far, so hard, so fast . . .

He saved my life and then he broke my heart.

"This can't be real," I choke out, but deep down I understand more. Suddenly. Like a clap of thunder and lightning that makes the landscape bright in a flash, revealing parts unknown, the sound echoing in a ripple of cacophony, *now* I get it.

I get it.

"He can't date me because I remind him of his mother," I say.

Amy raises one skeptical eyebrow. "You look nothing like her. For one, she has cheekbones more prominent than Heidi Klum's."

I wave my hand in the air between us. "No, not that I look like her. The sting. She had an anaphylactic allergy, I have an anaphylactic allergy. Declan can't handle it. Maybe I'm a trigger?"

Amanda makes a noise that tells me she's not convinced. "He would have dumped you right after the ER incident, then."

"It's a miracle he didn't," Amy adds with a snort. "You nearly decapitated his second head."

I give her a look that shuts her up. "Maybe he was just being nice. Not breaking up with me when I was in a medical crisis."

"That doesn't explain Easter," she declares.

We sit in brooding silence. Amanda takes action and starts googling furiously. I take action by searching through all the open mystery shops available at work to see if there's one at a bakery. I have a hankering for muffins suddenly.

"What are you doing?" Amy asks, peering over my shoulder.

"Discovering my ex-boyfriend's mother died from the same allergy I have always makes me crave baked goods, you know?"

Amanda ignores us both. "You two leave me alone for an hour and I'll have an answer."

"What the hell am I supposed to do for an hour while I wait to find out the one little piece of information that could put all the puzzle pieces together?" I demand.

"Eat ice cream," she says.

"Okay." Good answer.

"How about we go for a nice power walk?" says my sister, Richard Simmons. In about fifty years she'll look just enough like him with that curly reddish hair . . .

"Power walk or ice cream. Power walk or ice cream. That's like asking if you want to have sex with Sam Heughan or just use your vibrator, Amy."

She blushes. "Some vibrators are pretty damn nice."

"Like the one I got at the sex toy shop with Shannon last week!" Mom chirps from the main door.

"You summoned her. Say the word 'vibrator' and if she's

within three miles, she just appears," I hiss. To be fair, Mom came to my rescue at the sex toy shop. The trauma of seeing Jessica with Declan, then creating a minor traffic catastrophe that thankfully missed being covered on local news, meant I was completely useless by the time we'd reached the store's parking lot.

Instructions memorized, she went in and spent ninety minutes doing a fabulous customer service evaluation of the store, and came out with a lifetime of orgasms in a surprisingly compact shopping bag.

"Look at this puppy! While Shannon was having her breakdown in the garbage-covered car, I was a professional and handled everything for her," Mom announces with glee. She fishes a pink and white vibrator out of her purse.

It is bigger than a compact umbrella.

"Jesus Christ!" Amy screams.

"No, he's the butt plug." Mom pouts. "I didn't have enough in my budget for him."

The three of us stare at her, mouths agape.

Make it four. Even Chuckles' jaw drops just a little.

"They make a Jesus butt plug?" Amanda asks in a shaky voice.

"See why I wanted you to go with her?" I say with more viciousness in my tone than I'd planned. But it's sincere.

"See why I blackmailed you?"

Fair enough.

"Let's go for that walk while Amanda stalks your ex boyfriend to learn how his mom died," Amy says in a shell-shocked voice.

Mom marches into the living room and searches through the coat closet.

"What are you doing?" Amy asks.

"I need to hide this," Mom announces.

"Oh, God, we don't need to watch that!" I shout.

"Not in my body," Mom says with disgust. "In your closet. It's a surprise for your dad."

"Oh, that would be a surprise in bed, all right. It's basically a third partner."

Mom brightens. "That was my thinking, too!" She frowns. "Why are you researching how someone's mom died?"

"We're making plans," Amy whispers. "His mom came home with a giant vibrator one day and BAM!"

"I heard that." She shoves the vibrator inside a bag with great effort, shoving once, twice, three times.

"Give the poor thing a cigarette after all that," I mutter. "You didn't even buy it dinner."

Mom makes a sour face at me, then brightens as she sees Amanda at the laptop. "Are you really researching how Declan's mother died? Did James do it?" A bit too eager with that question, isn't she?

"Hey, wait a minute. You never finished telling me how Declan nearly became my stepbrother."

Amy does a double take. "What? Wouldn't that make Shannon and Declan's relationship incestuous?"

"No, more like Marcia and Greg on *The Brady Bunch*."

"Ewwww," Amy and Amanda say in unison.

Mom pretends not to hear us.

"Mom? James? You said you dated him."

"When did I say that?"

"The day Steve appeared at the ice cream shop."

She frowns, then grins like an idiot. "You were so commanding with Steve! So fem dom! I'll bet if you got one of those strap-ons at the sex toy shop—it turns out they're not just for lesbians!—you could have . . ."

Her voice trails off when she sees the looks on our faces.

"Walk!" Amy announces. "You'll spill your guts while Amanda does her cybersearching."

"Where are we walking?"

"Not where. What. The plank." She shoves me out the front door.

The big orange fireball in the sky is so interesting. I haven't seen it for days, holed up in my apartment, and I'm tempted to wave hello, like it's some neighbor I've known for years but haven't chatted with for a long time.

"*Some vibrators are pretty nice,*" I taunt Amy. "You had to say that, didn't you?"

"Sometimes it's true." She won't back down. Sheesh. Little sister syndrome. When in doubt, dig in your heels.

"Something is very wrong with you," I mutter, but we go for a walk. Because she's right.

Not about the vibrators, but about needing to get out of the house.

"Tell the story about James, Mom. I can't believe you let a real billionaire get away." She misses the obvious sarcasm in my voice.

She chuckles. It's not a happy sound. "He wasn't a billionaire back then. Far from it. I was an artist's assistant in some crappy squatter's building where we were all avant-garde painters and he was with the real estate company that was trying to turn our run-down warehouse into fancy loft apartments. If he could get the building, he could make his first fortune. Only one thing stopped him."

"You?"

"Rats."

"Rats?"

"Rats." She says that single word like it explains everything.

" **G** O ON."

"You want me to go on about rats?"

"Could you please connect the rats to James?"

"Isn't it clear?"

"No."

She sighs heavily. "The building was overrun with rats."

Amy and I both shudder and gag. I shudder, she gags. Then we trade.

"And the only way to keep the rats away was with cats."

"Is that where we got Chuckles?"

She snickers. "No, but Chuckles could be the baby of one of the babies of one of those old warehouse cats. There were so many."

"Rat killer thrice removed," Amy says.

"Get on with it. The James part." I'm impatient. My life is hanging in the balance here. Amanda's researching what the hell happened with Declan's mother, who died in a most fragile way and one that could kill me, too. Meanwhile, my mother spills the fact that she once dated (slept with?) Declan's father, and she's blathering on about rats.

"So when he saw how we controlled the rats, he went to the humane society and adopted fifty cats. Set them loose in the building. Except he didn't think about the stray dogs in the neighborhood."

"Dogs?"

Mom's laugh is infectious, and I study her profile. The years strip off her face and she looks like she's twenty again. Sunshine frames her face and I hold my breath, enraptured.

"All these dogs started sniffing around the building, howling. They wouldn't kill the rats, but they loved to chase the cats. We slept on these little pallets in the art studios and it reached a point where you didn't know if a rat, a cat, or a dog was running over your body at 3 a.m." She makes a funny frowny face. "Or if it was the residual effects of the hit of acid from that night."

"Are you sure any of this is true?" Amy asks. "Maybe it's all just an elaborate flashback."

Mom whacks her lightly on the arm and Amy yelps with manufactured injury. "It's all true. You can ask James."

"I can't ask James anything," I argue.

"Sure you can. He's still your client."

"What about you and him? How'd you start dating?"

"He came to the building one day and was horrified to find that it had become a doggie hotel. The cats were in hiding, the rats were gone, and a ton of homeless women had followed the dogs who were so starved for attention that they curled up in everyone's laps. There was one, named Winky—this cute little mangy Jack Russell terrier. That thing was smaller than some of the rats he managed to kill."

"A rat-killing terrier?" Amy's laughing.

"Mom! Dating!"

"He came over one day to assess the mess and I told him he had to take care of Winky's vet bill. The poor thing had an infected paw from a rat bite. James thought I was crazy."

"You are crazy," Amy and I say in unison.

"James agreed." She smiles. "I got that man to take me and Winky to a downtown veterinarian who treated him with antibiotics and stitches, though. James paid the bill, then asked me out for dinner."

I stop smiling. "When was this?"

"About a year before he married Elena."

Elena. Mom knows her name. Mom knew all this time about Declan and played dumb. The sidewalk dips and cracks from old tree roots along the tree lawn, and I halt, one foot higher than the other on a slab of concrete. Being off kilter makes sense.

"You've been lying this entire time," I blurt out.

"Not lying, honey."

"Don't call me honey! Declan called me honey!"

"I haven't lied, Shannon. I just . . . didn't tell you."

"A lie by omission is still a lie." Throwing that in her face gives me a certain satisfaction, because it was what she always said to us when we were kids and didn't tell the whole truth.

She sighs and looks up at the sky. A massive jet leaves contrails that spread out like a zipper opening, white fluff filling in the space.

"You're right. I didn't know how to tell you."

"All this 'marry a billionaire' and 'you can love a rich man as much as you love a poor man' crap has been because you regret being dumped by James McCormick a million years ago?" I snap.

Angry eyes meet mine.

"That's not true."

"How the hell am I supposed to know what's true, Mom? I dated Declan. I brought the man to Easter dinner and you pretended not to know his mother is dead! A woman whose name you know because you dated his dad."

"I had no idea Elena had died! I haven't seen James McCormick in thirty years, Shannon. Aside from the society and business pages of the newspapers."

"And Jessica Coffin's Twitter stream."

Her cheeks pinken. "He's in there sometimes."

I'm so livid that words turn into angry balloons in my head. I march forward, Mom and Amy rushing to keep up. We're halfway around a giant loop we walk in my neighborhood, and if I have to spend one more second being patronized I'm going to scream.

"'Marry a billionaire! Billionaire babies! Farmington wedding!' Jesus, Mom, you're one big, fat hypocrite." I come to such a sudden halt that Amy slams into my back and squeaks.

"Does Dad know you dated him?"

"Of course. Jason's the reason I broke up with him."

Awestruck. I'm awestruck, and Amy looks like she's just

been hit by a bolt of lightning. Are we smoking? We should have tendrils of fine white smoke pouring up to meet the jet trails.

"You dumped James McCormick to be with Daddy?" I gasp.

"Well, he wasn't *the* James McCormick back then. He was just an arrogant man who was hungry to make a deal and launch himself in the business world."

A pink flower catches my attention. Then the drip of a lawn sprinkler. A dog barks in the distance once. Then twice. The pneumatic wheeze of a dump truck starting to move after being stopped at a red light fills my ears. This cannot be real. My mother cannot be telling me that—

"You mean he was the equivalent of Steve? Like, the 1980s version of Shannon's ex?" Amy says.

Mom swallows, her hand fluttering at the base of her throat, eyes troubled. "I suppose so. I never thought of it that way, but yes."

I slump against a giant, knotted oak, a triple-truck so gnarled and scarred it looks like it saw combat. "That explains so much."

Mom leans against a shiny patch of pale yellow wood where the bark has been picked clean. Sheared off. "I guess it does. I wanted you and Steve to work out because he reminded me of James."

"And when I brought Declan home?"

"I wanted that even more."

I snort. "Because it was like reliving James. For you. If I got together with Declan it was James, once removed."

"No!" Mom's face flushes bright red, almost purple, and her eyes turn so angry. All that youth that captured her levity and light in her laughter moments ago is banished, replaced by an outrage I rarely see. "Don't conflate the two. I wanted you to be with Declan because it was immediately apparent from spending ten seconds in both your presences that something very unique is there. The air around you two is charged. You don't see that often."

"You didn't have that with James?"

"No." She blinks, hard, working to control her emotions. This is a side of my mother I've rarely seen. In fact, I've *never* seen this.

"What did you mean Daddy's the reason you broke up with James?" I ask quietly. We resume our walk, taking long strides, measuring our speed. Amy's eyes are alert and perceptive; she's taking it all in without saying much.

Mom looks at the sky again. "You can't choose who you fall in love with."

"And you didn't fall in love with James?"

"I tried." Without elaborating, she lets that hang there. A child flies by on a scooter and we move to get out of his way, the wind whipping through his hair, pure joy on his face as he races his dad, who is on his bike on the road. The dad is pedaling slowly, moderating his pace so his son can win.

We all smile at the sight. Mom's face folds in fastest, though, going somber, her eyes a bit haunted. "I tried," she repeats. "But you can't force yourself to love someone if it's not right."

"And maybe that's what's happening with Declan."

"You're not forcing anything, Shannon," she says, gently touching my arm.

"No—not me. Him. Maybe I really wasn't enough." I let a frustrated sigh burst out of me. "Or I was too much." His words ricochet in my head.

"Do you really believe that?"

We round a corner and watch the dad and son fade out over the big hill we're about to climb.

I can't answer. My mouth has gone dry and my throat aches. So much information. Too much history. Mom dated James? Mom rejected James? Mom watched me bring Declan home and didn't say a word? Was that really out of respect or was there something more?

"How did James take it when you ended your relationship?" I ask, deflecting. I don't want to answer her question.

She gives me a rueful smile. "Not well. James doesn't like to lose."

I laugh so hard I trigger a bunch of dogs behind a fence, their furious barking making me laugh even more. "That's an understatement."

"He didn't have a choice. I chose." Her eyes go to a place I can't even see, where a love that has lasted more than thirty years lives. Dad's in there somewhere, and he and Mom have their own world where they are each other's sun and moon, orbiting each other.

Amy pipes up finally, as if she's been holding back all along from asking a question that's burning a hole in her head. "Mom?"

"Yes?"

"How did you meet Dad?"

Her smile broadens. "He was the vet tech for Winky."

WHEN WE GET BACK from our walk, two issues are clear:

1. We're still going to eat ice cream.

2. Amanda's struck out.

"I have the best Google skills this side of the Mississippi," she groans. "But there's just this obituary. Not even a mention in the society pages. It's . . . weird."

We're shoving mouthfuls of sex substitute (and no, not vibrators) into our mouths, my caramel chunks a poor replacement for a man's mouth, but hey, I'll take it, when Mom shouts, "Jessica Coffin!"

I inhale a solid piece of chocolate-covered frozen caramel and the world begins to swirl. Can't breathe. Can't think. I thump my chest and stare, bug-eyed, at Mom.

"Look at Shannon do her *Planet of the Apes* imitation," Mom jokes.

Dark spots fill in the edges of my vision. I seriously cannot breathe, and Mom's face changes as she realizes I'm not making a sound.

Amy jumps up and is across the room in seconds, arms wrapping around me from the back as one thought fills my mind:

Death by chocolate is very, very real.

You take first-aid classes and learn the Heimlich maneuver and wrap your arms around a dummy and pull toward you. You practice on another human being without hurting them. In the seconds between life and death in real life, though, you don't realize how hard you have to pull, the force it takes to dislodge an errant chocolate caramel, or the panic that you feel as blood's cut off from your brain, your entire life in the hands of the baby sister who used to break the heads off your Barbies and roast them on a stick in the fire in the wood stove.

If I'm going to die, there's a certain irony that it's like this and not from a bee sting.

Amy, fortunately, turns out to be as much a hero as Declan, and with one rib-cracking yank the chocolate climbs up my throat, scrapes against the back of my tongue, bounces off the top of my mouth, and flies right into Chuckles' eye, sending him sprawling off the back of the couch and into a wastebasket next to the front door.

A hole in one.

Whoop! I inhale so long and hard it's like the sound a hurt toddler makes as they gear up for a big old outraged cry. Chuckles beats me to it, scratching his way out of the trash can and howling with outrage.

"My God, Shannon, are you okay?" Mom asks, rushing over with a glass of water.

Everyone ignores Chuckles. He marches over to the front door and begins peeing in Mom's purse. My throat is raw and I can't say anything, but a weird hitching sound comes out of me, tears rolling down my face as sweet, blessed air makes its way where the frozen caramel just perched.

"Eye," is all I can manage, pointing at the cat, who is now peeing on Amy's shoe. The new Manolo knockoff.

Amy's studying her hands like they're an Oscar statue. "I can't believe I did that," she whispers. Mom gives her a huge hug and they all watch me, Amanda behind me, her hand on my back with a supportive touch.

Normal respiration resumes. By the time I'm okay, Chuckles has moved on to peeing on a plant, a doorstop painted like a bunny, and someone's stray Target bag filled with dish soap. Equal opportunity sprayer, he is.

He hates everyone equally.

"Jessica Coffin made you choke!" Amanda declares, trying to be funny. She fails.

"Why did you shout her name?" I ask. The words make sense to me, but everyone acts like I just spoke in Farsi.

Somehow, Amy understands what I'm asking and repeats it.

Mom frowns. "We can talk about that later."

"Now," I croak.

"Okay, well . . ." She really doesn't want to say this. "When you're recovered."

I drink all the water in the glass she's given me, heart slowing down. "Thank you," I say to Amy with as much gratitude as my damaged voice can muster.

"Anytime."

"This makes up for the Barbie," I say in a shorthand only siblings understand.

"Finally!" She throws her hand up like an Olympian winning a gold medal. "It only took fifteen years and near-death!"

"That was my favorite Barbie," I rasp. We share a smile. I inhale deeply and turn to Mom.

"Jessica Coffin?"

Amanda points at Mom. "You're right! Perfect!" The two share a look that goes right over my head.

"Care to share?"

"She's the hoity-toity gossip queen. If anyone knows what happened to Elena, it's her. Or her Mom. They both use gossip like it's currency."

My throat nearly closes up again with the implications of what they're saying. "You want me to go and see Jessica Coffin to pick her brain for the answer to how Declan's mother's death is connected to his dumping me?"

All three of them nod.

"You are all in a *folie a deux*. A *tres*," I amend, because all three of them are nuts.

"What's that?" Amy asks.

"It's French for 'batshit crazy,'" Mom explains.

"You speak French?"

"No. But you're not the first person to use that phrase with me."

"And I won't be the last."

"If you don't see her," Mom threatens, "I will."

I give her a dark look. She's unpredictable enough to do it. The shock of seeing Jessica with Declan in Northampton was bad enough. The woman is pure, social media evil. But Mom and Amanda have a point. If there's some secret, some lynchpin to understanding what Declan's mom's death has to do with his breakup with me, then . . .

"Give me my phone."

And with that I tweet the only woman in the world who resembles my old Barbie.

Before its head was roasted on a stick.

chapter
ten

"YOU TOLD ME THIS would be a bunch of hot men running around covered in mud while scaling wooden walls like they do in Army basic training camp commercials," I grouse as I fill the 1287th paper cup with Gatorade. Amanda is slicing oranges and shoving them into little paper cups that will be summarily squashed by the fists of runners and flung in our faces.

And we have to cheer for those same people.

"Amy said that if we volunteer and hand out rehydration we can go to all the after-event parties and meet cool people," Amanda explains. A bee begins to hover over her hands, lazy and drunk, and I back away slowly.

We're at this 10k running event in downtown Boston, surrounded by a crowd that cheers on the runners. Amy's one of the athletes, and Mom and Dad are somewhere nearby, Dad with a camera so big and old it might have a black cloth you have to drape over it, and Mom's wearing four-inch high heels that scream *I Am So Not a Runner*.

The race is for a charity run to raise money for some medical condition I've forgotten already. The runners shoot through mud runs, climb crazy ropes courses, and engage in a manufactured obstacle course that is carefully cultivated to generate maximum filth and photogenic fun.

I just came to help out because Amy's on my case about turning into one of those women they profile on a cable reality television show, the kind with three hundred dolls in a living museum in their basement, or the woman who grows her fingernails out so long she can pick locks across the street.

"And that's my cue to leave," I say softly. Amanda jerks suddenly at the sight of the bee, and I step backward slowly, sticky hands in the air.

"You have your EpiPen?" she asks, giving me a concerned look.

"Three."

"*Three?*" As if on cue, two more staggering bees come over and give the air around her hands an ominous feel.

"Mom's new thing. And the doctor wrote the prescription out happily." I back away and head toward the building where the runners all register. I know there are volunteer spots in there to help with answering questions, directing people to bathrooms, helping with finding outlets to charge dead mobile phones, and to listen to people complain about everything from the dye in the Gatorade to questions about whether the oranges have GMOs in them.

Ah, Boston. Don't ever change.

I can't avoid bees and wasps in May in New England. Impossible. Unlike Declan's brother, I have no desire to live my entire life in some self-created bubble where I never go outdoors, never feel the sun shine on my skin. Being fully aware and carefully prepared for stings and medical responses is one thing; never taking the tiniest risk and being unable to enjoy the vast majority of what it means to live a rich, fully human life is quite another.

A pang of sadness fills me as I make a beeline (pun intended) for the bathroom. Declan. He was the cornerstone of what I thought would be that kind of life, one filled with fun and hope and love. I set the feeling aside like an errant child who needs to be put on Time-Out. I go to the bank of sinks to wash off the sugar.

The past week has been one long string of rejection, starting with Jessica Coffin, who completely ignored my direct message on Twitter and my carefully worded email through the Contact Us form on her website. Nothing. Nada. My dreams have shifted from sexy times with Declan to pitchforks and torches, Barbie heads on spikes and ogres noshing on jointed Barbie legs.

The new system at work that Josh carefully designed has been spitting back every single report my shoppers submit, and Chuckles hates my guts even more, refusing to sit in my lap after I hocked up a chocolate projectile and gave him the kitty version of a black eye.

I can't win.

Scrubbed clean and no longer a bee or wasp magnet, I walk out to a long hallway and look up to see Declan and his brother, Andrew, standing at the end.

Speak of the queen bee.

Optical illusion, right? My brain created it. They take three steps to the left and disappear, the long white floor making a channel of white light into a tunnel that feeds into a glass-covered wall at the building's exterior. I feel like something out of a movie about death and the afterlife.

Like being reborn.

What would Declan be doing here? It's a Saturday, and we're across the bay. There's no reason for him and his brother to be in this high-rise business building unless . . .

My eyes scan the walls near the bathroom doors. If I'm right, I'll find it in under a minute. And . . . yes. "Employees Only."

And next to that door is a small placard that reads:

"Managed By Anterdec Industries."

His company owns this building, and there are five thousand runners and friends using it for the race's headquarters, which means my heart starts to race and my palms sweat, because I am about to see him for the first time since our disastrous last meeting.

All because of a few bees outside.

Maybe Andrew's got it right. What if sealing yourself off from the rest of the world because you know there's one lethal enemy out there that is sociopathic and ready to destroy you with one touch is the right move after all? What if one sigh, one hitched eyebrow, one frown, one dismissive huff could crush you?

Would you do everything in your power to get away from them—forever?

Reason would dictate that any person of average intelligence and with a little common sense would do so.

Especially my heart. Because while I won't go to his extremes to protect myself from the absolutely random, utterly errant, highly unpredictable sting, I might hermetically seal up my heart because—

This is just too hard.

Suddenly, I understand Declan's brother better. Screw the world—I'll just build a bubble around myself and not even try to justify it. Make the world bend to me. Team Andrew all the way.

I should get some oranges and Gatorade and toss them his way. Maybe a little to the left, though, where Declan's standing.

I walk slowly down the hall toward the sunlight, glad now for my tennis shoes, which make not a single sound on the floor. Two men's voices murmur softly to each other, and I slow down. What a dilemma.

Walk past them and acknowledge their presence, or march on past and pretend I'm not there?

I'm not there.

Notice how I said that? Not pretend *they're* not there. Me. I make myself invisible because I don't know any other way.

"You should say something to her," Andrew says. I freeze. A handful of people run to and fro in the space at the end of the hall, all of them wearing jogger's shorts and carrying clipboards. The leaders are only a few minutes away and I need to go somewhere to help.

Missing this conversation, though, is worth incurring the wrath of Amy.

"Jessica's here. I don't want to add fuel that fire." *Her* is Jessica? Boo. Hiss. She's here? I'll go back outside and risk the bees and wasps to get a giant container of Gatorade and go Belichick on her ass. Pin her down and make her talk. Pry open those Botoxed pork chop lips and—

"You're not dating Jessica, though." *He's not? Whew!*

"And I'm not dating Shannon." *Oh! Oh! So* her *is me!*

"Which is stupid." *TEAM ANDREW! I knew I liked this guy!*

"What? My love life isn't any of your business."

"Following Dad's orders isn't exactly your standard operating procedure, Declan."

James? What the hell does James have to do with Declan's dating me? Orders?

I am sliding against the textured, wallpapered wall like a ninja, but with a rack like mine I resemble a silent warrior mastermind who can make himself seem invisible and discreet about as much as LeBron James resembles Mother Teresa in the humility department.

I try anyway, because eavesdropping on this conversation is the mystery shop of a lifetime.

"Dad didn't make me stop dating Shannon and you know it damn well, Andrew." A long, slow, angry sigh comes out of Declan, and I can imagine him, even if I can't see him, running a shaky hand through his hair. It's been a month since we've been together and I can't get a good look now. Is his hair growing out a bit from his super-short cut? Does he get it clipped regularly? Does he still smell like—

Andrew laughs, the kind of noise only a sibling can make. "Then you're being even more ridiculous than I thought. Not pissing Dad off is one thing. Dumping the first woman I've ever heard you really fall for is just asinine, and your reason is stupid. Plus, she has a hot friend."

Falling for? Reason? Hot friend? He thinks Amanda's hot? I need to tell her so she can run away from the killer bees and come in here and—

Wait—WHAT REASON? Maybe I don't need to kidnap Jessica after all. I crane my neck, inches away from the end of the hall, now exposing myself to certain discovery but not caring. I have to know. I need to know. He wouldn't tell me when I asked, and now this casual conversation tells me more than anything I've guessed.

"Dad's wrong about plenty of issues, but not this one," Declan says.

"Dec." Andrew's voice is suddenly so pained it makes me pause. Sometimes one syllable can have more emotion in it than one thousand words.

An involuntary sadness fills me. "It wasn't your fault," Andrew continues. *What* wasn't his fault? Our breakup? Because it damn sure was Declan's fault! I didn't dump him in the hallway of his company while Mail Boy rubbernecked with a cart creakier than a rusted Tin Man.

This is one of those moments where blood rushes to my ears, I can count the molecules in my breath, the ceiling seems lower suddenly, and the walls expand as if they seek infinity.

The moment when my life unfolds, for good or for bad.

"You keep saying that," Declan responds. "Been saying it for ten years."

Ten years? He's only known me for a month.

"And I'll say it for rest of my life," Andrew adds. I hear him take a deep breath to say something more, and just when I think I'm about to understand how the world works, how all the gears fit into place to turn the crank and function, why Declan broke up with me, and how maybe—just the tiniest taste of maybe?—I can find my way back to him, I hear:

"Oh. Hello." Declan's voice goes tight. He's clearly talking with someone he didn't expect to see. Did Jessica crash my conversation?

Mine.

Because they're talking about *me.*

"Declan." The voice is low, gravelly, and very angry.

That voice is my dad's. Controlled and wound, he introduces himself to Andrew, whose voice shifts down a half-octave, like a bunch of younger gorillas meeting a new orangutan they've never seen before, but one who disrupts the social order not only because he's strange looking, but because he's communicating pretty clearly that you don't mess with him.

My *dad*. The one who let me paint his toenails pink when I was seven and who walked around at the beach in flip-flops? The former vet tech who stole Mom away from Declan's dad?

Andrew says his goodbyes. *Please don't need to pee. Please don't need to pee. Please don't need to pee*, I pray, and he doesn't turn the corner. If he did, we'd be able to kiss, because my ear is that close to the edge of the hall.

My ex and my dad are about to square off. A rush of heat and terror spikes my skin. If I ever imagined a parent calling Declan out if would be Mom, like she did with Steve at the ice cream parlor. Not . . . my dad.

"How are you?" Declan asks conversationally. His voice is so neutral it sounds like a series of sound bites, like phone trees at major corporations. How—Are—You? He couldn't sound more robotic if he tried. I've seen him in enough tense situations to know that this is not his normal reaction.

"You don't need to engage in meaningless pleasantries," Dad replies. His voice is so deep, so filled with implied rage. Danger pours out of that mouth, and I'm hearing a side to him I didn't know he possessed.

A long time ago Mom told me something I didn't understand. She said, "Marry a beta-alpha."

"A what?"

"A beta-alpha. It's a kind of man. You know what an alpha male is, right? The dominant, self-assured, slightly arrogant guy who annoys you just enough to hate him but he's so powerful and commanding that against your better judgment you want to sleep with him. Desperately."

"Uh, sure." She'd said this to me right after Steve dumped me, and if I was going to sleep with anyone, it would be Ben & Jerry.

"A beta-alpha is different. He's the man who seems more docile. Whipped, even."

"Like Dad."

She had laughed. "Like your father, but don't ever be fooled, Shannon. Jason is the one in charge when he needs to be. We're equals—always have been, always will be—and he just doesn't care about the trivial stuff like I do."

"Dad has an alpha side? Where does he hide it? In your purse?"

She'd held up one perfectly manicured finger and wagged it

in my face, hard. "And that's your mistake. With your father, you can push and push and push and he won't push back until you cross his line. That line is way, way farther back than most men's lines, but it's there."

"A line?"

"You cross a beta-alpha's line and the alpha comes out. And it takes a long, long time to make it go away. And don't ever think that it's lesser just because he's a beta most of the time." She'd given me a long, hard look. "Beta-alphas always, always win."

"Over a what? An alpha-alpha?" I'd snickered.

Her wistful smile had made my heart pause. "Over every other man who thinks they have the right to cross the line of anyone your father loves."

I think Declan just found that line.

"Pleasantries." Declan's not asking a question, or requesting clarification. "No."

The abject silence that follows his final word makes me feel like I'm floating to the ceiling, like gravity ceased to exist with that single declaration of "no," like all the laws of physics don't matter any longer, because my father and Declan are facing off over me.

Me.

"Good. I'm not here to yell at you or exact revenge, or"— Dad blows a long puff of air out, and I can imagine him shifting his weight onto one hip, his toes curling under as he struggles with something he doesn't want to face, but makes himself do it anyhow—"but I'm here to tell you that if you broke up with Shannon because of what happened to your mother, then you might want to rethink that."

Your mother? Dad knows what I've been trying to figure out for the past week? It's like God took the world and shook it, hard, like a snow globe.

"Excuse me?"

Dad laughs, not the gentle laugh of my childhood, or the boisterous, rumbling sound of comedy, but a more nuanced sound, one that is masculine and just the tiniest bit dangerous.

"Steve was the last man to hurt Shannon. I never liked him."

Dad's voice goes raspy. Confidential. I see his fingers twitch at his hip, as if he's holding back from grabbing Declan's elbow and pulling him in closer to tell a secret.

"Never liked him," Dad continues, eyes narrowing. "I faked it. Pretended he was fine, but there was always something not quite right with him. Slimy. He was a user. The kind of man who views people as fleshbags they manipulate for their own purposes, then chuck aside when they're done."

Declan makes an ambiguous sound in his throat that sounds like Man Code for "go on."

"You, though, are nothing like Steve."

I can hear Declan smile.

"I liked you the moment I met you, and I know Shannon fell for you. Hard. You don't get that in life more than once, you know? That moment when your eyes meet a total stranger's and you realize you're a goner. Done. You just met the love of your life and forever isn't some fantasy people weave to get through reality. It's staring at you over an injured dog."

"Huh?"

Dad laughs again. "Long story. In your case, it was staring at you over a men's room toilet."

Declan snorts.

I can't stand it. Inching slowly, cheek against the wall, I position my eye so Dad comes into view.

Dad's face goes deadly serious so quickly it's like he's rebooted his emotional core. "But maybe I misjudged you. Maybe you're more like your father than I ever imagined."

"What the hell does my father have to do with anything?"

"I think you damn well know James has a great deal to do with what *you're* doing to Shannon right now. And I can't do a damn thing to stop you, but I won't keep my mouth shut, either."

Their conflict has my heart ricocheting around my ribcage, and I feel like I'm floating as the two men I care about most in the world are going head-to-head. Dad's face is so red he looks like he'll have a heart attack, and Declan's nostrils flare like a bull's.

"You're just like your father," Dad says, delivering the KO punch.

Gravity does, apparently, cease to exist, because I fall over in shock, my body flying forward and out into the lobby, shoulder and knee cracking against the polished floor, my shriek of surprise echoing in the enormous, airy building like a gunshot ricocheting.

I'm on my side and my hip and shoulder are screaming. I look up to find my father completely dumbfounded, with his jaw hanging so low it's resting next to me like a pillow, offered in shock.

And Declan is smiling.

chapter
eleven

H E CAN'T FAKE IT, no matter how hard he tries to hide the grin that just spontaneously popped on his face, but the smother job he does is pretty damn good.

"Just testing out my Lucille Ball imitation," I say as I roll onto my back, afraid to stand up. This is far less conspicuous than any limp, anyhow.

"Can I step on her, Mommy?" asks a little toddler as his mom drags him by the hand on the way to the bathrooms.

"No." She's dressed in all-white running clothes, and the little boy is wearing nothing but white, too. "You might get dirty," she snaps.

"You must be Jessica Coffin's sister," I call back to her. She ignores me.

Declan's eyes light up, though he doesn't smile. Dad bends down to help me stand up, but I wave him off.

"You two were about to compare penises, so don't let me interrupt you."

I didn't think Dad's jaw could fall open any more, but somehow it does. Half of Declan's mouth inches up with a quirked look, his eyes on me, conflicted but determined at the same time. He looks like a stern headmaster at a girl's prep school, the pinnacle of authority and a role model for how to comport oneself at all times.

Yet just as likely to take the older girls to his office for a spanking when they're naughty.

Parts of me that aren't supposed to be warm right now feel

like sunspots. And parts of me that aren't supposed to be wet
are. All in front of my father, who is grasping my elbow like he's
pulling me out of the rapids on the Colorado River in the middle of a flash flood.

"Shannon!" Dad exclaims, his voice shifting from the dominant fight tone he just used with Declan to the kindly, concerned
father tone I know so well. All the information Mom's given me
about him and James from thirty years ago swirls around inside,
a churn I can't contain. No one can pivot readily from one stance
to another, though; his muscles are corded steel underneath his
middle-age paunch, and he has a look in his eyes that makes me
a little afraid for Declan.

Once that alpha is unleashed . . .

"Why are you talking about penises, Shannon?" Declan adds,
then shakes his head. A fight between two approaches to me
and my father is brewing inside him. I can see it. Mr. Cool is trying to win, but Mr. Ass is giving him a run for his money.

Penitheth, I think, but don't say. Then I giggle as I get on my
feet, nursing my sore shoulder. Green eyes narrow and he goes
somber. Challenging.

Mr. Ass is, apparently, taking over. This is the same guy I saw
a month ago. The one who gives no quarter. Dismissive and
closed off, he won't be worth talking to.

And then Declan surprises me.

"Jason," he says, turning to offer Dad a hand to shake. The
two grip each other like a stripper hanging on to her pole after a
high heel breaks. "Good to see you."

Dad is dismissed. His eyes harden, and while he's older and
softer, he's not going anywhere. "Good to see you, too, Declan."
Both of them look at me for a microsecond and, like synchronized swimmers, cross their arms over their chests, brows lowering, necks tight, mouths set.

Who are these people?

I don't want to hurt my dad's masculinity here, but I also
don't want to miss out on the first chance to talk to Declan in
what feels like forever. Because my brain shuts down in overwhelmed moments like this, I blurt out the first thing that

comes to mind:

"Andrew thinks Amanda is hot?"

Declan lowers his head, biting his lips in that super-sexy way that he thinks is somehow suppressing a laugh but that just succeeds in making me want him even more.

"Eavesdropping? My dad was right."

A flame of fury engulfs me. He's itching to find reasons—really stupid reasons—to make our breakup my fault. *So* not my fault. Even when it's on fire, my heart beats for him. Damn it. Time to extinguish it with just the right words.

Which are . . .

Not there. Because I'm so happy to be a few feet from him, to look at him, to have his eyes on me. I can't come back with a retort because there are no retorts. If I say something—anything—right now, it will probably be a string of babble that makes me sound like I'm speaking in tongues at an evangelical revival.

So I just stare at him like Dory the fish. Just keep staring, just keep staring . . .

And he stares right back.

Dad clears his throat and gives me a look of consideration, the kind of glance you give someone who impresses you. Like he's underestimated me and has reconsidered based on evidence I don't know I've provided.

"I'll leave you two to talk," he announces, and gives me a wink. Have I neutralized the beta-alpha?

Or did Dad just defer to me because he knows he's secure in who he is?

I'm not nervous. Not anxious or worried or scared or—anything. I am present. Here, fully, in the company of Declan.

And ready to talk.

"Your dad was right about which topic?" I ask Declan, who frowns slightly, confused. One hand slips into his pants pocket and the other opens, palm flat against the wall as if he's holding it up.

Propping up the world.

Andrew's words pump through my mind, analysis impossible

right here, face to face with Declan. I can't smell him, breathe in his air, watch the movement of his body under his suit and shirt while dissecting what his brother meant moments ago.

All I can do is ask the source and see if he will reveal any new truths to me.

Then again, why should he? In his mind I'm just the woman who used him for his money and connections.

"What do you mean?" He's being coy. He knows I heard his conversation with Andrew, and instead of tipping his hand he's tipping my heart. Upside down, shaking it like a pickpocket rolling a victim.

"What isn't your fault? What was Andrew talking about? Something happened ten years ago and you're blaming yourself for it."

Blood drains from his face, but he doesn't change expression, eyes hard now, mouth immobile. No answer. No reaction.

Just a silent *no*.

I refuse the no, though, because I've decided that I can do that. Other people have the right to live according to their internal core, and so do I.

So do I.

What I want is equally important, and if someone else has a different opinion then they can express that and instead of living life as one big chain of reactions to other people's reactions, I'm going to act.

Act.

And process it all later.

My hand covers his, the one pushed against the wall. When our skin connects I feel his trembling. A little too good at making the surface look placid, he keeps all the ripples underneath.

He doesn't have to do that with me.

And he doesn't move his hand. If he had, he would drag my heart with it, and right now I can't handle the road rash.

"Declan?" I prod, my voice as tender as can be. "Where have you been?"

His mouth is set in a firm line, tense and unforgiving, but those eyes narrow with a questioning look, reading my face, and then the tension in his jaw lessens, as if a single layer is peeling back.

His lips part, a thin line of white showing between them as they start to form a word, the beginning of a sentence that will break through whatever wall has been built between us.

"Validating myself." He says it with such nuanced dryness that I'm not sure whether to laugh or be offended.

And then—

"You're not supposed to be here," says a woman's cold voice behind me.

It sounds like death.

I turn around.

Close.

A Coffin.

Declan doesn't move his hand. I cling to that single fact. It's all I have, literally, to hold on to right now.

"Here to take out the garbage? Don't you need that weird little car that looks like you're carrying a bowel movement on the roof?" Jessica says with a sneer.

"No," I say, eyes on her, hard as rock. "If I need a piece of crap to do my job," I say, looking her up and down slowly, "I can find one anywhere. Even on Twitter."

Her eyes lock on my hand. The one touching Declan. The one he's not moving.

Hardened again, he stares at me, then lets his glance dart to her. "You interrupted us," he says coldly.

Is he talking to me? No. I interrupted him and his brother, not him and Jessica. Instead of opening my mouth and stammering a nonsensical apology, I inhale slowly, as silently as I can, and just keep my eyes on Declan, pretending Jessica doesn't exist.

Turnabout is fair play.

"The race is ending. We have photo ops to attend to." Her tongue rolls inside her cheek, the movement so masculine it makes her look like Ann Coulter for a moment.

Declan blinks exactly once, but his fingers move just enough to squeeze mine affectionately, grasping me. "I'll be there."

Her eyebrow arches and the look she gives me makes it clear she thinks I deserve my car. "Don't waste your time. We have more important things to deal with."

He makes a small, derisive sound. "The world won't end if I'm not in a picture at the finish line, holding a ribbon."

She looks like she's been slapped.

"When your company donated heavily to support this charity, it meant—"

"I know what it meant." He is iron. Steel. Titanium. But his thumb caresses the back of my hand, and for all his hardness, I turn soft, my insides a twist of silk sheets, my mind airy with a floating feeling that makes it hard to breathe.

"Don't ruin this for everyone, Declan," she challenges.

"You should take your own advice, Jessica," he says, cool as a cucumber. "How's business?"

She storms off in a mumbling fit.

I don't know what to say. He's standing before me, touching me, my hand the center of the universe, his eyes a distant sun. A million questions race through my mind but I can't capture any of them long enough to read them and translate into coherent speech.

A man's shout from near the front door cuts through the air.

"Jesus Christ! Get it out of here!" It's Andrew, backing away toward the elevator.

"It" turns out to be what looks like a fly, but I know it's not.

It's so much more.

Declan's face goes slack again.

"I'm sorry," he says. "I wish this could be different, but my father is right."

And with that, he grips my hand hard, his face filled with regret, then lets go, the hard clap of his shoes on marble like gunshots.

chapter
twelve

L IMPING UP THE STEPS to my Soviet-bloc business building makes me feel like one of those over-muscled women
on the weightlifting team for Belarus. Except I'm limping
and whimpering, and I feel like my pectoral and gluteal muscles
have been sent to Siberia for re-education.

For the past three weeks—since right after I saw Declan—
my life has been a series of gym shops. Forty-seven of them in
twenty days, to be exact. That is more than two per day, which
equates to screaming quads and exposing more cellulite per
hour than you see on a Cape Cod beach in August.

Rumors of ongoing and persistent underperformance by
personal trainers at a particular chain of gyms in the area mean I
have to pretend to be a new customer who wants to try the "first
hour free" promotion. The gyms generally send the least-senior
personal trainer to do these jobs, though the one I just left was
quite different. I got a seventy-eight-year-old professional female
body builder who had more muscle than my dad, Steve, and
possibly Declan combined, and whose skin was the color of the
old leather armchair in dad's Man Cave.

Smelled like it, too.

Her teeth had gleamed like polished Chiclets gum and her
eyes were remarkably alert and bright for someone born before
WWII. No loose skin under the eyes, no bags at all. Her jaw was
so muscled she looked like an aging bulldog.

That woman worked me like Jillian Michaels with a group
of mouthy teens sent to some Christian re-education camp in

Utah. I haven't had my inner thighs quiver like this since . . .

Declan.

Damn it. I was trying so hard not to think about him, but leave it to my overactive adductor muscles to make him float into my mind. Three weeks have passed without seeing him, hearing from him—and yet he's in my mind, embedded in my skin, deep in my heart.

Still.

I use both hands to physically lift my right leg up the first cement stair. There are nine of them. Nine. As in my legs are screaming *"nein!"* Pain makes me bilingual.

I'm on stair number four when Josh appears next to me. His legs function. He can hop up those stairs like a cage fighter who just drank five Red Bulls.

"What's wrong?" he asks with glee, knowing damn well why I am suffering. We can't pawn any of these gym shops off on him because the assignment requires female guests.

"Not enough fiber in my diet," I mutter.

His face goes blank. "I thought it was all the gym shops you're doing." He snorts. "I know it's not from really good sex."

"At staff meeting today I'm telling Greg he needs to give you the role of supportive father-to-be on all those cord blood bank shops that are coming up."

His pale face makes me grin inside, because Josh can't stand hospitals. "You wouldn't!"

Before I can reply, he puts up a palm and shakes his head sadly, "Actually, you would," he says, leaping up the remaining stairs like Peter Pan and holding the heavy door open for me.

"Thank you. Just stand there for about thirty-seven more minutes and I'll get there."

A strange scuffling sound from behind us makes us both turn. It's Amanda, kicking a box the size of a small ottoman across the parking lot.

"What are you doing?" Josh calls out.

"I no longer have arms," she whines. "Just shredded, noodly appendages."

"Gym shops?" I shout. Using my diaphragm makes the

muscles between my ribs hurt. Now it hurts to talk? I need combat pay for this job, I swear.

Josh drops the door handle and runs down the stairs.

"Hey!" I protest.

"*Please*," he calls back. "I could drive to Starbucks and get us all lattes and return and you'll still be on the eighth stair. I can help Amanda."

He's got a point. I feel like a turtle with fibromyalgia.

Josh comes whizzing up the staircase with the box in his hands like he's Superman. Balancing Amanda's stuff on one arm, he uses the other to hold the door for me.

"Show-off," Amanda and I say in unison. I look at her and gasp.

"What are you wearing?"

She looks like the human embodiment of the coffee bean/piece of excrement on the top of my car.

"Car wash uniform. I have to go and pretend to be a counter employee for the rest of the day."

"With non-functioning arms?"

"That's what I said! Greg's being unreasonable."

"And that's the uniform?" Josh squeaks, laughing. "I haven't seen that much polyester since I watched the movie *Boogie Nights* with my boyfriend."

Amanda and I pause, which isn't hard. "Boyfriend?" We're in stereo.

Josh blushes. "Well, you know—YES! I have a boyfriend!" he squeals.

We all squeal.

Greg opens a window and sticks his head out. "You guys sound like you're replaying that scene from *Deliverance*. You okay?"

"We're just talking about our cars and how much we love driving in tin cans of humiliation," Amanda shouts back.

Thwack. The window snaps shut.

Josh starts to tell us all about Cameron the New Boyfriend while I make it to the seventh step and realize that Josh—geeky, smart, goofy, socially deficited Josh—has a boyfriend.

And I don't.

Tears prickle at the edges of the soft skin around my eyeballs, taking the immediacy of my aching muscles away from my attention. I inhale slowly through my nose and grasp my leg, pulling it up. Eight. One more stair to go. Just don't cry until—

Too late.

"You look great!" Josh says as I pull my leg up to reach the top. "All these gym shops are toning you."

"It's all neutral. I'm eating more ice cream to compensate."

"For what?" Amanda snorts. "You'd have to work out thirty-seven hours a day doing CrossFit to make up for the amount of ice cream you're eating."

I'm about to answer but she makes it up the stairs and is right behind me, nudging me with her shoulder. I'm forced to stumble forward and take three steps in a row.

"You look like you could star in *The Walking Dead*."

"You sound like you could star in *Honey Boo Boo*."

"What does that even mean?"

"I was aiming for 'offensive.'"

"You sailed right past it and hit the 'lame' target."

We get to the stairs. No elevator. Josh and Amanda slip past me and I am grateful for the peace. It takes me seventeen minutes to get to the office. I'm late for the staff meeting.

Just as I walk in, I hear Greg say two different sentences:

"Shannon and you can go to the Catch My Vibe store with her mother."

and

"The Fort shop goes to Shannon per James McCormick's instructions, no matter how much you threaten me, Amanda." Greg flinches just enough to show he's worried.

Both freak me out, though not enough to drown out the screaming pain in my legs.

"Wait—what?" I ask. Three faces turn toward me, Amanda's hostile.

"She can barely move!" Amanda argues, gesturing wildly

with her head, her arms immobile.

"Pick up your pen and write your name," I say in a quiet voice.

She's been taking glare lessons from Chuckles, I see.

"It's done," Greg announces. "You get your shot later in the summer," he explains to her. She leans down to drink out of a straw someone shoved in her can of diet soda.

As I bend to sit in my chair, I hear my hamstrings snap like a high-tension cord on a crane. *Ping!*

Greg eyes us warily. Josh adjusts Amanda's straw.

"What's wrong with you two?" Greg finally asks, though he sounds about as eager to know the answer as I am to know the specifics of my parents' sex life. And, like me, Greg is about to hear more than he ever imagined.

"I just had more weight swinging in and out between my legs than you could ever imagine," Amanda wails.

All the blood in Greg's face drains out, like low tide during a tsunami, rushing back in so fast that he looks like a big red beet.

"Um, I meant what's wrong *professionally*. I don't need to know about your sex life," he clarifies.

"This *was* for work! That Bulgarian ex-Olympian at the gym on Union Avenue made me do forty-pound kettlebell reps until I couldn't stand it anymore!"

Greg sighs with relief. "*That* kind of weight between your legs!" He's so relieved.

"What did you think I meant?" she demands.

"Never mind," me, Greg, and Josh say.

"I thought you were upset about The Fort."

"I'm upset about that, too," Amanda adds. "But mostly I just want to get laid."

"Don't look at me," Josh says, palms out.

"Or me," Greg murmurs so quietly only I can hear him.

"I think we're swinging away from professionalism," I whisper in her ear.

"It's the damn sex toy shop I did with your mother!"

"Anyone want coffee?" Greg shouts. Josh jumps up with him and they rush out of the room.

"Note to self," I say. "Mention sex life, get free coffee from men at work."

"Oh, and here," Amanda says, as if uninterrupted. She flails one arm toward her a giant Vera Bradley bag, hands hanging down like a T-rex, ineffectual and useless. Normally I would take pity on her, but I'm kind of enjoying her pain.

After what feels like an hour, she pulls out a water bottle. One of those big, pink-and-white plastic water bottles that . . .

Has a giant mushroom cap on the end of it, and a Power button.

"Is that a—OH MY GOD, AMANDA!" I scream, shoving the monstrosity out of my way. It falls to the ground and in the impact, the Power button is pushed. A slow vibration rubs against my foot.

"What? It's from the sex toy shop. You act like you've never seen a vibrator before!"

"Not at work! Here! With Greg and Josh around." I've never met a vibrator I didn't like, frankly, but this is a bit much.

"Your mom used part of her product allowance to give this one to you." Mom's been assigned to seven different sex toy shops now because of the way she handled my breakdown in Northampton. Her evaluation was perfect and the client asked for her to do most of the rest of the shops.

I'm so proud. It's like having your mother win the Nobel Peace Prize.

Almost.

I stare at the buzzing monstrosity and I just . . . I don't . . . words disappear. The earth implodes. A supernova of nothingness replaces my consciousness. I did not just receive a hand-picked vibrator from my mother. *Nope nope nope.*

"See? It has a backwards 'D' on the tip. Marie wanted it to remind you of Declan."

"Remind me of . . . what?"

"Plus, the curvature of the letter makes hitting the G-spot easier." She says this the way a home party product specialist might describe a decorative candle.

"Shut up."

"Why are you so hostile?"

"Some product designer actually thought this was a good idea?" I challenge.

"Your mom said the sex toy shop owner told her it was so your man could leave his mark in an intimate place."

"Where? On your *cervix*? That's like being branded! You know a man designed that," I fume.

The vibrator twitches on the ground, but I can't stop it. My legs won't move. I've been sitting here just long enough for atrophy or entropy or oldladykickedmyassery to set in, and all these gym shops have collectively rendered my leg muscles so useless I can't even kick a vibrator with enough power to make it come within range of my hand so I can turn it off.

Bzzzz. "Amanda, can you help me? Reach under there and—"

"Reach? REACH? You ever bench-press eighty pounds, then do ten minutes of high-intensity rowing while a Bulgarian screams in your ear? I'm lucky my arms are still attached." She looks down. "Okay, good. Still there. Hello, hands. I love you!" She looks up at me. "Just checking."

Bzzzz.

"Greg and Josh will be back any second, and I'd really prefer neither of them has to pick up a vibrator that my mother gave me."

"It's pretty impressive," she says. "Has an anal probe attachment that's shaped like an octopus tentacle."

Greg walks in as she says the end of that sentence. He stops so quickly that hot coffee sloshes out of the tiny sipping holes in the tops of the two take-out cups he carries. His ears perk up and he tilts his head, searching for the sound.

And then his eyes find it.

"Is that a robot vacuum cleaner?" he asks, poking his head under the table to catch a look. "Judy's been mentioning getting one. Says it could really make things better at home, because I've been slacking, and we need something bigger."

"Uh," is all I can say. Just as he bends down, Amanda kicks the vibrator, hard, but her aim is off.

It hits Josh squarely in the shin as he walks in carrying two more coffees. Josh looks down at the bleating white-and-pink flesh penis, then looks at Greg, who has a perplexed look on his walrus-like face.

"That doesn't look like a robot vacuum," Greg says.

Josh is nonplussed by the non sequitur. He looks at Amanda, then me, and asks:

"Do they make that in purple?"

N O AMOUNT OF BEGGING, pleading, or offers to clean anyone's shoes with my tongue—including Chuckles'—has made a difference. I am stuck driving my poop-topped car to my mystery shop for The Fort.

Why does this matter, you wonder? Because when you mystery shop a hotel, most clients want a detailed evaluation of every service offered in the hotel. For high-end luxury properties, that begins with valet parking.

That's right. I have to hand off my Turdmobile to a guy who makes more in tips parking Teslas and Ferraris in a day than I make in a week.

And while I'm sure these valets have seen some novel vehicles, including electric-powered Hummers and cars with batwings for doors, a compact car with a big, brown coffee bean that looks like a piece of feces is going to be a new one in their repertoire.

Which throws being inconspicuous out the window.

Even Greg wouldn't relent, making up some sob story about how he needs his car to take his mother to her hip rehab appointment. *Pffft*. Excuses.

The Fort is a massive building of wonder and beauty, blinding in the bright sunshine and shining like a beacon on the edge of Boston's Back Bay. Located right on the edge of all the fun in the city's core, you can walk to fine steakhouses, Faneuil Hall, see the boats come in, go to the aquarium, and have everything at your fingertips.

But first you have to talk to a valet named Guido who looks just like your ex-boyfriend.

Guido—according to the name tag—makes me do a triple take, because if Guido were a few years younger and had green eyes instead of brown, he'd be Declan.

"Holy—*what*?" I exclaim as I climb out of the car, keys in hand. The semicircular driveway in front of the glittering bronze-covered entrance seems like it's made of polished marble. As my high heels clack on the ground, I realize it *is* marble. Actual marble.

And because it's just rained, and various car tires have brought water onto the ground, I go flying in the air, keys arcing like they've been ejected from a stomp rocket, arms and legs flailing to grab on to anything so I don't crack my assbone in half.

Two strong hands wrap around my waist and save me from permanent butt damage. The red jacket Guido is wearing unbuttons and reveals a slim waist, broad shoulders stretching the fabric. His hair is a thick, wavy brown like Declan's, eyebrows thicker, a strand of grey here and there peppering his hair. His eyes are kind and worried, though there's a suppressed mirth there, his mouth twitching.

He sets me on my heels, my knee turning inward. I'm dressed in business clothing, the client insisting I assume the role of a C-level female executive traveling for business, in town for the night. And valet parking is the start.

"You hurt?" Guido asks in a bass voice that makes me jolt. If he had poured warm caramel sauce on my nipples I couldn't have had a naughtier response. That voice must get a lot of women out of their pants for him. I, myself, will be using the bathroom clothesline to dry my panties shortly if he speaks again.

"I'm, um, fine," I say, breathless. He steps across from me to retrieve my keys from the ground, giving me a chance to really look at his butt, er . . . at him. His face. His face! His cheekbones are broader than Declan's, and he's confident in that loose way men who work with their hands for a living have about them.

"Your car?" he asks with arched eyebrows.

"Business car." I smile with more perk than I really feel. I've already developed an excuse for the piece-of-crap car. "Testing a new advertising model for a client."

He nods, like he's in on some joke I don't know about. "I see, Ms. . . ."

"Jacoby."

"Jacoby." He smiles and gives me a small bow. "Does the market test include aromatherapy as well?"

"What?"

"Never mind, Ms. Jacoby." He jingles my keys and looks at my car with amusement. More amusement than I've ever felt. "I'll park your company car and keep it safe from harm."

"Really? Actually, I'd prefer you just park it on the street. Maybe someone will steal it and then I'd—" The words are pouring out of my mouth before I can stop them. Something about Guido is so casually comfortable, so companionable, and the facade of being an executive fades away without my even thinking about it.

He smirks and instantly looks nothing like Declan. What was I thinking? I clearly can't get him out of my head, so I'm inventing men who look like him. But when Guido's face goes back to semi-serious, it's like a shadow of my ex is there.

I'm going crazy, aren't I?

Driving the crazy piece of sh—

"I'd lose my job if I did that," he says in a low conspirator's voice.

I swallow, my mouth dry. All the moisture in my body migrates south. "Just kidding."

He eyes me in a way that makes me feel like I felt the first time I ever met Declan.

Inventoried.

"I suspect you aren't. Kidding, that is." And then he just stands there, watching me. It doesn't feel sensual, though. More of a neutral acknowledgement of my existence, for which I'm grateful, because if he starts sending out sexual signals of any kind I'm going to fall over in a puddle of my own goo.

The awkward pause makes me realize he's waiting for a tip. Of course! We have a mystery shopping procedure for this, so I pull out the $5 bill and hand it to him. He frowns, then glances at the other valets. What kind of parking dude doesn't take the bill and slip it in his pocket with a quick thanks?

My skin starts to tingle. Something doesn't make sense here.

As if I'm handing him a piece of raw steak at a vegan restaurant, he takes the five and puts it in his breast pocket, wincing. Wincing! What kind of guy—

Oh. Hmmm. Maybe $5 is an insult in a place like this? No one explains tipping guidelines, so staying in an $800-per-night suite might mean that a $5 valet tip—which would be healthy anywhere else—is like pissing on his shoes.

I reach into my purse and pull out a second $5 bill, handing it to him with a smile. "Thank you so much, Guido. Take good care of her."

The other valets laugh and Guido takes my bill with confusion clouding those rich chocolate eyes. "You're giving me more?"

Didn't expect that. "Yes. Is that okay?"

Finally, one of the other valets comes over and taps him on the shoulder. "Dude. Take the money, thank her, and let's go park the piece of—"

I snicker. "We call it the Turdmobile."

Guido laughs, eyes on me the entire time. "You're funny."

If he's flirting, he's horrible at it. But so am I, so maybe the weirdness is me? I can't juggle being "on" for work, doing a mystery shop, and figuring out whether the valet is horrified or attracted to me. Too much input. So I do the simplest thing and just walk away. One step, two step, and down I go—

Splat. *Riiiiiiip.*

I'm showing more ass than J.Lo in a g-string. Guido wasn't there to catch me this time, and I have one leg stretched out with my skirt split so high you can see where Niagara Falls visited my panties.

"Shannon!" Guido calls out, racing to my side.

Now, hold on there. I never told him my first name. But

that takes a back seat to the fact that I am staring at the chandelier-topped canopy and a Range Rover the size of my parents' house is about to squish me like a bug.

Guido and his valet friends rush over to me, and four sets of man hands lift me up, making me feel like I'm in one of those romance novels where the woman has more men touching her than she has holes for them to occupy.

"I'm fine," I protest, struggling to control my own body and realizing it's useless. Like synchronized swimmers they set me upright, someone grabbing my carryon and computer bag, another picking up all the items that rolled out when I fell.

Including Mom's vibrator.

"Um," Guido says as he hands it to me. It's the one Mom picked out, with a tip shaped like a backwards J, from the Alphasex Series. The one Josh wants to order in purple. But it's pink, so . . .

"How did that get in there?" I squeak out, and I'm serious. I have no earthly idea how it got in my laptop bag. Maybe Chuckles is playing an elaborate joke.

A vague memory of Mom in my closet that day after the sex toy shop in Northampton. J?

Oh. My stomach roils.

J for Jason. Mom got me one with a D on it, too. I crane my neck, twisting around, eyes on the ground. Where's that one? If one vibrator magically appears in my bag, I'm sure there are more.

"I've seen some crazy tips before, but . . ." Guido jokes. I shove the damn vibrator in my bag and decide that the best way to handle this with grace and dignity is to walk away without another word.

"I hope your stay is a pleasant one, Ms. Jacoby! You can believe all the *buzz* about The Fort," he says as I walk away. I swear he winks. And in the recesses of my professional mind I think:

Reminded me to have a pleasant stay? Check.

Sigh.

chapter
fourteen

ANOTHER VALET, MIKE, REMOVES my luggage from the trunk of my car and escorts me into the lobby. "Lobby" is an understatement.

The first wonder of the modern world is more like it. Grey Industries couldn't come up with something this fine if they tried. I can tell James McCormick has stamped his touch on this place in the most subtle of ways, from the enormous Persian rug that covers a quarter of the lobby to the old world map imprinted in the arched ceiling, a deep cupola made of highly polished oak and bronze highlights screaming with his style. It looks just like his office at Anterdec Industries.

All of the lights are dimmed, with sunshine from the sky-light adding just enough to make the lobby ethereal. I feel like I'm in a steampunk mystery, the blend of old-world flavor and modern technology so exquisite I could be in a slightly different dimension, couldn't I? Just tilted enough to be between two possibilities.

Check-in goes smoothly—Mike disappears with my luggage—and I'm assigned to room 1416, which means climbing into one of the elevators of doom. You know the kind. Major hotels have them. You punch in your floor number and the smart elevator system tells you which one to go on. Inside, there is no panel of numbers for floors, because the system is designed to assume that you are a pathetic, stupid human with inferior reasoning skills, and that the engineers (almost all male) who designed the system are smarter than you.

Which means that if you get on the elevator and a harassing asshole is on with you, you're stuck in elevator purgatory until the Machine of Superior Intellect decides to spring you out of your misogynistic prison.

I ascend to the fourteenth floor without incident, noting the condition of all the common areas (pristine), then enter my room. The bed is covered with fine chocolates from a Swiss company that uses slave-free cacao, and the towels are twisted to form a gorgeous rendering of the *Mona Lisa* in 3D.

I plop my carryon on the bed, and the valet has already delivered my rolling bag. One of the first steps I take in any hotel room I enter is to check out the balcony, if there is one. The thick black-out curtains take some serious muscle to pull apart, but the work is worth it. A stunning view of the city rolls out before me. Opening the sliding glass doors, I let the wind whip through my hair and carry my worries away.

A gentle knock at the door compels me to open it. Mike is standing there, smiling. He looks nothing like Guido, and resembles Merry the Hobbit mostly.

"Everything to your liking, Ms. Jacoby?"

I know the drill. I slip him a five and assure him all is well. He tips his hat to me and walks calmly down the hall.

My nineteen-page (*nineteen*-page!) list of instructions for the twenty-seven-page evaluation tells me exactly what to do for the night I'm here. If you mystery shop a lower-market chain of hotels you typically get your room free, about $25 in pay, and reimbursement for one dinner and a tip for housekeeping.

This place involves:

Valet parking

Tipping the bellhop

Drinks in the bar (two, minimum)

A full dinner from room service, from appetizer to entree to dessert

Breakfast buffet in the morning

Housekeeping tip

A massage in the spa
Tipping the bellhop on check out
Valet parking tip upon checkout

This is how the other half lives? If so, how do I join them? But that's not all.

Like relationships, you learn way more about customer service by testing them via problems. Any hotel or restaurant can run smoothly when it's quiet, when they're fully staffed, and when nothing's gone wrong.

The true test of a business is how its employees react to crisis.

Even manufactured crisis.

And my job is to manufacture a series of them, starting with the bathroom. I read the instructions, which were written by Amanda:

Facilities and Engineering: Create a problem with a fixture in the bathroom, a problem great enough to require a service call from one of our facilities workers. For instance, separate the chain from the ball in the toilet tank, or remove the nut that secures to one of the bolts on the underside of the toilet seat. Tuck the loose nut under the wastebasket.

The goal is to test the friendliness of the front-desk clerk, the response time of the facilities worker, and whether their service is friendly and efficient.

Okay. Standard operating procedure for a hotel mystery shop. I've done this tons of times before. My old standby is a little more creative than these suggestions, for I typically just make it so the toilet handle doesn't connect to the flushing mechanism.

Easy peasy.

I make the call first, eager to get this out of the way so I can move on to drinking at the bar . . . er, to the next task for my job. The hotel has an ice bar—an entire nightclub carved out of ice. The hotel desk clerk (Celeste) takes my call in stride, apologizes for the inconvenience, and at 3:56 p.m. promises that someone from their maintenance department will respond within ten minutes.

Great. I have ten minutes to break something. I'm Shannon; how hard can *that* be?

Something buzzes in the next room. My phone. I search the room and my eyes locate it, but it's not lit up. No text.

Bzzzzz.

Weird. What could be buzzing like that?

My carryon starts to move of its own accord, edging toward the end of the bed. I open it and—

A giant, carved J stares at me. It's pink.

Oh, yes.

Mom's Special Surprise.

The Power button appears to be jammed, and no matter how hard I try, I can't get it to pop up and stop vibrating. My fingers worry the little button, and in frustration I bang it—hard—against the edge of the desk.

BZZZZZZZZZZ.

I appear to have whacked it into hyperdrive. If it were the Millennium Falcon then Chewbacca would be turning all the thrusters on for Han Solo.

That sounds *soooo* dirty.

The vibrator is buzzing so loudly I'm sure the people in 1414 can hear it loud and clear. Removing the batteries should do the trick. I turn the cylinder over and—

Screwdriver needed.

Damn.

Tap tap tap. Someone's at the door.

"Maintenance!" a man's voice calls out.

I look at the clock. 3:58 p.m. Great. Of all the times for me to get the overachieving hotel maintenance dude. The only one on the freaking planet. I race into the bathroom and shove the top of the toilet tank off with one hand. Not being strong enough, I set the vibrator on the counter.

BZZZZZZZZZ. That only amplifies the sound.

Tap tap tap.

"Ma'am? It's maintenance. The front desk sent me," he says, a little louder. His voice is muffled and my hearing is slightly obscured by the rush of panic that makes the room start to spin. I break into a sweat as I grab the vibrator to stop the roaring sound and reach inside the toilet tank to loosen the chain from the handle. In mere seconds, I manage to do it, but as I stand up from my crouch I lose my balance and—

Splash!

Drop the giant pink vibrator into the toilet.

The J stares up at me, a bit of a blur as it motorboats inside the bowl.

The distinct sound of the electronic key being shoved in the slot of my door happens in slow motion, the sound like a series of guns in a firing squad being loaded, then locked on me.

I crouch down again and shove my hand into the tank to grab the vibrator, scanning the room for something I can use to mute it. Snatch it out of the toilet and wrap it in a towel? Maybe. Best plan I have.

But the door to my room opens and a familiar man's voice calls out.

"Hello?"

"I'm, uh . . ." I try to kick the door closed to buy time, but all I accomplish is a slow slide on the tile in my heels, my skirt dragging up to show the edge of my panties. I'm elbow deep in the toilet bowl, my hand smothering my mother's sex trophy meant for my *dad*.

And then a very familiar face appears with two highly amused, sparkling green eyes.

He looks at me, eyes scanning my half-acre of leg and thigh, my arm buried in the toilet, and says:

"We have *got* to stop meeting like this."

chapter
fifteen

DECLAN'S FACE, HIS EYES, his voice, that saucy grin do not compute with the blue workman's shirt he's wearing. Red embroidery on a yellow name tag says Alfredo, and he's wearing Dickies work pants with tan construction worker's boots.

He looks like any generic guy from my neighborhood back home. Like the dads of my friends. Like my male friends grown up now, in their early twenties, working in auto shops and framing houses.

"Layoffs at Anterdec got you working with your hands?" I say, leaning against the toilet bowl like it's all good. Casual. Nothing to see here. Just drowning a sex toy to put it out of its misery.

"I thought I'd develop a new skill to fall back on." He cocks one eyebrow and leans forward to see what I'm doing. "You drop your phone again?"

"Yep!" I chirp. "Sure did! Silly me, you know how I—"

Ring!

I changed my ringtone to that antiquated tone that sounds like a rotary phone.

Clearing his throat, he states the obvious because hey, that's what you do when you corner a woman who is insane: "Your phone is ringing."

"I'm not exactly going to answer it like this, now, am I?" I snap.

"Why don't you get up and . . . hmmm," he says, assessing

the situation. His head turns to look in the room, then over my legs at the toilet, hands planted on his hips as he judges the situation and determines that there's something wrong with finding me in a compromising position with the toilet.

"Are you drowning a tiny pink pig in the toilet?"

"Science experiment!"

Ring!

Does he have to look so damn hot while he's dragging out this moment of impending humiliation and doom? It's bad enough to be caught with my hand in the toilet—again!—but this time I'll pull out my mom's battery-operated boyfriend and go through the triple embarrassment of being turned on by the tight hang of his work outfit along his hips, how the cloth contours to those muscled thighs, the way the shirt is unbuttoned just enough to show his sprinkling of chest hair, and how the short sleeves showcase biceps that used to slide under my body and prop me up for his mouth as he—

Grabs my arm and pulls it out, dripping and buzzing from a gasping sex toy.

"You were drowning a . . . *that*? What the hell *is* that? A Barbie doll?"

I toss it at him. What do I have to lose at this point?

He sidesteps it neatly and it lands on the rug, turning to the left like a drunk driving in a roundabout.

"Definitely not a Barbie doll," he says, laughing.

"I stopped playing with those a long time ago," I say.

"I see you still have your favorite toys, though," Declan replies. "And why a 'J' on the tip? No 'D'?" he says, leering.

All I can do is glare. My heart is buzzing in my chest like a— well, you know—and he's looking at me like I'm a human being again. Like he likes me. Like he actually wants to interact with me.

"Why are you here?" I demand.

"The front-desk clerk said the toilet was broken." He holds up a small toolkit. "We have a completely different set of tools for malfunctioning vibrators."

"There's a protocol for *that*?" I gasp. Wow. And I thought I'd seen it all as a mystery shopper.

He nods and says dryly, "Yes. We just grab an EpiPen and shove it in there as hard as possible."

My turn to size him up. I'm standing here with a dripping arm (again), toilet water soaking my sleeve (again), and Declan's in disguise like he's dressed up as a superintendent for some very pervy Halloween party.

"Why are *you* answering my maintenance call?"

He seems surprised to be asked. "Amanda didn't coordinate this with you?"

"Amanda?" I say dumbly. "*Amanda* Amanda?"

"Is that really her last name? Cruel parents," he says with a low whistle.

"No, her last name is not—quit changing the subject!" I demand, turning away. My jacket is ruined, so I slide out of it to review the current state of my clothing. White silk business shirt—one arm wet. Jacket wrinkling rapidly on the floor—needs to be dry-cleaned.

Suit skirt split just like the first date—business dinner—whatever you call it.

My life is one big repeat, isn't it?

And here I am, all twitterpated because the ex-boyfriend who inexplicably dumped me is giving me some attention.

My life is one endless loop.

I can stop this, though. I can make choices that don't let other people do this—whatever this is—to me. Declan thinks he can waltz in to my hotel room dressed in uniform and smile and make me go weak in the knees and I'm just going to take the table scraps he's throwing my way like a good little doggie.

Ruff ruff.

"Why are you dressed in that uniform and responding to my service call?" I demand again.

"Because Amanda suggested that as part of measuring and following customer service standards to aid in marketing pushes with conventions, I perform some small version of that reality TV show, *Meet the Hidden Boss,* and go undercover in my own company's property."

I frown. "Didn't some CEO here in Boston do that recently?"

He nods. "Mike Bournham."

Bournham. Playboy. A sex tape that went viral. Something about a poor, naïve administrative assistant.

Utter disgrace and a resignation from him.

"That went *soooo* well for him, didn't it," I say with as much sarcasm as I can.

Declan shrugs. "Amanda was convincing."

I get the feeling she didn't have to push much. A flicker of emotion in his eyes shifts the tenor of the room, the bathroom instantly small in the blink of an eye. I'm washing my arm now—both arms—and all I want to do is get him out of my room so I can take a shower and cry.

BZZZZZZZ. As if reanimated by Dr. Frankenstein himself, the damn vibrator goes into high gear. I stomp across the bathroom, nudge Declan aside, and kick the damn thing as hard as I can.

When I was in middle school, for three years, I played goalie for my soccer team. Haven't done anything more athletic than that in a decade, but my feet must remember how to point the toe and scoop up for a serious drop kick, because that vibrator catches my toe and grabs some serious vault and air, sailing across the room, high over the bed, and flying through the open sliding glass doors, over the balcony railing and—

Down fourteen stories into the street.

We can hear the screech of tires and men shouting, then a few blares of horns.

Declan and I must look like a pair of owls, eyes wide and blinking.

I am speechless.

Declan's not.

"Good that you don't have a dog."

"Huh?"

"Because that could have been one game of fetch gone terribly, terribly wrong."

"You're making sick jokes after that just happened?" I point to the balcony. People are screaming at each other in the distance.

"Is there a more appropriate time to make sick jokes?"

"Why are you here?" I demand in a voice with more munition in it than I thought possible. I'm shaking with overwhelm, adrenaline, embarrassment, and excitement.

He starts to answer me. Repeatedly. Four times, in fact. I count each one, and with each new false start I feel a tiny rosebud, tight and contained, start to unfold inside me. One millimeter.

Just one tiny budge.

"I told you," he says in a rush, clearly flustered now, arms crossed over his chest, eyes hooded again. His hair is longer— like in my dream, but still fairly short. Not the rakish, hedonistic man I conjured in my subconscious. In my bed.

Bed.

My eyes flick over to the enormous king bed in the middle of my room, covered in more pillows than a sultan's sex den.

Declan's eyes follow mine. His arms drop. He blinks rapidly, focused on me now entirely, still maddening. Still not answering.

"Surely you haven't changed your name to Alfredo and taken up plumbing," I joke, regretting the intrusion instantly.

He gives me a wan smile. "Maybe I've become a mystery shopper."

I shrug, trying to hide how my heart is trying to break free and go hug his. "I've worn plenty of uniforms before during evals. You wouldn't be unique."

"So I'm not special?"

I measure my answer carefully as a cloud of calm coats me. He's here, and I want him so much, but I can't bridge that gap without an apology. Or even an explanation. Letting men waltz back into my life and resume as if there aren't pieces of broken, bloody glass made up of my soul isn't working for me lately.

Isn't working for me *ever*.

"If you mean are you like all the other men I've dated? Yes."

He flinches, guarded eyes showing a series of quick snapshots of hurt, confusion, atonement.

"Yes? I'm on par with *Steve*?" He says his name like a curse word.

I can't do this. I cannot have this conversation with Declan right here, right now. Who does he think he is? My mind scrambles to come up with a pithy comeback, witty repartees that will make him regret what he's cast aside, but instead I fall back on the one approach that comforts me most. That makes me feel real.

The truth.

"What are you doing, Declan? I'm not playing games with you. I don't play games. You chose to break up with me because you didn't know who the 'real' Shannon is. Because you thought I was using you to get ahead in business. Because—"

"Because I'm an idiot," he interrupts, taking one resolute step forward, bridging the gap between us by half. A thick gust of wind billows the stiff curtains inward, the sun flashing off some piece of glass on the desk, and the scent of seawater, the rush of cool air makes the moment seem so ripe with possibility.

"Idiot?"

"Idiot."

One more step. *Please take one more step*, I think. The Shannon inside me that knows I can't be walked all over is fighting with the part that wants him to kiss me, that wants to lose myself in his touch, our lips, a joining of bodies that banishes the clashing of minds.

Does it have to be either/or?

Declan's own struggle is reflected in his eyes, one strong hand moving to his hip, the other reaching up to push through hair I wish I could stroke. I still don't understand what happened a month ago in the hallway outside that meeting. Probably will never understand. But if he could just give me one reason, one tiny sliver of—

And now he's kissing me.

Good reason.

Very good reason. I arch into him, absorbing his warmth, lips parting to let him taste me. As my body softens against him

I feel the pull of my heart toward his, like a magnet gathering iron shavings, as if his touch could summon the disparate parts of me and bring them together, whole.

Yes, with just one kiss. And then another. And another, until there is no separation between them. No divide, no marking point where one warm, soft sigh and brush of a tongue and an eager embrace begins and ends. They all blur together, like seconds blur into minutes, minutes into hours, hours and days into the woven cloth of a life well lived.

And loved.

He smells so nice, like Declan. His own branded scent, like tasting him in the air. Hot, eager hands pull me to him like he's planning never to let me go, and the rush of being so close, so deliciously close to him doesn't subside when it should.

If this were a movie, I'd pull back, smack his face, and he'd yank me close and kiss me again.

But this isn't a movie. And he still has not answered my question.

I pull back, the kiss lingering on my mouth like a layer of silk as I ask, "You broke up with me because of your mother, didn't you?"

Another kiss replaces his answer. I slide my hands around his waist and there is this one spot where his shirt has pulled up just enough from his waistband to give me a glorious inch of hot, taut skin to touch, my thumb caressing it, my palm wanting so much more. Bold now, my fingers track upwards along the ropy muscles that parallel his spine, feeling the power of his shoulders as his arms envelop me.

Damn it. He did it again.

Breathless, I pull away just as he steps forward, pushing me gently until the backs of my calves hit the bed. I want to bend. Oh, how my knees want to fold just enough to sink us both into the down-filled duvet, to wake up in the morning with pillow mint wrappers stuck in my hair, and not because I ate a bag of them alone while watching the first episode of *Outlander* repeatedly and crying about how there are no good men like Jamie.

"No," I whisper, making him look at me. "Not yet. You can't

waltz in here like this and expect me to let you pick up where we left off, because you left off in a spectacularly crappy way."

He pinches the bridge of his nose and steps back, warm breath coming out in waves as he fights to control his panting. "Yes. You're right."

"That's a good start," I mumble. The United States of Shannon is a federation of states all working together, but a few parts of me—all below the waist—are calling constitutional conventions to discuss secession.

Traitors.

"Are you going to listen to me, or just crack wise?" Declan asks in a tight voice.

Record-scratch moment. *Screech!* Hold on.

"If you're here because you want to get back together, you have some explaining to do," I say, ignoring my clitoris, which is attempting to call the secession meeting to order for a vote. Man, is it banging that gavel. Hard.

"So do you."

"Me? What do I have to explain? I tried to explain. No, I never wanted you for your money or for business contracts. No, I'm not a lesbian. Yes, I have a bee allergy. What else do you need to know? Those are all parts of the very real Shannon who is standing right in front of you."

He points a finger at me.

"Don't muddy the waters. The problem is that you took what could have been a simple situation and twisted it into Gordian knot-like complexity," he says in a matter-of-fact tone.

I have no desire in this exact moment to admit that I have no idea what a Gordian knot is, so I say, "How did I make it complicated?"

"You caught Jessica's attention. Anytime she tweets about someone it has to have triggered a rash of rumors so strong it gets back to her," he declares.

"That's my relationship crime? That my ex's ex who is hot for your rod tweeted about my pretending to be gay? You broke up with me for that?" I laugh. I'm genuinely not upset, because that explanation is so freaking lame that I know it's not true.

"No."

"Then why?"

"Because you never bothered to tell me about your allergy."

"It was our *second* date! Don't you think you're being a bit unreasonable? Allergies aren't a second-date thing."

"Second-date thing?"

"You know, kiss on the first date, show your student loan debt on the second, intercourse on the third. There's a timetable for these things. Deathly anaphylactic bee allergy isn't slated until date number seven, filed under Batshit Crazy Relatives and Genetic Predispositions to Hammertoes."

Peering intently at me, he ponders this. I can tell he's debating, his eyes moving rapidly, his teeth sinking into the soft inner flesh of his lip. I've made a cogent point and he has to either react with reason or—

"Not good enough."

Assholery.

"Not good enough? You get to unilaterally declare my explanation 'not good enough'?"

"Yes."

chapter
sixteen

" **N** O!" I BLURT THE word out and whip around, grabbing the mints on the pillow and unwrapping them. The erstwhile wrapper goes flying near the wastebasket, wafting down as I shove the chocolate in my mouth, fuming at him.

"Cute. We can argue and shout 'yes' and 'no' at each other all day, Shannon, but you have to admit to yourself that—"

"I remind you of your mother, who died from a wasp sting, and you can't handle that." In finishing his sentence for him I've chosen a path that leads either to the end of everything between us, or a real beginning.

Real.

"Who told you that?"

"Google." I let the tension release from my shoulders. "I'm sorry."

"What else did you read?" His voice is so tight he could string a guitar with it.

"There isn't anything more," I answer, bewildered. "No matter how hard I tried, I couldn't dig anything else up. And Jessica was of no help."

"Jessica?" His carefully constructed facade begins to crack, his face betraying him as he starts to show a few slivers of emotion beyond desire. "What the hell does Jessica have to do with my mother?"

The whole scheme sounds ridiculous now, but I figure I should share. "We thought because she's a gossip girl, she might know what happened ten years ago, so I asked her. Got no response whatsoever. I guess she doesn't know."

"No. She knows what happened. Her non-reply is because she can't stand you."

Nice. At least he's being truthful.

"Then why can't you just tell *me*, Declan?" I ask in a quiet voice. "You've told Jessica. But not me? This obviously has a lot to do with us."

"Us?" The second that syllable is out of his mouth I deconstruct it, finding 17 different meanings when you include vocal inflection, tone, and pacing. "And I never told Jessica," he says with a growl. "She found it out on her own and confronted me with it."

"Confronted?" What is the big secret?

He storms away from me, onto the balcony, bracing his arms on the railing, leaning into the wrought iron in a way that makes his arm muscles bulge, his shoulders spread. Tipping his head down as I join him, he can't—won't—meet my eyes.

I touch him, my hand on his shoulder. He twitches just enough to make me remove it.

"Are you sure you're safe out here?" he asks in a flat voice.

"Safe from what? Flying vibrators?"

He laughs, clearly against his will. Yet he won't look at me. His gaze shifts to the water, eyes tracking a sailboat that glides smoothly on the waves.

"No. From a bee sting."

Anger pours into me like it's been attached to an IV drip bag and administered as medicine. "You can't let it go, can you?"

His head snaps up. "What?"

"You can't let go of the fact that I have this . . . thing. This allergy. This curse." I feel the rant coiled deep inside, ready to unfurl. "It's not like I have a choice. I didn't ask for this. It's part of who I am, and I take every precaution imaginable—"

"Not every precaution."

I tilt my head and stare at his profile. Red dots of fire kiss my cheeks. Blood courses through me like a spewing firehose.

This? *This* is what's stopping him?

"You liar," I spit out.

His eyes light up with a mixture of confusion and indignation.

"Liar?"

"Yes. Liar. You lied to me a month ago. You told me that you thought I was a chameleon, that I wouldn't reveal the real Shannon."

"What does that have to do with my lying about—"

"*This* is the real Shannon. The *real* Shannon can die if she's stung by a bee. The *real* Shannon has boobs that touch the bed when she lies on her back. The *real* Shannon needs to wear Spanx to fit into a comfortable size sixteen. The *real* Shannon hates Transformers movies. The *real* Shannon thinks Jessica and Steve and your father and fake people who have overinflated egos and are out of touch with reality."

He isn't showing even the tiniest hint of emotion as he listens, expressionless. His hands are tight fists, though, held close to his thighs, and his nostrils flare as he breathes silently. No reaction.

Oh, yeah? I'll make you react.

"And the *real* Shannon thinks you're a total emotional wuss for thinking that hiding your emotions makes you more of a man," I add. A parting shot, if you will. I want to kiss him again and knock some sense into that handsome face, using my tongue and hands and heart if I have to, but I see, now, that it's no use. He's clinging to his secret and if he won't tell me what's going on, I can't keep playing this game.

My heart isn't a toy.

And with that I storm out of my own room, snatching my purse and instruction sheet.

It's time to evaluate the bar.

IT'S AN ICEHOUSE IN here.

This time—literally. I'm fuming and so red-hot on fire that as I walk into the carved-ice bar I fear I'll melt the entire place down with my very presence.

As I step into the sculpted ice room, I realize it's like a cave. The bar has barstools—made of ice. The bar itself is one round-edged sheet of ice. Shelves? Ice.

It's magical.

My nipples tighten from the cold and I look down. All I'm wearing is the thin white silk shirt I have on, the one that got wet a few minutes ago. My soaked sleeve is like a frosted blanket, and I can see my own breath as I exhale. My jacket is back in my room (with Declan) and my skirt is split up to my panty line.

No wonder the girls just went tight and high. It's *cold* in here.

I don't care. My mind can't stop spilling over with a thousand words, most of them profanity-laced diatribes about Declan.

How dare he?

How *dare* he!

Show up and interrupt the most important job I've ever had, mock my profession by pretending to be a maintenance man (yeah, right . . . like Amanda put him up to it!) and then have the audacity to kiss me. A lot. And then blame me for not telling me what on earth his dead mother has to do with his dumping me.

I need a scotch. Bad.

I sit down gingerly on the cold, hard, ice-topped bar stool. The bartender's back is to me, and he's whistling some tune I don't recognize. The lighting in the bar is a series of cool blue LED bulbs carved into the ice. The entire room is like something out of the set of a new Star Trek film.

The music is soft jazz with a jaunty, bluesy tone to it. The kind of music that gets you warmed up to go to bed with someone. To throw inhibitions into the wind and let your impulses carry you to a new place.

Like a hotel room upstairs.

My skin tingles from the rush of emotion that clings to me, my lips raw from those kisses, my heart shredded and beating like it holds time itself together. Like my heart is responsible for the counting of seconds that pass.

Tick. Tick. Tick. Tick.

That's too big a burden.

Need to drown it in alcohol.

I clear my throat. "Excuse me? Could I order a—" As the bartender turns around and I get a look at his face, I cut my own words off.

It's Andrew.

Declan's brother.

"What are *you* doing here?" I ask, incredulous. A few heads, all male, turn toward the sound of my fairly-loud, and quite demanding, voice. They turn back to their drinks and conversation when Andrew leans in toward me and puts his hand over mine, like we're old friends.

Where Declan is dark and intense, Andrew is lighter and blank. Generic. Now that I've seen pictures of their mother, I understand who Andrew takes after. He's not quite blonde, and the eyes are pale brown, like a fine whisky. The broad planes of his face are Declan's, though.

"Would you keep your voice down? When you go undercover you're supposed to blend in."

"I'm blending in!"

"I meant me. I'm acting, and this is my first time, so don't blow it." He's mocking me, pretending to be serious. "I don't want to have to pretend to be a lesbian and have that blow up in my face," he adds.

"You're an asshole."

"Nice language."

"Wait until I have my two drinks in me."

That makes his face crack open in a smile and he sweeps an arm toward the myriad bottles on shelves in front of a highly-polished ice wall. "How may I serve you?"

"Two fingers of scotch. Neat." I've heard my dad order this way at fine bars, so why not?

He pours about two big shots into a tumbler and slides it to me.

I take a sip. The burning feeling does not square with the ice cold chamber I'm in, so I decide to go all-in and just chug it, slamming the glass down on the bar.

"That's it? Two warm shots in a glass?" I gasp as the liquid feels like lighter fluid pouring into my belly button.

"That's what you ordered. Want a wine cooler next time? Or a drink with an umbrella in a coconut?"

I glare at him. "Anything that might attract the attention of a bee would be great."

His eyes go cold, but he looks around the room, then says, "Not in here."

"Not anywhere in your life, so I've been told."

"Dec never was good at keeping his big mouth shut," Andrew shoots back, which makes me snort in surprise. If Declan's too talkative about, well, anything, then what kind of family did they grow up in? The handful of sentences I can pry out of him about his feelings, his past, his mother are the exact opposite of what Andrew's saying. As the alcohol hits me and fills me with a loose sense of curiosity, I decide that alienating the one person who might give me some insight into Declan McCormick is a mistake.

A big one.

"He's pretty good at keeping his own secrets close to the vest," I say in a conspirator's voice.

Bingo!

Andrew leans in. "Yes, he is." This gives me a chance to get a good look at him. He's wearing a white, collared shirt, a black vest, and a name tag that says "Jordan."

"Why are you and Declan pretending to work here?" I ask. Not the original question on the tip of my tongue, but right now I'm feeling all squiggly and casual with him. Aside from staring across a board room table at him and hearing about his OCD-crafted life to avoid being stung by a bee, I know nothing about Andrew.

"Your friend set it up. Amanda." His lips spread in an instantaneous smile that he tries to turn into friendliness as her name pours over his lips, but I'm not deceived. Two questions fight for positioning in me, and the one that wins is:

"Amanda?" I cough out her name.

Brilliant, right?

Andrew pours two more shots in my glass and stares at me,

hard. My eyes struggle in the dim light to find Declan in him, but all traces are gone.

Another patron at the bar flags for his attention, and he shrugs an apology, leaving me for a minute to pour a requested Guinness. I sip gingerly from the tumbler and remind myself that this is a job. I am working. My smartphone comes in handy and I pull it out, retrieving the evaluation form from my app and as Andrew helps a second customer with a martini, I answer questions with the background noise of the shaker.

"You look like Princess Elsa," a slurry voice says to my right.

I look up, disoriented, and find the face of a man about ten years older than my dad. He's bald, wearing stylish glasses with a black line straight across the top of the lenses, and has an earring in his right ear. Tattoos cover his forearms and he's wearing a plaid button down. It's like L. L. Bean, Mr. Clean and Keith Richards climbed into a Vita Mix and got poured out into a Man Mold.

"You're hitting on me by using Disney movie characters in your pick up line?" I answer, trying to summon outrage as I tuck my smartphone back into my purse. None appears. The whisky just makes me find this all amusing.

My skirt melted part of my bar stool and as I shift, the cloth stays put. My thigh, though, decides to give the female equivalent of The Full Monty. Good thing I'm wearing underpants.

He lifts one shoulder and smiles, revealing two gold teeth. Both canines. "Can't blame a guy for trying. Great line in a bar made of ice. You got a room here? And a sister?"

"A sister? Why, you have a friend for her?"

"No." His hungry eyes are trying to tell me something, and as I sip my scotch I try to figure it out.

Can't.

"Pete, get the hell out of here," Andrew growls, reappearing quickly. "Quit hitting on people who graduated high school in the twenty-first century. And stop suggesting threesomes."

"She's legal. You're legal, right?"

I'm flattered he might think otherwise, but I'm also trying to process what Andrew just said. Threesomes? "If you think I look like I'm under eighteen, Pete, then you need to get those glasses checked," is all I can think to say.

Andrew hands him a glass of something clear on the rocks. "Go find someone else to bother."

"She yours?" Pete barks out, rotating his look between me and Andrew. "Lucky man. You get those thighs wrapped around your head and you couldn't hear a tornado coming even if it plowed through your building."

I don't have a brother. Don't have a brother-in-law any more. So the look on Andrew's face doesn't make sense to me in the moment, though in later years I'll come to understand it better.

"Get the hell out of here," Andrew says, eyes flicking up to get the attention of the plainclothes security dude at the main door. His name is Jerry (I checked when I walked in) and Jerry's at the counter in three seconds.

"I'm a paying customer," Pete slurs, loose eyes taking me in as I try—and fail—to cover my legs. "Who's your boss? I'll have you fired."

"*I'm* my boss," Andrew says as Jerry escorts (drags) Pete out.

Compassion and a kind of wariness coexist in Andrew's eyes as he looks at me, but seems to struggle to make eye contact at the same time. "You okay?"

He seems more upset than I am. "Me? Yeah. Sure. He's just another asshole man who hits on women." The thigh comment rings through my mind. I don't know whether to be offended or flattered.

Andrew's mouth hangs open a bit. Oh. I guess I said that part aloud.

"Would you be offended?" I add, drinking the rest of my second scotch. "If someone said that about your thighs?" I pull out my phone, not waiting for an answer. "Let me ask Amanda. I wonder if her thighs are big enough to block out sound when she's—"

Andrew turns bright red at the mention of Amanda's name. Aha.

"Amanda," I say.

Red.

"Amanda!"

He flushes again.

"Oh, this is fun."

"What is?" he asks. "Talking about women's thighs?"

"How about *Amanda's* thighs?"

Red.

"It's warm in here," he mumbles. "Need to turn down the temperature or the ice will melt."

"The temperature isn't the problem. Amanda is."

"She sure is. This is all her fault," he announces.

Declan's words from earlier ping through me. "Declan said she set this all up. Is that true?"

He nods, then chuckles. "That friend of yours is a determined one, I'll tell you. Marching into my office like that yesterday."

"WHAT?" I motion to the wall of bottles and tap my glass. The mystery shop says to order two drinks, but what the heck— I'll pay for my third.

He gives me a single shot in a glass and upturned eyebrows. "That's it for now."

"Tell me more about Amanda barging into your office!"

"She came to find out the story about Declan and how our mother died." Something in him dials down a bit. The bar's emptying out and I look at the clock. It's early dinnertime, and people are either commuting or getting ready to eat.

"We know how she died," I say with as much sympathy as I can.

"Amanda wanted the whole story."

"Did you give it to her?"

"Yes."

"And. . . . ?"

"And told us we needed to go undercover for this mystery shop. To get Declan to see you."

"Huh?"

He runs a frustrated hand through his light-brown hair and looks like a younger version of Declan. It makes me smile. Then again, the television news could show footage of a serial killer and I'd smile. What's in this scotch that makes the world so . . . good?

"Shannon, I have never seen my brother so happy with any woman before. When he was dating you he was happy. Happy and Declan don't go together. Not since Mom died and Dad blamed Dec for her death."

"Why would he?" I gasp, horrified at the thought. "He was eighteen and a wasp stung her—what did Declan have to do with that?"

The eyes that meet mine are haunted. Just like Declan's.

"Because on that day, I was stung and so was Mom. We only had one EpiPen."

No.

"And we were at one of my soccer games, just goofing around. There were these long trails on the outskirts of the playing field, most of them two or so miles long. Mom loved to walk along the paths and see the creeks, stand on the bridges and listen to the water rush by. She said it was a welcome reprieve from the craziness of business life with Dad."

My own inbreaths feel like icicles entering me and piercing my heart.

Andrew clears his throat. "The three of us were walking, a good mile away from the soccer fields, when a swarm hit us. Just blasted right over our heads, but a few strays stuck around. Mom was stung twice, I was stung three or four times. We knew about Mom's allergy. She had an EpiPen."

I'm stone cold sober suddenly.

"But we didn't know I was allergic, too, until that moment." His voice has a sing-songy quality to it. He's reciting a well-honed story, one that took telling and retelling to shape.

I can imagine it all in my mind. All too well. Because I just lived it with Declan a very short while ago, in my own way.

"One of my stings was near my eye, another one on my neck, and Mom worked to find her EpiPen for herself, in her giant purse. By the time she found it I was wheezing. Declan started ed screaming about running back to get help, get an ambulance. I didn't have my phone with me, and I think we later realized neither did Dec, but Mom had one in her purse."

A sick dread fills me.

"And?"

"My wheezing got worse and I remember black spots filled my vision." He shakes his head, hard, like he's trying to force the memory out. "Mom was panicking and shaking, and then she dropped to the ground. Dec came running back and kept shouting. I don't remember the words. Then he grabbed Mom's purse and found her EpiPen."

He gave me a rueful smile. "Mom trained us all—repeatedly—on how to inject her in an emergency."

"Of course," was all I could croak out.

"But when Dec went to her she pushed him away and pointed at me. It felt like I was breathing through a coffee stirrer by then, and the force of blood pumping through me made it sound like—"

"You were under a waterfall," I say, interrupting.

We give each other a knowing look. My words seem to make him stop and close down a bit.

"Can you guess what happened next?" he asks. "Do the math. One EpiPen. One mile from help. One mother's decision."

A painful rush of emotion rolls up the muscles of my throat into the roof of my mouth, through my sinuses, making my eyes water. "Oh, Andrew. Oh, my God. She made Declan inject you, didn't she?"

He closes his eyes and his jaw tightens.

"Yes."

His phone buzzes in his pocket and he grabs it, desperate for a reason to be done with this conversation.

"Gotta go," he says in a clipped voice. Then he pauses, tongue rolling in his cheek, lips parted slightly. His eyes have gone neutral, a skill he shares with his brother.

"So now you know," he adds. "Dad blamed Declan. Said he should have treated Mom."

"But your mother insisted!" Any good mother would. I know my own mom would have done the same, exact thing. Know it with all my heart.

"I know she did. Or," he pauses. "I know she did at least once. I blacked out and woke up in the hospital."

"And your mom . . ."

"Died the next day. Dec injected me, searched Mom's purse in case there was something he could help her with, found her phone and called for help. Then he ran back to the field. By the time they got to us, it was probably too late for her. But he did everything he could have done. Everything."

"But not enough for James."

Andrew shakes his head slowly. "Never enough for my dad." And with that he purses his lips, breaks eye contact, and steps out into the main lobby, leaving me shivering.

But I'm not cold any more.

chapter
seventeen

I T'S 5:17 P.M. NOW and I decide that maybe I should have a wee bit more than five or six shots of scotch in my stomach as I struggle to comprehend what Andrew's just told me.

Fortunately, part of my job here at The Fort involves eating dinner in the main dining room. Testing whether they'll seat me without reservations happens to be built in to the evaluation, which is great, because not only did I not think ahead to schedule any, my mind is like a series of shrapnel bits spiraling through space after the grenade Andrew just lobbed at me.

A friendly, helpful, extremely insightful grenade, but a dangerous weapon nonetheless. Declan's words from our fight, the day he broke up with me.

I took a chance on you.

Of course, I thought he meant it the same way Steve did—that I was too rough, too jagged-edged, not fit for the upper echelons of society.

Declan meant it in such a different way.

As I approach the restaurant a coiffed, sleek woman who looks like Jessica Coffin's twin, fast-forwarded thirty years, graciously offers me a table. She does not say "for one?" with any condescension, which is important. Business travelers routinely dine alone, and alienating them is not in anyone's financial interest.

I just need a steak and a salad and some equanimity. I think the first two are on the menu. I know the third is not.

I'm seated at a lovely table with a glass waterfall to my right, the water trickling in perfect ribbons onto a Zen rock garden, peaceful and serene. Water lilies—real—float on the pools filled with koi fish, and I inhale deeply, muddling through the thousands of details, snippets of conversation and feelings, that fill me now.

A white-jacketed waiter brings me water and says,

"Enjoying your stay, Ms. Jacoby?"

I flinch and startle, flinging my arms wide, hitting the wine goblet he holds out to me, sending a spray of water all over his very familiar, lined face.

James McCormick.

"What kind of joke is this!" I sputter.

"That was supposed to be my line, Shannon," he mutters as he uses the napkin on his arm to wipe his face.

Whether it's the scotch or the mind blowing story Andrew's just told me, or the aftereffects of just seeing and kissing Declan, I let loose without thinking.

"How could you blame Declan for your wife's death?"

"You don't mince words, do you? I dated a woman like that once. It didn't work out."

"I know. Because she dumped you."

His eyes turn into wrinkled triangles. "What are you talking about?"

"The name Winky mean anything to you?" Andrew opened the floodgates with the truth. Well, technically, Amanda did. My head hurts. Too much to tease through, so instead I'll just bulldoze James.

He deserves it.

Reflexively, he looks down at his crotch. Is this a male thing? "Winky? Like that children's television character?"

"Winky the dog."

He sits down next to me, moving just slow enough in that way people in their fifties—even the really fit ones, like my mom—have.

"What kind of joke is this?" He's studying me carefully.

A little too much scotch, way too many revelations, and a flying vibrator that stops traffic have made my day one big, giant crater. "The name Marie Scarlotta mean anything to you?" Mom's maiden name.

James' eyes widen and he searches my face avidly. "My God! I knew you looked familiar." He laughs through his nose. "You're Marie's daughter? And Jacoby is your last name?" He leaps up and disappears around a corner, headed for the kitchen.

That was remarkably anticlimactic.

A worker brings a breadbasket with artisanal options that carry a layer of seeds and nuts on top thicker than an energy bar. James returns, carrying two tumblers of scotch.

Neat.

He holds one out to me and with a shaking hand I take it. Seems like the best idea ever, especially right now.

"A toast."

"To extraordinary fathers," I say.

He beams. "Why thank you."

"I was talking about mine."

His smile fades, but he shrugs. "To Jason."

Our glasses crash together, retreat, and then we empty them.

"*He* never accused me of killing someone," I say viciously.

"Is that the baseline for being a good enough parent?" James fingers the rim of his glass. "If so, I've failed." Standing, he pulls off the white jacket and rips off his bow tie. Fit and trim, like Declan, his stomach is flat, shirt a bit askance after his partial undressing. Shrewd eyes meet mine as he raises one hand and a waiter attends to us instantly.

I cover my glass with my hand and shake my head 'no.'

James smiles, baring teeth. He's just wolfish enough to scare me. Not in a sexual predator kind of way.

Just a plain old predator. He's dangerous. Any man who would blame his own son for—

"I regret it. I never should have said that to Declan, and even now, ten years later, I find I can't help myself. It slips out. I'm really angry at me. Not him."

The confession feels insincere.

"You don't believe that." I pull a piece of bread bigger than my head from the basket and take a bite. The crust is so hard you could use it to stone rape victims in backwards countries with misogynistic laws. I think I just cracked a tooth. Good thing I have whisky to help with the pain.

"What do I believe, Shannon?"

"You're pissed at your wife."

"Because she chose to save Andrew? What kind of a father would feel that? I'm not a monster."

"No, not because of that. Because she died. Period. You're just pissed. Anyone would be. It's human. You're allowed to be human."

He sighs slowly and looks angry.

"And so is Declan," I add.

"If I'd been there, I might have—"

"What? Been racked with guilt like Declan?" I shake my head. "It's a freak accident. They happen. In fact, if Declan hadn't done exactly what his mom told him to do, you might have lost Andrew, too."

"I know."

"And you told Declan to stop dating me because I'm too similar to his mother," I mutter, making the connection.

The booming laugh that greets my statement rattles my teeth. "You? Similar to Elena? No."

"But we have the same affliction."

"Yes."

James worries the glass in front of him and glances at the ice bar, where Andrew's back in place, this time in a suit and tie, talking with what looks like a manager.

"Do you have any idea what it's like to have a child or a wife or a loved one with a severe, anaphylactic allergy like this, Shannon?"

I point to my heart. "Ummm. . . ."

"No." He sighs. "I am absolutely not trivializing what you live with, day in and day out, but no. It's not the same as loving someone who has it."

I frown. Where's he going with this?

"When we learned Elena was severely allergic we went to the best specialists. Took all the preventive measures. Trained the boys and had them tested. I took every damn precaution known to man, mitigated risk as much as possible, and—" He spreads his hands out in a gesture of supplication. "Look what happened."

"You can't live in a bubble," I say, helpless.

"Do you understand," he says through gritted teeth, "what it is like to live in constant, vigilant fear that the person you love can, through the simple, random accident of brushing up against a bee or a wasp, be taken from you? To twitch every spring and to sigh with relief every fall at the first frost? To live in that state incurs a kind of madness."

I really don't know what to say, so I finish my drink and eat more bread.

"Trust me," he says, his eyes searching for and finding Andrew, who is polishing glasses at the bar. James returns his attention to me, his eyes red-rimmed, the loose skin of an old man making him seem even sadder. "That's no way to live your life."

"Neither is cutting off your nose to spite your face."

Resentful eyes meet mine. "Ah, if only life were so simple."

I stand, my appetite long gone, legs wobbly but mind very, very clear. "You make it more complex than it needs to be, and you are teaching your sons all the wrong things. What about love? You loved your wife, didn't you?"

He leaps to his feet. We're making a scene. So much for professional standards. At this point, the ruse that I'm mystery shopping anything other than my own freaking life is over.

"Of course I loved her. More than life itself."

"People say that, but it's not true."

He just stares at me, red-faced and angry.

"If you love anything more than life itself, that means you'd rather be dead. And you're not. You chose to live after her passing."

"That wasn't an easy decision."

"And now you're emotionally crippling your sons!"

"I don't need you to play armchair psychologist with me, Shannon," he spits out.

"You need someone to play psychologist, Dad," says Guido,

who has mysteriously appeared behind us. One look at his face, then James' angry eyes, and it all clicks.

"Terrance," I whisper. "You're not Guido."

He gives a twisted smile. "And you're not an executive here for a night."

"What is this?" I demand. "Why are you both and Andrew and Declan all pretending to be hotel employees?"

"Amanda told us—" James starts.

"Really? This was set up by Amanda?"

"She suggested we each take two hours to learn more about the inner life of our property."

"And have you?"

"I've learned quite a bit, Shannon," James says over his shoulder as he leaves. "More than I ever wanted to know."

I take a few shaky steps and stumble. Terrance/Guido grabs my elbow.

"How many drinks did you have?" he asks in that deep voice. My panties are wet, though that might be from the melting bar stools from before.

"Enough to tell your father off."

"That many? I'm impressed." He helps me walk toward the elevator and asks for my floor number. I type in 14 and step back.

"Terrance," I say simply.

"Call me Terry. Impressive," he says, his eyes combing over me.

"You're going to hit on me, too? I'm kind of done with that, thanks," I sigh. Between Declan's kiss and Pete's thigh comments I think I'll become a nun.

"No, just . . . Declan's spoken so highly of you. Plus you have a really interesting vibrator. I've never seen one before that can fly and stop traffic like that." Those words come out of his mouth just as an older couple comes to the bank of elevators and starts to press the buttons for their floor. The man halts in mid air, finger an inch from the numbers.

Mercifully, my elevator arrives and Terry escorts me on to it. The older couple doesn't join us. We ride in quiet, the enclosed space spinning just a bit, my body warming up to him. Of Declan's brothers he looks the most like him, and for as angry as I am at Declan, I want him, too.

Terry gets me to my room and says, "Nice meeting you, finally."

I snort. "Not that it matters. Declan dumped me. But nice meeting you, Guido."

And with that, I key into my room, flop down on the bed and everything fades to black.

I took a chance on you.

SOMEONE IS KNOCKING ON my door. I sit up, disoriented. The wind's blowing the curtains and moonlight streams into the dark room.

Darkness. Nighttime. When did that happen? I climbed onto the bed in the day time, and now . . .

A glance at the bedside clock tells me it's 10:22 p.m.

What?

I sit up as the person outside the door knocks again, harder this time, like a man banging with the edge of his fist.

"Room service," says a muffled man's voice.

Room service? Did I order room service? I know I was supposed to as part of the mystery shop, but I don't remember it.

I sit up, my mouth dry, and rub my eyes repeatedly. A deep inhale and I launch myself up. A gurgle, deep inside my belly, makes me realize I'm ravenous.

Maybe I did call and order dinner? If so, what the heck am I about to eat?

I open the door and there's Declan, standing behind a room service cart loaded with covered dishes.

I close the door in his face.

Not *that* hungry.

Back pressed against the door, I fight my way to full wakefulness, heart slamming against my breastbone. I'm still mad at him, aren't I? By all rights I should be. And yet as the details from my conversations earlier in the night come flooding in, a calm sense of equivocation fills me. I bite my lower lip, hard, trying to wake up. To shake some sense into me.

Tap tap tap.

"Shannon?" His voice is contrite. This is new. "Please? You need to eat. Andrew and Terry are worried about you."

Worried?

"They said you were drinking quite a bit, something about a guy hitting on you in the bar, my dad being an asshole and . . ." His voice winds down into a frustrated snarl. "Just let me in. Take the food. I want to make sure you're well."

"What's on the tray?" I ask through the door.

"Filet mignon. Mashed potatoes in a reduced fig and balsamic vinegar sauce. Mocha caramel cheesecake."

I moan. Can't help it.

"No white wine, though. Andrew insisted." There's a big question in his voice. I rub my cheek against the door and take a deep breath, deciding.

Cheesecake wins.

The click of the door sounds like a choice, and I open it, stepping back. Declan rolls the cart in and gives me a half smile as he sets the cart next to the desk and unloads the trays onto the bed.

"Eat."

"You don't have to worry about me, you know," I insist, but as he pulls the top of the first tray up the scent of steak and spices makes my stomach scream the opposite of my words.

He laughs.

"Just eat."

After he sets the cover down he steps back and looks me up and down. "Nice nap?"

"No. I kept dreaming about a killer bee coming to get me in Antarctica. And a ferocious wolf."

"What a mystery," he deadpans. "No need to guess what your subconscious is struggling to get out."

"What do you dream about, Declan?" I pick up a fresh strawberry from a fruit plate and eat it, grateful for something to fill my mouth after asking.

"You."

"Nice," I say, tipping my chin up, hurrying to swallow. "Really. Great line."

"It's not a line." I take a bite of potato and then another, suddenly starving. Declan pulls the desk chair away from the keyboard tray and turns it backwards, straddling it.

Oh. He's staying. And we're talking.

So that's how it is.

I cut into the steak and take a bite. It's like eating butter, just right, the perfect cut of tenderloin. "Tell me more about your dreams," I insist as I eat, then I stop. "Would you like some?"

"I already ate." His voice is raw. "I enjoy watching you."

"Dreams," I demand. "Dreams."

chapter
eighteen

"WHEN I DREAM ABOUT you, it's all sweetness and light. I don't remember the dreams," he confesses. "Not the way normal people do. I see pictures. Still images. Flashes."

"Not like a movie reel? That's how my dreams work. The parts I remember," I explain. The filet is the size of a silver dollar and I finish it in five bites, then move on to the potatoes, then some julienned vegetables. Our conversation is so . . . normal. Concrete.

Cradling his jaw in his palm, he leans his propped elbow against the back of the leather chair. "No. Even as a kid. I compared notes with Terry once and he ribbed me about it. Said I was weird for not having dreams like him and Andrew." Declan shrugs, eyes a little too bright, throat tight. I pause my dinner and take a long, slow drink of water, enjoying the moment to look at him.

He's nervous.

Nervous.

My soul starts to hope.

I unveil a piece of mocha caramel cheesecake that could feed a small village in Southeast Asia. Grabbing two forks, I hold one out to him like an olive branch.

"Have some with me."

"I'm not hungry."

"Look at that! It's a work of art. If you don't want a single bite of it, then you're not human," I joke.

We simultaneously take a bite and groan together. Mutual mouthgasms. They're rare, but when they happen, they're unbelievable.

He gets to the cheesecake before me for a second bite.

"I thought you weren't hungry," I tease.

"God, I've missed you," he says, vulnerable and watching me like I'm the only woman he's ever seen. I swallow and stop, fork jabbed into the dessert, hanging in suspension. My shaking hand reaches for the water goblet and I finish it, Declan's breath tortured, the air in the room singed with anticipation.

"If you missed me," I say in a hoarse voice that seems to come from a place nine inches away from my mouth, "why haven't you called? Or texted? Or sent a bat signal?"

"Remember that whole idiot thing from earlier today? Yeah. That."

"And then there's your mom."

This time, he doesn't flinch. Just closes his eyes and sighs, then opens them, fighting for composure. I want to reach out, to touch him, to connect my skin to his but he has to make the first move. Simply knowing what happened ten years ago and making the connection doesn't mean he's here to reunite.

He has to be the one to say it.

Leaping to his feet, he begins to pace. There's a nervous tension in him, like an animal that has been caged for so long it doesn't know what to do when freed. Three times he traverses the small room, words pouring out.

"You know my mother died from that damn wasp sting. Andrew was stung. First time he had a full-blown anaphylaxis." The medical term comes out in a robotic voice, but as he continues he becomes more emotional. "Mom kept pointing from the EpiPen to him. She fought me off when I tried to jab it in her leg. Fought me. She couldn't speak by then. The words came out as grunts. Andrew was panicking and they were both dying."

"I know." I walk to him and stop him, reaching for both his hands. "I know."

"That day when you were stung," he says, eyes wild, pulse beating so hard I can see it in his neck, right under his earlobe.

"When you were stung and your EpiPen came out my first thought was Thank God, only one person. Only one person who I am responsible for. The odds aren't stacked against me."

"And then I stabbed you," I say with a choked, horrified snort, squeezing his warm hands.

"And I thought that was it. But you had a second one." He doesn't need to say what we're both thinking. The room goes cold with a huge gust from a brewing storm on the bay. If only . . .

"Fate," I blurt out.

"Fate," he says without question. "Fate is a cruel mistress."

I look at him with a questioning face.

"Of all the women I could have met with their hand down a toilet at one of my stores, it had to be the one with the same allergy that. . . ."

"Yeah. It's pretty freaking weird."

"I shouldn't be with you."

I freeze.

"But I can't do this."

Do what?

"I can't stay away. Dad tried to convince me that I'm signing up for nothing but heartbreak with you. That the genetics are stacked against us—"

Genetics?

"That our children have a higher chance of—"

CHILDREN? Did he just say *children?*

"And I'll spend the rest of my life in fear of—"

In a mad rush I tackle him, the kiss desperate and urgent, my body launching into his with such force that we fall onto the bed, a mass of pillows rolling off and bouncing, pelting our legs as his mouth meets mine, rougher with each second, claiming me.

"I can't be without you," he says in a hurried gasp. "I've tried. You're forthright and honest and the most upfront woman I've ever met. You have an inner core that makes you turn toward the good. You make me want to be good, too." He kisses the end of my nose and pulls back, half in shadows and half in moonlight.

The room is timeless, his face pensive. Thoughtful.

"And you have a very weird family."

"And a malicious cat," I add, peppering his jaw with kisses.

"You don't give a damn what people think, at the same time you care about what people feel. And you took on my dad." I can feel his grin through our kiss. "That's when I fell in love with you."

"The same day you *dumped* me you fell in love with me?"

"Love isn't rational."

I fell in love with you.

"When you said you took a chance on me, that was . . ."

"My being an idiot. Not the taking a chance part." He pulls my shirt out from the waistline of my skirt and rests his palms against my back. The feeling charges me, making my skin hum. "The jumbled mess of thinking that I should just walk away. That the pain of being with you outweighed the joy."

Joy.

"And you're here because . . ."

"Because I couldn't stay away."

"You had to pretend to be Alfredo the Plumber in order to tell me this?"

"Did it work?"

"I don't know. You'll have to ask me again. At breakfast." The smoldering look he gives me as he pulls me to him in a kiss makes my toes tingle. Dishes on the tray rattle and he sits up, moves the tray, and stands in the moonlight, the lines of his clothed body like a work of art.

I stand, pressing in for a kiss, and begin to unbutton his shirt. "Forthright, huh?" One knowing touch as I reach down makes him suck air in through his teeth.

"I like a woman who knows what she wants."

"Then you must *really* like me, because I know exactly what—and who—I want."

My own breath is foreign to me, the spellbinding touch of his fingers on my cheek like a caress from a different world. He's different now, deeper and richer in his intents, and I want to believe him. Need to believe him. My body responds before my heart, so quick to react that I pause, listening to the beat of blood pounding through me, all rushing to the surface of my skin to get closer to him.

I hold nothing back now and invite him to cast aside whatever keeps him from surrendering to the new reality we've woven just by being together, right here. Right now. I don't need to hear him tell me he loves me—it's too soon for that—but I need him to show me.

Show me.

His hands take in my skin like a man in charge, grasping what he wants, possessing it. As I reach for his pants and unsnap them, his fingers make quick work of undoing my bra, then his heat is on me, warm palms cupping my breasts, the pleasure of being together and intimate nakedly on display in the look he gives me, open and revealing.

Trust. He trusts me, now, and joy pours through my body like liquid fire, my lips quivering from emotion, my whole being at rest and yet in eager motion. He slips my shirt, then bra, off my shoulders and onto the floor as he steps out of his clothes. We're both naked and raw before one another in the blink of an eye, and we both feel it. The shockwave of peace and hope, of arousal and yearning.

Of coming home.

"This is what you want," he murmurs against my shoulder as he seeds it with tiny kisses, repeating my own words back.

"Yes."

"Me, too. More than anything. This is . . . everything. You are everything."

"Then let's be everything together."

"High standards."

"I know you're an overachiever."

His deep, throaty chuckle morphs into something more sensual as he gently guides me to the bed, the full length of him covering me. All my jokes disintegrate, replaced by a moment-by-moment awareness that makes me feel ancient, alive and immortal, regenerated kiss by kiss, stroke by stroke, lick by—

"Oh, there," I whisper, the sound half groan, half sigh, as

he makes me speechless once more. We're just kissing, but it's so much more, his mouth sensual and alive, our hands roaming and remembering, searching and loving. Each lush kiss makes me go to a level inside myself that I didn't know I possess, and Declan's right there with me, a fiery, passionate presence.

"You know," he says as my hands ride up from the grooves of his hipbones, over his sharp belly, abs like inverted shells under perfect, musky skin, "this isn't part of your evaluation."

I laugh as he kisses the base of my throat, my fingertips memorizing him, reaching down to feel his tight ass. "How do you know? Maybe this is in my app."

"Do you find the lovemaking aesthetically pleasing?" he asks, his hands making damn certain that I do.

"I need more time and observation to make that kind of de-termination," I say in a faux-prim voice.

The teasing fades as he kisses me again, then dips his head down to tongue one tight rosebud nipple. Again? This is new. Then again, we've never had all the time in the world, our own hotel room, and a bed the size of my backyard.

"As you wish," he adds, showing me exactly how to perform exemplary customer service, the rough rasp of the soft hair on his thighs and calves tickling my hips. We're a slow, languid twinning of warmth now, and Declan stops to look at me.

Really look at me.

No modesty, no walls to hide emotion behind. We watch each other for longer than is decent, the air telescoping to a pin-point, his eyes a cavern of delight. He's inviting me to join him with this look, and I intertwine my fingers in his, shift my thigh just so to stroke him, the resulting gasp the only answer either of us needs to give.

The moonlight spilling into the room gives me all the visual access I could wish to revel in, my eyes feasting on the sharp lines of his body, how muscle dominates in all the empty spac-es between bones. Fluid and graceful, Declan moves like a man who knows himself, and I adopt the same, even as it is not in my nature.

Who says it's not?

His kisses travel lower, attending to my breasts, then down

the valley and into the fertile lands where his mouth makes me arch up in surprise and pleasure. He takes his time, hands under me, generous with his effort, erotic with his skill. My hands find his shoulder blades, admiring the fine, artistic lines of his muscled back, then stroke up the nape of his neck to bury in his hair. He is at my essence, tasting all I have to offer, and he is giving in bold, breathtaking ways.

My release is so close, a glow that fills me from top to bottom, and I reach down, curl up, and pull his mouth to mine, wanting more intimacy, wanting him face-to-face. His lips are tangy and savory, his smile all mine, and I nudge him to lie down on the bed, pulling myself up onto my knees.

In full glory, oh—I can't quite catch my breath, the handsome, powerful pull of his skin and blood next to me magnetic. I want him to belong to me. I want to be claimed.

I want.

I want.

Declan tugs gently on my knee and guides me to straddle him. He turns to take care of practicalities, a condom on him quickly, and I am on him, not leaning forward with rounded shoulders and self-conscious posture, but riding high, sitting straight up, breasts gleaming in the shadow of the city lights and the moon's eye.

"You are . . ." He finishes the sentence with a sighing sound more gratifying than any word. Eyes the color of Irish hills gaze at me with an intensity that brands me. I am his. He is mine.

I don't need to hear the word love. Not yet. Because I know that someday I will. The certainty inside me is so solid, so secure that as he fills me, our connection complete, I will the words to span between us without being spoken. Appreciative, smoking eyes take me in as he pushes up, touching my core. We are one. One flesh, one heart. I feel it beating, strong and pattering under my hand, pulse pounding as we rock to ecstasy.

This is how we find each other.

We tremor together on a frequency of our own creation, and then, with dawning awareness, find the divine within.

chapter
nineteen

"**Y**OU HAVE SUCH NICE hands." In the morning light, his big hands look like an artist carved them, the thick veins and muscled thumb pad like an artifact you would find in a display case in a Greek museum. I'm pressed against him under the covers, a handful of pillows under our shoulders and heads, and we're luxuriating in the sheer quantity of skin that can touch each other when we're naked, in a bed, and alone.

The way life should be.

He inhales slowly and stretches like a big lion, the thick triceps in his arms bulging and thinning out, making a deep groove in his arm as the muscles pull away from each other. Does the man have any fat on him? I have plenty for us both, I suppose. As if reading my mind he reaches for my ass and gives it a love pat.

My phone buzzes.

"Ignore it," he groans, breathing with a slight sound of deep satisfaction. "I don't want to deal with people just yet."

"What about me?" I pretend to pout.

"You're not people."

"What am I, then?"

"You're prey." With a playful roar he pins me beneath him, demonstrating that all of his body isn't nearly as sleepy as he's pretending to be. Some parts woke up a bit earlier and are standing at attention, ready to, er. . . . plunge into the day.

Bzzzzz.

And then my hotel phone rings.

We look at each other in alarm. "I have to answer that," I say with a pleading tone.

"Of course." He lets me go and I grab the receiver.

"Hello?"

"Shannon?" It's Amanda.

"Who is it?" Declan asks just loud enough for her next words to be:

"YOU HAVE A MAN IN YOUR ROOM WITH YOU?" She screams so loudly I fling the receiver across the bed and hold my palm over my ear, moaning in pain. Declan winces and sits up, scrambling for the phone, which slides off the bed like a paralyzed snake with no ability to save itself from plummeting.

"Amanda? It's Declan. Shannon will be back in a second. She's just sewing her eardrum back together."

The ringing in my ear isn't fading, and Declan gives me an awkward look. I'm completely naked and his eyes drift down.

Now he looks like a wolf.

"Fine, and you?" he says, making strange small talk with the woman who mysteriously set last night's events into motion. I have a million words for her, most of them involving some combination of "thank" and "you," but right now I'm staring, agog, at my naked—boyfriend?—talking about the weather with Amanda.

I snatch the phone back and wave him off to the bathroom. As he stands, his ass muscles make me whimper.

"Ear hurts that bad?' she asks softly.

I wipe a line of drool from my mouth as I get a very nice view of Declan making coffee in the Keurig. "Um, yes. It's torture. Why are you calling me in my room? You can't do that. It could break my cover. Plus, what the hell did you do? Andrew told me you barged into his office and demanded to know about Declan and his mother's death, and then I came here to do this mystery shop and it's a plague of McCormicks! Terry and Andrew and Declan and James all pretended to work here."

Silence.

"Amanda?"

"Um." Her tone of voice is hesitant. If she were calling

because someone got hurt, she'd say so. This is business, and a cold dread fills me.

"What's going on? Tell me why you set all this up."

"That's not why I'm calling."

"Then why?"

"Greg's been trying to call you. Me, too. Shannon, go get your smartphone and log in to your Twitter account."

"Say what? I don't need to read any more crap from Jessica Coffin right now." I give Declan a once-over as he makes the second mug of coffee. "Especially right now."

"Yeah, well, it's about your mom. And Jessica. And the credit union client."

"What do those three completely unrelated things have to do with each other?"

"Marie made them not-so unrelated last night."

"Speak in English, please."

"Well, she, uh . . ."

"Spit it out!"

"Your mom started taunting Jessica Coffin on Twitter and insisting that you were pretending to be a lesbian for the credit union shop, and Jessica looped the client in, and now they're insisting Greg fire you."

I asked for the full story and got it. In one sentence.

"Say that again," I peep. Declan's frowning now and he hands me the hot cup of coffee, a concerned look on his face.

She takes a deep breath and repeats it, word for word.

"I'm *fired*?"

Declan's eyebrows shoot up and he mouths the word. I shrug. None of this makes sense.

"Not yet, but when Greg calls . . ."

"Was this because I didn't do the mystery shop I'm on right now correctly?" The words come out of my mouth and I know they're wrong, but what she's saying doesn't make sense.

"No, honey. It's because your mom and Jessica publicly blew your cover and the client basically needs to save face. It's all public relations. They need a fall guy. And that's . . . you."

"*I'm* the fall guy?"

She sighs. "Yes. I'm so sorry," she adds in a rush. "Greg feels awful about it and argued with the client forever, but they are absolutely adamant. The credit union called the client and it's turned into a nasty mess."

"Have you talked to my mom?"

Amanda pauses mid breath. "She, uh, didn't really understand what a see-you-next-Tuesday Jessica could be."

My jaw drops. "She didn't realize that? After everything we've dealt with?"

"I think your mom just turned into a Mama Bear and went crazy."

"Like that's different from . . . what?" Declan crawls on the bed and starts massaging my shoulders, which are two big lumps of granite right now. Fired. I'm fired.

Fired for doing my job.

Fired for nearly losing the man who is right behind me, touching me with tenderness and compassion, trying to massage the crazy away.

Fired for being loved by a mother who has the business skills of a sno-cone salesman in a blizzard.

Bzzzzz. I haven't even reached for my phone to look at the Twittermess. I can only imagine. But Declan reaches across me, smelling like sex and spice and mmmmm, and hands me my phone.

Greg.

"Is that Greg on your phone?" Amanda asks with a pitying voice.

"This is real. You're serious," I whisper.

"I wish I weren't. Trust me."

Declan peels the receiver from my fingers carefully. "Answer the phone, Shannon. Get it over with. It's like ripping a Band-Aid off. It's better to just do it." The look he gives me is no-nonsense, but understanding at the same time.

I take a deep breath, hit Talk, and say, "You don't have to say it, Greg. I already know."

Declan heads to the bathroom to give me some privacy. I hear the shower turn on as Greg blusters and apologizes, rants and overexplains. His words pour over me as I wonder how my life could pivot like this in less than twenty-four hours.

I get my (ex) boss off the phone quickly so I can go shower with my (ex-ex) boyfriend. Just as I knock on the door the water stops. Great. He's one of those people who can take a three-minute shower.

Freak.

"Come in." I open the door a crack and poke my head in. He's toweling off. His face softens into a look of compassion.

"You okay?"

"I'm fired."

"Come here." He opens his arms and I walk into his embrace, still in a state of shock. Even my libido is stunned, because the press of his clean, wet wall of skin against my body isn't making me hump his leg.

"I have more student loan debt than you could ever imagine. Plus credit cards, and now I won't have a car because I have to give the Turdmobile back. And as bad as it was driving that piece of—"

"Shhhhhh," he urges. "It'll be fine."

"Fine? No, it won't! You try finding a good, steady job in this economy. I have a marketing degree. I'm lucky I haven't spent the last year handing out new product samples at Costco for $15 an hour!"

"You'll find a better job," he says with confidence.

For some reason, his reassurance is annoying. "I hope you're right."

"I know I am." He rests his chin on my head. "Because I want you to come work for me."

My laughter makes my breasts bounce against his chest. "Ha ha."

He pulls away, eyes dead serious. "I mean it. Come work at Anterdec. Assistant Director of Marketing."

"I really don't need you to make fun of me right now."

"I don't joke about business. We'll pay you more, Anterdec has great benefits, and you'll get stock options, bonus, and a great maternity leave package." He winks.

"I can't believe you're saying this." I feel numb.

"Did I overdo it on the maternity comment?" He makes a sheepish face. "Didn't mean to over play my hand."

"No, I mean that you'd think I'd just jump right in and take a job working for you, that you'd ride in on your white horse and rescue me."

"That's not what I—"

I start to shake. Can't control it, can't mute it. Just . . . shake. It's all too much, from Guido being Terry to my confrontation with James to reuniting with Declan and now I'm fired?

And Declan wants to wrap me up in gauze and make me his little porcelain doll.

Nope.

"I, um, need a shower. Don't you have a business meeting or something you need to get to?" I mutter as I turn on the water and climb in. I couldn't hint any more if I shoved him out the door and threw his clothes at him.

Declan's face appears between the tiled wall and the shower curtain, like Jack Nicholson breaking through the door in the old version of *The Shining*. Okay, not quite that bad, but . . .

"You're not getting rid of me that easily," he says, and climbs on in with me.

"You just showered!" I protest. The slick feel of his skin against mine as he holds me from behind is at odds with my righteous indignation, which I'm holding onto by a thin thread.

"I can get wet again." He turns me around, the hot spray glorious against my back, my hair hanging in limp strands against my cheekbones and shoulders, Declan's second head definitely not limp. "And my eyes are up here," he coaxes.

I raise mine. "Oops."

"You're ogling me."

"Yes."

"Good." He kisses me so deeply I think my toes have curled into themselves. "Don't be mad. I really mean it about the job. I thought about offering it to you a while ago."

"How long ago?"

"The day you showed up at that meeting after the toilet incident."

"That long ago?" I eye him with suspicion. "Why?"

"Because you're smart."

"Pffft. That's not a good enough reason! No one gets a great job with a huge megacorporation because they're *smart*," I say, making a dismissive sound with the back of my throat.

"Then how do you get a great job with a megacorporation?" he asks.

"By knowing someone—" I groan. "Networking."

His hands squeeze my ample ass. "Is that what they call this?" He kisses the hollow at the nape of my neck. "Networking?"

"You can't give me a job just because you're sleeping with me! What kind of feminist would I be if I did that?"

"An *employed* feminist?"

I stop and consider that for a moment as his hand does unspeakable things. Really. He's making it hard for me to speak. "Would I work under you?"

He makes a suggestive sound.

"How about we conduct a little employee orientation right now?" he whispers.

And then he schools me.

chapter
twenty

"CHECK OUT THAT HEADLINE," Josh crows as he slaps a morning paper on my desk at work. Um, former work, technically. I'm here to clean out my desk.

Unidentified Flying Orgasm screams the newspaper headline, with a giant picture of a crushed vibrator on the ground next to the bumper of a taxi, two men arguing over it.

"Nice."

"Funny how that happened at the exact hotel where you were working," he adds with a sly look.

"The world is made up of unremitting coincidences."

"And you have an awful lot of them following you around." He walks out of my office and into his. Keyboard keys click furiously in the distance.

I make a dismissive sound in my throat and continue putting my personal stuff in a box. Greg isn't here today, but he's called me three times in the past two days to apologize profusely. I get a month's severance and can continue to mystery shop for him, but he can't chance losing the second-biggest client for Consolidated Evalu-shop.

I get it. I really do understand. And there's a silver lining. A big one.

Carol's taking my job. She screamed in my ear after Greg interviewed her, and Mom and Dad can fill in for child care during the occasional non-school hours she has to work. It's a relief to know that even as my own career turns to shambles, at least my sister and nephews are in a better place.

"Hey," Josh whispers, carrying his laptop with him. I'm about to hand mine over and he'll back up all my personal files, then wipe it clean for Carol. "I need to show you something."

He clicks on a tab with Twitter open. On Jessica Coffin's profile. I groan.

"No, no, just look," he assures me. His eyes are lit up and he's so animated, which means I'm about to learn all about Linux sftp protocol scripting or he'll explain some intricate detail about how the darknet will take over the world when the Millennial Illuminati gain power.

"I really have no desire to even think about Jessica Coffin again."

"She's getting completely trashed online. Twitter, Facebook, Pinterest, Tumblr—you name it. There's a long, long thread on Reddit calling her out."

Now I'm interested. "What happened?"

He waves his hands in front of him with glee, face consumed by the glowing screen. "Someone," he says in an arched tone, "appears to have hacked into her Twitter account and is posting all of the direct, private messages she's been receiving for the past year."

"Huh?"

"Basically, people have been feeding her gossip and now they're all being outed by her. Her Twitter stream, that is."

"Why would she do that?"

"She's not doing it. A cracker did it."

"A cracker?"

His harsh sigh makes me feel stupid. "A hacker."

"So do I know this 'someone'?"

Pride shines through in his upright posture and he strokes his chin. "I can't imagine knowing anyone who would do such a thing, but you never know. Could be 4chan, or . . ." He goes on and names a bunch of groups I've never heard of.

I stare at the screen and read some of the messages.

Many are from Steve. Busted!

A wide smile stretches my face as I turn my own computer

off and hand it to Josh. "Thanks."

"For what?" He looks at the ceiling and pretends to be innocent.

I stand on tiptoes and kiss his cheek. "For helping to balance the world a little more fairly." My keychain rattles in my hand as I palm it off on him.

"Company car?"

"Yep. You can take the Turdmobile and hand your car off to my sister when she starts working here. Though my nephew, Jeffrey, would be disappointed. He wants to drive around in a 'pieth of thit car'."

Josh laughs, then swallows, hard. "I'm going to miss you."

"I'm not disappearing."

"But you won't be here. You and Amanda are this amazing duo. Someone has to huddle with me in the winter to stay warm."

"Carol's a big girl like me. You'll do fine."

We hug.

My phone buzzes. It's Declan, outside, in a limo. Josh walks me to the main doors and peers out at my mode of transportation.

"What the hell am I worried about," he declares. "You're leaving this place and the Turdmobile to get into *that*?" A low whistle and a high five ends my visit, and I turn to Declan with my personal belongings in a box, walking away from the very job that made me meet him.

Car tires screech in the parking lot as Amanda arrives. She parks across two spaces and jumps out, running to me. Josh stands in the doorway, gawking.

"Wait! Stop!" Breathless, she leans over and puts her hands on her knees. Declan climbs out of the limo and takes the box from me, a curious look passing between us.

"Mystery shopping emergency? Did someone fail to deliver a drive-thru order in ninety seconds or less?" I joke.

"No." She's in tears. "I just didn't want to miss you before you left."

"You could just text me," I say slowly, trying to keep the joke going because if I don't, I'll dissolve into a puddle of tears, too. "You didn't need to pull a Hollywood moment where you rush in and—"

Too late. We're sobbing. Two strong, masculine arms wrap around me and Amanda and then we hear the whimpering sound of Josh crying, too.

"It's not going to be the same," he wails.

Declan unbuttons his suit jacket, crosses his arms, and leans back against the limo. His eyes roll skyward. "It'll be a few minutes, Lance," he says to the driver through the open window.

"That's right!" Amanda squeaks, flashing indignant eyes at my boyfriend. "You get her for the rest of her life. We only have her for a few more minutes."

"We're all going to that tapas bar in Waltham at seven tonight, remember?" Declan answers dryly. "If you can suffer through five hours of not seeing Shannon."

"That's not the point!" Josh gasps, wiping his eyes. "It's just the end of an era. You don't get it."

Declan nods slowly. "You're right. I don't." He gives me a warm grin and cocks an eyebrow like he's saying *WTF is up with your friends?*

"He's right," I say to Amanda and Josh, laughing through tears. "It's not like you'll never see me again. We'll have chevre-stuffed pimentoes in a few hours."

The three of us compose ourselves, give final hugs, and they walk into the building while I climb into the limo with Declan, where he's sitting, waiting for me.

Arms outstretched and tissues at the ready.

The drive over to Anterdec involves a lot of hitched sobbing and, fortunately, no eyerolling.

"I'm fine! And no, I haven't officially decided." For the past week Declan's been pestering me to just say yes and come work for him.

And for the past week I've dug my heels in and told him I

hadn't made a decision.

My terms: a meeting with James to make sure I can tolerate working here.

In Declan's mind this is a done deal.

In my mind it's an open case. Nothing is settled. Putting all of my emotional and financial life in the hands of one man is a risk that involves an extraordinary amount of trust, and while we're back together and it's clear—so clear—that we're meant for each other, I'm a pragmatist at heart.

A little OCD, even. Which is great when it comes to managing 34,985 details for marketing campaigns, but not so great when it comes to taking flying leaps of faith and love.

Working for Declan means working for James, and I didn't exactly leave off on a good note the last time I saw him.

I'm fairly cleaned up and halfway decent by the time the limo pulls in to the Anterdec private garage. Unlike the main entrance, this is a quiet, subterranean section of the parking labyrinth that I would never know existed if it weren't for Declan.

I say so.

He looks at me, eyebrows crowded, and shrugs. "Isn't that the point?"

I laugh, the sound like ping pong balls being dropped on a trampoline. "You really have no idea how real people live."

"Your mom is taking me thrifting, remember? I'll be sure to have Jeeves scuff my shoes just so and to forget to shave." His pretend British accent and locked jaw make me laugh harder. Sweat covers my palms, my makeup's long been cried off or kissed off (I much prefer the latter), and I wonder just how raw I must appear.

An audience of James McCormick in this kind of fragile state is really not appealing.

"Mom will make you dumpster dive if you're not careful," I warn him.

Very real horror fills his face. "What?" He looks a bit sick. "I thought that chicken tasted a bit odd when she had us over for dinner last night."

I punch him. We get out of the limo and board the elevator. "Not food. She goes behind florist shops and card stores and comes home with a mountain of stuff to add to the mountain of stuff in the basement."

He pauses and reaches for my shoulders, locking eyes on me. "Are your parents okay financially? Do they need—"

I press my index finger against his lips. "The fastest way to wind up dead and decomposing in a 55-gallon drum in Dad's Man Cave is to offer financial help to my parents."

He gulps. "Understood. But—dumpster diving?"

"It's a hobby. Mom does this. Wait three months and she'll get over it. Last year it was the whole Extreme Couponing thing."

We ride up a few floors in silence and he turns to me with a look of dawning recognition. "Extreme Couponing. Is that why you have what looks like hundreds of deodorants jammed in the drawers of your bathroom?"

I wink. "You connected the dots."

"I just thought you were obsessive about not having smelly armpits . . ."

"She goes crazy on triple coupon day. You should see her stash of sex lube."

With that the elevator doors open.

And there stands James McCormick, who clearly heard my and Declan's last words.

"Make her take the job, Dad," Declan announces, face impassive as he leans over and kisses my cheek. My fingers grope for his arm but he's slick and eludes my attempt.

"Not if she has smelly armpits," James jokes. We walk quietly to the private door to his office where he motions toward two enormous wingback chairs pointed toward the windows.

"Please. Sit. Coffee?"

My hands are shaking. Don't need to add a caffeine injection. "No, thank you."

He sits next to me and leans forward, forearms on knees, eyes perceptive. "Declan tells me you're hesitating on taking the Assistant Director of Marketing job."

"Yes."

"Because of me." It's not a question.

Honesty is best here. "Because I don't want to be too dependent on Declan."

One eyebrow slowly rises. "Go on."

"There isn't any more to it." I shrug. "It's that simple. We're together, and I'm concerned about mixing business with . . ." I frown.

"With life." He nods, rubbing his hands together slowly.

"Yes."

"Declan tells me you're good." He clears his throat. "With marketing."

He *really* didn't need to elaborate. Now I'm self-conscious.

"And he is willing to take a larger risk than you, Shannon. I think you need to take that into consideration." There's a hard edge to his voice, but it's encased in a velvet tongue.

"What?"

"Not in business. But in choosing to love you. To stay with you. To—perhaps—build a life with you."

Love.

"I'm not in a pity relationship," I answer bluntly. "He's not offering me a relationship, or a job, because—"

"That is evident." James McCormick doesn't listen to extraneous words. "My point is that Declan, who has one of the smartest, most rational minds I know, has decided that giving his heart to you is worth the risk that you may not be around to share it."

A cold rush pours through me.

"What does that—"

"While you dither and pretend you don't know whether to take the job, Declan is living his choice every day. He's taken a much bigger risk already than you would take if you accept the job at Anterdec."

I just blink.

"Take the job, Shannon. Worry about what-if later. You can't spend your life worrying that the devil you don't know might turn bad when the devil you do know already is. Unemployment doesn't suit you."

No. It doesn't. I've gotten so bored this week that Chuckles now has painted toenails and you can eat off my dad's Man Cave floor.

"Why are you urging me to do it? Take the job?"

"You make Declan happy."

"Nope. Not enough."

"Because you're Marie's daughter and it feels like karma."

"Still not enough."

He sighs. "Because of all the women Declan has dated, you are the first one I've met who is remotely interesting. And challenging. I don't surround myself with yes men and I'd prefer not to be surrounded by yes daughters-in-law."

Daughter in law.

"Therefore, I ask you to take some time to decide, and—"

"Yes."

"Yes?"

"Yes."

"That was fast."

"When you know, you know."

James looks over my shoulder and I follow his gaze. He's looking at a picture of his late wife. She's on the beach with all three boys; I'm guessing Declan is about twelve in the photo, braces on his teeth and a layer of baby fat in his face that says the long stretch of puberty hasn't hit yet.

It's a happy photo. A joyous one, even.

"Yes, Shannon. When you know, you know."

twenty-one

I SPEND THE NEXT few hours in Human Resources, kept busy on an assembly line of managers and coordinators, never once seeing Declan. The Associate Director for HR gave me my salary proposal, benefits information, and when my eyes bugged out of my head at the salary, she was polite enough not to tell me to shove them back in my head.

We're taught in business classes to negotiate. Always. But when someone offers you more than twice your old salary and a benefits package valued at nearly a year's pay—you just say thank you profusely. I'm sure Steve would argue the opposite, but Steve can go suck a box of rocks.

My phone buzzes in the middle of signing paperwork. Mom. I keep it to text.

You okay? She texts. *Need a chocolate intervention?*

Nope. Signing my new hire paperwork at Anterdec.

The phone rings. "You're coming to my yoga class on Saturday still, right? And bringing Declan."

"You cannot use him to sell more spots in your class, Mom. He's not a side show like a sword swallower or The Bearded Woman."

She makes a tsking sound. "We already have that! And Corrine is trying to get it under control with electrolysis, so stop making jokes about her."

"I wasn't!" The HR coordinator who is explaining my health insurance package comes back with her photocopies. "I have to go."

"Congratulations, honey! What's your salary?" The coordinator takes my empty coffee mug and motions, asking if I want more. I nod yes.

"Shannon?"

I tell Mom my salary.

"You make more than Jason!" she squeals.

"Will he feel emasculated?" I ask, worried.

"*Pffft.* If that man can stay married to me for nearly thirty years, he can handle this. Your father doesn't do emasculation. Well, not in public, anyhow."

"Mom," I growl.

"Fine, fine. I'll make a celebratory dinner tonight! Bring Declan over! We'll play Cards Against Humanity and I'll break out the new candles I found in the dumpster."

"Living it up!"

"I'm so proud of you, Shannon."

"Thanks, Mom."

The HR person comes back in and after two more hours, I have a photo ID, a start date, and a raging case of missing Declan.

Bzzzz.

Meet me where the limo is, he texts.

The receptionist guides me to the right elevator and I ride it down, completely drained. A happy kind of drain. The kind of exhaustion you feel when your entire paradigm about how to live your life has changed.

The elevator doors open and there's Declan, holding two EpiPens and a dozen long-stemmed chocolate covered strawberries (a mix of dark and milk, of course) in his arms.

And he's wearing a grin that makes my heart do jumping jacks.

"Do you, Shannon Jacoby, promise to be my Assistant Director of Marketing so long as your stock options may vest?"

"I do."

He kisses me with a freedom and abandon that makes the world disappear.

And I swear, somewhere, my mother is banging a spoon

against a wine glass, finger ready to dial Farmington Country Club to reserve a date in 2016.

Someone get Steve's mom some smelling salts. And a dose for him, too.

BONUS—CONTINUE ON TO READ *Christmas Shopping for a Billionaire*, which takes place about six months later.

When Shannon is called to the mall to work as a sexy elf, her billionaire boyfriend, Declan, gets roped into playing Santa. The mall mommies start tweeting pictures, and soon everyone is crashing the mall to have a seat on Santa's lap.

AMERICAN AIRLINES
BOARDING PASS

STRAWN/JESSICA

DALLAS FT WORTH
HONOLULU
AMERICAN AIRLINES

AA 123   P 10FEB905A

835A   15L NO

GROUP
4

AMERICAN AIRLINES

TSA PRECHK   US

STRAWN/JESSICA   10FEB18
XWC /DSM   DES MOINES

DALLAS FT WORTH   AA 123   P 10FEB905A
HONOLULU

****
*   *
*   YXELUC /AA   *
*   BOARDING PASS   *
*   DOORS CLOSE 10 MIN PRIOR TO DEPARTURE*
****

GROUP 4

SEAT 15L

PRIORITY PREM E ***********

****
****
****

2 001 7008632606 6   XWC /DSM

ABCD12345678

PRINTED IN U.S.A. BY MAGNETIC TICKET & LABEL CORP., DALLAS, TX

christmas
shopping
for a
billionaire

chapter
one

THE CALL TODAY FROM my old boss, Greg, two days before Christmas at 2:12 p.m. should have tipped me off. I *should* have let it go to voicemail. I *should* have ignored it and not stopped decorating the Christmas tree in my boyfriend's apartment. The tree that Declan had ordered from some place in Nova Scotia where all trees look like something out a movie set and the super-nice Canadians hire Tibetan refugee monks to rub the trunks down with virgin coconut oil and chant "Om Mani Padme Hun" for universal nirvana.

That is, before they chop the tree down to ship it by helicopter to a waterfront high rise on Long Wharf in Boston, where it will look pretty for two weeks and then get the chipper treatment at a recycling center. That's a form of reincarnation, right?

But I *don't* ignore Greg's call even though I might be a little intoxicated by the sight of my man wearing a Santa hat, tight jeans, and a snug green cashmere sweater that makes me want him to hurry up my chimney tonight.

(C'mon. You knew the pun was coming).

"Hey, Greg. What's up?" I answer.

Declan is hanging one of the new ornaments I bought him, a candy cane made from glued cloves. Mom's friend holds a Sustainable Free Trade Christmas Fair every year, and I'd been told a young African girl made the clove ornament to raise money to buy a three legged-goat for milk to feed her family, or something like that.

The details are fuzzy because I couldn't listen through my

sobs as I handed fistfuls of money to Mom, who just picked out a few items and patted me on the back, mumbling something about how I am just like my father. He had been banned from the fair two years ago when he bought all five hundred hand-made Christmas cards from the Ivory Coast refugee who was promoting slave-free chocolate, sobbing with guilt and apologizing profusely for his KitKat addiction.

"Did Carol call you?" My old boss sounds frantic. Greg isn't the type to descend into hysteria. A chill runs up my spine, and it isn't from the nine inches of snow that blanketed Boston yesterday. I know that tone of voice.

That is the tone that got my hand shoved down a toilet in the men's room of a fast food restaurant when I worked for him as a mystery shopper, evaluating customer service at stores and companies.

The tone that gave me a brand-new car that looked like a Goliath took a steaming dump on top of it when we were doing branded advertising for a website.

The tone that made me listen to podiatrists wax rhapsodic about toe fungus as they eyed my feet like I was starring in a fetish story from one of my dad's old *Hustler* magazines that he kept stored in his backyard Man Cave.

That is the tone of desperation.

"No. Carol did not."

Declan looks at me, tilting his head to the left and making a low voice in the back of his throat that indicates displeasure. While I work for Declan's company now, I fill in for the occasional mystery shop. My oldest sister, Carol, has my old job now and sometimes does the *really* professional maneuver where she calls and begs and whines and pleads and threatens to tell my boyfriend all about that time I bought a chest enhancer and got my budding nipple caught in the springs, in order to get me to take on a shop.

Yeah. Professional like that. Carol would make a great women's prison kitchen chef.

So Greg is a step above. "Carol had a mystery shopper no-show on her, and she can't come in because of your nephews.

Something about needing a babysitter—"

"We can go over and watch Jeffrey and Tyler!" I say in an overeager voice as Declan continues his vocal imitation of Jamie Fraser from the *Outlander* series, making more guttural sounds than a female sea lion with strep throat.

Of course, I offer to babysit. Because the alternative is . . .

"That doesn't work. Something about one of the kids having the bubonic plague," he adds. Carol can get a wee dramatic, but I vaguely remember Mom telling me one of the kids had something that generated more snot than a bunch of postmenopausal women watching *Steel Magnolias*.

"Did you try Josh?" Josh is the company technogeek, and he almost never gets pulled into mystery shopping. Right now, though, I'll throw him under the bus if it means staying here with Declan for the rest of the day, my eyes memorizing the tight little ripples of muscle between his lower ribs as he stretches up on tiptoes to hang an ornament. His sweater pulls up enough to make his torso look like it was finely carved from tanned alabaster.

On the first day of Christmas, my true love gave to me
A humping in the bedroom so fine I forgot my name.

(So what if it doesn't rhyme. Just go with it).

"We need a female," Greg stresses. I look down at my overflowing bosom, tightly encased in a green wrap shirt that makes my cleavage pour out like a split muffin top. Damn. For once, having breasts *qualifies* me for a job.

"He looks really good in drag," I tell Greg.

Declan halts in mid-stretch and plants his feet firmly on the floor, turning to me. He points to himself and shakes his head slowly, eyes steely green.

Not you, I mouth.

"Good," Declan says with his hands on his hips, one knee bent, like a man in pose to argue, the male equivalent of Talk to the Hand.

"Josh *does* that stuff?" Greg asks, incredulous.

"No," I confess. "I just don't want to do whatever it is *you* want me to do."

"We need a sexy female elf."

"A sexy female *elf?*" Did I hear him wrong?

Declan appears instantly at my side, suddenly *very* interested.

"You would be a very good sexy female elf," Greg and Declan simulcast in my ears in two completely different tones of voice. Both, though, carry the tiniest hint of desperation.

"Who's there?' Greg asks. His words are a bit muffled, as if floating through cotton.

"Why are you talking so weird?" The cinnamon-scented Christmas candles on Declan's sleek marble mantel send a glow high into his arched ceiling. The city is spread out before us on one side of the high-windowed penthouse, the ocean on the other side. Panoramic views are fine and all, but the best scenery is two inches away, his lips closing in on my neck.

"It's the beard," Greg says, jolting me out of my turning into a maid a-milking, my hand reaching for Declan in a place that makes him inhale sharply, then smile against my ear.

"Beard?" I ask.

I twist my way out of Declan's arms and make a pouty face. He joins me, looking disturbingly like my cat, Chuckles. I didn't know Declan had a Grumpy Cat face. You date a man for eight months and then one day you discover he looks like a cat doing a Paul Ryan imitation. Thank God that's not his O face.

I shudder and Declan mistakes that for my being cold, wrapping his arms around me.

"I'm Santa," Greg explains. "We're evaluating the customer service quality of the Children's Christmas Village set-up at the mall. Our Santa no-showed and I had to jump in."

"You've got the body for it." Greg doesn't just have a bowl full of jelly—he's the entire Smucker's plant.

"Hey!" He sounds genuinely offended.

"You can talk about how I can be a *sexy elf* but I can't mention your beer gut?"

"It's not a beer gut!"

"Fine. *Wine* gut."

He lets out a long sigh of resignation. *"That's* better."

Because it's true.

"You want me to come in and put on a sexy costume to play the female equivalent of Buddy the Elf at the mall two days before Christmas because no one else will do it?"

"Right."

"Why?"

"Why *what*?" Greg's breath is coming in huffs of nervousness.

Grumpy Declan sees me wavering and finishes my hot toddy for me, returning to the tree to decorate.

"Why should I do it?" I challenge.

"It pays $30 an hour and you get a free picture with Santa."

"I make more than that working for Anterdec Industries now, and I am not sitting on your lap."

"I didn't ask you to! I'm only here for a little while longer, and then the new Santa comes on board. You can sit on *his* lap." He pauses. "Wait. You make more than $30 an hour now?" He seems more scandalized by *that* than by the idea of having me in his lap.

"You can sit on my lap right now, for free," Declan murmurs, nibbling on my ear.

"He's paying $30 an hour." I point to the phone.

"You want me to pay you to sit on my lap?" Pulling me into it, he shifts in just the right way. I groan, inhaling cinnamon and sex, exhaling weakness and loyalty.

"Shannon, please? Please?" Greg is begging. "Carol said she might be able to come at five o'clock and take over for you, but I'm really stuck here. All these kids are lined up, their hopeful little faces cheering for Santa, and they want to know where the elf is."

"Awwww." Declan's hot tongue in my mouth makes it hard to answer.

"And the dads are asking, too."

"Ewwww."

I push Declan away and eye him closely. He'll make one hot dad someday. I imagine a little girl in his arms, Declan carrying her to the Christmas Village for a visit with Santa, me waddling behind pregnant with our first boy. It's a pleasant vision, and one that Declan seems to share, if I'm reading the look in his eyes right.

Christmas at the mall is such a cornerstone of my childhood that I begin to weaken. All those kids. All those parents. And if I don't go in . . .

"Bottom line is that there's suspicion that one of the photographers is stealing cash payments here, and some of the Santas have been coming in drunk, so in the interest of making the holiday a joyful experience for every single kid—kids like Jeffrey and Tyler—if you could get your butt down here and help your old boss, I'd really appreciate it." Greg's voice shifts from pleading to commanding, and the combination means—

Damn.

A long sigh escapes from me, making Declan freeze, his tongue perfectly centered now on that soft spot of skin beneath my earlobe, the gateway to all things warm, wet, and naughty.

"Where are you?" I ask Greg.

Declan's turn to groan, and so not in the good way.

Greg names a mall about twenty minutes away.

"I'm on my way."

I hang up to find that I am suddenly on my boyfriend's Very Naughty List. I deserve a spanking, but I'm about to get a tongue lashing instead, and not the kind that makes me rip the sheets off the bed.

I give him *my* best Grumpy Cat look.

"You're leaving? You're seriously going to push aside this carefully planned day so you can go dress up in a sexy elf costume . . ."

His voice shifts from self-righteous anger to aroused intrigue, the morph so gradual yet distinct. His green eyes match his sweater, dark hair recently clipped in a style that makes his face even more masculine, the cut jawline lickable. Long eyelashes frame steady, sharp eyes that comb over my body with more suggestions than a waiter trying to upsell you on the chef's special.

Meeting the son of Boston's most famous billionaire while

conducting a mystery shop eight months ago was the best stroke of luck I'd had since counting the right number of M&M candies in the contest jar at Dad's favorite auto parts store when I was nine and bringing them home, but this was better.

Because I can eat this prize without getting a stomach ache.

Wait. That doesn't sound right . . .

"Yes." I shrug helplessly. "He wouldn't call if he weren't desperate."

Declan's mind is a million miles away, his eyes smoking hot and aimed right at me. And then I realize he's not a million miles away. He's five miles away, at the mall, listening to "Rockin' Around the Christmas Tree" with visions of something way dirtier than sugar plums dancing in his head.

"Do they let you bring the costume home?" he asks.

I whack him hard with a fistful of tinsel. It flies up in the air and whirls around us, like a piñata filled with Angel Dust and disco balls from the 1970s.

Which is about on par with what we experience when we arrive at the mall.

chapter
two

YOU KNOW WHAT THE North Pole smells like? Frightened kid pee, scented baby wipes, and Tiger Moms.

What are Tiger Moms? The same women who rule over their piano-playing prodigies, the kids mastering Chopin before they were weaned, who make Yo-Yo Ma look like a drunk homeless dude playing a broken recorder in East Cambridge, who raise soccer players who make Luis Suarez look like Rainbow Brite—and they're lined up here at the mall with their kids, and they're not taking "no" for an answer.

To anything.

"Tycho! Tycho!" screeches one blonde mother who looks disturbingly like Jessica Coffin with under-eye bags. "Tycho, don't you dare sit down. You'll crease!"

Crease. She's dressed the kid in all white and he looks like a cross between President Snow from *The Hunger Games* and a Ralph Lauren ad. He's three. *Three.* And you put him in white? Mommy Masochist.

Creasing is the least of his problems. Most three year olds can't follow a two-step command, or watch an entire episode of *Bubble Guppies* without wiping nine boogers on the couch cushions, and she expects him to not *crease*?

"I don't like waiting! You said your waiting app told you we wouldn't wait, Mommy. Give me your phone. I want to play Paplinko!" Tycho whines. "Eat at P.F. Chang's! I want to order from your app!"

"Manners!" his mother snaps back.

Her eyes glow red with the kind of intensity that only a well-educated, over-entitled *Nanny Diaries*-type mother can cultivate. My own mom suddenly seems cuddly and harmless, like Mrs. Brady with a side of Mrs. Weasley and a touch of Peg Bundy.

Okay, a *lot* of Peg Bundy.

"We were told, in the app, that there would not be a wait!" she yells at me. I am standing in front of Santa's throne, a veritable pantheon to the advertising geniuses who have turned Christmas into a religious holiday, serving the new gods: Visa, MasterCard, Discover, and American Express.

"App?" I ask, resisting the urge to pull the butt floss out of my crack. Butt floss? Oh, yeah. After Declan dropped me off at the main doors to go hunt a wooly mammoth . . . er, find a parking spot (either were equally likely on December 23rd at 3 p.m. in this particular mall parking lot), I'd found Greg, who had wordlessly handed me the elf suit.

I've seen models on GoDaddy Super Bowl commercials wearing more than this.

"App!" Mommy Masochist screams, texting while she's yelling at me, her eyes on the screen but her lips devoted entirely to me. "The app!"

"An app for . . . what?"

Demon eyes flash at me and she holds up one perfectly French-tipped finger. "One second," she says with a supercilious air that makes me want to crack that fingernail in half and use it like a ninja star to shave off that arched eyebrow. She's blonde, hair pulled back in a twist, and she is wearing all red, open-toed shoes in December in Massachusetts, where nine inches of snow means everyone I know wears Fuggs and looks like a Jawa for four months of the year.

Red stiletto heels, open-toed and with these crazy ankle strap things that make her feet look like red flamingoes. If that's fashion, then my Salvation Army wardrobe is starting to look good.

She ends her textfest and centers all her attention on me, taking as much time as she pleases to size me up. Her eyes catalog my bright green, satiny outfit, with sequins that spell out *Ho Ho Ho* across my boobs.

A careful examination under the blinking fluorescent lights of the employee bathroom two hours later will show that yes, indeed, I walked around the mall for three hours with just *Ho* on each nipple.

But I digress . . .

The green fabric cuts into my armpits, the shelf bra was designed for a ten-year-old gymnast, and what might have been appealing in a Mae West kind of way as the bustier pushes everything up instead makes me look like a can of Pillsbury biscuits.

One that someone pulled the string on.

And twisted.

The green, shimmery stockings are two sizes too small, and the crotch threatens constantly to pull down about six inches lower, which would make me look like I am wearing harem pants . . . except I'm wearing the closest thing to a g-string anyone can imagine, a tiny little red taffeta skirt circling my crushed hips like a bad case of eczema.

The costume design department for *Blades of Glory* is weeping with jealousy right now for not coming up with this.

Or maybe they did . . .

"Nice outfit," Mommy Masochist says. "I need to speak with your manager," she adds slowly. Her eyes cut away. "And tuck in your nip."

I look down. Yep—headlight escaped, pointed right at the security guard by the service desk, who starts to stroke his billy club suggestively.

"Thanks," I mutter, because one good turn deserves—

"Manager," she snaps. "You're useless. And slow." Her face softens a little. "Are you—do you have a helper? An aide who works with you? I think it's great you have a job and all. Is there a program manager I can—STOP IT, TYCHO! DO NOT SIT ON THAT BENCH! CREASE! CREASE!"

A cold rage replaces the scent of peppermint and pine that the mall is piping through the heat registers. I'm breathing ice and frost and I wish I had Elsa's power, because I could freeze a bitch right now. Turn her into a mall Han Solo.

"I am not developmentally disabled," I say, searching for Santa, er . . . Greg. He's gone, and the line of moms, a few dads, and tons of kids is getting longer.

"Then you're just stupid *and* useless. Why is there a wait? We paid the exclusive premium for Santa's Special Delivery, and—"

"Ho, ho, ho!" Greg busts out, materializing from the direction of the bathrooms. Either he's pretending to be Santa or he's reading my breasts.

In full Santa costume, he's pretty amazing. Breathtaking, really. His belly fills out the costume perfectly, his eyes twinkle in a warm, inviting way with the skin wrinkling around them in a calm, compassionate manner, and his beard is fake but so realistic I want to tug it, just to make sure he didn't magically grow it overnight.

"Your elf is ruining Christmas!" Mommy Masochist announces in a voice loud enough to make several children, and one dad, start to cry. I suspect the dad is her husband, Daddy Doormat, because Tycho runs over to him and buries his face in the man's knees.

"Crease, Thomas! Crease!" Thomas the Daddy Doormat is wearing white jeans (those are a thing? For men?) and a white turtleneck, with a red wool sweater the exact color of Mommy Masochist's shoes.

"I've never had an elf ruin Christmas," Greg booms, his voice so Santa-like that shoppers slow down from their fast clip through the mall, pull phones away from ears to gawk, and come to complete halts at the baritone that fuels old dreams tucked away long ago.

He's kind of magical.

"In fact, Shannon the Elf here has come to our rescue to help make sure every good little boy and girl gets their turn." It's working—she's thawing and smiling now, her eyes a bit frozen in place as she realizes she's the center of attention but not in control of it. All those years of Greg playing Santa at the community center are paying off.

"Thank you," she says softly, giving him a look that says she could just as soon hug him as sever his limbs and hide them in the Verizon kiosk. "But the app says we're supposed to be here on time."

"App, Santa?" I ask helplessly.

Greg pulls me aside. "There's this new app the owners rolled out. For $79 you can sign up in advance and come at your appointed time and jump the line. No waiting."

"So the rich get to buy their way to no lines but the people who can't afford it have to wait for eternity? How is that fair?"

"Is it fair that when I was a kid Santa brought one toy and my neighbors all got five? Santa's an unfair bastard."

"What?" Mommy Masochist asks, eavesdropping. "Please keep your voice down!" she snaps at Greg. "I can't have Tycho tormented by nightmares about hearing Santa talk about . . . *Santa,* and calling him a bastard!" She throws her hands up and then reaches into her purse for her phone, muttering something about getting a refund and how nothing works properly these days because employees don't know how to do their jobs.

I look at the enormous sea of wiggly children, tired parents, and crabby mall workers.

"What now, Santa?" I ask.

"Off we go," Greg says, walking past Mommy Masochist and letting out a loud "ho ho ho," to the children's delight. The throne has a place for Santa to sit, and I'm there to hand out candy canes, keep people in orderly lines, and encourage the kids to look at the photographer, who charges $39 for a blurry photo of your kid sitting on the lap of a man who hasn't gone through a CORI background check.

(Actually, *Greg* has, but not the average mall Santa).

Tycho is first in line. He looks at my chest and points, shouting, "I want nanas!"

Doormat Daddy gives my breasts a nervous grin and says, "Tycho, we're all done with nanas. Remember? We had your weaning party—"

Greg turns the color of his beard and I turn the color of my elf suit as we both realize what "nanas" are.

"Want nanas! Want nanas!" Tycho screams. Visions of a three-year-old vampire-diving into my overflowing nanas and drinking direct from the tap—a decidedly dry tap—make me cross my arms and push back my breeding date by, well, *never*. How does never sound? Sorry, Mom. No billionaire grandkids. I'm too traumatized by being turned into an unsuspecting wet nurse while wearing a naughty elf costume.

"Crease! You're creasing!" Masochist Mommy cries out.

And that's kid number one in a sea of them.

Merry Christmas.

chapter
three

O NE HOUR LATER I am ready to give myself a tubal ligation with a mascara wand.

Sex ed classes shouldn't teach abstinence, or the mechanics of sex, or even birth control. They should march those teens to the mall two days before Christmas and make them play Santa's Helper for a few hours. That would drop the teen pregnancy rate by a good fifty percent, *tout de suite*.

I love kids. I do. The world revolves around Jeffrey and Tyler when I'm with them, and in my thirties, after I make director or vice president, I plan to have a couple. Whether Declan wants them or not is still a mystery, because we don't talk about it. Ever. There's this shadow between us that seems to have formed not by intention but more by omission.

The longer we don't bring it up, the bigger it becomes.

The photographer, a lovely older woman named Marsha, who dresses in a Mrs. Claus outfit that makes her look like Betty White, approaches me and Greg.

"My shift's over," she says, a bit nervous. "The new photographer is talking to the parents."

We look at a man in black jeans, a grey leather jacket, and a collared business shirt talking to parents in line. Twenties are changing hands.

Greg stands and we put up the "Santa is Feeding the Reindeer—Back in Five Minutes!" sign. Parents groan, but the new photographer seems to be keeping them occupied.

"You know him?" Greg asks Marsha, who shakes her head.

"Never seen him before, but he says he's a sub the owner sent. I texted the owner and he hasn't replied, so . . ." She reaches for a clipboard on the small counter behind Santa's throne and starts writing numbers on a spreadsheet.

Greg and I exchange a skeptical look. "We need to document this," he whispers to me. "They either pay through the app or at checkout. Cash isn't supposed to change hands." One of the many sour aspects of being a mystery shopper and customer service evaluator is that you end up busting people who are embezzling, or cheating customers. It always involves cash.

Marsha looks at me with agitation and pulls me aside. "Your nipple is, um . . ." She points down and I growl, shoving the girls back in place.

"Thank you." If this were a Dickens novel I would be the Ghost of Christmas Nip Slips Present.

"Jory was less . . . buxom," she murmurs.

"Jory?"

"The old elf. The one who always worked here before. So much turnover." She slings her purse over her shoulder and gives a wave, looking repeatedly at the new photographer, then shrugging. "I'm doing some shopping, so I'll pop back in after a while and see how it's going. I've been here for nine seasons and I can spot someone who isn't going to work out."

Greg and I share a knowing look, and he turns away from the crowd to text the client and let them know what's just gone down.

Marsha crooks one finger at me and whispers in my ear: "This Santa is too nice. Betcha he won't make it two more days." She has no idea who we are, so I play along.

Greg is texting the client, but then stops, alarm crossing his face. "Shit!" he exclaims.

"Hush!" I hiss. "Santa doesn't say 'shit'!"

"He does when the replacement Santa is stuck in the parking garage! Says he's been in there for more than forty-five minutes and can't find his way out."

"I believe it," says a familiar voice. Warm hands are on my shoulders, and Declan adds, "This parking lot is designed by planners who hate human beings."

I laugh. He doesn't. But he plants a kiss on my cheek and lets go of me, walking around and emitting a low whistle.

"*Whoa.*" His eyes rest on the overflowing volcano of flesh that is my chest line.

"Ho," he says as he looks at one breast. "Ho," he says for the other. "Nice. It's like a Christmas eye doctor's chart."

Greg's texting furiously, then looks at us, horrified. "He says he just came out of the exit to the mall near the turnpike and he's heading back home! Says it's not worth it!"

Declan shrugs, eyes glued to my breasts. "You said *sexy* elf costume," he says in a weird voice.

"This isn't sexy?" My eyebrows are buried in the mall skylight.

"This is a *slutty* elf costume."

I glare at Greg. "Told you." I turn to Declan. "I'm sorry. I know it's a bit much—"

"What are you apologizing for? Slutty beats sexy any day." His hands slip around my waist and he pulls me into a kiss.

Greg texts and clears his throat. "Um, guys? I have a serious problem here. No replacement Santa, and I have to take Judy to a doctor's appointment." Greg's wife is a long-term breast cancer survivor, and while I don't know the details, everything has been in a good place for a while. The look on his face makes my stomach sink, though.

Declan goes somber, too.

And then Greg and I turn simultaneously and give Declan the once-over, like Clinton and Stacy on *What Not to Wear*.

Except we're doing the Christmas Mall Edition: Santa Style.

"Oh, no," Declan says, reading our minds. "No."

"It pays $30 an hour and you can get a free picture on the next Santa's lap."

"I make $30 every time I cough," Declan snorts. I've never heard him snort before. Today is a day for discoveries and revelations. Grumpy Cat looks and snorts. What's next? Farting in bed and not excusing himself? Or, worse, pulling the covers over my head and Dutch Ovening me?

Mom says men save that for the second anniversary.

"Your nipple is, um . . ." Greg says. To me. Speaking of revelations. I tuck it back in. I might need to walk over to the scrapbook store and get a little rubber cement so these puppies will stop trying to escape.

"What's your currency, man?" Greg asks Declan, gone from begging to outright negotiation. "You've got me by the balls."

"I've got my own balls. Don't need yours."

The parents in line are murmuring louder and louder. "If there's no Santa, the entire mystery shop is compromised, and twenty kids out there are going to start crying," I say to Declan, pleading.

His eyes rake over my body, angry and determined, the deep "no" in there. He means it. I know he does. I use the only leverage I have.

"Greg says I can take the costume home with me. If you fill in for Santa." I reach between us and make a suggestive stroke. The North Pole does indeed exist.

Declan groans. "Ho. Ho. Ho."

I stand on tiptoes and lick his ear. "I will be one for you if you do this. It's only for an hour or two," I plead.

"I look nothing like Santa," he says in a hard, flat voice, but arousal flickers in his eyes. He looks behind the wall and sees the sea of kids. Those green eyes look worried. He's an old softy underneath this granite-like appearance.

I think. I hope so.

"Name your price," Greg adds, already taking off the costume, handing Declan the hat.

Eyes the color of my suit flash at Greg, angry and exasperated. "Quit calling her for mystery shop jobs. Forever."

Greg's hand shoots out. "Deal." He takes the jacket off and hands it to Declan with a warning. "It's hot in the suit, so you might want to take your sweater off."

"I don't have anything on under it," Declan explains.

"That's fine," I peep. My mouth waters. He gives me a glare. I stand by my words.

"Where's the pillow?" Declan asks as he slips into the Santa pants. Luckily, he's wearing black leather shoes that are perfect.

"What pillow?"

"The pillow for my belly."

Greg laughs, his real belly shaking. "I didn't need one. I think there's one back on the counter." And then he's gone, calling back, "Merry Christmas to you, and to you a good hour."

"You are going to pay for this," Declan grouses. "And these pants are a little wet." He sniffs one leg. "Is that pee?"

"No," I lie.

He's standing just behind the wall on the back of Santa's throne, jeans peeking out from his Santa suit, red suspenders hanging down. In one fluid movement, like something out of a stripper show, he reaches for the hem of his green cashmere sweater and slowly pulls it up, biceps flexing, his skin gleaming under the calibrated Christmas lights in the mall.

It's one of those moments that should have a soundtrack attached to it, something Barry White. Slow and sensual, the kind of music that gets you wet and throbbing. Time stops, and all the moms walking by telepathically communicate the presence of my hot boyfriend taking his clothes off, pecs on display, a free peep show at the most stressful moment in the Christmas rush.

A regular community service Declan's performing here.

Out of the corner of my eye I see Mommy Masochist taking pictures and texting someone. Whatever. Tycho managed not to crease for his photo and now he's running around with a $9 cupcake from the gourmet bakery in the mall, chocolate smears everywhere. He looks like a Tide commercial.

The sweater makes Declan's thick, dark, wavy hair stand up a tiny bit with static electricity, and he reaches one perfectly sculpted arm up to smooth it back. I hear a decidedly female moan from behind me, and then look. *Really* look at the moms around us, most biting their lower lips and squirming.

That's right. Look all you want. I'm the one who gets to touch.

He slides the red suspenders up over his shoulders and looks like something in a Santa firefighter's calendar. If he had a big hose in his hands right now.

Boy does *that* sound porny.

Let's try again: "Hey!" I murmur, sliding up next to him and placing a strategic hand on his hip. *Mine*, I communicate telepathically in a voice designed to make all the other women's heads explode like a cantaloupe dropped from a second-story window.

Mine.

"Hey what?" He's still pissed. Doing the Santa bit, but pissed.

"How about you bring the suit home, too? We can play Santa Disciplines the Naughty Elf," I whisper in his ear as he dons the fake beard.

"That's one of your father's favorite games," Satan says from behind a fake ficus across the way.

chapter
four

" **M** OM?"

"Just look at you two! I knew Shannon was here as a beautiful little perky elf, but Declan as Santa! You two were meant to be together," Satan, a.k.a. my mother, says, reaching in to give Declan a kiss, ignoring my protests.

My sister Amy is with her. "Perky is right. Shannon, your, um, headlight is . . ." I look down. One is pointed toward New Hampshire and the other toward Antarctica.

I turn around and readjust. "What are you two doing here?"

"Amanda texted to let us know."

"I hate her."

"She's your best friend. You can't hate her."

"Why isn't she here doing the elf impression?"

"She's delivering toys to needy kids."

"Flimsy excuse." I look around the wall and see that Mommy Masochist is back in line, dragging a very chocolate-y Tycho. The line's gotten a lot longer suddenly. Doubled, even.

"Wow," I say. "The line's really getting long."

"Blame it on Hot Santa," Amy says, pointing to Declan, who scowls.

"You look just like Chuckles!" Mom gasps.

It makes Declan's frown darken. Even Mom backs off.

"Please don't call my boyfriend 'hot,'" I chide Amy. "It's gross."

"No," she explains, pulling out her phone. "#HOTSANTA.

Some mommy blogger who's here at the mall started it on Twitter with pics of Declan getting dressed, and now Jessica Coffin's made it go viral."

"What?"

She's holding up a picture of Declan in all his broad-chested, thick-pec glory, adjusting one red suspender and looking good enough to ride.

Like Santa's sleigh.

"But, but—" he protests. "That was five minutes ago!" He's rattled, and Declan doesn't *do* rattled.

"Five minutes is like a day on Twitter. You could end up with a flashmob," Amy says.

"Hot Santa, huh?" I smack his ass and send him on his way. "Time to go make some good little girls and boys very happy."

"I think he's got mostly naughty girls out there," Mom says.

"Humph," is all I can reply. I see the photographer out there, working the longer line, more cash changing hands. Greg trusted me to get this right, and I will. I march out there, ignoring my mom and sister, wondering if the day can get any weirder. By the time I get to the guy, he's worked his way to the front of the line.

The new photographer ignores my outstretched hand as I try to introduce myself and says something in a clipped, accented voice to the mom standing with her little boy. She smiles nervously at him, clearly not understanding a word he says. He sounds like a mix of a Russian hit man and the Swedish chef from the Muppets.

Which means he'll probably shoot me dead with a silenced gun and have my body made into something they serve at the shady burger joint in the mall food court before he finishes a cigarette.

"Come here! Look here!" he says in that severe accent, his eyes dead. The guy could be anywhere from twenty to fifty, with a face so angular you could use it to dig a hole under the Berlin Wall (circa 1988).

The little boy who is about to perch himself on Declan's lap begins to cry as the photographer sighs, throws his hands up, and spews a stream of foreign-language invective that might well be the words to *Goodnight Moon* but sounds like a laundry list of all the ways he's going to cook this boy's pancreas for dinner.

"We have our own photographer, actually," the mother says nervously as she comforts the sweet boy, whose eyes are teary. He has bright blonde hair and a giant cowlick on his forehead hairline. The green eyes make me think of Declan.

The photographer starts screaming in what I now realize really *is* Russian, making a handful of kids in line start crying, parents on smartphones texting and calling and trying to look like they're doing something.

And then: Santa starts shouting back at the photographer. In Russian. Declan speaks *Russian*?

The Russian man spits on the ground. Santa hands the kid off to his mom and stands, grabbing the photographer's arm and pulling him behind the wall on the other side of Santa's chair.

A massive wave of anxiety and fear spills through me as Amy and Mom hide behind a planter and my nipples decide to try to run away, too. I can't catch my breath and everything happens so fast I feel the room spin.

There is this 1980s movie that Mom and Dad loved to watch over and over when we were teens. It's *A Fish Called Wanda*, and there's this scene where John Cleese speaks Russian to Jamie Lee Curtis and it makes her so hot and horny she turns into a sex machine. I always giggled with embarrassment, and later lots of eye rolls, at the idea when we watched the film.

But finding myself horny, wet, and suddenly turned on from zero to humpgirl by the sound of Declan speaking Russian makes me see that Jamie Lee Curtis and I are soul sisters.

Getting *that* aroused while wearing a too-tight elf costume that turns into a g-string when I stand up straight is all kinds of *wrong*.

Declan's hissing in his deep, clipped voice, so angry and cold looking that I wonder if he's really a Russian hit man and the American stuff is just an act. Maybe he's not actually the VP of marketing for his father's mega-billion corporation. Maybe he's a secret double agent working for some shadow government and I'm just his cover.

I take a careful inventory of my elf costume.

Green satin. A skin volcano up top. Sequins unthreading. High heels with candy cane striped stiletto points. If I'm a double agent's cover, then the Illuminati are in really big trouble.

The photographer tosses his camera onto a chair and barrels down on Declan, snatching Declan's Santa hat off his head and throwing it down, stomping and spitting on it. His face is inches from my boyfriend's, red rage all over as the Russian words are flying back and forth in a volley that is making my little red nub try to break away and drown itself in a fifth of vodka.

The Russian dude wrenches Declan's arm, then rips his red jacket off Declan, who is now shirtless and bearded, fighting this guy.

"Beat his ass, Santa," one of the dads in the crowd shouts. A bunch of the fathers have let go of their kids' hands and are craning to catch a view of the fight. I grab the first thing I can use as a weapon, just sitting there on the counter, and run after, whacking the Russian dude over and over.

With the belly pillow from the Santa costume.

And then the photographer reaches for something on his hip, and everything goes into slow motion. Declan grabs his arm and twists it, hard. The guy headbutts Declan, a sickening crack breaking through the pan-flute version of "The Little Drummer Boy" that fills the mall's sound system. Every parent is still, eyes wide and mouths shaped by shock.

Blood trickles into Santa's beard and down his bare chest. I scream.

Declan ignores the blood and reaches for the guy's hip just as a swarm of overstuffed mall cops (any of which could easily play Santa) arrive on their Segways. He lifts up the guy's jacket and exposes the hip where he was about to reach and—

A gun.

As the security guys cuff him and call for police backup, some of the dads have phones high in the air, taping everything. Not a single mom or dad has covered their child, pulled them behind a post or a piece of furniture, or walked away. Fortunately, the kids just stayed in line, good little do-bees who haven't had every Santa fantasy crushed.

Something falls out of the photographer's pocket as he's half dragged off. A giant pile of money. Then another.

"Hey! We paid extra for the good pictures!" a parent calls out. "You can't take the photographer away!" The mall cops step in and try to calm the crowd while I run to Declan.

"You speak *Russian*?" I gasp as Declan walks toward me with a swagger. Either that, or he's staggering.

"My nose is fine, thank you," he says, irritated. "And yes, I speak it. Have since high school." He glares at me. Mom and Amy run up, Mom holding out a tissue. He takes it and presses it against his nose as he tips his head up, eyes locked on me. "I go through that and all you can ask me is . . ."

"What the hell was that?" I snap. "You speak Russian to some angry photographer and next thing I know you turn into Jason Bourne!"

"You figured it out," he deadpans.

People are golf clapping. "Go, Santa! America! America!"

"What does America even have to do with—" Amy starts to ask, but Mom cuts her off.

"All those children! Santa can't be ruined for them!" Mom clucks, grabbing the Santa jacket and working to help Declan back in it. There isn't much blood on the beard, and Mom dabs at it, frantic. "We need to get you back in that chair."

"Mom's just worried we won't get a picture with you guys," Amy says drolly.

"Picture?" Declan asks in a ragged voice. The mall cops come over and I walk away to answer questions. The long line makes this all tough, with a million questions that need to be addressed. Declan casts a long look my way. I can't tell if he's more upset about his injured nose or being left alone to converse with my mother.

I dispense with the mall security by begging for an hour to clear the line, which seems to have tripled. Declan's peeling himself off Mom and Amy is texting. He settles in Santa's chair to thunderous applause and I realize: we have no photographer.

Great.

As if on cue, Marsha walks past carrying some shopping bags. She comes over behind the Santa chair and reaches for her clipboard.

"I'll take over. As long as I get to sit on Santa's lap for an extra long time," she says with a wink. I have no leverage here, so I just nod. Noddy the Elf.

"Hot Santa," Amy says as I walk past him to join her, shaking her phone at me. "Word's getting out. Look at all those women in line."

I peer into the crowd. "They don't have any kids with them."

"So?"

"Shouldn't you bring a kid to see Santa?"

"I think they just want to sit in Santa's lap and visit the North Pole, if you know what I mean," Amy says, snickering.

"She means they want to sit on Declan's penis," Mom translates.

"THANKS, MOM," I COUGH, "for the explanation."

"Just being helpful! Oh, look—there's Agnes!" Mom runs off toward the end of the increasingly long line. Agnes is a ninety-something regular in Mom's yoga classes.

Declan is warm and gracious with each child who comes through, and if I weren't completely gobsmacked by how helping Greg out has turned my boyfriend into a Special Ops CIA dude who speaks Russian, I would pay more attention to my ovaries. They appear to be clapping, cheering, fanning themselves and putting on makeup for a special occasion with Santa, because damn if Declan isn't amazing with the kids.

Charming and fatherly and sweet, yet ruthlessly efficient. The perfect blend of high-powered executive and Chevy-commercial dad.

He's made to be a father.

A giggly woman *sans* child asks if she can sit in Santa's lap and he says, "I'm taking all the little kids first, and then we'll work our way through the big kids," adding a wink.

I look through the line. There are about ten kids sprinkled in among the forty or so folks queued up. I walk out and pull the kids and grateful parents forward.

"Hot Santa is kind of a dick," the rejected woman mumbles, walking away.

My mother hands her a candy cane and a yoga business card. "Merry Christmas!" The woman just glares and mutters to the other women in line. The single women in line thin out, about half leaving.

"Once you're done with the kids, can senior citizens be next? This bladder isn't as young as it used to be," shouts a familiar voice.

"Ho ho ho," Declan shouts, then mumbles to me, "I've been peed on enough. Don't need to add Agnes to it. Do whatever she wants."

"What is Agnes doing here?" I ask Mom, who turns out to be remarkably helpful, handing out candy canes and directing people to the pay station. Amy wanders off to huff the Lush bath products.

"I canceled yoga today when I learned you were coming here, and when they asked why there was a huge stampede of people who figured they might catch a glimpse of Declan. No one ever dreamed they'd get to sit in his lap!"

"Neither did he."

Her eyes take in my costume. "You're a little bigger than me, but not much. You get to keep that costume? Can I borrow it?"

Declan waves me over and I walk away from her without a single word, because I know why she wants to borrow it, and while costumes can be cleaned, brains can't. Once that image is imprinted in my mind—of Mom and Dad playing Santa and the Naughty Elf—I might as well get an official Red Ryder Carbine Action 200-shot range model air rifle—

And shoot my eyes out.

We get through the kids and Declan begs for a short break. Out comes the "Santa is Feeding the Reindeer—Back in Five Minutes!" sign. Declan walks around back and stretches. The mall cops seize on the chance and come over to explain that the Russian dude was a garden-variety scammer, telling parents that for an extra $40 he'd make sure they got their pictures to them on CD on the spot. He'd pulled the same scam at five other malls this season.

And a fingerprint check showed he was part of a mafia ring, too.

"Russian? You speak Russian? We've been dating for how

long and I don't know this?" I bark.

He shrugs. "There's a lot we don't know about each other. What foreign languages do you speak?"

"Southie and Pig Latin."

"See! I didn't know that. You polyglot."

The security force people leave us alone and Declan takes a minute to hydrate and just breathe without a little kid on his knee. I look down the long walkway in front of us and do a double take.

"This section really brings out the crazies," I say.

"Your mom's a bit weird, but crazy might be an overstatement—"

"Not her. I mean, she is, but—see that guy walking toward us?" I point to a tall, older man wearing glasses and a brown down coat. He walks slowly, shoulders hunched, and is carrying a cat in his arms.

A cat wearing reindeer antlers, and as he gets closer—

"Is that cat wearing a red nose that lights up?" Declan whispers out of the side of his mouth.

"Holy smokes!" I peep. "What a nutcase." The guy comes closer and avoids eye contact. The area is loud and the glow of red and green Christmas lights makes everything a bit dim, but he stands out. I've never seen a cat so angry before, either. So grumpy. So pissed off.

So—oh my God.

"DAD?"

Chuckles tips his eyes up at me, the red light from his battery-powered nose making his irises glow evil red, like Dracula's cat come to kill Santa Claus and steal the Spirit of Christmas.

And, frankly, I can't blame him.

"What are you doing to Chuckles?"

"More like what is your mother doing to my manhood," Dad mumbles just as Mom comes over and makes a big to-do of the cat.

"Look at Chuckley-Wuckley!" Mom squeals, holding him out from her, arms stretched with a limp animal planning how to smother her in her sleep, his eyes glowing with hatred and

LED-inspired evil.

"Chuckles is figuring out how to pull your liver out through your nose and snack on it while you writhe in death throes, Mom," I say. My cat nods slowly and Dad shivers.

"He's so cute, though! The family Christmas picture will be so perfect."

Dad cuts me a look that says *Don't even say it* as he pulls his jacket off in the stifling mall.

But I say it.

"Family Christmas picture?" I turn fifteen again. Mom has this way of making me turn into a screaming teenager with a persecution complex. "What family Christmas picture? There will be no family Christmas picture!"

"Especially if your nip is hanging out like that," Mom says.

Amy comes back smelling like avocado, coconut, and way too many rose hips mixed with Ralph Lauren's Polo. Like Jamba Juice meets Milton Academy.

"Walked through the perfume counter at Macy's, huh?" Dad asks her.

"WHAT CHRISTMAS PICTURE?" I thunder as I shove my hand down the front of my bustier.

"Is that Josh over there? In line?" Amy asks me as I wrestle my own boobs like I'm the female lead in a tentacle porn movie.

"Josh?" My old coworker? Technogeek Josh, the one I tried to throw under a bus and get Greg to call today instead of me? A red wall of fury fills me. He should be the humiliated one here, with nipple slips and peeing kids and . . .

I look over and sure enough, he's in line in a group of three guys, all way too stylish to be straight. I march over, hand still down my front.

"What are you doing here?" I demand.

He looks up, face friendly. Like his friends, he's wearing all black and grey. In a mall swimming in green and red, they're a welcome reprieve.

"Hi, Shannon! We're here for Hot Santa. What are you . . ." He and his three buddies watch me giving myself a breast exam. "Um, do you need some privacy?"

"Why are you guys in line? Do you have little kids with you?"

They instantly look uncomfortable. "No," Josh confesses. "We're here to see Hot Santa." He, like my sister, holds up his phone. The same damn picture of Declan in red suspenders.

"Where did you learn about this?" I demand.

"Jessica Coffin," Josh and his friends intone.

"You realize you're about to sit on my boyfriend's lap!"

Josh goes from embarrassed to mildly horrified. Then kind of interested. "Really? *Declan* is Hot Santa?"

"Declan McCormick?" one of his friends asks, fanning himself. "Oh, hot, hot, smoking hot Santa! I've got a lump of coal he can turn into a diamond by letting me shove it in—"

"Yes!" I shout. "Mine!" I growl savagely. "MINE!" My girls are in proper place, but the g-string cuts into my ass, giving me a Brazilian. It's like a built-in Epilady string.

"That is hot," Josh says in an admiring voice.

"No. Just . . . no." I can feel a complete public meltdown coming on.

"You wear jealousy well," one of his friends murmurs. He looks at his phone. "Hey! Coupon for Lush!" They all skitter off and I wonder what I'm missing with this whole Lush craze.

I'm not about to find out, though. Something far more lush is in my immediate future.

A strong, insistent hand circles my forearm. "Ho, ho, ho, little elf, Santa needs your help," Declan says in a jocular voice. A bunch of kids, all of Josh's friends, and ten women in line wave at Santa, who is now dragging me off to the employee break room, where he slams the dented metal door shut and deadbolts it. He rips the beard off, slips out of the Santa jacket, and—

Hot Santa's hot mouth is on me. Hands roam over the slutty elf costume, soon finding their way inside the bustier, and Declan is not just readjusting my headlights. He pulls one breast out and tongues the nipple, making it rock hard.

"We can't have sex in here!"

"You'd prefer I ravish you on Santa's chair, in public?" He pulls my other breast out and sucks lightly. My entire body tightens and twangs like a plucked guitar string. "Kinky." He pulls back and gives my body a visual once-over. "I *like* kinky."

"I'm not having sex in the Christmas Village of a mall!" My words come out more like a moan than a protest, because his mouth feels so damn good on my caged breasts, the slick heat of his warm tongue forcing my blood to pound through me like the 1812 orchestra, cannons at the ready for the big finish.

"Then this will have to do." He pulls the tight costume down my body, the cold, painted concrete wall behind me stinging my shoulders, back, and hips. His mouth is all over me, his chest pressed against my belly, those suspenders rubbing against just the right parts as he deliciously peels me out and I'm standing there in nothing but fishnet thigh-highs.

"Oh my God, Shannon," he whispers, eyes eating me up. "You are so beautiful." My red nub is beeping so loudly it sounds like Rudolph's nose. I grab the red suspenders and slide them off each shoulder and he drops *trou*, then he drops trou, and oh, Santa baby—

"I'm going to explode if I can't get in you, Shannon," he hisses as his naked body becomes a wall of hot, silky flesh pressed into mine.

I reach between his legs and cradle him. "I can tell you're Santa," I murmur.

"Huh?"

"Santa's sac." I make a move that makes him groan and chuckle.

"What does that—"

"It's so big because he only comes once a year."

"You're making Santa scrotum jokes when we're—oh, you naughty girl." And he pulls back and spanks me, hard, the sound like a thunderclap of erotic dreams come to life. Somehow a condom appears in his hand. Perhaps it's a little holiday magic.

"That stings!" But I open my legs, and he's in me in seconds. Jokes fade, our bodies releasing all the pent-up lust and frustration.

"You are so hot," he mutters in my ear, thighs tensing, his body primed for climax. We have mere minutes, and while I normally need more foreplay than one spank and a ball fondle (for him), my orgasm is at the ready, eager for Santa to empty his sac at my place.

The friction and the slick of our bodies working together, all fire and need, the clench of his hands on my hips, the slow drag of my fingernails against his back are almost enough.

"Speak Russian to me," I beg, and he does, making my core clench instantly, his tongue on my earlobe the final touch that makes me burst into fireworks. His body tenses and I feel his heat pour into me, even through the condom, his shudder and hoarse cry caused by me. Me.

Mine.

As we slump against the wall, the snickering starts.

"Oh, Santa!" I moan.

"Oh, Slutty Elf!" he groans.

I burst out laughing so hard I push him out of me as he finishes, giggles overcoming us as we give in to the absolute absurdity of the past hour and a half.

"You're amazing, you know that?" he whispers in my ear, fingers grazing my bare shoulder, tracing a line down to my nipple. His hot breath tickles my hair as he kisses me slowly, finally finding my mouth.

"You aren't too bad yourself, Santa," I whisper when we break apart, warmed through.

"Chuckles in a reindeer costume," he laughs, reaching down to remove the condom, tie it off, and throw it in a trash can next to . . . another condom. Oh, gross. Who has sex in a mall employee break room—

Oh.

People like us.

"What did you say to me? In Russian?" I ask as I straighten my stockings and try to squeeze myself back into the sausage casing that masquerades as my elf costume.

He's buttoning his Santa coat and doesn't look up, just laughing to himself.

"Declan?"

He won't look up. "Let's just say Santa's sac will be visiting you quite a bit more often than once a year, and I need to look up the Russian word for 'slutty.' I only know the word for 'whore.'"

"You called me a *whore* while we were having sex?" I twist around to catch his eye so fast the g-string nearly gives me a colonoscopy.

"Not on purpose." He opens the door and we walk out into the industrial hallway toward the public bathrooms.

"Not on purpose? You mean, like, 'Whoops! I called you a whore in Russian while buried balls deep in you,' like you might say, 'Whoops, I forgot to pick up milk while I was at the store'?"

My words echo down the linoleum-floored hallway. And then I realize we're not alone.

"See?" Mom says to Dad. "I told you we're not the only ones who play The KGB Agent and the Bond Girl."

chapter
six

"I AM GOING TO pretend I never heard that," Dad says, making a beeline for the men's room. He hands a still-fuming Chuckles over to Mom, who strokes his fur and hums "Hark! The Herald Angels Sing" while Chuckles raises one paw and—if he had claws—looks like he's imagining how he'd stroke Mom's vocal cords and shred them while singing "Kumbaya."

In that reindeer getup he looks an awful lot like Anthony Hopkins playing Hannibal.

"We need to get back to work!" Declan announces, storming off.

"Sounds like Santa was already in someone's chimney, busy at work—"

"MOM!"

I storm off and follow Declan. We come to the end of the hall and into the main part of the mall to raucous applause. The line is twice as long now, but no one has kids with them. It's all elderly women and gay men.

Declan goes behind the Santa chair and I realize I need caffeinated reinforcement. I stumble over to the espresso cart near the service desk and dig into my breasts again. I can store anything in there, including a sweat-soaked twenty.

At least, I hope that's sweat . . .

Two double Mexican mochas later, I come back to find Declan already in the chair, Amy and Mom there to help, and a series of old ladies from Mom's yoga class tittering. I drink as much of my spicy-hot nirvana as I can before setting it down and getting back to work.

"You don't smell like Santa," one of them giggles, making fun of a line from the movie *Elf*. "You smell like beef and cheese!"

"Actually, he smells like sex," Mom says cheerfully. I kick her.

"Elves can't kick people!" Amy informs me. I kick her, too.

"Shannon the Violent Elf," Amy mutters as she hands a candy cane to yet another old lady who just got more male muscle contact from my boyfriend than she'd had since he was born.

And then:

"Hi, Auntie Thannon!"

I look at Mom and Amy. "You have got to be kidding me."

Mom kicks *me*. "What's good for the goose is good for the gander. Now smile!"

"Smiling is my favorite," I say as I frown. Chuckles nods.

"Auntie Thannon!" Jeffrey and Tyler sprint through the crowd and both of them leap into my arms at the same time, knocking me backwards onto my ass. Something in my costume rips.

"Day-um!" Amy says just as Dad appears, his face shocked as he quickly looks away.

"Um, honey? Cross your legs. No one needs to see your clam," Mom whispers in my ear.

"You have a clam?" Jeffrey asks. "I have a hermit crab. What's your pet's name?"

"What a nice surprise!" I shout in an overly friendly voice. Carol comes up behind them, eyes turned to triangles, narrowed with laughter at my appearance. "I thought the kids were too sick for you to work here."

She ignores that comment. "Shannon the Christmas Can-Can Dancer. How nice."

"At least there's no nip slip," I mutter.

"Lip slip," Mom says, pointing to my crotch. A three-inch tear in the costume has, um, made private parts of me not so private.

I look around frantically for anything I can wear, then spot it. Perfect.

I wrap Declan's green cashmere sweater around my waist.

"That's cashmere!" Mom gasps. "It will pill!"

"My labia are on display in a place where people are snapping pictures at a rate faster than the paparazzi following Lindsay Lohan."

"But it's cashmere!" She's scandalized. I don't care.

"We're here to see Santa and take the family Christmas picture," Carol explains.

"There is no family Christmas picture!" I scream. My cries echo through the high-ceilinged mall at the exact moment the Muzak system cuts short and the service desk announces:

"We will now start the canine Santa time. I repeat, bring your favorite furry kids on down to Christmas Village and get some bow-wow-wow holiday cheer." The clerk says this with the enthusiasm of a Brazilian announcing Germany's win in the World Cup.

"Let's give Tyler and Jeffrey a turn first," Mom pleads as a slow trickle of dogs on leashes, attached to green-and-red-covered owners, makes its way to the Christmas Village.

Carol grabs five-year-old Tyler, marches over to Declan, and unceremoniously plunks him down. Tyler hates strangers. Despises face hair. Can't stand loud noises. And yet he looks calmly at Declan with absolutely no facial expression whatsoever, eyes blinking.

"What do you want Santa to bring you, buddy?" Declan asks in a soft voice, familiar with my nephew's language disorder. For a kid who can't say much, little Tyler looks Declan firmly in the eye and says:

"You need to pee."

Tyler confuses "I" and "you" and is potty trained, but . . .

Declan jumps up and Carol swoops in, hurrying my little nephew off to the bathroom as his older brother, eight-year-old Jeffrey, climbs shyly onto Declan's—er, Santa's—lap.

"I don't need to pee," Jeffrey assures us. His lisp that was deeply pronounced just eight months ago has faded, a hint of it left. His features have broadened and he's in third grade now, on the cusp of being a bigger boy. This might even be his final year in Santa's lap.

Mom snaps picture after picture, ignoring her duties and reveling in being Grandma. Dad beams and records the whole little moment as Jeffrey chatters on and on and on, giving Santa a list of requests longer than anything you'd find on the wish list of one of the wives in those fancy reality television shows about over-consuming rich people.

Carol rushes back with a (hopefully) emptied Tyler as we all hear Jeffrey loudly request the latest video game system, and then he goes quiet.

"But I have one final thing, and Santa?" he whispers.

"Yes?"

"First of all, I know you're really Declan, because Santa needs lots of helpers, and you're one of them."

Declan, er . . . Santa just smiles.

"But, um, I'll ask anyway." He goes still, his face falling. I swallow, my mouth dry, and all the ambient sounds of the mall fade to a series of whispers, like time slows down.

"I don't need any of those video games or systems or points. I don't even need the robot. What I really want is my dad."

Tears prick at my eyes, and Carol's hand floats to her mouth, trembling.

"Can you tell the real Santa I just want my dad for Christmas? Or, maybe"—Jeffrey's eyebrows connect in concentration—"maybe if he's too busy, like Mom says, maybe just *a* dad?"

Declan's eyes register so many emotions—surprise, anger, compassion, confusion, befuddlement—but he manages to stay composed as Mom, Amy, Dad, and I try to secretly wipe tears away. Dad's spare hand is in a fist, the other one still taping the scene. He's angry not at Jeffrey (of course), but at Todd, my older sister's ex-husband who took off and who hasn't seen his sons in far too long.

Casting his eyes about, Declan catches mine and I shrug in solidarity. I don't know what to say, either. Whatever Declan says is fine, because no one can do the right thing here.

Other than Jeffrey and Tyler's father, and he isn't exactly in the running to provide a Christmas miracle.

"Tell you what, buddy," Declan says quietly. Carol is furiously wiping tears away and turns her back on the scene. Mom's standing there, sniffling. Amy is looking at me, our exchange one that doesn't need words.

"What?" Jeffrey says, eyes down. A rumble of dog sounds builds around us as big dogs and little dogs, hairy dogs and shaved dogs, all line up for their chance at Santa.

"I'll tell Santa what you want, just like you asked me to."

"You will?" Jeffrey's eyes light up, his face completely changing to one of pure joy. "Do you think he'll help bring my dad home?"

Declan widens his eyes, the fake white eyebrows covering for a multitude of emotions no eight-year-old could understand. Hell, the adult man in the costume is clearly struggling to comprehend.

"Um, well, Jeffrey, I don't know. Santa isn't all-powerful, but I know—I *know*—he'll try."

Jeffrey nods somberly. "Okay."

"But I know something else."

"What?"

"Even if your dad doesn't come for Christmas, I can't be a dad for you, but I can be an uncle."

chapter
seven

MOM GASPS AND SHOOTS her eyes my way. I drop the candy cane in my hand. Everyone stops breathing. Declan's eyes are only on Jeffrey, whose head is bent so close their foreheads are touching.

"Uncleth are great! I've never had one before! My dad only has sisterth. Mom only has sisterth. I have a ton of aunth so I don't need any more, but an uncle is wicked cool!" His lisp comes out when he's excited.

Declan envelops Jeffrey in an enormous bear hug. His eyes are glistening with undropped tears as he says to the boy, "Be good for your mother, and nice to your brother."

Jeffrey whispers something in Declan's ear. It makes them both smile, and Declan says, "You bet."

And then my little nephew scampers off, leaving the rest of us with shattered hearts. Declan looks at me and winks, then addresses the crowd.

"Ho, ho, ho, Merry Christmas," Declan bellows as he sees the crowd of dog owners lined up. If we weren't so crushed for time I'd try to talk to him—

Uncle?

—but we can't. The new Santa is coming in fifteen minutes, but we have to do this last bit.

Mommy Masochist comes running over with a yappy Bichon Frisé in her hands, perfectly white (of course), uncreased, and wearing green and red bows.

Dad drops Chuckles to the floor and I realize the poor cat is on a leash. No wonder he's plotting more violent deaths for us.

"I reserved my time for my family picture with our dog, Mr. Puffinschmitz Snowfighter III at exactly 4:55 p.m., which is in exactly one minute, and I expect—"

"Is she wearing ankle laces?" Dad asks under his breath, just as—

"AAAAIIYYYYYYYY," Mommy Masochist screams as Chuckles pees all over one ankle. She kicks Chuckles across the room, where he lands right in Santa's lap. Declan shouts and Chuckles hisses, back arched to the full in a complete and utter feline imitation of Mommy Masochist, who is screaming in a pitch made only by dog whistles.

Two giant German Shepherds break free from their owners and descend on Chuckles and Declan, one of the dogs encasing the cat's head entirely with its mouth, though Chuckles maneuvers just so, leaving the dog with a mouth full of antlers, clinging to Declan's lap.

"Off! Down! Ho ho ho!" Declan shouts. Chuckles sprints to a giant water fountain and springs into the air, landing with a furtive grace on the very edge of the top marble tier of a five-layer water cascade. He pauses to lick a paw as if it were the most natural thing in the world.

"Chuckles!" Mom screams, racing to the fountain. "Get down!"

SPLASH! A Great Pyr jumps into the fountain, followed by a rush of dogs that resembles something out of *101 Dalmatians*. A gaggle of Segway-powered mall cops appears, blowing whistles and accomplishing absolutely nothing as Amy, Dad, Carol, Jeffrey, Tyler, me, and Declan all run to the fountain to try to do, well, *something*.

Tyler crawls into the fountain and shouts "Wa-duh! Wa-duh! Da dog is in da wa-duh!", splashing with glee.

Carol stares in surprise. "That's a new sentence!"

Mom, Dad and Amy grin as Jeffrey jumps in, too, and begins scooping his hands into the water and stuffing handfuls of something in his pockets. He's soaked, and tiny dogs swim past him in the eighteen-inch-deep water, their heads tipped up, eyes on the prize of Chuckles, who now rules over his domain.

The King of the Mall.

"Money!" Jeffrey shouts. "Fwee money! Look, Mommy. It's fwee!"

I hear laughter behind us as a crowd of mall shoppers just takes in the scene, a few taping it. Josh is laughing in the crowd, across the large fountain from us, and he pulls his phone out. He snaps a ton of pictures as Mom cries out for Chuckles and the rest us just laugh, the kids throwing handfuls of "fwee money" from the wishing well into the air.

A white-haired old man lingers by Santa's seat, and I realize it's Declan's replacement. He's standing next to a shapely young woman.

"Hi!" I ask. "Are you the new Santa and elf?"

She eyes me up and down. "I, uh, brought my own suit."

"What's 'O O' for?" the old man asks, looking at my boobs. I look down.

"Great. More sequins fell off," I mutter. My breasts tell people what to say when they're coming. Excellent. Directing the replacements to the changing area, I sigh a big, long blast of relief. We're done.

We made it through the miracle of Christmas.

Two strong arms wrap around me, bending me backwards in a dip so low my loose hair brushes the carpet. Soft, hot lips cover mine and a fake beard presses into my face, a welcome tongue exploring and teasing as Declan's hands hold me in place, his heart cradling me, too.

He pulls back and I look up, dizzy with desire and joy. "I love you," I say.

"I love you, too," he says back, then leers. "And you're bringing that costume home."

"My family Christmas picture! It's ruined!" Mom cries.

Josh comes over and says something to her, the two hovering over his phone. He taps a bunch of times, then does one final tap.

"I got one. And I think it's the best family Christmas picture ever."

And it is.

But I don't appreciate it when Josh sends it in to the website Awkward Family Photos, because, um, I have another wardrobe malfunction.

And their caption when they post it?

Jolly Old Saint Nip.

THE END

Thank you so much for reading Shannon and Declan's story. What started out as a short novella turned into a 600+ page saga of life, humor, and crazy love.

Readers have asked me to continue the story of Shannon and Declan, and so I have. You can read about Declan's proposal in the next book in the Shopping series . . .

Shopping for a Billionaire's Fiancée

All of our best dates end up in the emergency room. . . .

I planned the perfect proposal. Plenty of lobster, caviar, champagne and—her favorite—tiramisu. The perfect setting. The perfect woman. The perfect *everything*.

Dad gave me my late mother's engagement ring, platinum and diamonds galore. Shannon wouldn't care if I slid a giant hard-candy ring on her finger instead of a three-carat diamond designed to impress.

But my future mother-in-law, Marie, will pass out when she sets eyes on that rock, which will give us two minutes of blessed silence. That woman talks more than Kim Kardashian flashes her naked backside on the internet.

I was going to make it perfect, from the color of the tablecloth to the freshness of the roses. And it *was* perfect.

Until Shannon swallowed the ring.

Shopping for a Billionaire's Fiancée gives near-billionaire Declan McCormick the chance to tell his story in this continuation of the New York Times and USA Today bestselling Shopping for a Billionaire series.

about the author

NEW YORK TIMES AND USA Today bestselling author Julia Kent turned to writing contemporary romance after deciding that life is too short not to have fun. She writes romantic comedy with an edge, and new adult books that push contemporary boundaries. From billionaires to BBWs to rock stars, Julia finds a sensual, goofy joy in every book she writes, but unlike Trevor from *Random Acts of Crazy*, she has never kissed a chicken.

She loves to hear from her readers by email at jkentauthor@gmail.com, on Twitter @jkentauthor, and on Facebook at facebook.com/jkentauthor

Visit her website at http://jkentauthor.com

Text JKentBooks to 77948 and get a text message on release dates!

CPSIA information can be obtained
at www.ICGtesting.com
Printed in the USA
BVOW08s1705081117
499878BV00007B/518/P